Faithful
LIES

Chelly Bosworth

Faithful Lies
By Chelly Bosworth

Grateful acknowledgement is made for permission to quote from 'Jeremiah Weed' by Dos Gringos. Copyright © 2007 by Viper Driver Productions, LLC. All rights reserved. Used with permission.

Transcendent Publishing
PO Box 66202
St. Pete Beach, FL 33736
www.TranscendentPublishing.com

Transcendent
——Publishing——

ISBN: 978-1-7332773-2-7
Library of Congress Control Number: 2019910627

Printed in the United States of America.

For Daniel Clair Buckingham.
You're unforgettable.

CHAPTER 1

Mary took one last look around the kitchen to make sure all was in order. The chicken Marsala was slowly simmering, the garlic bread was warming, and the wine was ready to pour. Olive oil and rosemary scented the air with its special welcoming aroma.

She glanced at the clock and nervously tugged at the short, silky negligee that was barely visible beneath her apron. Any second now, Owen would be home. Mary loved these moments, just before he walked in, when she could envision the perfect reunion, when she could let her husband know how much he had been missed. She had begun the tradition in the early days of their marriage, when Owen, then a young navy pilot, returned from deployment. She would cook his favorite dish, keep the wine flowing, then fall into bed with him for the remainder of the day or night. Although lately… lately, that hadn't been happening as often.

The door opened and Owen's tall, handsome presence filled the room. Powerfully built, with chiseled features and an angular jawline, he was the quintessential soldier. He also never failed to set Mary's heart pounding.

"Owen," she said happily, though it sounded more like a gasp of pleasure.

Roger, their giant black Boxer, came racing across the wood flooring and flung his huge body at Owen.

"Roger!" he said, laughing as he stooped down to hug the dog. "Roger boy! I've missed you!"

Mary stood back, her smile frozen in place. There was a time not so long ago when poor Roger would have been brushed aside while Owen gathered Mary in his arms and placed gentle kisses all along her neck and cheeks. "Mary, I've missed you so much," he'd say, then his lips would be pressed to hers and, Marsala forgotten, they would make their way down the hall to their bedroom.

Now Owen disentangled himself from the joyous Roger and looked across the room at his wife. Mary saw the stress lines around Owen's eyes and mouth. He appeared to be stifling a yawn, then sniffed the air appreciatively and offered a tired smile. Had he even noticed what she was wearing? It didn't seem so.

Still, her heart quickened as he strode across the room, his blue eyes fixed on her. He placed his large hands on her bare arms, giving her a chill, then placed a rather disappointing kiss on top of her head.

Mary's heart sank. After three weeks apart, she had been hoping for a rekindling of their romance. Absence makes the heart grow fonder and all that. Instead, she felt like she had been reunited with an old friend. There wasn't any spark or excitement crackling in the air. There was no unrestrained yearning tugging at their bodies. There was just familiarity and comfort. Nice, but not the sensuality she missed and craved.

Roger barked insistently and Owen pulled away. He bent down, picked up a tennis ball and threw it into the dining room. Roger scurried off eagerly.

With a sigh Mary turned to the stove. One strap of her negligee slid down her shoulder as if to remind her that Owen hadn't even noticed. And to think she'd spent an hour in the lingerie department. As she began to dish up the Marsala, she heard a chair scrape the floor in the dining room. He was sitting down, waiting to be served. She suddenly felt uncomfortably warm. When had her marriage turned into a friendship? Was this normal? Did other wives feel this way?

They had married hastily, right out of high school and before Owen left for boot camp. That had been fourteen years ago, but sometimes Mary felt like it was much longer. Since then, they had lived the life of military nomads, beginning with a move from their native Arizona to Pensacola, Florida so he could attend flight school. After that it was Norfolk, Virginia, followed by rainy Washington state. Owen worked odd and inconsistent hours and she never knew when the navy would summon him away or how long he would be gone. For Mary it was a lonely life; she never seemed to fit in with other navy wives, and just when she did feel like she had made some friends, they were on to the next place.

Mary admired these independent, strong women who took their life of service in stride. She knew they worried when their husbands were deployed to God-knows-where, but somehow they managed to put on brave faces as they went about their business. Mary spent much of her time fantasizing about the day when Owen would leave the military and they could settle into a more normal existence. Instead, he had gone right from the navy to a job with AirSec, a defense contractor, which took him away even more. Sometimes he was training other pilots somewhere in the States, but other times he flew on missions she knew little about but assumed were very dangerous. She desperately wished he would do something else, but Owen wouldn't hear of it.

She told herself she should be happy. And who wouldn't be, living in the laid-back surfer town of Encinitas? She loved their spacious two-story townhouse of stucco, terracotta clay tile roofing and a lush patch of green grass, all within walking distance of the beach. She told herself that the same job that took him away from her was the same one that paid for this life. Everything was a tradeoff, right?

She used to tell herself that the long absences kept the passion in their marriage. His kiss before he left on a mission always had a slightly desperate quality, as if he knew it might be their last. He was so tender then, holding her close, letting her cry if she needed to, and gently wiping away her tears. But lately, whenever he left, he would simply drop a quick, impersonal kiss on her cheek. He barely looked at her as he eagerly ran out the door to his next adventure.

She carried carefully arranged plates of chicken Marsala, garlic bread and salad to the table. Owen had already nabbed the wine bottle and uncorked it. He poured himself a glass and sipped it slowly, not seeming to notice Mary's empty goblet across the table from him. Suppressing a sigh, Mary slid into her chair.

"I'm exhausted," Owen told her as he cut into his chicken.

"You'll be glad to sleep in your own bed tonight."

"That's for damn sure. Tex snores louder than an F-16 taking off."

"Maybe we can sleep in tomorrow and then go out for breakfast. There's a new brunch place in La Jolla we could try." Mary's amber eyes sought out her husband's, but he was engrossed in his food.

"Can't," he said, tearing off a piece of garlic bread. "I have a briefing at five a.m. Horse is picking me up at four-thirty and we're going to swing by Rudy's and get a bunch of chorizo burritos and coffee for the flight crew. Those guys have been working their asses off."

Mary could feel hot tears behind her eyes. I am NOT going to cry, she told herself, and in that moment, her sadness was replaced by anger. Was it resentment of his job, or of Owen himself? It seemed the two were indistinguishable. Ever since becoming a fighter pilot, his identity had almost ceased to exist. Being a pilot WAS his identity. The sweet boy she had married all those years ago had been gradually replaced with an analytical, career-obsessed man. Their life revolved, first around the navy and now on the security contractor, and Owen wholeheartedly gave himself over to its demands, his superiors and his men. There was, it seemed, less and less left over for Mary, and she was tired of it.

"But Owen, you just got back and -"

He cut her off. "I hate to bring this up right away, but have you gotten your period?"

Instantly, the anger rushed out of her, replaced by humiliation. She let out a deep breath and didn't meet his eyes.

Owen speared a piece of chicken with his fork. "I'll take that as a yes."

A tear rolled down her cheek.

"Maybe it will happen next month," Owen said, but he didn't sound optimistic. Instead, his voice held a slight note of accusation.

Mary pushed her plate away. She didn't want to talk about the baby. The baby that didn't exist. The baby that didn't make an appearance month after month. Of course Owen wanted a family. He was an only child and his parents were desperately ready for a grandchild. All of Owen's military friends had babies. In fact, at thirty-two years of age, Owen and Mary were considered a bit of an anomaly.

Roger nuzzled Mary's leg under the table and she reached down to scratch his soft ears. *What would I do without you*, she thought, feeling a rush of love for the animal; he was her constant companion when Owen was away. How ironic that she felt even lonelier now that her husband was home. Would a baby ease her solitude? Bring Owen closer to her?

Owen finished his dinner and sat back, wine glass in hand. Mary looked across at him. She loved her husband. He was kind and strong and dependable. She could always count on him. Although he was not emotive, he had a strong sense of duty and loyalty. He would never cheat on her. Never leave her. He would always provide for her and protect her.

"Owen?" she said tentatively.

"Yes?"

"I missed you."

Owen's blue eyes softened. He got up from the table and came around to his wife. Gently, he cupped her face in his hands.

"We'll have a baby soon, honey," he said softly. "Then you won't feel so alone when I'm gone."

How about, I missed you too? she thought, but said nothing. She realized she was afraid to hear the answer.

Suddenly, as if seeing her for the first time, Owen pulled Mary to her feet and into his arms. He kissed the top of her head and ran a hand down her back. She leaned into him, loving the feel of his nearness, his strength. This was what she had wanted- to be close to Owen, to feel special to him. She pulled away slightly and traced his lips with her fingers.

"I love you, Owen."

"I love you too."

He bent his head to hers and kissed her lightly. It was not a passionate kiss, but it was comforting. Familiar. Mary sank her hands into his dark hair and Owen tightened his grip on her waist and pulled her even closer. Their bodies instinctively pressed themselves together and Owen's kiss turned sensual, teasing, almost possessive. Mary responded with a low moan and Owen picked her up and carried her up the stairs.

"Hey," he said, surprised, "that's one sexy nightie you have on."

Mary giggled. "Welcome home, baby."

Owen lightly tossed her onto their bed and began to kiss his way down her neck. "Maybe we *will* make a baby tonight."

In that instant, Mary lost all desire. She let Owen make love to her. She made all the appropriate noises and responses. She held him close when it was over. And as they lay basking in the glow of Owen's spent passion, Mary had never felt so alone.

CHAPTER 2

⌒

*T*he next morning, Mary awoke and reached across the bed. Empty. She curled on her side and wrapped her arms around herself, wondering if they had made a baby last night. She also wondered how she would feel if they hadn't. Shame. Emptiness and shame. Those two words seemed to encapsulate her life for the last year. An absent husband. An absent baby. An absent... wife? Emotionally absent, anyway. When had she last felt truly happy? Fulfilled? Excited?

She sat bolt upright. Did she even WANT a baby?

The thought stunned her. When they had talked about starting a family all those months ago she had agreed with Owen that it was time. They were in their thirties, financially stable and they'd been married for over a decade. All the stars were aligned. Yet she had never really given much thought to becoming a mother, not like other women who couldn't wait to give birth and start the most important part of their lives.

But WAS bearing children the most important part of a woman's life?

Mary got out of bed and pulled on a powder blue terry cloth robe. She padded into the bathroom and took a good look at herself in the mirror. Big, gorgeous amber eyes stared back, fringed with very thick, dark lashes. She knew her eyes were her most remarkable feature. Everyone commented on them when they first met her. Owen said they were the window to her soul and indeed, she knew every emotion she felt was reflected in them. Strange that Owen now rarely looked into them at all. And when he did, he didn't seem to read her like he used to.

She reached up and ran her hands through her long hair and thanked the hair gods for a natural beach wave. Mary knew many women who blew-dry, flat-ironed, curled and spritzed their hair into the style she had been naturally blessed with right out of the shower. One less thing to worry about.

When she had the baby would she have to cut her hair short? This was another thing a lot of women did. They said long hair was too time-consuming to take care of and they were tired of babies grabbing it, yanking it, chewing on it. Easier just to have it lopped off. What would she look like with short hair? She bundled it all up at the nape of her neck and turned her head from side to side. Not bad. But she loved her hair as it was.

What other things would change with the coming of a baby? No sleep, that was a given. No time to herself. No spontaneous date nights. Wait. There weren't spontaneous date nights anymore. Owen was always so tired from working, the few hours he was home he wanted to just rest.

Roger came running into the bathroom, snapping her out of her thoughts.

"Were you outside, big boy? Did you go potty?" Mary ran her pink fingernails up and down Roger's short, black fur. "Who's mama's good boy? Mama loves you."

Loud *wheeking* sounds emerged from Roger's throat and she giggled. He made the funniest noises sometimes.

"Do you want your breakfast?"

The stub tail was going a mile a minute.

Mary wondered how involved making breakfast for a baby was. Formula. How often and how much? And weren't you supposed to warm up the milk and then put drops of it on your wrist to make sure it wasn't too hot? And then you had to burp the baby. Wipe spit-up off your shoulder. Change the baby. Then what? How much and how often did babies sleep? She had no idea. Mary was an only child and had never been around children. Dogs, though… dogs she had been around her whole life. She knew almost everything there was to know about canines.

In the bright, sunny kitchen she poured Roger's food into his dish and he danced around the floor in excitement. She thought about breastfeeding. It wasn't politically correct to think so, but the thought of it freaked her out. She knew it was natural, but it looked so uncomfortable and way too intimate. Self-consciously she hugged her chest and shuddered. She remembered her friend Faith talking about how raw her nipples were after she nursed her last baby. Faith said it would keep her up at night because they burned so horribly. She'd even had to use some special cream. Mary's mouth had been hanging open, a look of horror on her face.

"It's okay," Faith had said, "it's beautiful and bonding. And breastmilk is way better than formula because it contains so many nutrients and antibodies from the mother. But you know what's really weird is the chaffing and then when the baby starts to get teeth-"

At this point, Mary's best friend, Lorelei, jumped in. "Faith! Can you not!?"

The three women had dissolved into giggles and the conversation moved elsewhere.

Mary's cell phone rang, bringing her back to the present. Roger was lustily slurping his food so she carried her mobile into the living room before answering.

"Hi, babe, would you like to meet for lunch today?"

Mary smiled just hearing Lorelei's energetic voice. "Yes, please."

"Pannikin?"

"Perfect."

There was a slight pause, then Lorelei said, "Did Owen get home in one piece?"

"Mmmm hmmm."

"That's not wifely excitement I hear."

"Lorelei, don't…"

"I'm just saying…"

"Please don't start in on me."

"Why? Because you're tired from all the crazy, mind-blowing welcome home sex you had last night?"

Mary blushed. "No… it's not that…"

"Look, I'm just worried about you… I know things haven't been so rosy between you two for a while now. It bothers me to see you so down."

"I know."

"Is it the baby stuff again?"

"Oh, Lorelei," Mary said, her voice catching. "He wants children so badly and there's all this pressure and -"

"We can talk about this at lunch, okay? We're going to chat this through and we're going to drink fortifying mimosas and lattes and then we're going to laugh. A lot. All right?"

"That sounds really wonderful." Mary sighed. "I don't know what I'd do without you, Lei."

"That's what best friends are for." There was a slight pause and then, "You're not bringing Roger, are you?"

"Yes. You know he wouldn't want to miss out on seeing his One True Love."

"Roger is like a bad date- he drools on me, ogles me and tries to paw my chest."

"He just wants you to pet him."

"Don't they all. See you soon."

⌒

"What the hell, Mary? He greeted ROGER first?! He didn't even notice you were practically NAKED?!" Lorelei Harper was in full-blown anger mode, her short, blonde curls bouncing with each word.

The two sat under a large blue umbrella outside Pannikin waiting for their drinks. Formerly a train station, the building, with its bright yellow paint and white lattice gables looked more like a stately family home than a local coffee shop. The relaxed atmosphere, old wooden beachy furniture and sprinkling of colorful umbrellas on the lawn made Pannikin a favorite amongst all North County San Diegans. It was also the scene of many shared secrets and laughs between Mary and Lorelei, not to mention a few very serious conversations.

A barista arrived, balancing a tray with two champagne flutes. He took a moment longer than necessary when setting down Lorelei's drink. Mary watched, amused, as the young man stared at Lorelei's voluptuous figure and stammered out, "Here's your mimosa, ma'am."

Lorelei's green eyes flashed amusement. "*Ma'am?* How old do you think we are? Early thirties! We are definitely *not* ma'ams."

"Uh, um… Yes, ma-"

Lorelei held up a hand. "No. Just no."

The red-faced barista took the rest of their orders - two omelets, along with a latte for Mary and a cappuccino for Lorelei; then, with another wistful glance at Lorelei, he reluctantly shuffled away.

Mary smiled at her friend over the rim of her mimosa. Wherever Lorelei went there was always some guy drooling over her or generally making a fool of himself.

They had met shortly after Mary and Owen moved to San Diego. Lonely in yet another new place, Mary had been exploring Seaport Village downtown and wandered into The Upstart Crow, a local bookstore. There she found a small group gathered around an author as he read an excerpt from his new novel. Delighted, Mary took a seat in the back row and quickly immersed herself in the world he had created. Novels had always been her favorite escape from reality, an escape she badly needed at that moment. Maybe she would linger after the reading and try to strike up a conversation with some of her fellow book lovers.

Midway through a climactic scene in chapter five, a loud crash came from the Biography section. "You bastard!" a woman yelled accusingly. "Who is she?! WHO IS SHE?!?!" Another crash. The author stopped midsentence as the entire audience craned their necks in the direction of the noise. Mary turned just in time to see a book fly across an aisle. This was followed by a dull thud that sounded like a fist connecting with flesh, then a man's yelp and, finally, the clack of high heels stomping across the wood floor.

Mesmerized, Mary watched as a very beautiful blonde came marching past the astonished crowd. The two women locked eyes, and the blonde suddenly smiled, winked and mouthed the word "drink?" Mary paused for a minute, then, amazed that for once real life was more exciting than a book, got up and followed her. Once outside the blonde started laughing.

Mary couldn't help but smile. The laugh was enchanting.

The blonde held out her hand, "I'm Lorelei."

"Mary."

"Are you up for a drink, Mary?"

"What about that man?"

Lorelei chuckled. "Oh, we're through."

"Yeah, I kind of picked up on that. You don't seem very sad about it."

"I was tired of dating him. He talked about himself too much and he made this really bizarre sound when he chewed."

Mary giggled. It sounded foreign to her ears. How long had it been since she had laughed?

Lorelei elegantly gestured toward a building south of where they stood. "I'm thinking Redfield's- they have a wonderful wine selection. We can just walk over from here."

"Sure, okay." Mary nodded. "Can I just ask a question? If you were sick of him why not just end it? Why cause a scene?"

"Oh that. I don't want him calling me again. I saw a picture of another woman on his phone and used that to freak out like a crazy bitch."

Mary laughed –this time, a real belly laugh, the kind that makes your sides hurt. It would be the first of many that evening, and she and Lorelei had been thick as thieves ever since.

Smiling at the memory, Mary looked fondly across the table at her best friend, who was still going on about the barista's offensive use of "ma'am." There was only one thing Lorelei loathed more than a weak man, and that was the idea of growing old.

"How is Brad?" Mary asked in between sips of the delicious drink.

"Who?"

"The, um… the tall one. I think he had a big tattoo on his arm?"

Lorelei thought for a minute. "Oh, *Brad*! I haven't seen him in a while."

"I thought things were getting kind of serious?"

"No. Absolutely not. You know I'm not ready for any kind of commitment. And speaking of commitments… can we talk about you and Owen?"

Mary hung her head slightly.

"That bad?"

"Do you think I'd be a good mother, Lei?"

"God, yes. Are you kidding! Look how well you take care of Slobber Roger over there."

The big dog picked his head up off the grass and looked lovingly at Lorelei.

Mary sighed. "There's a big difference between dogs and children."

Lorelei waved the thought away; both creatures demanded far too much of one's time. "My theory is that you have Only Child Syndrome. It's still interesting to me that you married an only child as well. You do realize your kid isn't going to have any aunts or uncles, right?"

"Auntie Lorelei?"

"Hell no! I know even less about children than you do. Remember the last time we were at Faith's house? I spent most of that horrific visit trying to dodge those four tiny savages of hers."

Mary giggled. "Her kids are a bit out of control. I don't think she'll have any more though. Jesse said they decided four was enough."

"From your lips to God's ears. Maybe one of them should get fixed just in case."

"Lorelei! You're terrible!"

"You're right. I guess someone has to populate the earth."

The barista returned with their omelets.

"Here's your brunch, ladies," he said, but his eyes remained fixed on Lorelei. "Fresh from the kitchen. I garnished the plates myself."

Mary thanked him but he barely acknowledged her as he backed away slowly.

Lorelei forked some of the fruit on her plate. "Be honest with me, Mare. Do you even *want* to have children?"

A seagull cut through the sky and landed close to their table. Roger let out a low growl and gave the bird a warning look. An ocean breeze picked up and blew around the lawn, offering the fresh scent of salty sea air. The gull's feathers ruffled in the wind and Roger raised his nose to sniff at the new smells wafting in. With a low, sad cry, the seagull flew away and Mary found herself wishing she could fly too. But where would she go? Somewhere she could be free. The thought startled her. She *was* free, wasn't she?

Mary shook her head slightly and realized Lorelei was looking at her with a concerned expression. She tried to smile.

"I'm fine. Really. I just... I guess I'm sort of sad about... some things."

"About Owen physically being gone a lot of the time? Or about Owen being emotionally gone *all* the time?"

Mary sighed. "Yeah."

"That's what I thought. Listen, Mare, don't have kids if you don't want to. That's far too big a decision to make just because *he* wants it."

"I thought I wanted it too."

"So do you want kids or not?"

Mary laughed. "You are direct, aren't you?"

"Would you have me any other way?"

"Absolutely not."

"Listen, I know Owen isn't around a lot. And I know he's saving the world and whatnot, and I fully support…whatever he does… but, Mary, if he's not making you happy when he's home then that's a problem." She paused for effect. "A problem that will not be solved by a baby."

Mary nodded, unable to deny the truth of her friend's words. "He just seems so sad I'm not pregnant yet. We've been trying for almost a year. Maybe he'll be, well, different, once I'm expecting."

Lorelei sipped her latte. "I hate to tell you this but he started being closed off way before the whole family planning gig. He's not the same guy you married out of high school- at least, not from what you've told me."

Mary picked at her omelet. "You're right. Being a pilot changed him. But the other military wives are so brave and so independent. I'm not at all like them."

Lorelei narrowed her eyes and spoke sternly. "I admire those women, but they are not my best friend. You are, and you still haven't answered my question."

Mary's amber eyes filled with tears. "I don't know if I want a baby," she said, her voice barely above a whisper.

"Then we have a pretty big problem."

"I know. Oh, Lei, I know."

CHAPTER 3

⌒

Saturday dawned overcast and damp. San Diegans referred to the May weather as May Grey and the June climate as June Gloom. This particular June morning was definitely gloomy. But it was a small price to pay for perfect weather the rest of the year, and besides, Mary enjoyed the cloud cover, the moist air and the slightly chilly ocean breeze. She stepped onto her patio and breathed deeply. A few feet away, Owen sat on one of their adirondacks, his long legs stretched out before him, a newspaper in one hand and the other gently scratching Roger's head. As always, Mary marveled at how her husband somehow gave off the vibe of being completely in control and alert even though his body language suggested only relaxation. Next to him, two steaming coffee mugs sat on a low table and Owen turned to look at his wife, offering her one.

Mary took it, grateful not just for the caffeine but his consideration for having thought of her. She kissed the top of his dark head.

"What are we bringing to the barbeque today?" Owen asked.

"I'm going to cut up some watermelon and throw together a potato salad."

"Aunt Francesca's recipe?"

Mary smiled. "Yes."

Owen licked his lips. "Mmmm. With the bacon in it?"

"Just for you."

"We should probably leave around ten-thirty. That'll get us to Horse's by eleven."

"Okay."

"What are you going to wear?"

"I don't know. Why?"

Owen sipped his coffee, his eyes slightly averted. "Nothing. I was just wondering. Last time we saw the guys you were sort of... well, kind of looking a bit casual." He set his coffee mug back on the table and held up his hands. "Not that there's anything wrong with that, but... it's just... Mare, I really want that promotion. I want to make a certain impression around those I work with and part of that is having a wife that looks very respectable."

"I am not the First Lady, Owen."

"I know. But I would appreciate it if you would tone down the surfer look a bit when we're around work people."

Heat rose in Mary's cheeks. "Owen. We live in a beach town. Everyone is in shorts and sweatshirts and flip flops. Half the people in Encinitas walk around in nothing but bathing suits. And besides, I was coming straight from work that day. Of course, I was dressed casual. But I didn't think I looked any different than anyone else."

"That's the point."

Surprised by the intensity of her anger, Mary looked away from her husband and up toward the grey sky. She didn't want to say anything rash, but at the same time she wanted to lay into him. How dare he tell her how to dress? What would come next? Would he tell her how to vote? How to scrub the floor? Or was being barefoot and pregnant going to be the next order of business? Wait... maybe it already was.

With an effort, she pulled back from her emotions and let her analytical brain take over. Owen was the provider. He was only acting this way because he was motivated, competitive and aggressively type-A when it came to his career. Fighter pilots paid strict attention to detail and quickly cut through any mountain of information in order to prioritize long mental checklists. That's probably what he was doing now. He's ready for that promotion, Mary thought, and my image is simply an item on the checklist: Make sure the wife is respectable enough to help me reach the next rung on the ladder.

Owen was silent, having gone back to his paper. Probably in his mind, the matter was settled. Mary wondered what it would be like to have a career- a *real* career. Sure, she had had jobs here and there, most of them part-time filing papers, working in a shop or something equally as mind-numbing, but nothing with any promise. How could she hold down such a job when the move to the next city was always hanging over her head? Things were better now that they had finally put down roots, and she loved being a professional dog-walker. Her honest eyes, fresh face and obvious love for canines resulted in each in-home consultation hiring her on the spot, and before long she had more work than she could handle. Yet she couldn't help but envy her female clients who dressed in suits and carried laptops. They always looked so put together; ready for a high-powered meeting or a court case or a day of crunching numbers in some big high rise downtown. Mary dreamed of having her own office, a neat and tidy desk, a loyal and helpful assistant and an intelligent boss who challenged her mind. She would keep her office walls bare, but for a framed poster of the Empire State Building. She'd have fresh flowers in a vase and a picture of Roger as her screensaver. Mary sighed, because that's all it was – a dream. She had no experience to speak of, had never even stepped foot in a college. What could she do with no education?

Roger barked loudly, his hackles rising at the sight of a pigeon that had flown into the yard. Owen glanced up from his paper, made a shooshing sound, and then returned to his reading. It was as if he didn't realize she was still standing there.

Mary drained the last of her coffee and went inside. There didn't seem to be anything left to say to her husband. Besides, she had food to prepare. And an outfit to carefully choose.

Horse and Corinne lived in a tiny blue house on Coronado, an idyllic island only a bridge away from the rest of San Diego. With a low-slung roof and ivy crawling all over the walls, their house was, like so many of the homes on the island, homey and welcoming. It sat on a stubby hunk of property with lush green grass and eclectic flora and fauna, surrounded by a white slatted fence. The house had been in Corinne's family for three generations, purchased by her naval officer grandfather back in the days when Coronado was affordable by those on a military salary. Today it would go for a couple of million.

A tiny wheat-colored dog hopped around the lawn, yapping and chasing a hovering butterfly. When the dog saw Owen and Mary pull up in their dark blue Jeep, it began whining excitedly. Roger's big head appeared over the Jeep's roll bar and he woofed loud and low. Before Mary could stop him, he jumped out of the back, bounded over the fence and ran straight to the little dog, only to stop short inches away. The two began sniffing each other, Roger's big nose practically lifting the small dog's feet off the ground. It was the customary greeting between these two old friends.

Corinne came out of the front door, a dish towel in one hand and a Tupperware container in the other. She was a plump woman with big dimples and frizzy red hair, but what people remembered most about her was her serene, captivating smile. Corinne literally radiated a love of life.

Owen swung himself out of the Jeep, then reached behind his seat and pulled out three six-packs of beer; Mary retrieved her bowl of cut-up watermelon and giant container of potato salad. They made the perfect all-American couple walking toward the house; Owen in his pressed khakis and blue golf shirt, and Mary in a demure light-green dress.

"Hello, my loves!" Corinne called.

A moment later, Mary found herself enveloped in a tight hug. She smiled, her earlier annoyance melting away. Like Corinne herself, the embrace was warm and maternal and made it utterly impossible to be in a bad mood. It had been that way ever since they first met, when Horse recruited Owen, who he had known since flight school, for the job with AirSec. Corinne, who had both grown up in a military family and married into one, had mastered the art of dealing with her husband's frequent absences, and she had taken Mary under her wing. Though the lessons hadn't really stuck, Mary was forever grateful for Corinne's guidance and had come to think of her as a wise older sibling.

Corinne led them into the living room just as Horse's bulky frame came around the corner of the hallway. He carried a shot glass and a bottle of Jeremiah Weed bourbon.

Owen put up his hands. "No way, Horse! This is a BBQ. A *family* BBQ."

Horse snorted. "Yeah, and it's my family and my house, so buck up."

Corinne rolled her eyes at Mary. "I don't know how they drink that stuff. Tastes like kerosene."

Horse began singing a Dos Gringos song in a loud, robust and completely off-key voice, "When I was a youngin', my daddy said to me... son, I wanna know what it is you wanna be...I said I'll never wear a tie, but I like the color green... I think I'm gonna wanna fly the fucking F-16!"

As if on cue, a voice boomed from the front door, "Fox One, when you've got nothing left! Fox Two, it's that heater in your chest! Fox Three, the only friend you'll ever need! That cocksucker motherfucker, Jeremiah Weed!"

"Tex!" Horse bellowed. "Get over here, you bastard, and have some hooch."

"Oh brother," Corinne said, but she was smiling warmly as she went to greet Tex, his wife and their three young boys. "Hello, Johnsons. So good to see you guys."

"Is Roger here?" the youngest child asked.

Mary smiled. "He ran around out back. He's playing with Jet."

"Mom, can I?"

Tex's wife, Ricki, nodded to her son. "Yes, and no running in the house."

The other two boys followed their brother through the living room and kitchen and out the back door. They mumbled greetings at the adults as they went.

Though her smile was carefully in place, Mary secretly thought the boys must be utterly exhausting. How did Ricki do it, or Faith, with her four kids? Four had to be worse, right? Then again, she thought, it only took one to change your life forever.

Tex and Owen were shaking hands. Tex was a short, compact man with a thick frame and bowed legs. Pointy cowboy boots peeked out from under his Wrangler blue jeans.

"How's my crew chief today?" Owen asked.

"Missing my jet."

Ricki laughed. "He'd bring that thing home if it would fit in the house. Sleep with it, bathe it, feed it, burp it, play with it…"

Horse snorted. "You maintainers think you own our jets even though *we're* the ones flying them."

"WE spend more time with those gorgeous hunks of metal than you do."

"And we appreciate you keeping them in top shape," Owen agreed.

"Thanks, Viper," Tex said, using the nickname Owen had had since his navy days. "I know ya do." He glared at Horse for a moment. "Bring that Weed over here, you pussy."

"You look stupid without your coveralls."

"If you're just gonna talk and not pour maybe you should let me have the bottle. Why don't you go mix yourself a Cosmopolitan?"

"Why don't you shut the hell up?"

The front door opened and a gangly blonde man with a bright smile walked in. "Hi, everyone!"

"JAMBO!" Horse yelled. "How's it hangin'?"

"Long, strong and... hey, did you break out the Weed already?" He looked at Owen. "We drinkin' early, Vipe?"

Towheaded ten-year-old twin boys ran through the door from behind Jambo. Their shorts had holes in them and their faces were smudged with dirt. A young, harried woman chased behind them. "Get back 'ere ya little buggers," she yelled in a thick cockney accent, "before I box yer ears!"

The boys ignored her as well as everyone else in the room and bolted for the back door. It slammed with a loud bang, then the sounds of childish voices mixed with Roger's deep barking and Jet's lively yipping wafted in through the open windows.

Corinne hugged Jambo and his wife, Happy. "So lovely to see you both." She winked at Happy. "Come into the kitchen – the wine is chilled and waiting."

"That sounds some good, lovey. Those boys 'ave got me knackered, they do. Run me off my feet and always into trouble."

Ricki snorted. "Boys are hellions. How I got saddled with four of them I'll never know."

"We have three boys, babe," Tex said.

"I'm pretty sure she was includin' you in there, mate," Happy laughed.

Owen and Mary's eyes met across the room. For the first time in a long time, Mary couldn't read what he was trying to signal. She stared down at her neatly clad feet, so feminine in pretty, strappy white pumps. She glanced at Ricki, Corinne and Happy, taking in their outfits - Ricki in capris and a tank top, her sandy hair pulled back in a ponytail; Happy, in a loose-fitting, faded sundress that looked like it had seen better days. Her ebony hair was a mess and she wore no makeup. And Corinne... she looked fresh, clean and relaxed in a pair of jean shorts and a well-worn t-shirt with "Navy Wife: Eat. Sleep. Wait." printed on the front. Her strong, plump legs were sun-kissed with a beautiful California tan and her wide feet were encased in a pair of bright white canvas sneakers. They all looked so casual, so comfortable, and so at ease with their lives.

Everyone made their way into the spacious kitchen, the largest room in the house. All of the curtained windows were open and the salty sea air blew in, balmy and refreshing. Horse began lining up shot glasses.

"You womenfolk having any?"

"Seriously, Horse?" Ricki asked.

"Don't wanna discriminate. I know you broads like to be treated as equals."

"Mary will not be having any," Owen stated casually. All eyes turned to him.

An awkward silence followed.

Finally, Happy spoke. "Well, this is a pregnant pause if I ever 'eard one." She turned to Mary with one eyebrow raised. "Somethin' to tell us, luv?"

Mary felt the heat rising to her face. "No… no… I… nothing to announce."

Not missing a beat, Corinne clapped her hands together and began good-naturedly barking orders. "Okay, let's get the meat going outside. Men, please take the ribs and chicken out of the fridge. Happy, you can help me open the wine. Ricki, you can heat up your baked beans – which smell delicious by the way. You must give me the recipe."

Ricki jerked her head in the direction of her boys' loud voices. "You think I have time for recipes? Those are from Kansas City Barbeque."

"Well, I'm not lighting up that grill until *I'm* lit up," Horse announced and began pouring Jeremiah Weed into four shot glasses.

"None for me," Owen said.

"What the hell, Viper?"

Tex jumped in. "Maybe he don't feel like drinking today, Horse. Lay off."

"I wasn't talking to you, cowgirl."

Jambo held his glass high. "One drink is good. Two at the most. Three I'm under the table. Four I'm under the host." He winked lasciviously at Corinne then tossed back the shot.

Horse raised his own glass. "Here's to nipples. For without them, titties would be pointless."

"Oh god," Ricki muttered.

Owen cleared his throat. "Fight on and fly on to the last drop of blood and the last drop of fuel, to the last beat of the heart."

"To the Red Baron!" Jambo and Tex said in unison.

Horse stuck his head out of the back door. "YO! Navy spawn! Get in here!"

Tex opened the refrigerator and began pulling out racks of ribs and chicken breasts, all delectably swimming in Corinne's special marinade. The younger boys trooped in and lined up to take portions of the meat from Tex and then headed back out toward the grill.

Happy saw Jambo grab the bottle of Jeremiah Weed and she whacked him on the chest. "Oh, no you don't. I won't be taking care of ye all night and nursing your hangover in the mornin'." She took the bourbon from him. "Go on, now."

A few feet away, Mary stood quietly watching the cheerful chaos around her. Suddenly, Owen was by her side. She looked up at him and he nodded toward the living room.

"Can we talk for a minute?"

For a moment Mary considered saying no, that she didn't want to hear what he had to say, but then she just nodded and followed him out of the kitchen. As soon as they were out of sight, Owen took her in his arms.

"I'm sorry, Mare. I'm sorry I said you couldn't drink- and in front of everyone. It was thoughtless of me. It just… came out."

Mary buried her face in Owen's shoulder, but it was to stop herself from issuing an angry retort rather than a show of affection. Once again, he had managed to bring her non-pregnancy to the forefront.

"I just didn't want you to drink anything because of the baby…" he began.

Something snapped inside Mary and she pushed him away. "There IS NO baby, Owen!"

"You don't know that! The other night we could have…"

"It's been ten months! You think two days ago we beat the odds all of a sudden?"

"*Beat the odds*? We are operating on the assumption that this *is* going to happen for us. We just don't know when. But, Mare, honey, I think we should start talking about you seeing a doctor."

Mary could feel hot tears starting to well up behind her eyes.

"We need some answers about why… why you aren't pregnant yet." Owen started toward her, but she put her hands on his chest to keep him at arm's length.

"What if I don't want to go to a doctor? What if I don't want to get tested for whatever it is they test for? Why don't *you* go to a doctor? Maybe it's you, not me."

Owen stiffened. "Okay, you're right. I should go in too."

"What if…"

She was about to say, *What if I don't want a baby,* but was interrupted by Horse's voice booming from the kitchen.

"Viper, get your ass outside with the rest of the men! You can talk to your wife at home!"

Mary began to cry.

"Please don't…" Owen said, reaching out to wipe her tears away.

"We should talk…"

"And we will. But not here and not now. I know you want children just as much as I do. This is hard on both of us, but we'll make it through. I love you, Mary. I know I don't say it enough and I sure don't show it very well, but I do. And I want nothing more than to have a family with you."

Mary said nothing, but her amber eyes burned with a thousand pent-up emotions. Owen saw only the tears.

"I have to go join the guys. We'll work this out. I promise." Owen kissed his wife's wet cheek then left her standing alone in the living room.

CHAPTER 4

"There you are," Corinne said, joining Mary on the plush tan couch and handing her a glass of wine.

"I'm sorry… I just needed a moment..."

"No apologies necessary. Happy just got ahead of herself. She knows it's been a struggle for you and was excited to hear some good news. And Owen," Corinne's lips tightened, "should not have said what he said."

Mary sniffed and smiled a bit. "It was awkward all right."

"That it was," Corinne laughed. "Now drink a little wine and come join us girls when you're ready. Can I get you anything?"

"I'm fine. And you are wonderful."

Corinne hugged Mary and then placed a gentle hand on her perfectly arranged hair. "It'll all work out. Everything does."

"The voice of experience."

"The voice of someone who has lived with Horse for too many years to count."

"Trial by fire?"

"As they say: The average fighter pilot is very much capable of such feelings as love, affection, intimacy and caring. Those feelings just don't involve anyone else."

Mary put a hand to her mouth and giggled. She'd heard the old aviation quote a hundred times, and it never failed to amuse her.

As Corinne left the room, Mary reached into her purse and pulled out her cell phone. There was a text message to Mary and Faith from Lorelei:

Drinks at George's tomorrow night. 6:00. Don't bring any dogs or children.

Mary tapped out a reply that she would be there, then put the phone away and took a fortifying swallow of wine. She held the full-bodied pino in her mouth, savoring it for a moment before setting it down on the table. Owen would be angry if he knew she was drinking. She paused for only a moment before picking it back up and draining it, allowing the warmth to course through her body. She then stood up, smoothed her dress over her hips and went into the kitchen. The women were gathered conspiratorially around the center island, wine glasses in hand.

"I *saw* her with him," Ricki was saying. "They were in a corner booth, holding hands."

Corinne took a sip of her wine. "Maybe they were talking about something very personal- like a death in the family. Perhaps he was comforting her."

Ricki's eyes narrowed. "Would you let Horse 'comfort' another woman? Alone? With his arm around her?"

Corinne raised her glass. "Touché."

"Sounds a bit dodgy to me," Happy said, "but maybe we shouldn't assume anything."

"She is *married*!" Ricki hissed. "She is married and at a romantic restaurant with another man. How do we not make assumptions?"

Mary leaned against the bar next to Corinne. "Who are we talking about?"

"Meredith Booker."

"You mean Meredith Hooker," Ricki said darkly.

Happy laughed and then dropped her eyes guiltily.

"I think we need to remember this is not our business," Corinne said. "Now, should we set the table? I just bought the prettiest new plates at a steal-"

But Ricki was on a roll. "I'm just saying that it's not fair of her to cheat on her husband. ALL of us struggle with our men being gone. That doesn't give us the right to a fling."

"Maybe it's not a fling," Happy suggested. "Not like they were shaggin' right there in the booth, were they now? Could be they're just jolly good friends."

"I saw them kissing!" Ricki practically yelled.

The women let out a collective gasp.

"Maybe you should 'ave started with that, luv..."

Corinne sighed. "Look, ladies, let's try to talk about something else. It isn't right to discuss someone else's private struggles like this."

She pointedly eyed Mary's empty wine glass. Mary glanced outside then back to the bottle, then she nodded.

"Private struggles?" Ricki's eyes flashed angrily. "They're anything but private. Anyone who's ever been married to someone in the military knows what it's like to struggle. And just when we think they're out of the military, they hire on with a defense contractor and are away for even longer periods of time." Happy grunted in agreement, while Mary gave another nod. It was as if Ricki was giving voice to all her woes. "We get lonely, we are sad, we miss them, we're scared, and we wonder if they're ever coming home. And what are we supposed to do? We're supposed to *wait* for them. Faithfully wait for them! Because that's what you do as a loyal wife. We are not only supporting our men, but our country. What happened to integrity and honor? Meredith isn't grappling with anything WE aren't! But WE aren't running around getting our needs met by... whoever we happen to..."

"Fancy?" Happy supplied.

Mary stared down at the countertop. Her wine glass had left a little ring of moisture and she touched it lightly with a finger. As the women continued to talk she drew small wet circles, her mind a million miles away. Ricki was right. Each of them dealt with these emotions in her own way- Corinne with her optimism and strength, Happy with her boundless energy and Ricki with her strong sense of duty to

God, country and husband. Mary thought about how she coped with Owen's absences and realized she just… well, didn't. She tried not to think about the loneliness, that awful feeling of always waiting for another person to return. It was better to concentrate on the positive – Roger, her dog-walking business, and her friends. Was that why she was becoming more disconnected from Owen? Because she was in denial of her feelings, not just for him but about what she really wanted out of life? Did she want to have a career? Be a mother? Why did the answers to those questions seem to always be just beyond her reach? Why did it feel like everything had been decided for her?

"Well, I will never speak to that woman again," Ricki was saying. "She is weak and disloyal. She's a disgrace to all us wives who work our butts off taking care of house and home and children while our husbands are out serving our country."

"One could argue that Meredith is serving too," Corinne said quietly.

"More like *servicing*." Ricki arched an eyebrow.

Mary looked out of the window and saw Owen throwing a football with a few of the boys. He was smiling and laughing. Roger ran around them in circles, enthusiastically barking, his stub tail cheerfully twitching back and forth. One of the Johnson twins intercepted a pass, stumbled into Roger, and then bounced off Owen's legs. The little guy went down with a thud and two other boys piled on top of him. There was a scream of "Get off me!!!" then childish shrieks of laughter. Owen began hauling kids to their feet and he looked so happy and relaxed that Mary's heart turned over. Her husband was a good man, she knew that in her core. So some of her needs weren't being met. Did any woman have *every* desire fulfilled by a man? Was there even such a thing?

She took a large gulp of her wine, finishing it off and resolving to push aside her trepidations about having children. Owen was right, it was time they became a real family.

Lorelei always picked the best place for drinks, and tonight was no exception. As Mary stepped onto the rooftop bar of George's at the Cove in La Jolla, the sun was just beginning to set. The sky was a fiery orange pink with wispy purple clouds. The tranquil sounds of lapping ocean waves blended contentedly with clinking cocktail glasses and friendly chatter. George's attracted the young, the rich, a few tourists and even the occasional celebrity.

Mary scanned the tanned, well-dressed crowd, searching for her friend. She was about to text Lorelei when her phone buzzed: *Look straight ahead.* Mary looked up and smiled, for seated at a high-top table in the middle of the open patio was Lorelei, looking stunning as usual in a short lavender dress. Diamond drop earrings sparkled against her neck, her curly blonde hair shone in the last rays of the sun and her long bare legs were crossed at the ankle. She gracefully held a dirty martini in one hand and beckoned Mary with the other. She looked like a 1940s film star. Smiling, Mary headed in her direction, but stopped short when she saw a man walk up to the table. He was not the sort of suave, stylish man that usually approached Lorelei, or the fashionable sort who frequented George's, for that matter. He was muscular and husky, with close-cropped sandy-colored hair and a formidable demeanor. A police badge rested openly at the waistband of his pants, as did a holstered semi-automatic pistol, and for a moment Mary wasn't sure whether he was there to hit on her friend or arrest her.

"Excuse me," she heard his deep voice say as she approached the table, "may I borrow your salt and pepper?"

Haughty look in place, Lorelei turned to look at him and was clearly surprised by what she saw. She started to speak, then stopped and handed him the shakers.

"Thank you so much, ma'am."

Mary heard the hated term and waited for Lorelei's typical retort, but none came. Instead, she continued to stare at the man in front of her as if perplexed.

"Lei?"

"Oh, Mary, you're here," Lorelei said; she sounded strange.

"You knew I was here, you just text -"

"Officer," Lorelei said with a pointed glance at his badge, "this is my friend Mary, and I am Lorelei Harper."

"Detective Williams," he corrected, but there was no ego in his voice. "Nice to meet you."

"Are you joining us for drinks?" Mary asked pleasantly.

"No, ma'am, I need to get back to my buddies over there." He jerked his thumb at a table a few rows down. "Enjoy your evening."

As he turned to leave, Lorelei's eyes widened slightly in surprise. "Hey," she said, "aren't you going to offer to buy me a martini? Ask for my digits?"

Detective Williams turned around. "Pardon?"

Lorelei flashed him a winsome smile. "You came over here to talk to me, right?"

"I came over here to borrow the salt and pepper."

"I assumed that was a ruse."

"My buddies are giving me some dirty looks, ma'am. I need to get back to them." His eyes were kind, and an amused smile played about his lips. "But let me just say that you are the most beautiful woman I've ever seen in person, and if I thought I had a chance with you I would ask for your number."

Lorelei cocked her head. "In person?"

"Well, I've never met Marilyn Monroe, but you sure remind me of her."

Mary watched the exchange with amusement, and to her horror, a bit of envy. When was the last time a man had hit on her? She looked down at the wedding band on her left hand and supposed that's what kept men from approaching her. At least she hoped that was the reason. She pulled at the rings and saw white skin underneath. Tan lines. Even if she took them off it would still be obvious she was married. No matter, she didn't even think she remembered how to flirt.

"I love Marilyn Monroe," Lorelei was saying. "What is your first name? Or do I have to call you Detective?"

"Frank. Frank Williams." He put out his hand.

Lorelei reached forward for a firm shake, but instead the detective gently placed a kiss on the back of her hand. Was it Mary's imagination, or was her friend actually blushing?

Suddenly a high-pitched, cheerful voice cut through the moment.

"Lor! Mary! I'm heeere! Sorry I'm late. Madison threw up on me as I was leaving so I had to clean her up and then change my shirt. I grabbed the first button-down I saw and didn't realize until I was halfway here that it's Jesse's. Just pretend I'm hip and single and I had a drunken one-night stand with some guy and had to come straight from his apartment wearing his shirt." Finally pausing to take a breath, she turned her attention to Frank. He was still holding on to Lorelei's hand. "Who are you? I'm Faith."

"Frank Williams. Nice to meet you."

Mary and Faith hugged hello. Faith sent a knowing look Lorelei's way and then whispered in Mary's ear. Something to the effect of "he can arrest me anytime." She and Faith giggled.

"Well, I should be going. Gotta get back to my buddies," said Frank.

"They probably want their salt and pepper," said Lorelei.

But Frank didn't move. Lorelei didn't pull her hand away. Their eyes never wavered from each other.

"What are you drinking, Mary?" Faith cut in.

"I haven't ordered yet, but probably the usual."

Faith hopped up on a bar stool and pulled up close to the table. "I'm starving. Can we order food soon?"

"As long as it doesn't require seasoning," Mary said with a wink.

Frank still stood, one hand holding the salt and pepper and one hand holding onto Lorelei's.

Finally he said, "I'll let you ladies enjoy your evening. Lorelei, it was nice to meet you." He kissed her hand once more and left them.

"He looks pretty good leaving," Faith said. "Check out that butt. Must work out. I wonder what kind of gun he carries. Glock? Smith & Wesson?" A waitress walked close by their table. "Hey! Can we get some menus over here?"

"Wow, Faith, you are just all over the place," Mary said.

"I've been kind of scattered and a bit tired lately."

"Is that why you need food so badly?"

"Something like that." Faith smiled and her face lit up, her skin glowing.

Lorelei sipped her martini. "He never did ask for my phone number."

"Well go over there and give it to him," Faith said.

"I don't think so." Lorelei tossed her lovely curls.

A server brought menus and asked for Mary and Faith's drink orders.

"Gin rickey, please," Mary responded.

"I'll just have water."

Lorelei looked at Faith over her glass. "Not Ubering tonight? You can still have one drink and be okay to drive, so long as you eat something."

"Nah, I'm good." Faith shook out her long red hair. It was tousled as usual, but beautifully thick and soft. She was tall and uncoordinated, like a newborn colt, and her wardrobe was always a mix of colors and patterns, some of which didn't go with each other. Faith couldn't care less how she looked, which made her all the more alluring. Her vivacious spirit, unabashed zest for living in the moment and lack of verbal filtering drew people to her. She was always busy with her kids- running them around town to soccer games, Boy Scout and Girl Scout meetings, toddler playgroups, gymnastics and Joel's unfortunate drum lessons which didn't seem to be improving his skill level whatsoever. Mary was often surprised the entire family wasn't deaf.

"Is Madison okay? Why did she throw up?" Lorelei asked.

"Oh, Joel found a frog outside and told her if she held it in her mouth for two minutes he'd give her ten dollars."

Mary made a face. "Isn't that kind of dangerous? Aren't some frogs poisonous?"

"It was a dirty plastic frog- I think one of the neighbor kids' toys. I don't know how it got over to our yard. Anyway, Joel doesn't even HAVE ten dollars. I swear that kid -"

"So," Lorelei interrupted, trying to get the story straight, "she put the frog in her mouth and then vomited?"

"Yeah. She put it too far back on her tongue and accidentally started to swallow it. Her gag reflex kicked in and she barfed."

Mary's eyes went wide. "Maddy could have choked!"

"If I had a nickel for every time one of my kids cheated death I'd be richer than Oprah."

"Your life is maniacal," Lorelei said, examining her French manicure. She stole a covert glance at the back of her hand, where Frank's lips had been moments earlier. "I don't know how you get through each day with so little sleep, so little time for yourself and endless kid-related responsibilities. It's a wonder you have so much energy."

Mary nodded. "Don't you miss things like… pampering yourself? Hot bubble baths, sleeping in on the weekends, making love whenever you want, wherever you want, watching movies that don't have cartoon characters…"

"Are you trying to depress me, Mary?" Faith asked, but she was laughing. "Come on, guys, you know I love having kids."

Lorelei rolled her eyes. "Name one thing you miss about being kid-free."

"Going to the bathroom by myself." Faith sighed longingly. "There's no privacy. Someone is always knocking on the door or sticking their fingers under it trying to wave. Sometimes I can see an eyeball looking up at me."

Lorelei pulled an olive out of her martini. "You also mentioned the little ones sometimes crawl into bed with you and you wake up in wet sheets."

"Oh yeah, that's a real treat," Faith snorted, rolling her eyes. "But they can't help it, poor little things. Jesse started sleeping in the spare bedroom."

Mary gasped. "You're not sleeping together?"

"Oh, we're still having sex. But, yeah, he said he didn't want to wake up drenched in pee anymore and he moved all his stuff out of our room."

"Isn't that sort of a big deal?" Lorelei asked.

"Of course not! As long as he's happy I don't care. At least he's still sleeping in the house."

Their server brought Mary and Faith's drinks as well as menus.

"Do you guys know what you're eating?" Faith wanted to know.

Lorelei rolled her eyes at her. "We haven't even looked!"

"We come here all the time. You know what they have."

"What's your rush? Get an appetizer if you're so hungry."

"Good idea." Faith turned to the blonde waitress. "I'll take the calamari to start off with."

Mary tasted her gin rickey and sighed with contentment. She loved girls' nights. Catching up on her friends' news, their lives, listening to their banter, the three of them giggling together. She stared out over the ocean waves, wondering whether they would see the green flash this evening. The green flash only lasted a second or two, right as the last of the sun dipped into the sea. Mary had never seen it, but Lorelei had and said it was worth waiting for. No blinking, Lorelei had instructed, you have to stare right at the horizon the whole time so you didn't miss it. Mary sighed contentedly and looked around the cozily lit bar before focusing her attention back on her friends.

Lorelei's eyes were narrowed at Faith. "You're ravenous. You're drinking water. You're talking lovingly about your insane children."

Faith smiled hugely, smug with delight.

"What?" Mary asked. "What's going on?"

"I'm pregnant!"

Lorelei put her drink down. "Judas Priest! Again?"

Mary hugged Faith. "Oh, I'm so happy for you! I didn't even know you guys were trying- I thought you had decided four was enough...?"

"Well, we did. I mean, Jesse did. But a few months ago I passed out on the couch after Joel's tenth birthday party and -"

"That was a shitshow," Lorelei muttered.

"...and you guys know, there were like thirty boys there and twenty adults and the house was so messy and I was just exhausted from cleaning all evening. Jesse saw me sleeping and when he covered me with a blanket I woke up. He was so sweet- told me to stay where I was- he would check on the kids and make sure they were all tucked in. After he did he came back and said they were all zonked out and he ran his fingers through my hair and told me I looked beautiful. One thing led to another and it all happened so fast that we didn't even think of birth control."

Lorelei made a gagging sound. "I will never sit on that sofa again."

Mary hugged Faith again. "I'm happy if you're happy."

"I am. I've kind of missed having a baby around. I mean, Scotty is two now and already becoming so independent. I love having a baby in my arms. I love the way my babies smelled, all sweet and powdery, it's the best smell in the world. I was sniffing Scotty's head the other day, but all I could smell was peanut butter and petulance."

Mary laughed.

"Well you'll find out soon enough. You and Owen are still trying, right?"

Lorelei and Mary exchanged glances across the table.

"No?"

"Fay, I don't really know if I want kids..."

"Of course you know! Deep down you know. People lean one way or the other. Cut through the crap and visualize what you really want."

Lorelei sighed. "I don't think it's that simple."

"Sure it is. Look, Mare, the unknown is scary. But that doesn't mean you don't actually want to be a mom."

"But what if it does? You always knew you wanted to be a mother."

"True, but I grew up around a ton of kids. You were an only child and…"

Faith trailed off, but Mary mentally finished the rest of the sentence: *…and you grew up without a mother…*

Though unspoken, the words smarted. Mary had had a wonderful childhood, yet she felt the absence of her mother keenly, even more so since she had been trying to have a child of her own.

Faith squeezed Mary's hand. "You are one of the most responsible, dependable, *loving* people I know."

Mary stared into her gin rickey. "I've sort of been thinking these past few days that maybe… maybe I don't actually know what I want out of life."

"That's because all of your decisions have been made for you, babe," Lorelei said. "First by the Navy, now AirSec…" She shot Mary a look. "And then there's Owen himself…*Owen's* career, *Owen's* goals…"

"And I'm just along for the ride, right?" Mary questioned, a hint of sharpness in her words.

Faith shook her head, her pretty red hair tumbling around her shoulders. "No, no, no. Just tell Owen how you feel. You guys can talk this out. Maybe wait for a few years to have kids. Does it have to be now?"

"Owen wants to start a family as soon as possible," Mary said simply. "He says we've waited long enough already."

"How much does this have to do with Charles and Ellen?" Faith asked.

"Yeah, there is that." Mary sighed.

"How Owen came away from that family semi-normal beats me," Lorelei said. "Ellen Crossfield is a domineering bully."

Mary giggled. "She can be pretty mean sometimes."

"Sometimes?" Lorelei derided. "Remember that Thanksgiving she freaked out because your dinner plates were mismatched?"

"She is just very cultured and she likes things to look nice."

"She's a snob."

"I can still remember the horrified look on her face when Joel ran up to her with green beans shoved up his nose, yelling, 'I'm the Booger Man! I'm the Booger Man!'" Faith said. "He was trying to make her smile because she had such a frown on her face that day."

Lorelei raised her martini glass at Faith in a mock toast. "Your children are such refined creatures."

They all laughed.

"Seriously, Mare," Faith said, "this is about you and Owen, NOT his parents."

"I know. I do. But they want grandchildren and I get that."

"They want the Crossfield name passed on," Lorelei asserted. She then tightened her jaw and in a tone that was startlingly like Mary's mother-in-law said, "You *are* aware that the Crossfields can trace their roots back to the Winthrop Fleet in 1630 during The Great Migration…"

The three erupted into laughter again, with Mary and Faith applauding their friend's nearly flawless imitation.

"And since Owen is their only son…" Lorelei added.

Faith held up her water glass. "Well if they want to share a chunk of that money they're rolling in, they can send it my way and I'll have one of my kiddos change their last name to Crossfield."

The waitress glided up to the table and set a pearly white platter of steaming calamari on the table. Her eyes excitedly wide, Faith grabbed a fried squid, dunked it into the cup of cocktail sauce, and popped it in her mouth. A guttural moaning sound came from her throat.

"Mmmm… that is soooooo good."

Lorelei rolled her pretty green eyes. "Get a room."

Mary giggled and picked up the menu, though it was a formality. She'd spend a few minutes fantasizing about burgers and fettuccini with cream sauce, all the while knowing she would order the grilled chicken salad with lots of strawberries and low-cal vinaigrette dressing on the side. Mary had never been overly concerned with her weight, not until a few months ago when Owen mentioned that she had gained a few pounds. Of course she had noticed – her shorts were a little tighter and her tummy was a bit bigger – but she didn't think much of it. She was a normal-sized woman with a healthy body. Who cared? Owen cared. At first she thought it was about her appearance, but no, he was worried she wasn't consuming the right foods for "the baby." He had asked her to please stop eating things that had fat, grease, sugars, too many carbs, and anything else he'd read in the several pregnancy-related blogs he subscribed to. He had even given her printouts of what pregnant women should have for meals and snacks- lean, grilled meats, fish, eggs, beans, tofu, cheese, milk, nuts, whole grains, lots of fiber, iron and B-vitamins. Within a month, Mary had dropped fifteen pounds, but she couldn't lose the hurt of Owen's disapproval and his micromanaging of her diet.

With a sigh, she set down the menu, resigned to another grilled chicken salad, when a handsome bartender approached their table, a dirty martini in his hand. He set it in front of Lorelei. "Compliments of Detective Williams."

"Oooh…" Faith started singing, "Frank and Lor sittin' in a tree…"

"Oh, shut up." Lorelei looked back at the table where Frank's buddies had been, but it was empty.

"He asked me to bring it after he left. Also this." The bartender pulled a business card out of his pocket and handed it over.

San Diego Police Department
Detective, Homicide Frank Williams, Jr.
Major Crimes Division

The office phone number had been scribbled out and a different number handwritten next to it, along with an arrow, directing her to turn the card over. On the back he had written:

I'd love to take you out. Call or text me any time. Gentlemen really do prefer blondes.

A smile played about Lorelei's lips, but she handed the card back to the bartender. "I don't want this. Thanks anyway."

"What are you DOING?" Faith cried, snatching it.

Lorelei fluffed up her blonde curls. "I don't call men. Men call me." She picked up the martini. "Now this..." Her eyes widened as she took a sip, "...is delicious!" She looked at the bartender. "This is not Grey Goose."

He regarded her, amused. "No, it is not. The gentleman specifically requested Beluga Gold Line."

"Well, la-di-da!" Faith said. "Last time Jesse and I went on a date night he bought me a Coors Light- and that was on happy hour prices."

Lorelei snickered. "That's because you're a lightweight, not because he's cheap."

Mary took the business card from Faith and read the message on the back. It really was very sweet. She felt another slight surge of jealousy. What must it be like to have this kind of attention from men?

The bartender nervously shifted from one foot to the other. "Um, if you don't want to call that guy, I'd be down if you called *me* some time." He produced a pen and wrote his phone number on Lorelei's cocktail napkin. "I'm Adam." He smiled charmingly, revealing adorable dimples, and then quickly walked away.

Faith grabbed the business card back from Mary and waved it under Lorelei's nose. "You're *gonna* call that detective. You liked him! I can tell." She glanced down at her still flat stomach. "Are you going to tell a pregnant woman no?"

"Yes, as a matter of fact, I am." Lorelei took an elegant sip from her martini glass, savoring the pure, distilled taste of excellent vodka. A smile played about her lips as she recalled Frank's scorching touch.

Then again, maybe not...

CHAPTER 5

*M*ary frowned when she saw the white envelope lying by the front door, the all-too-familiar HOA insignia clearly visible. The HOA –or more accurately, the HOA president -was the one thing Mary disliked about living in their lovely beach community. Imogen, a despotic harridan with Shar Pei wrinkles and far too much time on her hands, was always patrolling the neighborhood for an errant weed in the yard or, God forbid, a piece of chipped paint. Mary refused to answer the door when she stopped by, and she handed any HOA letters over to Owen, who would pay Imogen a visit. One look at the handsome fighter pilot was enough to melt her icy demeanor. She'd fall all over herself, serving him coffee and a piece of cake, and promptly forget all about her complaint. After a snack and a lovely conversation, Owen would return home and inevitably ask Mary why she couldn't get along with such a sweet old lady.

Mary opened the door and placed the unopened letter on the table. Their entryway, much like the rest of their home, was classically decorated in soothing ivories and rich browns. Owen liked calming colors, nothing too bright or showy. There were candles in wrought iron holders throughout the rooms, muted paintings on the walls, leather couches, chairs and cushions in the living room. Gauzy ecru curtains hung above all the windows and beige Pottery Barn rugs were sprinkled ubiquitously over wooden floors.

Roger came running at Mary from the kitchen, whimpering excitedly. She crouched down and hugged him, rubbing his ears and murmuring, "How's mama's big boy? Mama loves Roger."

"Hi, hon!" Owen called from the living room. "Have fun with the girls?"

Mary stood, walked toward her husband and kissed him on the cheek. "Yes, it was really nice. And guess what? Faith is pregnant."

"Who's the father?"

Mary laughed and plopped down on the couch next to Owen. "What are we watching?" Roger jumped up and placed his head on Mary's lap, licking her hand contentedly.

"The High and the Mighty."

"I love John Wayne. He always reminds me of Daddy."

"Your dad is a badass, all right. Made me quake in my boots back in high school. Sometimes still does." Owen put his arm around Mary. "He is very protective of his little girl."

"Who's not so little anymore."

"No, you are not. Now you are a sexy woman with a gorgeous body."

Mary turned to Owen, placing a hand on his leg, her amber eyes earnest. "Am I really?"

"Now why would you ask that?"

"I don't know... I just... sometimes I feel very ordinary. Maybe even invisible."

Owen put his hands on either side of her face. "To me, you are the most beautiful woman in the world. You always have been." He kissed her softly on the lips, his breath warm, his mouth so very tempting.

Mary leaned into him, her arms going around his neck, while Owen gently shoved Roger off her lap.

"Come here, little girl," Owen said as he pulled her to him. His hands cupped her bottom and she straddled him, kissing his neck and then running her tongue up to his ear. He made a rumbling sound in the back of his throat and Mary reveled in the way he melted under her touch. This is what she wanted- the passion, the closeness, the romance of physically loving the only man she had ever been with. As their kisses intensified, so did her desire for him. She wanted his hands all over her body, exploring it like it was the first time. All thought and sound faded away as she let herself go, consumed in a cloud of desire.

Owen crushed Mary to his chest and said gruffly in her ear, "Tell me what you want."

Mary whispered, "You, I want you..."

Owen's mouth silenced her with a deep kiss. Her world went dark until there was nothing but her hunger for him. She shuddered when he tore his lips from hers and rasped her name. He gathered her body to his and pushed her down on the couch, lying next to her, encircling her with his strong arms. Mary arched into him, savoring the feel of his body trembling against hers.

Owen began to kiss his way down Mary's neck to her chest, his hands moving over her, firm and certain, unbuttoning her blouse. She shivered in anticipation and sank her hands into his dark hair. As he tugged at her jeans he looked into her eyes. "Mary, my love, you're mine, you belong to me..."

"I belong to you," Mary repeated in a whisper. Owen removed all of her clothes and she lay naked on the couch.

"You are so damned beautiful," he said, his eyes taking in every inch of her, his fingers caressing her face, trailing down her neck, making a titillating path across her breasts to her quivering stomach, and then...

Mary gasped and clutched at the sofa. Owen expertly brought her to the pinnacle of her endurance. He knew her body so well, knew exactly how to deftly send her swirling into the ocean of desire, wave after thrilling wave washing over her, carrying her higher and higher until the tide of release pushed her over the edge. She screamed, trembling and crying out with pleasure.

Owen quickly removed his jeans and was inside her in an instant. Immediately Mary was swept out to sea again, but this time in a different, magical way, this time she was not alone and she drifted along with Owen, their bodies so in tune with one another that they easily found mutual satisfaction, mutual pleasure together.

With each movement, each sway, each push and pull of their bodies, their hands all over each other, their mouths and tongues unable to get enough, Owen and Mary pulsed faster and faster until they reached that ultimate peak, that uncontrollable oblivion. They'd been there many times before together - years of love, years of practice, years of knowing exactly how to please one another.

Owen collapsed on top of Mary, spent. He buried his face in her soft hair and she ran her fingertips lightly down his back, loving the feel of his heated skin.

"I love you, Mary."

"And I love you, Owen."

"You're amazing."

"As are you." She pressed her body as close as she could to his, a smile on her lips, her eyes sparkling with happiness.

Owen said something into her hair, but she couldn't understand it. She didn't even care what it was. Every part of her body was singing. How long had it been since they'd made love like this? How long since she had felt so desired, wanted, and adored? She floated along on a tranquil lake of satiation and serenity.

Owen pulled himself up onto his elbows. "Did you hear what I said?" he asked, grinning.

She reached out and traced a finger along his strong jawline and shook her head.

"I said, 'I bet we made a baby tonight.'"

⌒⌒

Mary pushed Owen off and stumbled to her feet. She stood naked, looking down at him, her hands clenched into fists.

"STOP TALKING ABOUT THE BABY!" she shouted.

Owen's eyes widened in shock. "What's wrong?"

"Can we just have sex without mentioning 'the baby'? Can we have sex because we love each other, not because we're trying to make a life?" Mary pressed her fists to her heart. "Can you make love to me and think ONLY about me?"

"What are you talking about, Mare?" Owen sat up on the couch, completely bewildered. "There isn't anyone else- I only think about you..."

"But you are constantly bringing up the baby. What about ME?"

"What about you?"

"Do you want to have sex with me?"

"Of course I do... we... just did... You're not making any sense."

Mary looked down at the floor so he wouldn't see her fighting back the tears. "I feel like you care about some non-existent baby more than you care about me."

Owen stood and tilted Mary's chin up so that he could look into her eyes. "I care about you. And I care about the baby. I don't understa-"

"There IS no baby!" she shouted into his face. "Stop it! Just stop it!"

Owen's eyes narrowed, a sure sign of his waning patience. "I don't know where all of this is coming from, Mary. We agreed to have a family almost a year ago and you want to have children as much as I do and -"

"Do I? Do I want to have children?" Mary stood to her full height, her shoulders back.

"What is that supposed to mean? Of course you do."

"Did we talk about it a year ago? Or did *you* talk and I just went along?"

Owen put his hands on his hips. "WE talked about it."

"No, WE did not," Mary countered.

"What are you saying?" Owen's voice was dangerously low.

"Maybe I don't want kids."

"What the hell are you talking about?" Owen bellowed, startling Roger. The big dog made a whining noise from his dog bed across the room, his ears pricked with concern.

Mary held her head in her hands and whispered, "I don't really know if I want to have a baby or not."

Owen lost his temper. "This is ridiculous!"

"It is not!"

"How can you be saying this? After months of trying and months of planning and..." Owen began pacing the living room. "My parents keep waiting for me to tell them a due date... I keep having to let them down every four weeks by saying you're not..."

Mary cut him off. "I'm not what? I'm not fertile? I'm not woman enough to carry a child? I'm not trying hard enough to conceive? What reason do you give them for my inadequacies?"

Owen spun around mid-pace. "I never said you were inadequate!"

"But it's my fault, right? Isn't that why you wanted me to go to the doctor?"

"I said I would go too!"

"After I mentioned it."

Owen looked up at the ceiling. "I don't want to do this, Mare. I don't want to fight. I love you. We're perfect together. I make a good living. We're young and happy and healthy. Why wouldn't we have children?"

Mary sighed. "Sometimes I feel like my life has been all planned out for me and I don't really have a say, or any choices..."

"It's my work, Mary. You knew that when I enlisted that this was not a passing thing for me. That our lives were not going to be our own."

Quietly Mary said, "But I didn't think it was going to be forever. You're not in the navy anymore, but your career is still dictating my life, and when it's not, YOU are."

Owen's mouth flattened. "Are you saying I'm controlling?"

"Yes."

"I can't believe this…"

"I just want you to listen to me…"

"This is so out of left field."

"…I feel disconnected from you and…"

"It makes me wonder what else you're keeping from me."

"…like you don't even really care what I want…"

They stared at each other- Mary's eyes pleading, Owen's hard and angry.

"I feel like you've betrayed me," Owen said finally. "Why lead me on and make me think you wanted kids if you didn't?"

"I'm not saying I don't want children. I'm saying I don't KNOW if I do." Mary reached for Owen's hand but he pulled away. "Please listen to me. I just need some time. I need to know that if I decide I don't want to be a mom right now that you will be okay with it. I should have given this more thought ten months ago."

"This isn't fair." Owen turned his back on her and she saw his shoulders hitch up defensively.

"It hasn't been fair to me for a long time."

"What is that supposed to mean?"

Mary spoke softly. "I feel used when we make love. Like it's just for the goal of having the baby, not because you love me or you want to be close to me."

"You feel *used*?"

Mary lowered her eyelashes. "Yes."

Owen turned back to her, his face set, his tone caustic. "Did you feel used when you were screaming my name a few minutes ago?"

All the blood drained from Mary's face and a hush settled over the room, punctuated only by the rhythmic tick-tock of the grandfather clock in the corner. Why wasn't the TV on? Had they turned it off before they started to make love? Mary couldn't remember. Her heart was beating very slowly; she could distinctly feel each heavy thud. Roger gazed anxiously at them from his bed by the fireplace.

Mary shivered and realized she was still naked and suddenly very vulnerable. Instinctively, she wrapped her arms around her torso, a physical gesture that did nothing to protect her from the anger on her husband's face. Owen stared at her for a long moment, then turned on his heel.

As he stalked from the room he said over his shoulder, "I'm going over to Horse's. Don't bother waiting up."

Mary remained still until the door slammed, then sank to the floor, hot salty tears pouring down her cheeks. Roger was at her side in an instant and she buried her face in his soft black fur.

~

Bonjour Mama,

I'm sorry it's been so long since I've written you, I've just been so distracted and out of sorts – still am, actually – but then you came up at dinner with Lorelei and Faith tonight and I knew it was time to pick up the pen again. I didn't tell them that, of course. They don't even know I write to you, and I've certainly never told Owen. He would just think it was strange, and who knows? Maybe it is. I know you'll never see these letters. I don't even know who you are, where you are, or if you're even alive. I don't know if you ever cared about me. I don't know anything, really, except that for some reason it feels good to confide in my mother. Then there's that other part of me that wants to hate you for leaving me, but I won't get into all that now, because what good would it do? Besides, Daddy gave me the best childhood anyone could ever have. Anything I needed (or thought I needed) a mother for, Aunt George provided. Did you ever meet Aunt George? Did you know her at all? I imagine maybe you didn't since you and Daddy were only together a short time. He said you and he met through a mutual friend, you guys had a whirlwind romance and then you disappeared after finding out you were pregnant.

I know you were/are French. You had long, light brown hair and large hazel eyes. Dad said you were very curvaceous (like Sophia Loren) and that you loved listening to chanson réaliste (mostly Eugénie Buffet and Marie Dubas) while you painted. Your parents were bohemians and you were a free spirit, kind and generous and flighty and cultured and artistic. Your clothes were flowy and comfortable and always from some secondhand store. You usually wore a scarf in your hair, some colorful bit of silk that added to your gypsy-like appearance.

I know this because I've been asking about you ever since I can remember. Not so much anymore, but when I was a kid I was relentless. I had a million questions, and I drank in every detail.

Daddy told me you were shocked to find out you were expecting; I wasn't unwelcome, just a life-changing event you never saw coming and didn't know how to deal with. And I'm so grateful that you did the right thing - ringing Dad's doorbell and handing me off in my onesie along with a small suitcase of bibs, diapers, pacifiers, bottles and Similac. Not everyone would have had the courage to admit they're not cut out to be a parent. I just wish you had left something of yourself, something personal, in that overnight satchel.

Of course I still sometimes wonder about you, especially lately, when I'm struggling to figure out who I really am and what I want out of life. Owen and I are talking about having our own child... well, more like fighting about it, if I'm being honest. It's not that I don't want children– at least I don't think it is – it's more like I'm not sure I'm ready to be a mother. I wonder, how much of that hesitation has to do with you?

You ran away.

Why not me?

Does the apple fall very far from the tree?

Oh, Mama, I guess I still have questions, but these only you can answer. I can only hope and pray that I will eventually find my own way, and that if and when I do have children I will be half the parent Daddy was to me.

CHAPTER 6

From: Willow Kleszczynski / WillowStarflower@willowreadings.com
To: Mary Crossfield / Mary@rogersleashbrigade.com
Subject: Re: Patchouli's Schedule

Peace Mare,

Thank you for your response! Patch is very excited that you will begin seeing him twice a day now instead of just once. He told me how positive your aura is when you're walking him. He feels very connected with you and believes the Universe brought you into our lives. I do as well, and I'm grateful you take such good care of my little magical mutt.

Also, I wanted to let you know I recommended you to a friend of a friend. His name is Thomas and he has a French Bulldog named Voltaire. Thomas is a bit of a celebrity and sort of eccentric, so he might be rather high maintenance. I've met him a few times and he has good karma, so don't worry. He'll be calling or emailing this week.

See you tomorrow at 9:00.

P.S. I had a premonition about you last night. We should chat about it in person.

⁓

From: Lorelei Harper / L.Harper@empireandmalkininc.com

To: Mary Crossfield / Mary@rogersleashbrigade.com

Subject: Are You Okay?

Hey Babe,

Just checking in. Have you heard from Owen today?
Let's meet for coffee by my office. 2:00?
Love you.

Lorelei Harper
Commission Accountant II, Brokerage Revenue Division
EMPIRE & MALKIN, INC.
200 Market Place I San Diego, CA I 92101
619-555-9222 (direct)
www.empireandmalkininc.com

⁓

From: Mitchell Morrison / Mitch@morrisonhomebuilders.com

To: Mary Crossfield / Mary@rogersleashbrigade.com

Subject: What's New Pussycat?

Hi Princess,

When are you coming to visit me? I miss my little girl. Flights to Phoenix are running $68 next week. You fly, I'll buy. Fly... get it? Ha!

Georgette texted me last night- something about a letter our grandpa wrote to our grandma back in the early 1900s. I don't know what she's talking about. And I don't know why she has to text- my fingers are too big for that. Wish she'd just pick up the damn phone and use it for what it's for- PHONING people.

I have a new contract next month for a couple of custom builds in Flagstaff. I'm looking forward to working in cooler weather for a while. Hotter than hell here in the valley- 115 degrees yesterday.

Dale and I shot some pool down at The Boozy Turkey last weekend (I know, I know, but your debonair dad gets to drink and smoke cigars every once in a while) and I met a very nice lady named Roberta (she goes by Bertie) with a southern accent and a nice rear end. I got her number and I might ask her out. She wasn't your typical Turkey female patron- she had all her teeth and real fingernails. I reckon she's a lady because her manners were impeccable. She even thanked me when I bought her a drink and shook my hand at the end of the night. Oh! And she said she's an editor! I told her my daughter's dream is to write a book. I hope that was okay. She seemed interested when I told her you're very talented but have never been published. I'll let you know if I see her again. I probably will. Your old man has still got it, you know. (I can hear you saying, "Dad! Grosssssss!!!")

Say howdy to Owen for me and give that dumbass dog of yours a couple pats from his grandpappy.

I love you,
Daddy

———

From: Imogen St. Perux / I.StPerux@odiumscapemanagementllc.com
To: Mary Crossfield / Mary@rogersleashbrigade.com
Subject: FW: THIRD ATTEMPT – HOA Increases

Mrs. Crossfield,

Please respond immediately. This is the third email I have sent you. The board is meeting next week to count ballots for the monthly HOA increase and I need to ensure you and Lieutenant Crossfield will be voting in favor of bumping the amount paid each month in order to keep up with the annual rate of inflation as measured by the Consumer Price Index for all Urban Consumers.

Attached is a spreadsheet listing the details of the proposed budget. As you can see, a 30% increase in dues is much needed.

I know you and your husband will vote in support of keeping our community beautiful and in tiptop shape. Please acknowledge this email without delay. I will be following up with a home visit and look forward to discussing with you.

Imogen St. Perux, HOA Board Member President
Odiumscape Management, LLC
(619)555-9000

⌒‿

From: Thomas McQuillan / T.McQuillan@ThomasMcQuillan.com

To: Mary Crossfield / Mary@rogersleashbrigade.com

Subject: Pet Nanny Services

Hello Ms. Crossfield:

Your services were highly recommended to me by Willow Kleszczynski, an acquaintance of mine.

I am in need of a professional to walk and entertain my French Bulldog while I am working. I don't know how much Willow told you about me, but I am a writer and cannot have Voltaire disrupting my creative flow. You must be willing to exercise him as much as possible so that he is too tired to bother me.

More importantly, I need to know that you are discreet (Willow assures me that you are). My life is very private and I intend to keep it that way.

Please plan to meet me at The Marine Room Friday night at 8:00 to discuss the particulars.

Best regards,
TMQ

⌒

When Mary saw the name on the last email she let out a loud gasp. *A bit of a celebrity*?! Willow had given new meaning to the word understatement. Thomas McQuillan was only one of the most admired and successful writers in the world, not to mention one of Mary's personal favorites.

Several of his books had been successful, but it was his novel *Souls in Collision* that had catapulted Thomas McQuillan from author to household name ten years earlier. It was number one on The New York Times bestseller list for several months, during which a powerful Hollywood producer purchased the film rights. McQuillan was heavily involved with both the screenplay and the film itself, which topped the box office week after week. After winning an Oscar for Best Adapted Screenplay, McQuillan's handsome, rather intense features seemed to be on every talk show and news program, his work praised and lauded, his life as a bachelor – and some said womanizer – exposed. For months he was photographed with several supermodels and actresses, even the occasional Playboy Bunny. Since then, Thomas McQuillan had faded into obscurity. He had written no other books, and he no longer appeared on TV or was mentioned in articles, except the occasional speculation that he had lost his talent. Mary refused to believe that, preferring instead to assume that he had wearied of the spotlight and quietly retired.

Telling herself she was doing her due diligence on a new client, Mary picked up the phone to call Willow.

CHAPTER 7

When she heard the soft knock on her office door, Lorelei's head whipped up from her dual computer screens. She was working on a tight deadline and had asked not to be disturbed, but, as usual, her request had been ignored.

Her annoyance evaporated when she saw Simone standing in her doorway. In the few months she had worked at Empire & Malkin, Inc., the cheery twenty-something had quickly become one of Lorelei's favorite people in the office. Of course, Lorelei knew Simone had been hired less for her demeanor and more for her shapely legs, long silky hair and large innocent eyes. Empire & Malkin was notorious for having only the prettiest receptionists, no doubt because of their allure for high-powered commercial real estate brokers. Unlike most of the others, however, Simone was not there to attract a wealthy husband, but to make her way in the industry. Lorelei respected her for that.

"Margaret is holding for you on the main line. She said she's called your direct number several times and can't get you."

Lorelei leaned back in her white leather chair and rolled her beautiful green eyes. Though Margaret's official title was commission analyst – meaning she reviewed deals that generated over one-hundred thousand dollars in gross revenue - the woman's true calling was condescension. She worked out of Empire & Malkin's Manhattan office and, in Lorelei's opinion, was enough to give commission analysts everywhere a bad name.

"Good grief. Tell her I'm still working on the LevTrust Building commission and the calculations are a real bitch. I'll call her when I'm done, and not before."

"Will do. I'm going to Starbucks on my break - can I bring you back a latte?"

Lorelei smiled warmly. "No, dear, but thank you. I'll be leaving for the day a little before two."

Simone wiggled her eyebrows. "Hot date tonight?"

"Not this time. My best friend needs me."

"Oh." Simone's face fell at the serious tone. "Everything okay?"

"I'm sure everything will be fine." Lorelei turned back to her dual computer screens, putting an end to the conversation. She never gossiped about friends, and certainly not Mary. "Thanks again for the latte offer."

Simone nodded, then pulled the door closed, shutting out the sounds of typing, phones ringing and people bantering in their cubicles. Lorelei looked up at the ceiling and sighed, reveling in the privacy of her own space. She was as fastidious about her work environment as she was her home; there were very few personal affects, though her awards and achievement plaques were prominently displayed. In addition to the two massive computer monitors, her desk housed a giant old-fashioned calculator, a steel nameplate and a trendy polished nickel table lamp.

Lorelei sighed again, this time with frustration. Margaret would probably call again.

Her insistence on taking a look at the LevTrust numbers before they were final was simply a power move - to try to give advice where it wasn't needed, critique Lorelei's comprehension methods or attempt to control how Lorelei should extract the monetary verbiage for calculation. It was ridiculous, really. Lorelei had been reading leasing contracts and sales agreements for years- pulling out rent schedules, abatements, square footage rates, dissecting broker commission language, checking for contingencies and detailing out percentages. She was a master at commission accounting - thorough, precise and efficient and already the darling of the revenue commission division.

She was also more than qualified to do Margaret's job; the problem was, Margaret knew it.

There were fifteen commission accountants throughout the company, all of them spread out over different states. Lorelei was by far the best, and over the years she had gradually taken on five regions. She welcomed the extra responsibilities, relished the challenges and enjoyed working with her own brokers in San Diego as well as her "extended family" in the other sectors. Lorelei was called upon often by the other commission accountants when they needed help navigating through a particularly difficult deal file. They knew they should approach Margaret for assistance, but most were wary of her lofty tone and long-winded responses. Lorelei was always quick to help, concise and clear in her answers and never patronizing.

She had just turned back to her screens when another knock sounded on the door. Lorelei was about to tell whoever was to go away when the door opened to reveal Simone, this time carrying two dozen lavender roses.

"I'm soooooo sorry to bother you, but these just came and I thought you'd want them right away." Simone set them down carefully on Lorelei's desk. "I wonder who they're from…?" She stood expectantly.

"Well, we know they're not from Margaret," Lorelei said.

Simone giggled. And continued to wait.

Lorelei looked at her pointedly. "I need to get back to LevTrust."

"Of course! So if you need help opening that card…"

"Simone."

"Okay, okay! I'm out." She twirled away, softly closing the door behind her.

Lorelei leaned forward and smelled the beautiful flowers, then reached out and gently touched the silky petals of one particularly stunning bloom. A quote she had once read floated through her mind: *The fragrance always stays in the hand that gives the rose.* Who had said that? Her eyes rolled skyward as she thought back to her college days. An accounting major, she had taken a few literary classes to ease the pain of macroeconomics, auditing, taxation, cost management and business valuation.

"Belle-lettres…" she said softly, recalling the phrase she had used to describe those enjoyable hours she had spent escaping mathematics and luxuriating in the garden of language. Always a voracious reader, she had diligently carved out time from her studies and very active social life to dive into the latest novel or collection of poetry. Later, she and Mary had spent many an afternoon or evening discussing books they had read, sharing articles or blogs with each other and fantasizing about Mary's dream of becoming an author one day.

A smile touched Lorelei's lips. Lavender angel face roses. Her absolute favorite flower.

She opened the card, scanning the scrawled message:

"Perchance he half prevailed
To win her for the flight
From the firelit looking-glass
And warm stove-window light.
But the flower leaned aside
And thought of naught to say
And morning found the breeze
A hundred miles away."

I'll be your winter breeze if you'll be my window flower.
I'll leave behind the ice and snow if you'll ditch the silence.
Come away with me for an evening.

Then her gaze fell on the scribbled name. For a moment her heart fluttered, then, brow furrowing, she quickly put the card back in its little envelope and pushed the roses aside. She had no time for such distractions, she told herself, not with LevTrust and the threat of Margaret's next call hanging over her head. Within seconds, the flowers and their charming note were forgotten, replaced by a flurry of aggregate rates and compensation figures.

CHAPTER 8

"Nancy and Bob adopted a new dog," Mary said, referring to two of her clients who were professional clowns and excellent pet owners. She and Lorelei were sitting on the patio of Le Parfait Paris, a trendy patisserie in the Gaslamp District. Lorelei looked sleek and professional in her tailored business skirt suit and expensive heels. Men frequently glanced over at her admiringly as they walked past the two women.

Mary was wearing a white hooded sweatshirt and blue running shorts, her long honey hair on top of her head in a messy bun. With her tanned legs and a sprinkling of freckles across her nose she looked like a typical Southern California surfer girl. No one would have ever guessed she grew up in the hot, dry desert of Phoenix, surrounded by saguaros and a plane ride from the ocean.

"Why is Roger here?" Lorelei asked grumpily as the big dog placed his head on her favorite Walter Steigers. She shoved him off and he excitedly licked one of her legs, his tongue leaving slobbery kisses and drool lines on her calf. "Gross! Mare, control your animal, please!"

Mary smiled as she reached down to pat the dog, but there was no light in her eyes. When she looked back at Lorelei, she found her friend regarding her with a mix of concern and anger. She knew Lorelei wanted to ask her about what was happening with Owen; she also knew she was waiting for the right way, and the right moment, to bring it up.

"So, the Harrises got a new dog, did they? That's nice. Are they still clowning around?" Lorelei winked, trying to elicit a smile from her best friend.

"Yeah. They just entertained at that big Houghton wedding."

"That's right! It was in the paper. Looked like a bunch of rich socialites showing off for each other. So ostentatious. Lots of Botox going on. I can't believe they hired clowns."

"Apparently the bartenders were all dwarves and the officiant was dressed like a ringmaster. Nancy told me a few weeks ago it was going to be a circus theme."

Lorelei made a face. "Wow. Well, to each their own." She slowly stirred her latte. "Any new clients on the horizon?"

Mary averted her eyes. "Not really."

"Well, that was mysterious," Lorelei teased. "Has dog-walking suddenly become a clandestine operation?"

Mary smiled, but she barely heard what Lorelei was saying; she was too busy thinking about the conversation she'd had with Willow Starflower the day before. After taking Patch for his morning walk she had tried to pump Willow for more information about Thomas McQuillan, but her client was uncharacteristically tight-lipped, saying only that Mary had to "step out in faith." A little annoyed, Mary was about to say goodbye when Willow reminded her about the premonition.

"Oh, right," Mary had said, immediately intrigued. "Is it about Owen?" she asked, then paused. "Children?"

"Now, Mary," Willow said, sidestepping the question, "I want to preface this by saying that I don't tell you anything unless it has the potential to help you reach your best and highest good."

"Okay, Willow, you're scaring me…"

The rest of the conversation was a blur, though Mary remembered clenching her hand so tight her nails had cut into the flesh of her palm. Willow had "downloaded" the message that Mary's soul would shatter into a thousand pieces not once, not twice, but three times by the end of the year and that she should prepare her heart for love, for death and for betrayal. Willow could not give her any specific details, she just reiterated that these things would all be lessons for the growth of her soul.

Now Mary's eyes looked over Lorelei's shoulder as she wistfully watched a young couple strolling by. The girl was telling her boyfriend some sort of story, chattering and making wide gestures with her hands. The guy was watching her intently, his eyes lighting up whenever she smiled. Suddenly they both burst out laughing and the girl joyously flung her arms around the young man's neck. He kissed her cheek and her whole face glowed and sparkled with happiness. How long had it been since Mary and Owen had shared a moment like that? After what Willow had hinted at Mary wondered if they ever would again.

"How about some petit fours?" Lorelei tempted, knowing it was Mary's favorite dessert. "I'll run inside and buy two to go with our coffees. Chocolate for me and pink champagne for you?"

"No, I'm good."

Lorelei narrowed her eyes. "Are you still on that diet, Mare?"

Mary nodded, looking miserable.

"Damnit! I have about had it up to here with that..."

Lorelei trailed off, but Mary knew she had been about to say something nasty about Owen. Lorelei didn't open her heart to many people, but when she did she was fiercely protective. It was one of the things Mary loved most about her. Now, though, she was relieved Lorelei hadn't finished the sentence; she might have found herself agreeing with it.

Roger started to make whining noises, his big lips puffing out with each breath. A well-dressed older woman was strolling by with a diamond-collared white poodle. As the poodle got closer Roger's cries became louder. The poodle completely ignored Roger, prancing right by as though she knew she was being watched and making the most of it.

"She's too stuck up for you," Lorelei told Roger and he looked up at her adoringly, wagging his stub tail.

"He's always had a thing for poodles," Mary said, "but he'd give them all up for his One True Love."

"You should stick to your own species, slobber boy." Lorelei advised, then turned to Mary. "So…" She pulled a card from her purse and held it out to her friend. "This came with two dozen flowers today at work."

Mary took the card, her eyes growing wider as she read the lines. She looked up at Lorelei when she was finished. "He quoted Robert Frost."

"Yes."

"It's so romantic." Mary handed the card back. "What kind of flowers?"

"Lavender angel face roses."

Mary's eyebrows shot up in surprise. "Your favorite!"

"Indeed."

"But how did…?"

"Yes, Mary, *how did he know*?"

"What? Wait! No, no… it wasn't me! I mean, I haven't talked to…"

"Faith!" Lorelei muttered darkly.

Mary's eyes went wide. "When did she… how did she…?"

"Let's find out." Lorelei pulled her cell phone from her purse, dialed Faith's number and pressed the speaker button.

After a few rings a piercing scream came from the phone, followed by loud wailing and a little boy shouting, "That's mine! That's mine! That's mine! Give it back! GIVE IT BAAAAAACK!"

More sobbing, and then Joel's voice: "It's Mom's cell, Hank. Let go. Let go!" Scuffling sounds ensued. "LET GO of it, butt face!"

Madison's bossy little girl voice came on the line. "Auntie Lor? My brothers are SO dumb! Do you want me to get Mommy?"

Lorelei had been staring at her phone in distaste, but she smiled at the sound of normalcy. "Hi, Maddy, you sweet thing. What is your mother doing? Can you put her on?"

"She's trying to get the blood out of the curtains in the dining room. Hold on, I'll get her."

Mary looked at Lorelei in alarm but Lorelei merely waved her hand in dismissal and shook her head. "I'm sure it's fine," she mouthed.

After several long moments, Faith's cheerful voice rang out, "Hey, Lor!"

"Finally! What the hell is going on over there?"

"Mrs. Fartington caught a gopher and dragged it into the house. The kids are a little wound up."

"That's disgusting. Listen, Mary's here too."

"Oooooo, hi, Mary! Where are you guys?"

"Hi, Fay! We're at Le Parfait."

"So I would like to discuss with you, *Faith*, how Detective Frank Williams knew not only where I worked, but that I love poetry and lavender angel face roses?"

A loud happy squealing noise burst through the phone's speaker. "He sent you flowers? That's so exciting! He really liked you, Lor. I could tell you two had chemistry."

"And he had a nice bottom," Mary threw in; she and Faith giggled.

Lorelei's head came up when she heard Mary's chuckle, as if relieved to finally see a genuine smile, then she turned back to the phone with a scowl.

"I will repeat my question. How did Detective Williams know three things about me that he couldn't possibly have known after our brief encounter?"

"Oh," Faith breezed, "that was easy. When you and Mary weren't looking I snapped a picture of his business card. I called him after I got home."

"For crying out loud!"

"Oh stop. I did it for your own good." Faith grew thoughtful. "But I actually didn't tell him you like poetry. What did he write?"

"'Wind and Window Flower,'" Mary said.

"Expound, please."

"Robert Frost. It's about a winter wind who is hopelessly in love with a window flower."

"Or, more accurately, it's about unrequited love," Lorelei maintained. "Not technically romantic at all."

Faith let out a contented sigh. "I think you two are meant to be. So when are you going out? Next weekend? Where are you going? Dinner? The theatre? His place? Your place? Hubba hubba…"

Mary's cell phone chirped.

"You are annoyingly meddlesome, Fay, you know that?" Lorelei scolded.

"I do know it," Faith said cheerfully.

Mary was staring at her ringing phone, her face suddenly drawn and pale.

"Fay, gotta go," Lorelei said and abruptly ended their call. "Mare, are you okay? Is it Owen?"

Mary nodded. "I haven't talked to him since he left the house last night. He didn't return any of my calls or texts."

She paused for another beat as if debating whether to answer, then she got up from the table and walked to a quiet, unoccupied corner of the patio to take the call.

CHAPTER 9

"Mary, I love you. I'm sorry for everything."

"I'm sorry too, Owen. Why didn't you call or text me back? Are you... are you coming home?"

"I just walked in. Roger is with you, I assume? I always miss the big guy when he's not here to greet me."

Mary's shoulders slumped. "But you didn't miss seeing *me*?"

"That's not what I... Listen, when will you be home? I want to take you out to dinner, somewhere romantic, where we can talk. Would that be okay?"

Mary looked across the patio at her best friend. Lorelei's slender legs were crossed, her body language confidently composed, her blonde curls perfectly arranged and unruffled by the slight breeze, and her eyes, well, her eyes looked a bit... murderous. They were fixed on Mary and seemed to shout, "Hurt my friend and you will deal with me!" Mary forced a cheerful smile and a wave, but Lorelei rolled her eyes, unconvinced.

"Mare?" Owen's voice cut through her thoughts. "Are you there? I really am sorry about last night. I lost my head. I was just surprised by your... your confusion about the baby. I know you didn't really mean what you said. We'll work this out, I promise."

"Did you just say my '*confusion*?'"

"Right. Yes. Whatever is happening with you, I'm sure it will pass. Maybe it has something to do with hormones." He paused. "Like PMS?"

Mary's mouth dropped in shock. "What?!" she exclaimed, her voice carrying across the patisserie tables. Several people turned their heads.

Lorelei was on her feet in an instant, manicured hands balled into fists. Roger seized the opportunity to lick one of her legs.

"I'm just saying," Owen continued, "that I understand you might be feeling some things right now that aren't -"

"How would you know what I'm feeling when you won't even *listen* to me?" Mary threw Lorelei another weak smile, silently communicating that everything was fine and she should stay at their table with Roger.

"I *am* listening to you, which is why I want to talk tonight. I want you to be excited about the baby."

"THERE IS NO BABY!" Mary screeched angrily, then hung up the phone and powered it off so Owen couldn't call back. Suddenly she felt as though she couldn't catch her breath. She put a hand to her head and leaned forward a bit, the world around her tilting imperceptibly.

In an instant, Lorelei was beside her. "Are you okay, Mary? You look like you're about to pass out. Marion Grace Crossfield, look at me!"

Wet amber eyes lifted to meet infuriated green ones.

"I'm taking you home," Lorelei said, wrapping an arm around her shoulders.

"I don't want to… go home."

"Is that where that bastard is?"

Mary nodded.

Lorelei gritted her teeth. "I don't even want to hear what he said right now. I swear to God…"

"It's okay, Lei, everything's fine."

"Like hell it is." Lorelei led Mary back to the table, where she collected their purses and Roger, who was begging an elderly couple for their crepes. As upset as she was, Mary couldn't help but appreciate her friend's efficiency as Lorelei guided them to her Lexus, then expertly maneuvered the red car through the downtown streets of San Diego. Within minutes, they had pulled into the underground garage of the high-rise she lived in.

Lorelei got out and opened the back door for Roger, noting with dismay the trail of dog hair and drool on the previously pristine leather backseat. They took the elevator up to the twenty-eighth floor and made their way down the carpeted hallway to her condo.

"I love coming to your place," Mary said, sinking onto a crimson couch.

It was the perfect space for Lorelei, just minutes from work and with a fantastic view of San Diego Bay. Mary knew Lorelei leased it for a ridiculously small amount from her Uncle Bart, a wealthy investor who spent most of his time in France and could care less about the few properties he owned in the States. He had told Lorelei she was doing him a favor by moving into the condo so that "someone was keeping an eye on it." He let her decorate however she liked, encouraging her to think of the place as her own. He kept promising to come visit but there was always some financial imbroglio crashing through his schedule that he had to fix, resolve or invest in. Lorelei's only complaint about dear Uncle Bart was that he owned no properties in New York.

Mary looked around the room, thinking that the décor was a perfect reflection of Lorelei herself – boldness mingled with understated elegance. The condo was stark white throughout with bright red furniture, cobalt blue paintings of the sea and a sprinkling of contemporary objets d'art on side tables, kitchen counters and windowsills. There was no television taking center stage of the spacious living room, but rather an immense industrial-looking metal and wood bar stocked with unique bottles of vodka, tequila, rum, whiskey and wine. Trendy glasses of all shapes, sizes and colors lined up at the ready on the bar shelves, while three modern red leather-topped wooden stools stood invitingly under the lip of the bar. A small circular staircase stood between the living room and the kitchen, cozily curling up to Lorelei's huge loft bedroom.

Lorelei went immediately to the bar and poured two glasses of Puech-Haut Prestige Rose. She kicked off her heels and settled herself on the couch next to Mary. They clinked glasses and Lorelei said, "De meilleures amies, soeurs pour toujours!"

Mary tipped her glass all the way back and drained it.

"Wow, babe," said Lorelei, staring. "I've never seen you do that before."

Roger woofed and ran to the sliding glass door by the kitchen. He pawed at the latch and panted excitedly.

Mary got up and went to let him on the balcony. Roger rushed out, chasing off a seagull. Pleased with himself, he jumped up on one of the two chaise lounges and gazed out over the railing, his nose excitedly sniffing the ocean air. Mary hugged him, earning a wet kiss for her efforts, then patted him on the head and went back inside.

"What do you want?" Lorelei was snarling into her cell phone.

Mary threw her a questioning glance.

"Yes, she's here and no, you may not talk to her." There was a pause. "I don't care, Owen! Why don't you slow down for a minute and think about your wife." Another pause. "Of course not! What goes on between you two is private. I only know she's sad and that *you're* the reason for it."

Mary stood in the middle of the room, unmoving, unsure of what to do. She was still upset, but a desire to talk things out with Owen was winning over. She loved her husband. Fighting was too distressing, too awful. They'd never really argued, and she had no idea how to navigate this unfamiliar and very painful terrain. Mary preferred her vision of Owen as her rock, her soulmate and friend, even if he hadn't lived up to the role lately.

"Over my dead body, Owen," Lorelei was saying. "You come over here and I'll have security throw you out on your ass!" She stood up, pacing rapidly on her white plush carpet as she listened to whatever it was Owen was saying. "All right. Yes. I understand. I will have her call you if she wants to. No, she's right here. No, I am not giving the phone to her. She will use her own phone if and when she decides to talk." A short silence ensued. "Okay, but you had better be nice to her and for God's sake use your damned ears for once instead of your mouth." Lorelei swiftly hung up before Owen could respond, retrieved her wine from the glass coffee table and took a delicate sip.

Mary offered a smile. "Thanks, Lei."

Lorelei shrugged casually. "Friends look out for each other."

"No, you're special. I am very lucky. You go above and beyond."

"You do too, babe. Listen, enough mushy stuff. Why don't you go upstairs and rest for a bit, relax, take a nap? You can call Owen later if you want to. If not, you know you can stay for as long as you need."

Roger came in from the balcony, plopped on the floor at Lorelei's feet and began licking her toes.

"Well," Lorelei said, looking down, "that's disgusting." She moved away quickly and Roger rolled over on his back, twitching this way and that, scratching all of his itches on the plush white carpeting.

"I think I will call Owen now, Lei," Mary said. "I want to work things out; we love each other and… and… maybe I'm overthinking everything. I will go to dinner with him tonight and see if I can get him to understand my feelings."

"Good luck with that." Lorelei peered up at the ceiling.

Mary laughed. "There's that eyeroll again!"

"Couldn't help it. Where will you go to dinner?"

"He said somewhere romantic."

"That should be interesting. He's the least romantic person I know."

Mary returned to the couch and tucked her legs underneath her. "Over the years he's become so…I don't know…black and white." She sighed. "Oh, I know it's because of his work – pilots can be more analytical than emotional – but…"

Lorelei finished her sentence. "…but it doesn't make marriage any easier, does it?"

"No, it doesn't," Mary said quietly. "But I married Owen because he is a good man. He is practical, concrete, responsible…"

"What if you need more?" Lorelei said simply.

Mary's head snapped up. It was as if Lorelei had read her mind. "What do you mean?"

"You're a romantic. Always have been. What about fascination and passion and excitement?"

"Those things are great, Lei, but it's different when you've been married for a while. Marriage is comfortable and secure and…"

"Boring," Lorelei finished.

"Sometimes." Mary smiled. "But it's worth it. It really is. To have that bond with someone, to be a part of a team, to walk through life with…"

Lorelei made a big show of yawning enormously and Mary threw a red couch cushion at her.

"I know what you need…" Lorelei said and walked over to a bookshelf on the far side of the room. "You need some smut in your life." She pulled a thick, slightly tattered novel off the shelf and held it out.

Mary peered at the title – *A Viking's Ardor: Asvald Takes a Wife* – and burst out laughing. "My favorite!"

Reading romance novels out loud had always been a guilty pleasure of theirs, though in truth their books of choice were less about romance and more about lusty sex scenes.

Lorelei bounced onto the couch and opened to a dog-eared page. "His manhood sprang longingly from his loins and pointed toward Priscilla with a come-hither glint in its one eye. Priscilla stared feverishly at the rod of desire, fascinated by its strength and power. Her thighs trembled violently as Asvald entered her wet, slick cave of ecstasy."

Lorelei paused and dramatically threw a hand over her forehead as if she was about to swoon.

"Maybe you should read that to Detective Williams," Mary said mischievously.

Instead of protesting, a slow smile touched Lorelei's full lips. Such a suggestion was very enticing indeed. She remembered Frank's warm mouth pressed against the back of her hand at George's, the feel of his rough fingers brushing her own soft delicate ones, his blue eyes, intense with interest.

She shook her head slightly, her blonde curls dancing. It wasn't like she was going to see him again. Better to keep her love life as it was – under her control.

CHAPTER 10

itchell Morrison stood barefoot in his spacious kitchen, brewing coffee and softly whistling an old Waylon Jennings tune, much as he did every morning. Outside, the air was hazy, promising another Phoenix scorcher. Yet something felt different – he felt different. Mitch had been blessed with a serene soul and a natural contentment most strived for all their lives, but he had not been filled with this kind of excitement in years, and he knew it had everything to do with the woman lying in his bed.

There had been plenty of women over the years. Women older and younger than he, and of all shapes and sizes, nationalities and cultures. Mitch found them all endlessly interesting, for each had a story to tell, a background filled with intriguing circumstances and peopled with fascinating characters. Each had her own way of kissing, of loving. No two women were alike. That was the draw.

And they found him irresistible as well, for Mitch was very handsome and tall, with deeply tanned skin; his body was heavily muscled from a life spent in construction. Even now, in his early sixties, he seemed to draw female attention wherever he went.

He turned to look through the open door of his bedroom where she was sleeping peacefully, her raven hair spread out on a pillow, her breathing slow and even. He rubbed a hand over the stubble on his chin, wondering what made Bertie Collins different.

He had known the moment they'd met at The Boozy Turkey that he wanted to see her again. When he called to ask her out for the following weekend, she was equally direct, accepting his invitation to dinner in her husky southern drawl, with no pretense of having to check her schedule, no coquettish beating about the bush. Last night, he picked her up in his old 1964 Stingray Corvette and sped up the 101 toward the trendy eatery where he had made a reservation. The top was down, and he loved watching the way Bertie's ebony hair blew in the wind, the way her chocolate eyes danced as she laughed at his jokes. He didn't want it to end, and as they approached the exit for the restaurant he asked her if she was in the mood for a little adventure. In response, Bertie nodded and placed an elegant hand on his leg, where it remained for the next few hours, driving Mitch to distraction.

The air grew cooler as the old Stingray hugged the winding roads north of the city, and Bertie inched closer to him as if seeking warmth. The moon and the stars illuminated their path, making them feel as though they were the only two people on earth. It was so magical that Mitch was almost disappointed when they reached L'Auberge, the most exclusive resort in Sedona.

They dined at Cress, L'Auberge's restaurant nestled right against the banks of Oak Creek. Bertie had never been before, and her eyes lit up with delight as they were shown to a wooden candlelit table next to the burbling creek. Over dinner, Mitch told Bertie about his business, his love of building and the happiness that working with his hands and being outside brought him. Bertie entertained Mitch with stories of dealing with demanding publishers and late-night editing sessions that sometimes ended in more than a few tears. Like most creatives, she explained, writers were notoriously temperamental, and highly sensitive about "killing their darlings."

She stopped talking about her work abruptly at one point, put her hand to Mitch's face and said, "You have the most gorgeous eyes. I can't think what color they are... not brown..."

Caught off guard, he mumbled, "Amber."

She smiled, blinding him, and he leaned toward her, catching the sweet scent of her perfume.

The waiter arrived with a delectable meal of escargots fricassee and roasted beef tenderloin and afterward, a dessert to share and two coffees with brandy. The dessert was a beautiful chocolate lava cake with whipped topping and dark chocolate shavings.

Bertie dipped her finger in the whipped cream and brought it to Mitch's lower lip. She smeared it across his mouth, delicately, slowly, erotically. His eyes fixed on hers, Mitch reached out and stroked Bertie's neck, his hand going back into her thick beautiful hair. He pulled her close and she languidly licked the whipped cream from his lips, deliberately teasing him, tempting him, inviting him...

Mitch placed his hands on either side of Bertie's face and kissed her deeply. She responded in kind and they explored their desire by tasting one another, letting the kiss intensify and then playfully allowing their tongues to dance and skip with leisurely abandon. Her hands grasped the front of his shirt, their kiss becoming more fervent. Every nerve in Mitch's body was screaming to have this woman, but he pulled away reluctantly, tenderly, for Mitchell Morrison was a gentleman.

Bertie leaned back in her chair, reached for her coffee and smiled devilishly. "I've been wanting to kiss you all night."

Mitch forked a bite of lava cake, willing his body to control itself. "You're a good kisser, Collins."

Bertie raised an eyebrow. "Likewise, Morrison. You know, we don't have to eat that dessert here. We could take it back to your place."

"Is that what you would like to do?"

"I'd like to take all of your clothes off and then eat that cake off of you."

Mitch's fork dropped to his plate with a clank as he turned around swiftly in his seat and called, "Waiter!"

The drive back to Phoenix had been filled with lighthearted banter. Mitch liked to tease and Bertie gave as good as she got. They exchanged barbed wit as though they'd been joking around their whole lives. Bertie's hand rested on Mitch's thigh as he drove and sometimes when he made her laugh she would grip his knee and then trail her fingers back up his leg. One time her hand had wandered dangerously close in the other direction and he had distractedly drifted onto the roadside rumble strips. As the Corvette bounced loudly and jauntily off the bumps, Bertie drawled, "Driving braille tonight, Morrison?"

Mitch parked in his three car garage and led Bertie into his expansive adobe home. She marveled at the architecture, the capacious rooms and the auspicious ambiance.

"What a charming place," Bertie admired, looking around. "I love the western décor. And you're very tidy for a bachelor."

"Maria comes in every two weeks and does a bang up job on the ol' homestead. She makes great tamales too. There's some in the fridge if you'd like to take some with you… tomorrow."

Their eyes met, still playful, still full of each other. The unasked question hung in the air, but they both already knew the answer.

Mitch picked Bertie up in his arms and carried her to his bedroom. He lightly threw her on the king-size bed and she laughed with happy abandonment as he stripped off his clothes and lowered himself next to her. He began to remove her dress, her bra, her delicate panties, his hands skilled, strong and intensely seductive.

"Make love to me, Morrison," Bertie breathed, her brown eyes raking down over his fit body. "Do it *now*."

The coffee maker beeped, pulling Mitch back to the present. The tantalizing aroma of fresh brewed coffee permeated the air and he sniffed appreciatively. His mom and dad had made coffee every morning their entire marriage and Mitch had grown up associating comfort and security with the scent of coffee. He pulled a clay mug out of the kitchen cabinet and filled it with the dark, fragrant liquid.

A husky voice from behind drawled, "Aren't you going to pour one for me?"

Mitch turned around to find Bertie leaning against the sink dressed only in the white button down oxford shirt he had worn on their date. Her hair was disheveled and messy and alluringly provocative. Bertie's lips were swollen and a little bruised from the hours of passion they'd shared the night before and her brown eyes sparkled with undisguised desire.

She hasn't had enough, Mitch thought to himself. Now *that* was exciting.

He handed her his mug of coffee. "Cream or sugar?"

"Black," Bertie said.

"Me too. Care to join me on the deck? I usually read the paper in the mornings."

"Should I put my clothes on?"

"No need. I own ten acres. My neighbors are too far away to see your gorgeous legs… or anything else you might want to show me outside."

Bertie laughed and took a sip of her coffee while Mitch pulled another mug from the cabinet for himself.

As they walked through the living room toward the sliding glass door, Bertie stopped when she saw a wall filled with pictures. They ranged from old black and whites to present-day snapshots and studio portraits. Each was encased in a smoothed pine wooden frame.

"These frames are lovely," Bertie said, touching one with a delicate finger.

"My father made them all. He was a carpenter."

"Ah, it runs in the family. Is he in any of the photos?"

Mitch pointed at a photo of two adults and three children- two identical little boys of about five and a teenage girl around sixteen. The adult male wore overalls and a toolbelt. The woman wore a shabby dress and a haggard look on her weathered face. They all stood in front of a barn and a cow was visible in the background.

"You are a twin!" Bertie exclaimed, and Mitch nodded. "And how far apart are you and your sister in age?"

"Eleven years. But you'd think it was thirty. She's bossy and overprotective."

"She loves you." Bertie surmised.

"If love means nagging then yes, Georgette loves me."

"Where are they all now?"

"Georgette lives in Tempe with her partner, Francesca. My parents are long gone, and my brother..." His voice caught. "...he passed away as well."

"I'm sorry." Bertie placed a hand on his arm.

"Mom and Dad lived good lives. They were good people. No regrets." He smiled, brought her hand to his lips and thoughtfully kissed her palm. "They live on in me and in my daughter. And, one day, maybe a grandbaby."

Bertie gave him a long appreciative look. "You'll be the sexiest grandpa I've ever known."

He wiggled his eyebrows roguishly and smacked her bottom. "Damn straight."

Bertie laughed and turned her attention back to the wall and the many pictures of an amber-eyed, honey-haired girl. "And this is your daughter? She's very pretty."

Mitch's voice softened. "Yes. She's my princess. Never knew a girl with a purer heart than my Mary."

Bertie studied a young man in uniform. "Her husband is in the military?"

"*Was* in the military. Now he's a pilot with a private company."

"Impressive. He's good-looking. Very all-American-hero type."

Mitch hedged a bit. "They were high school sweethearts. Married very young."

"You don't approve?"

"He's a good guy. He's changed, but I suppose we all do as we grow up. Owen's responsible and hard-working and a good provider."

"But…?"

"I don't know. Mary and I tell each other everything, but lately… I feel like she's holding something back. If she doesn't come out here soon then I'll fly to San Diego before the Flagstaff gig starts. Those custom builds will keep me busy for a while and I'd like to see her before they begin."

"You two are very close."

"I raised her alone. She's my world."

"Where's her mother?"

Mitch paused for a beat. "I don't know exactly."

CHAPTER 11

⌐⌐⌐

O n Friday night Mary stood in her walk-in closet trying to choose an appropriate outfit for her meeting with Thomas McQuillan. She considered a red, off-the-shoulder dress. No, too flashy. Maybe something more studious, like the classic brown pantsuit Owen insisted she buy and wear to an AirSec dinner party a few months ago. No, too boring. Jeans were out of the question. The Marine Room had a dress code. Strange that she'd never been to the upscale restaurant before and was now eating there twice in the same week - once with her husband, and again tonight with a very famous author.

Thomas McQuillan.

Roger squeezed himself into the walk-in closet with Mary, his stub tail wiggling ferociously against Owen's pressed and hanging pilot uniforms. Mary laughed and petted him, angling his rear end away from her husband's clean clothes.

"What time are you leaving, hon?" Owen called from the bedroom.

"In about fifteen minutes." Mary pulled a pale yellow dress from its hanger and looked it over. The fabric was shimmery and clingy, but very conservative in cut. The skirt would hug Mary's figure, but the length demurely ended mid-calf. The sleeves were long and the sweetheart neckline was feminine and unassuming. A slim silver belt showed off Mary's small waist and curvy hips.

She emerged from the closet fully dressed, slipping her feet into silver peep-toe pumps.

Owen called Roger away from Mary, but his whistle was for his wife rather than his dog.

"You look gorgeous!" he said, pride shining from his blue eyes.

She smiled and adjusted her earrings. "Thank you."

Owen reached out for her and drew her in. "And you smell delicious." He nuzzled her honey hair and kissed her ear.

Mary sighed happily. Their romantic dinner a few nights ago had gone well. Better than well; it had been amazing. Owen never once mentioned the baby, and he listened - really listened to what she had to say. She told him how her dream of writing a book -something she hadn't seriously thought about in years – had been on her mind more and more lately. She told him she had been feeling restless, that she loved walking dogs but she needed something more challenging; something that kept her mind sharp and engaged. She told him that she daydreamed about having the type of career Lorelei had. She said she was happy with her flat tummy and svelte body but she desperately longed for fried foods and desserts. They both laughed when she told Owen about driving down their street the other day and making a fast U-turn when she spotted Imogen St. Perux walking up their driveway. She even, after some internal debate, told Owen about Willow Starflower's rather disturbing premonition. Aside from her upcoming meeting with Thomas McQuillan she had thought of little else.

"What does she mean by *that*?" Owen had asked over dinner, suspicion creeping into his voice. He had nothing against Willow personally - he'd never met the woman and knew little about her work – but he had a general skepticism about all things spiritual. He laughed off anything to do with ghosts, aliens, the afterlife, astral projection, and so on. In fact, he seemed to lump all supernatural inexplicables together and believed the notion of heaven was just as absurd as the existence of Bigfoot.

Mary thoughtfully took a sip of her wine. "I don't think she meant it to be negative, more as a warning to me. She's such a kind person, Owen, full of love, and she truly wants to help others with her gift.

She told me to start meditating, maybe take up yoga. The idea is to learn to really center myself and to call upon the angels for guidance and protection."

Owen laughed and shook his head. "Sounds like a bunch of hippie mumbo jumbo to me."

"I know. But she's completely sincere and she has so many clients, most of them repeat customers. That says something. She can't be making everything up."

"So you believe in ESP? The sixth sense? Foretelling the future?"

"Maybe. Don't you want to believe there's something more out there? A spiritual world? God and fate and guardian angels and a divine plan for each of our lives?"

Owen dipped a forkful of his lobster in melted butter. "No. I see what I see. I touch what is real. *Reality* is real to me, Mare, not a bunch of nonsense that no one can scientifically substantiate."

"That's why it's called faith, I suppose. Believing in things we can't prove."

Suddenly Mary sat straighter in her chair. "That would make a great novel premise, wouldn't it?" she said, more to herself than to Owen.

"What would?"

"A romance with a paranormal theme."

"It would definitely be a work of *fiction*."

"I'm serious!"

"Pretty sure that's been done over and over. Vampire love? Sound familiar?"

Mary giggled. "No, not like that. Something deeper- more intense and introspective."

Owen shrugged. "Then write it."

"What do you mean?"

"You've always wanted to write. So write. What's stopping you? Just do it."

Mary looked away, her gaze resting on the other diners, the waiters, the floor. It was dark now and she could no longer see the ocean waves through the windows. "I don't know. It's just that… I've always been so scared to actually try my hand at writing. I mean, what if it isn't any good?"

"You write all the time. Emails to your family, a few poems here and there, you and Lorelei exchanging short stories when she went for her Masters. Not to mention your journal."

"Emails? They don't count. And even those other things are a far cry from writing an entire book."

"If you don't like it, no one has to read it. You can burn it if you like. But if this is really your dream you have to do it. There's nothing holding you back."

"Well, I have all my clients…"

"So stop taking new clients. Stick with your current schedule and write in between walks."

"You make it sound so simple."

Owen's eyebrows rose. "Because it is."

Mary let the thought sink in. Why had she never written a book? She sighed. She knew the answer – it was doubt in her ability. She was terrified that she would finally try the thing she had always loved, only to find she wasn't good at it. It was much safer to say she fantasized about being a writer rather than attempting it and discovering she had no talent at all.

"I guess I could just keep my regulars. But I have one new client possibly coming on board this week."

"That's great, hon!"

"It's a French Bulldog. I'm actually meeting the owner here."

Owen was skeptical. "You're meeting a client at The Marine Room?"

"Yes. Friday at eight."

"That's odd. Doesn't this person want you to come to their home so you can meet their dog?"

"The client is rather sensitive. A bit private. I don't think he wants me to know where he lives until he feels me out."

"A male client? You're meeting a male client for dinner at The Marine Room?" Owen's eyes narrowed.

"It's fine. It'll be fine. He might be a little eccentric or something."

"I thought this place would be special for you. New and romantic and..." Owen winked. "...expensive."

Mary reached for his hand across the table. "It *is* special being here with you and I feel very loved that you would romance me with a beautiful night out. Friday will be all business."

Owen squeezed her hand. "Okay, but I still don't like it. What's this guy's name?"

Mary averted her eyes. "I can't tell you. There's a confidentiality matter."

"Mare..."

"I know. I'm sorry."

"Cancel on him. Tell him you aren't taking new clients."

"I already said I'd meet him!"

"Refer him to another dog-walker."

"Owen... I want this job. Please."

"Why?"

Mary hesitated. Because she wanted to meet Thomas McQuillan. She wanted to talk to him about his books, about his writing career, about his creative muse and his technique. Because she wanted his advice and his knowledge. Because... maybe the timing was all coming together for her to finally realize her dream. It couldn't be a coincidence that she was meeting Thomas McQuillan the same week Owen told her to write a book. And hadn't her dad emailed her that he'd just met an editor at some bar? Was it all serendipitous? And if so, if this was her time, her chance, to follow her heart, then why would Willow say bad things were about to happen? Could one have anything to do with the other?

Owen wiped his mouth with his napkin and set it down on the table. "Look, Mare, don't worry about it. I'm just being a little jealous. This guy is probably an eighty-year-old tycoon who just needs help caring for his dog. We're not here to talk about your work or my work- we're here for me to tell you I'm sorry about everything and how badly I want us to move forward. I don't understand what's going on, but I know I love you and I'd do anything for you. You're my wife. I will take care of you always, Mary. Always."

"I'm sorry too. I don't want to fight. I just want you. I want us."

Owen looked pleased. "You already have me. I'm yours, now and forever."

Mary smiled, her heart soaring. It was like the old days- before Owen had become obsessed with his career, before there was talk of starting a family, before Mary had begun questioning what she wanted from life. She wondered if Owen would make love to her when they got home. Slowly, sweetly…

"Are you thinking what I'm thinking?" Owen asked, his voice low and intense.

Mary licked her lips, her heart picking up speed. "I think so…" She looked at Owen with longing, her eyes taking in his handsome face, his broad shoulders, his strong hands.

Smiling, he gave a decisive nod. "Good. I think you should splurge on dessert too. Take a break from the diet for one night. Should we split the Almond Dacquoise?"

Roger barked loudly and ran out of the bedroom, crashing noisily through the dog door and bringing Mary back to the present. She kissed Owen on the cheek and stepped out of his arms. He reached out and ran his fingers through her long, soft hair. The honey waves cascaded over his hand and spilled down her back, the color a pleasing contrast with the light yellow of her dress. They stood like this, silently, companionably, Owen stroking her hair over and over. Mary's eyes closed, her breathing slowed and she surrendered to her husband's gentle touch, relaxing into his hand and swaying slightly with his movements. There were few things that could relax Mary quicker than someone playing with her hair. It took her back to childhood, when her father would brush her baby-soft tresses each night until her head drooped with sleepiness. She had never felt so loved, so safe...

"You won't be too late tonight..." Owen said. It was more a statement than a question.

"I'm sure it will only be two hours, tops," she murmured distractedly.

"Okay, I'll wait up for you."

Roger came prancing back into the bedroom looking smug. His tongue lolled out of the side of his mouth and there was a feather stuck to one of his floppy lips.

"Uh oh..." Owen said, staring at the feather.

Mary shook her head. "Another pigeon?"

Roger panted happily.

"Well, I'd love to stay and help you clean up whatever is out in the yard, but..." Mary looked down at her beautiful dress in mock remorse.

Owen laughed. "I got it. Go on. I love you."

"I love you too."

CHAPTER 12

Bonjour Mama,

When I was in third grade I won the school's poetry contest. I had to read my poem in front of the entire student body - five hundred kids who couldn't have cared less about a rhyming story of a tiny purple fairy who lived in a tulip. Since I have no illustrative talent whatsoever (why didn't I inherit that gift from you?) the English department had a pretty blonde girl from second grade draw a picture to go with my poem. It wasn't a very good depiction, but this boy, Brian, who I had the hugest crush on, took an instant liking to Hillary's artwork, and to Hillary. Oh, I was so devastated! Later I found out Brian really just wanted to dress up like Hillary's fairy for Halloween. Recently I saw on Facebook that Brian married Nathan Redgren, who also went to our school, and they adopted three children from China. So he and I both married our Prince Charmings. All's well that ends well, right?

Anyway, winning that contest and having teachers praise my writing ability was a defining moment for me. I knew from that day on that I wanted to create stories. But the lackluster response from my peers was enough to fertilize the seeds of self-doubt.

Have you ever read "Little Women"? I did, when I was ten years old. There's a character named Amy who loves art and dabbles in it all through her younger years. When she reaches traveling age, she goes to Rome to pursue her passion, only to reach this conclusion:

"...talent isn't genius, and no amount of energy can make it so."

Those twelve words have stayed with me for well over two decades. Just because I love doing something (writing) doesn't mean I'm any good at it. I've always been afraid to try for fear of seeing in black and white just how possibly ungifted I really am.

Amy also said, "I want to be great or nothing. I won't be a commonplace dauber, so I don't intend to try anymore."

On this, I disagree because if only a handful of people enjoyed my writing it would be worth it. I will never be an F. Scott Fitzgerald or an Ernest Hemingway. Many say writers are born- you either have the talent or you don't and you have no say in it. Did Fitz and Hemmy know why they were so brilliant? Or was all their work simply innate- an amalgamation of the genius within them pouring out onto paper?

Wow, this entry has become very philosophical and introspective. And boring, I fear. What I'm trying to say is that I need to stop hoping and wishing I could be a writer and instead, do *something about it. If I discover I have no literary ability at all, well then it's about time I found that out and moved on with my life, whatever that means.*

I know it seems like I'm rambling, but in a strange way I feel like things are starting to come together. For one, I told Owen how badly I've always wanted to pen a novel and he was actually supportive of it! He even told me I should cut back on my dog-walking and take time to work on my book. Which brings me to this other completely synchronistic thing that's happened. Last night I had dinner with Thomas McQuillan- one of the most important writers of his generation – perhaps several generations. I've always been a voracious reader, but his book Souls in Collision, *was seriously compelling and insightful and I could NOT put it down. His imagery, his choice of words, they were almost lyrical -I mean, he literally changed the way I thought about novels. I know, I know, I am such a gushing book nerd, but I've probably read that book fifteen times over the years. It's that incredible. So you can imagine how excited I was to meet him.*

Well, let me tell you, it was nothing like I thought it would be. I valet parked at The Marine Room, which is a fancy restaurant in

La Jolla right on the water. The tide comes up and over the win-
dows when you time your dinner just right, which of course Thomas
McQuillan did. He also had our table angled in a private alcove
right against the glass. I got the feeling this is where he usually sits
when he's conducting business meetings. All of the staff knew him
and they were very quiet, using as few words as possible when ask-
ing for his order or checking in to see if he needed a drink refill or
if all was to his liking. The manager came by several times, not to
chat, or to even look at us, but to eye our table and assess we had
all we needed. When the tide was at its highest, and the waves beat
against the windows, I tried not to appear frightened even though I
sort of was. The glass vibrated and shook and the noise of the ocean
was so loud it sometimes drowned out our voices. It was totally dif-
ferent than when I went there with Owen earlier in the week, and
not just because of the tide. That night was all about him, and our
marriage, and the fact that he cared enough to take me out on a date.
With Thomas, it was a completely different kind of magic. It was as if
being with an author I admired heightened my senses. I noticed the
beauty of the warm candles glowing throughout the restaurant; the
taste of the delicate fish we were served left me craving to try every-
thing else on the menu; the smell of the wood burning in the fireplace
and the crackling of the flames made me drowsy with contentment.
And the man himself, well, he had the sharp intellect I expected, but
he also had a cynical sense of humor. He was definitely guarded, and
excellent at deflecting any questions away from himself and back to
me. He was mellow and surprisingly easy to talk to. And handsome!
So very, very handsome. Not in the classical way. Not in the clean-
cut, pedigreed way like Owen, either. No, Thomas McQuillan looks
like a surfer, tan and athletically lean with thick, sandy-colored hair
that falls to his shoulders. His eyes are hazel and very intense and
there are crow's feet at the corners that add to his air of worldliness,
or perhaps world-weariness? I got the feeling he's seen and done
everything exciting there is to see and do.

As we ate, I kept staring at his hands, wondering what they looked like when they were typing. Or did he create his books by handwriting the first draft? No, too laborious. But still, I looked for a writer's horn on his middle finger just in case. I didn't see one, for the record, but he caught me eyeballing his fingers and held his hands up in mock surrender. "Is there something you're looking for, Ms. Crossfield?" I was mortified! Did he think I was checking for a wedding ring? I then blurted out that I was married, which of course was extremely awkward and totally out of the blue. He just said, "That's nice," and then returned to the subject of Voltaire, his French Bulldog. Did I mention that's why we were meeting in the first place? He was "interviewing" me to be his dog-walker.

I'm afraid this is where our evening took a downturn because it is very apparent Mr. McQuillan is not one bit fond of his dog. He spoke of Voltaire as if he were a nuisance, an intrusion on his valuable time, which made me so mad! Why anyone would bother having a pet if he doesn't like it is beyond me!

He must have seen my look of disapproval because he said irritably, "Have you, Ms. Crossfield, ever been interrupted during a creative jag? Especially by an annoying animal?"

That stopped me in my tracks. I honestly didn't know what to say. I'd love to have identified with him and said, "Oh, yes! I hate when I'm working on my next bestseller and in the middle of a really great scene Roger barks, and I lose my concentration." One author to another, you know? We would wink conspiratorially to each other, bemoaning our tortured artist existences and the bothersome banalities of life that creep into our prolific worlds of visionary genius.

But, as it turned out, I didn't need to say anything. Thomas wasn't expecting an answer. He seemed to want to vent a bit of frustration so I just sat there and listened, absorbing all he said because I wanted to learn what I could about being an author.

"It's just…" Thomas raked his hands through his thick sandy hair and leaned back in his chair. He looked up at the ceiling and I found

myself leaning forward, anxious to hear what he had to say next. "I just... I feel like in some ways I've lost my passion. I need something to inspire me. Something to get me back on the page. I pound out word after word, read what I've written and it's... it's trash!" He banged on the table with a fist and our wine glasses jumped. "I have to keep going. I sit down to write and wait for my muse to show up. Letters turn into paragraphs that turn into chapters but it's not right... I don't like any of it. Where is my muse? Where is it?" He sounded so sad. "What do I have to do to get it back?"

I watched him very carefully, fascinated to see this bit of vulnerability from such a famous person. It was in this moment that I realized he'd never "retired," at least not in a way people thought. Had he really been trying to write for the past decade and come up bupkis? It's hard to believe someone of his talent has had writer's block for almost ten years. How is that even possible?

Thomas snapped out of his troubled mood pretty quickly. I'm sure he was embarrassed to have let his guard down in front of a stranger. He covered it up by being brusque and businesslike and returning to the matter at hand: his rambunctious Frenchie.

"Voltaire is trying my patience," Thomas said tersely, his back straight now, his head up and his eyes focused. His intense gaze was a trifle disconcerting. I didn't look away even though I wanted to.

"Is Voltaire a puppy?" I asked.

"If a one-year-old is still considered a puppy, yes."

"Has he had training?"

"I don't have time to train an animal, Ms. Crossfield," he said condescendingly, "nor the expertise."

"Please call me Mary," I said quietly, trying to inject some warmth into the conversation.

His mouth thinned. "Can you or can you not keep Voltaire busy while I'm trying to write, Ms. Crossfield?"

"I'm just saying that it may not only be exercise Voltaire needs. He may also require a bit of learned discipline. Dogs enjoy routine, rules, following commands, having a purpose."

Thomas laughed outright at me. "A purpose?"

"Yes. Like dogs who herd sheep or assist physically challenged individuals or belong to the military... canines live to please humans. Those animals, who are highly intelligent, need to focus their energy into a job."

"The only vocational 'skills' Voltaire can offer are being stubborn, aggravating and bad. He's a bad dog, Ms. Crossfield."

I totally bristled at that. "There are no bad dogs, Mr. McQuillan, *only bad owners."*

Thomas looked annoyed. "I am not hiring both a dog-walker and *a dog trainer. Can you exercise him enough to tire him out or not?"*

"Of course, but..."

"You must make yourself available to come whenever I need you."

"I don't understand. We should have a structured schedule; discuss how long you would like each visit to last and the days and times."

"You are right- you don't understand. I write on the whims of my imagination. Inspiration can strike at any time and I want to be free to conceive and flesh out ideas uninterrupted. I am telling you, you would be on call."

"That's not possible, Mr. McQuillan, I have other clients."

"So get rid of them," Thomas said carelessly.

I flared up at this. "I will not let all of my clients go and set them aside like they don't matter!"

"Why not? I will make it worth your while."

"They count on me. You can't... you can't just throw money around and expect people to do what you say."

"Again, I ask, why not?"

He was so smug, so self-contained. It was obvious his looks, his status, his wealth had given him anything and everything he wanted over the years. It grated on me.

"No," I said, shaking my head. "No. I will not do it. I will not give up several clients for one new client because he is famous and... and... used to getting his way."

Thomas sighed. "You are a very exasperating woman."

I have never had anyone call me that before! I tilted my chin up. "I won't be bought and I won't be dictated to."

"Something tells me you're already dictated to." He gestured toward my wedding bands. "What does your husband do for a living?"

"That is none of your business!" I said haughtily. The nerve! "But you know what is my business? The fact that you have a dog you don't like and don't pay attention to. Why even bother owning a pet? I feel sorry for Voltaire."

"This meeting is becoming tiresome." Thomas insipidly looked over at the flames in the fireplace.

"Well, Mr. McQuillan, I think our discussion has led to an impasse. Should you change your mind about scheduling, please let me know. Being 'on call' is out of the question."

"And you are willing to sign a confidentiality agreement?"

That stopped me. "What do you mean?"

"Surely you are aware I do not want you talking about me to your friends, your family or the press. I do not wish anyone to know what I'm working on, where I live, etcetera."

"Of course..." I stammered. "No one knows I met you here. I would never breathe a word to anyone about you or your private life." I paused. "You can trust me implicitly."

Thomas relaxed somewhat. He looked into my eyes for a long time, as though he were searching for any hint of deception. I let him. I let him swim into whatever thoughts of mine he wanted to read, if that's what he was trying to do. I have nothing to hide, nothing to be ashamed of, nothing but admiration for his talent and his work. But the man was completely frustrating.

I finished my glass of wine and placed my napkin on the table. "Now if you're done with your interrogation, I need to use the ladies' room." Then the strangest thing happened. As I stood up, I saw Thomas' eyes lazily glide over my figure. The fabric of my yellow dress, soft against my skin, coupled with his gaze, was oddly sensual- as though he and the dress were of like mind, both working together to create feather-like sensations on my shoulders, my stomach, my thighs. Abruptly I turned and walked quickly away before he saw the shallow breaths I was taking, the slight flush that was creeping up my neck and to my face. I know this is terrible, but I knew he was watching me cross the restaurant and I swayed my hips more than normal, twitched my rear end in that sexy way women do to tease. By the time I got to the restroom, I shook myself mentally. I was not a flirty schoolgirl! I was a married woman. So Thomas McQuillan was a genius with words. So what? I thought of his hands again... those strong hands that looked like they would be equally comfortable bracing a surfboard or flying lightly over a keyboard. What else could those strong hands do? I closed my eyes and imagined them running down my back, his fingertips traveling lightly up my spine... I really don't know what got into me. But then I remembered Meredith Booker and the way Ricki's face twisted with hatred when she talked about her. My blood grew cold instantly, and when I got back to the table I told Thomas that it appeared our meeting was at an end. I thanked him for dinner and for the opportunity to nanny Voltaire, and told him he should contact me if he wanted to set up a regular exercise schedule. Then, with a brisk shake of his hand, I made my escape. But as I drove home I couldn't help but replay the entire evening: Thomas' voice, his transformation from charming companion to vulnerable artist to arrogant ass and... his hands. Most of all, his hands.

Owen was reading in bed when I got home and after trying, unsuccessfully, to get some information about my meeting, he wrapped his arms tightly around me and fell asleep. I drifted off too, but woke up in the middle of the night. Not wanting to wake Owen, I lay still and stared at the ceiling, hoping the sound of his breathing would lull me back to sleep. My fingers itched to write to you and my brain started sifting through possible storylines - a few interesting, most ridiculous – that I might want to plot out for my book. I made myself stay put under the covers, trying to push aside the excited restlessness that was taking me over.

It was the first time in a long, long while that every part of my body felt alive. I know it's because I'm finally going to commit to writing. I AM going to write a book. Meeting Thomas McQuillan may have been synchronistic and provocative, but only because I admire him as an author. This rousing energy I feel, the excitement that's coursing through me, it has everything to do with writing, and nothing at all to do with the writer. I hope Mr. McQuillan doesn't contact me again.

CHAPTER 13

*M*itch was lounging on his big leather sofa reading *The Man from Skibbereen*, one of his favorite Louis L'Amour novels. Bertie was snuggled up next to him, her head on his shoulder as she scanned a manuscript from a client she referred to as Dangling Participle Dave.

Mitch's living room basked cozily in the late Sunday afternoon desert sunshine streaming in through the high and wide windows. Soft western tunes played unobtrusively in the background and the smell of fresh-baked bread wafted over from the kitchen. Mitch had the ceiling fan on so Bertie had thrown a fluffy Sherpa blanket over her shapely legs.

The couple had spent virtually every day together since their first date a little over a week ago. They just couldn't get enough of one another- the laughter, the banter, the almost palpable chemistry... the hours of love making. Mitch could barely keep his eyes off Bertie, or his hands off her sensual and responsive body.

"Hey," Mitch said, looking down at the lovely lady nestled against him, "you never told me what you were doing at The Boozy Turkey. Hardly seems like your kind of hangout."

Bertie took off her reading glasses, set her small laptop on the rustic teak coffee table and picked up her wine glass. "Research. Adverb Arthur wrote a new scene into his rewrite. The protagonist was supposedly at a dive bar in a small western town, but Arthur didn't quite have the descriptive ambiance the reader needs. I've driven by the Turkey before and thought it might offer me some insight into what Arthur is trying to convey in terms of a 'divey' atmosphere." She gave Mitch a reprising look. "And what were *you* doing at the Turkey?"

"Dale and I have been going there since college. It just never stopped being our hangout even though they don't have drunken Quarter Shot Nights anymore." Mitch winked at Bertie and placed a kiss on top of her head. "The clientele has changed over the last forty years, but beer, pool and good friends are constant. Besides, the building was erected in 1908 and you know I appreciate old school engineering. The Boozy Turkey was a saloon right up until Prohibition, and then again afterward; between 1920 and 1933 it was converted into a billiards parlor. But the construction of the place. . . that cast iron façade is brilliant and the damned cornice moulding is impressive." Mitch sighed with pleasure. "I love being inside a well-built structure."

Bertie cast a sidelong glance at him.

Mitch laughed, chucking her under the chin. "Hey, lady, you've got a dirty mind."

"I'm an editor. I'm naturally attuned to word play."

"And I'm naturally attuned to you," Mitch said, suddenly serious. Bertie's shirt had dipped down on one side, revealing a soft, tanned shoulder. Just the sight of her skin, however innocent, sent his mind reeling down a path of physical surrender.

Bertie looked up at him, her eyes molten with intensity.

"What's happening to us?" she asked, her southern drawl thick with emotion.

"I don't know." Mitch took her wine glass and set it on the table. He gathered her into his arms, holding her so tightly that her face pressed into his chest. He pulled the blanket around them and they clung to each other, letting the flurry of their magnetism flow in and around their bodies.

"I love being with you, Morrison," Bertie whispered.

"And I love being with you, Collins."

"This is all moving rather fast, isn't it?"

Mitch couldn't speak, for Bertie had begun to absentmindedly trace circles on his thigh with her dainty finger.

The heavily charged air was abruptly splintered by the buzzing of Mitch's cell phone. He was about to decline the call when he saw his sister's name on the screen. With a grin he picked up the phone.

"Hi Georgette," he said, placing the phone on speaker.

"We haven't talked in over a week," came a pleasant but no-nonsense voice. "I just wanted to see if you'll come out of hiding long enough to have lunch with me…"

"Sure thing." Mitch felt Bertie moving and shifted his body.

She mouthed, "Want a glass of water?"

He nodded.

"…and to see if you're going to San Diego to see our Mary," Georgette was saying.

"Yes," he said, his amber eyes softening at the mention of his daughter's name, "in a few weeks."

"That will be so nice for you both. Hitting up all your favorite restaurants?"

"You betcha."

"Good." Georgette paused. "I know this time of year is hard for you…I mean with your birthday coming up…"

Mitch frowned. *My birthday…and Claude's.*

"George, I don't want you worrying about me. Seriously. It's not… it's not something I like to really think about. I reckon it's gotten easier over the years, but I'm a big boy. I can take care of myself."

"I know you can. I miss him too, but it's harder on you. You were so close to each other."

Mitch stared out of his floor-to-ceiling windows at the dry, dusty desert. It stretched as far as the eye could see… cactus, dirt, tumbleweeds, small half-dead bushes. The Superstition Mountains loomed in the distance, their red and purple beauty baking in the hot Arizona sun. Mitch wondered where Claude was now. Could he see the desert that had been his home for so many years? Could he see the family he had left behind? Did he know how much he was missed?

"Sometimes I talk to him," Georgette was saying, as if reading her brother's thoughts. "I don't know if he can hear me, but I'd like to think he's sort of… my guardian angel."

Mitch felt his eyes dampen. "I talk to him sometimes too."

"You boys were always such good kids. Never into trouble. Claude dabbling in his paints and you following Dad around pounding nails, walking on trusses, caulking, lath and plastering…"

"Lath and plastering?" Mitch let out an amused chuckle. "That hasn't been done since the fifties, George. Drywall is all the rage now. You've heard of drywall, right?"

"Oh, ha-ha, make fun of me. I don't know all your trendy little construction terms."

"Uh huh," Mitch said distractedly as Bertie walked back into the room. His eyes were riveted to her every graceful move.

"Are you excited about the Flagstaff contract?"

"Uh huh," Mitch said again.

"And how long will you be up the mountain for it?" Georgette prompted.

There was an awkward silence.

Georgette became very bossy and older sister like. "MITCH! Pay attention! What are you doing? We are having a conversation here."

"Here you go," Bertie said quietly as she handed him the water, but not quietly enough.

"Who's that?" Georgette asked suspiciously, then added, "So *that's* why you haven't called me back. You've got a new woman, haven't you? And she's there now…?"

Mitch grinned at Bertie as she sank down onto the sofa next to him. "Yes…"

"Well, why didn't you say so? I can let you go." Mitch heard a garbled voice in the background. "Francesca wants to know if it's that nice lady from New Jersey? We liked the way she said 'whalk the dawg in the pawk.'"

Oh no! Mitch's eyes widened and he snapped out of his trance. No, no, no...

"We're on speaker now!" Francesca jumped in. "Hi Mitch, my lovey! Is Kelly there with you? Tell her I like my cawfee with cream and sugah!"

"No," Mitch said pointedly, "I don't see Kelly anymore." He glanced at Bertie, who was laughing silently. "And *you're* on speaker too so can we *not* talk about this right now?"

"That's too bad. Kelly was a nice girl. Although the skirts she wore were really too short. One time she scooched down to hug Georgie and I almost saw her biscuits. So who's there now?"

Mitch sighed. "Her name is Bertie."

"Is this why we haven't heard from you in over a week?" Francesca wanted to know.

"Never knew anyone to attract the women like our Mitchell," Georgette put in.

"Remember the fashion designer?" He heard Francesca ask his sister. "Susan, I think her name was. She had that little puffy mole on the side of her neck. The first time I saw it I thought it was lint and I tried to pick it off for her. She was all shrieking, 'It's attached! It's attached!'" Francesca harrumphed. "Well, I can't help it if your mole looks like a dust bunny, lady. I was just trying to be helpful."

Georgette laughed. "Wait... wasn't she the one who had a pet bird that could only say, 'Happiness is a crunchy cricket!'"

"No," Francesca said, "that was Jenny."

"That's right! Jenny the Squid!" Georgette agreed.

"She was in the mafia."

"I thought she was a stripper...?"

"Really, Georgette! A stripper named Jenny the Squid?"

"Enough, you two!" Mitch bellowed exasperatedly. "Don't you have better things to do on a Sunday afternoon than harass me?"

Bertie laughed outright this time, her whole face lighting up with delight.

"So," Georgette said, smugly. "She has a sense of humor, this Bertie. Hello dear."

"Hi," Bertie said, smiling. "Nice to meet you."

"Francesca is my partner," Georgette explained. "We live in Tempe and we simply adore Mitch."

"He's told me about you," Bertie said warmly. "I saw pictures of you both on Mitch's wall."

"Ah, so you know what we look like, but we don't know what you look like."

Francesca piped up. "If she's with Mitch you can bet your sweet bum she's a hottie."

Mitch dropped his head into his hand.

"How old are you?" Francesca asked.

"I'm forty-six."

"And what do you do for a living?"

"I'm an editor. Mostly fictional novels."

"And you're from the south?" Georgette chimed in, picking up on Bertie's accent.

"Yes, born and raised in Old Hickory."

"And do you have specific designs on our Mitch?" Francesca asked.

Bertie looked at the handsome man next to her and placed a hand on his cheek. "No," she said softly, "I just enjoy spending time with him. He makes me happy and he is a gentleman in every way."

"I like her," Francesca said to Georgette. "Let's invite her to lunch."

"Bertie, come to lunch with the three of us before Mitch goes to San Diego. We'll probably meet at Bandera in Scottsdale. Do you like chicken and cornbread?"

"I'm from the South, aren't I?" Bertie said.

"Hot damn!" Francesca said. "I can't wait to meet this one."

"Okay, well, I think this conversation is over," Mitch muttered.

"I have to go anyway," Francesca said cheerfully. "I'm off to my shooting class."

"Bye, hon," Georgette said, a kissing sound lightly coming over the phone.

"What kind of shooting?" Mitch asked suspiciously. "I hope she's talking about photography."

Georgette sighed. "Unfortunately, no. She bought a gun after the Hendersons were robbed a few weeks ago and she says she's going to protect the neighborhood."

"I don't think that's a good idea…"

"I know, I know. But you pick your battles when you're in a relationship. I can live with a gun in the house as long as she *only* fires it at the range." Georgette cleared her throat. "Listen, Mitch, I'd like to… discuss that thing we were talking about last month… the thing in regard to you telling Mary… that thing you should tell her."

Bertie started to get up. "I'll let you two talk in private."

Mitch reached for her hand and pulled her back down next to him. "Don't go. I know what Georgette is talking about." His voice became stern. "And Georgette knows my position and that I will not change my mind."

"I really wish you would rethink it. Mary is older now and she will understand. She must wonder about her mother and she should know-"

"No, George. I decided it was best she *not* know thirty-two years ago when Helene showed up on my doorstep."

"But don't you think she deserves to-"

"Absolutely not. She has such a tender heart. I never, ever want her upset."

"Being upset is part of life, Mitchell."

Mitch's jaw clenched. "This subject is closed."

"For now," Georgette said dismissively. "But I'd like to discuss this again later."

"No," Mitch said, his voice low and taut.

"I love you, little brother."

The jaw relaxed a bit. "I love you too."

"We will see you at Bandera… say… Wednesday? Six o'clock?"

Mitch looked at Bertie and she nodded silently in agreement. "We'll see you there, Georgette."

"I look forward to meeting Bertie. See you two soon. And Mitchell?"

"Yes?"

"I'm so proud of the man you've become. Never forget that."

Mitch ended the call and put the phone down on the coffee table. He leaned his head back against the couch and released a long, slow breath. He didn't like discussing Mary's mother. Certain predicaments belonged in the past. Mary didn't need to know the whole truth- it wouldn't bring her joy or closure- it would only serve to cause her confusion and grief. He couldn't understand why Georgette didn't see that; and he didn't know why she was bringing it up again after all this time.

Bertie uncurled herself from the leather sofa and stood behind Mitch. With strong, skillful fingers she began to knead and rub his shoulder muscles and he closed his eyes in response, letting his body unwind, allowing her peaceful presence to soothe him into a relaxed, dream-like state. She was very good with her hands and as they moved from his shoulders up to his neck, the calming firm strokes eased the stress from his body.

Drowsily, he reached up, took hold of her arm and brought her around the couch, guiding her body next to his.

"Rest with me," he murmured. "I want to hold you."

"I'm not going anywhere, Mitchell Morrison," Bertie said gently, pulling the blanket over them and letting her head fall back on his shoulder.

"I'm sorry about getting upset with George -" Mitch started, but Bertie cut him off.

"I like your sister. She's funny and she really loves you. I have a feeling she is as protective over you as you are over Mary. And I won't ask about what she didn't want to say in front of me. That's family business and I won't ever pry. No worries, no apologies."

"I don't want to keep secrets from you..." Mitch yawned, his eyelids very heavy.

"The only secrets that are important to me are the ones you want to share."

"I..." Mitch's voice trailed off as he succumbed to a blissful slumber, his arms full of Bertie, his heart full of emotion. Whatever he had been about to reveal would have to wait.

CHAPTER 14

Wyland's was full. Not busting at the seams with tables and booths squashed together so closely the servers could barely squeeze by- no, it was a languid, classy atmosphere filled with soft lighting, muted, winsome conversations and barely perceptible jazz playing in the background.

Lorelei stepped into the dining room, following the hostess to the spot Faith had reserved in the back by a window. Lorelei didn't know why she had never worn the dazzling blue dress she'd bought almost a year ago from an expensive Del Mar vintage boutique, or why tonight of all nights she'd pulled it out of the closet. But as she glided through the room she was vaguely aware of the stares it was attracting. Men looked at her appreciatively. Women looked at her admiringly. There were a few catty glances from younger, insecure women, but not many. Most nights, Lorelei would have enjoyed the attention; tonight she was too busy wondering what Faith was up to.

"I still don't understand why you're not inviting Mary," Lorelei had said into the phone.

"Because I have something personal going on that I can't tell anyone else about." Faith lowered her voice conspiratorially. "You know, I need special Lor advice.

"Hmmm... I just don't want Mary to feel left out is all."

Faith pretended to pout. "You two go out without me all the time!"

"Because we don't want a gaggle of kids listening to our conversation. For one, it's very hard to talk in 'code' when discussing adult subjects and for two, children are too disruptive and distracting- especially yours. We can't have real and meaningful dialogue when one kid is screaming, one is crying and one is yelling, 'Mom! Mom!!! MOOOOOOOOOMMMMMMM!' over and over and over. I get a headache just thinking about it."

"Well, my little loves won't be at Wyland's. It'll just be you and me."

"Ok, Fay, I'll meet you tomorrow night. But just so you know, I'm deeply suspicious."

"That hurts. You wound me..."

The hostess rounded the corner and said, "Here we are, Miss Harper." She pulled out a chair for Lorelei with one hand, a menu in the other.

It took a moment for Lorelei to absorb what she was seeing. The table was not for two, but for four. Faith sat in one chair looking particularly cheeky; her husband, Jesse, sat on her left and there, on her right, was Detective Frank Williams.

"Surprise!!!" Faith crowed happily, raising her water glass at Lorelei.

Lorelei blinked a few times in disbelief and Frank stood up. He took the menu from the hostess and held Lorelei's chair for her.

"You look beautiful," he said sincerely, his eyes taking in her stunning blue dress, her red lips, her gorgeous crown of golden curls.

Lorelei sat down, her eyes narrowed at Faith, an angry flush beginning to spread over her chest and neck. Frank pushed her chair in. He placed the menu in her hands and went back to his seat.

"Fay..." Lorelei was dangerously close to letting loose a string of terrifying cuss words followed by a malicious lecture filled with threats on how nosy, manipulative friends should mind their own business because if they didn't, terrible, horrible things could and would happen to them. But of course she couldn't do that in front of a restaurant full of people, or, for that matter, the presumably innocent Frank Williams.

Jesse put up his hands in mock surrender. "Sorry, Lor. You know how Faith is when she gets an idea in her head."

Lorelei turned her icy green eyes on Detective Williams.

"Frank didn't know until he got here," Faith breezed. "Don't be mad at him. And look how handsome he is in that jacket and tie! Don't you just want to eat him up?"

Frank cleared his throat. "It's true, I had no idea this was a setup." He cast an amused sidelong glance at Faith. "She said on the phone that she and her husband wanted to consult with me..." He cleared his throat. "... on a homicide novel he wants to write."

"Judas Priest! And you *believed* her?"

"I barely know her and, well, it sounded interesting."

Lorelei turned to Faith and said, with barely controlled rancor, "You have crossed the line and I will-"

"Oh stop!" Faith tsk-tsked with a merry wave of her hand. "This double date is going to be so fun! Frank is really nice and he was telling us this funny story about how he and some of his buddies made the new rookie take vital signs on an already deceased perp and when the rookie said the guy had already passed away, Frank and the other detectives started yelling, 'You let him die on your watch?! He was alive before you touched him! What the hell, baby cop!? Revive him! Revive him!' Then the rookie started doing mouth-to-mouth on this dead murderous arms dealer." Faith laughed delightedly. "Isn't that just hysterical, Lor?"

"Hilarious."

A waiter came over to take Lorelei's drink order.

"A Templeton Rye Manhattan, up with a twist."

Jesse gave Lorelei a sympathetic look, his arm around the back of Faith's chair. He was a big man, African-American and darkly handsome. His movements were easy and his eyes sharp and intelligent. He was clearly his own person, but it was obvious Faith was the brightly lit sun his world revolved around. Jesse knew his wife was full of carefree mischief and he had warned her that Lorelei might be very, very angry about this setup. Faith had blown him off saying, "It's for her own good. I think she and Frank are meant to be together. You should have seen the chemistry between them at George's! It was so romantic." And Jesse, taking in Faith's sparkling eyes and loving determination to finagle a fairy tale happily ever after for Lorelei, relented and agreed to attend the staged dinner.

Lorelei glanced around the table suspiciously. "Exactly how long have you all been here?"

"About a half an hour." Faith said. "We-"

Jesse coughed pointedly.

"I mean... *I* wanted to let Frank know what was happening before you got here."

"I see," Lorelei said staunchly. "Why couldn't it have been the other way around?"

"Because if you had gotten here first you would have left as soon as I told you the plan."

"True." Lorelei glowered at Faith and then shot Frank an apologetic glance. It wasn't his fault her friend was an intrusive buttinski. And Frank really did look handsome tonight. His big hands were clasped loosely on top of the table and Lorelei wondered what it would be like to reach over and touch him. She remembered the shot of electricity she had felt when he had kissed the back of her hand at George's, and a stirring warmth spread through her body, eliminating a lot of the righteous anger and indignation she felt toward Faith. A lot, but not all of it.

"Now," Faith said decisively, "let's figure out appetizers pronto because I need sustenance."

Jesse gave his wife a conspiratorial wink. "You need your strength for tonight, baby."

Faith squealed in delight and kissed her husband soundly on the lips.

"Oh god…" Lorelei muttered and looked around for their waiter, praying he would bring her drink soon.

Faith leaned into Frank and Lorelei and said in hushed excitement, "Wicky is staying the night tonight so Jesse and I can have hotel sex!"

Frank's eyebrows shot up.

"Fay," Lorelei hissed, "you do *not* have to tell everyone everything about your life. The detective here doesn't need to know about your personal… *activities*."

"Oh, why not? Everyone has sex. It's okay to discuss it amongst adults. I'm sure Frank has had sex before and knows what it is."

Lorelei wanted to crawl under the table. Frank shifted in his seat and straightened his tie.

"In fact," Faith went on, whacking the table with her hand animatedly, "let's play a game! Let's go around the table and each person has to say when the last time they had sex was. Frank, you go first!"

"Uh…"

"Three hours ago for me," Jesse interjected proudly.

"Faith, can I see you in the ladies' room for a moment?" Lorelei's voice was like steel. "*Now!*"

Their waiter appeared and set Lorelei's drink in front of her with a flourish. She picked it up and drained it. "Please bring me another as quickly as you can."

"Wow," said Jesse, his mouth hanging open. "Didn't that burn going down?"

Faith completely ignored Lorelei and spoke to the waiter. "I'm pregnant and need food stat. I don't know what everyone else wants, but I'd like to start with the poached pear and brassicas. And a small cheese plate."

The waiter nodded and turned to leave.

"OH!" Faith called loudly in a rush. "Wait! Can I have a plate of steamed asparagus as well?"

Jesse squeezed Faith's shoulder and smiled. "Good girl, getting your veggies in."

Faith put her hand on Jesse's arm and rubbed it affectionately. "Mmmm..." she purred, "I *am* a good girl. I'm *your* good girl and tonight I will show you-"

"FAITH!" Lorelei seethed, cutting her friend off. "There are other people present." Lorelei's voice turned sickeningly sweet, like a villain with nefarious intent luring its prey. "Why don't you and I visit the powder room now? I have something I want to show you..."

Frank, sensing a domestic violence scuffle was about to go down, jumped in with, "So, what or who is a Wicky?"

Faith smiled contentedly. "Oh sweet heavens, she is our angel of a babysitter! The kids just love her. She's a little unorthodox but she's a really great person- has such a big heart."

Frank picked up his beer and took a sip. He was keenly aware of the angst emanating from Lorelei and he wanted to somehow put her at ease. He could sense the heat of anger radiating from her lovely skin, the tenseness tightening her muscles and the fury she must have roiling through her mind at having been tricked into this double date. She had never called him after he'd sent the roses and he'd understood. Someone as beautiful and intelligent as Lorelei must be badgered by male attention constantly. He knew it had been a one in a million shot, but he could have sworn she had felt the seductive pull between them just as he had the night they'd met.

"And why is she unorthodox?" he asked, trying to keep the conversation light.

"Because she looks like Satan," Lorelei said darkly.

"Oh, Lor! You're so funny!" Faith giggled.

"Well," Jesse agreed, "she kind of does."

"She's just into the whole goth thing is all- black clothes, black hair, black lipstick, black eyeshadow, marshmallow white face," Faith explained. "And she wears a black dog collar with spikes and a dangly tag that says 'HERETIC.' Her friends nicknamed her Wicked, but my kiddos just call her Wicky. Her real name is Belinda, which is just so pretty! I think she's adorable. We all go through phases when we're teenagers."

"I went through a grunge stage in junior high," Frank offered.

"Lor, remember when your mom showed me that picture of you in high school and I couldn't stop laughing? You had crimped hair and a weird choker necklace on. Your mom said your style that year could only be described as 'slutty bohemian.'"

Lorelei's eyes narrowed into slits and she drummed her French manicured fingernails on the table. Where was that second drink?

Faith's mobile, banged up and covered with Bob the Builder stickers, began to ring.

Lorelei's mouth tightened and Jesse wouldn't meet her eyes.

"Hello?" Faith said very innocently into the phone.

Frank, aware of an undercurrent, took a casual sip of his beer and feigned interest in the delicious looking meals being served at the table next to them.

"Oh no!" Faith exclaimed dramatically and several diners turned to stare. "Well, oh my goodness! I can't... believe that happened! Gee, we should probably come home, Wicky. Oh myyyyyy... blood, you say? And pus? Yeah, that sounds bad. Reaaaaaaal bad."

Jesse covered his mouth with his hand and looked at the ceiling.

"Yes, yes, of course," Faith said. "We'll leave now. See you soon." She hung up and heaved a great sigh of anguish. "Joel fell down the stairs," she informed the table morosely, like a soap opera actress giving a eulogy. "He'll be okay, but he needs his mama." She stood up, swaying slightly, theatrically bereaved. "I must go to him."

"That was SO campy," Lorelei said. "I cannot... *cannot* believe you're doing this."

"I don't know what you're talking about, Lor," Faith said dolefully, gathering up her silky black pashmina and leather purse. "I'm so sorry," she said, turning to Frank. "I know we were supposed to talk about the book and then it turned into a double date and now it's a single date. It was nice to see you again. You seem like a lovely person.

I hope you can catch lots of perps next week." She kissed him on the cheek and turned to Lorelei. "Now you be nice to Detective Williams, Lor, and have fun. Don't do anything I wouldn't do."

"You mean like get pregnant?" Lorelei scowled.

Faith's eyes gentled and she leaned down to whisper in Lorelei's ear. "I love you. I will always love you. You are the best friend I've ever had." Faith ran her hand over Lorelei's curls, a gesture so maternal and caring that Lorelei softened for a moment. "Make tonight all about you. Have fun. Let go."

And just like that Faith and Jesse were gone.

CHAPTER 15

L orelei took a sip of her fourth Manhattan, her gaze resting contently on the moonlight rippling over the dark ocean waves just outside their window at Wyland's. The ocean never failed to calm her, especially when accompanied by fine whiskey. Of course, conversation with the charming Detective Frank Williams had helped as well. Indeed, the evening had turned out to be quite pleasant, perhaps even better than a date that has been planned for and anticipated, but that didn't mean Faith was off the hook for her matchmaking efforts. After her abrupt departure from Wyland's, Lorelei had silently plotted all kinds of revenge – not that she would ever follow through, of course, but it helped to diffuse her rage. So had the email she'd dashed off to Mary when Frank excused himself to go to the men's room.

It hadn't escaped Lorelei's notice how well Frank had handled her dark mood, which had lasted through two and a half Manhattans. He was laid-back and completely self-assured, drawing her out carefully, always maintaining eye contact and listening intently to what she said. He paid close attention to her mannerisms and her facial expressions, responding when it was appropriate and offering his own opinion or thoughts whenever warranted. He talked of interesting subjects, but nothing too serious, and he had a broad knowledge of many topics. Mostly he was just easy to talk to. *Maybe it's from taking all those confessions*, Lorelei thought wryly.

A waiter approached with a dessert menu and Frank leaned in close to Lorelei and asked if she would like to split the Berry Feuillete. Lorelei nodded, her breath quickening at his nearness. He had a very masculine scent about him that wasn't cologne or aftershave; it was natural and incredibly sexy, as was his presence, which was at once both mellow and commanding. Lorelei presumed he was the type of man who could unequivocally handle any situation. Perhaps because of his profession; perhaps it was innate. Whatever it was, it made independent, take charge, highly intelligent Lorelei feel dainty, feminine and protected. It was a new feeling for her and one that wasn't completely unwelcome in the midst of her cozy whiskey euphoria. She was warming toward Frank, her legs crossed in his direction underneath the table, her body subtly inclined to his when he spoke. She was smiling more, her face lighting up and her eyes dancing whenever he made her laugh.

After they had finished their shared dessert, and Lorelei sipped the last of her drink, Frank leaned in close again. He was careful not to touch Lorelei, for he feared crossing some imaginary line he sensed she'd clearly established. He'd been pleasantly surprised she hadn't left him alone at the table after Faith and her husband had gone- after all, Lorelei had been tricked into the get together and it would have been perfectly within her right to abandon him. He realized that the gorgeous woman next to him was more than beautiful and brilliant- she was also very kind. Although she'd been seething mad on arrival, she hadn't the heart to leave him all alone in a classy restaurant on a Saturday night. He briefly wondered what kind of bluffing Faith had employed to get Lorelei to Wyland's- surely Lorelei had been suspicious from the outset; she was too smart to be conned. He wanted to know how the two had become so close since they seemed to be complete polar opposites, but he held back on asking any personal questions. He was biding his time with Lorelei very carefully because tonight had turned out to be a gracious and lovely present dropped neatly in his lap. He didn't want to do or say anything that would make

Lorelei cut the evening short. And he hoped against hope she'd let him see her again.

The waiter approached and asked if they'd like an after dinner coffee. Both declined and the waiter nodded to each of them and said, "It was a pleasure serving you." He placed a black leather check presenter on the table and Frank reached for it immediately and opened it.

"Well, I'll be damned," he said, his lips twitching. He handed the leather bifold to Lorelei.

The check inside had a line through it that said, PAID, and there was a little sticky note on the top in Faith's handwriting.

"Frank and Lor sittin' in a tree... I hope you had a fabulous supper... and may there be k-i-s-s-i-n-g afterward. Hugs and much happiness, you two lovebirds! Dinner is on Jesse. I hope you'll be doing what we're doing tonight. WINK!!!"

Lorelei felt a blush creep up her arms and then her neck, but then she locked eyes with Frank and they both burst out laughing.

"That is some friend you have," Frank chuckled.

"She really is," Lorelei said, the last vestiges of annoyance toward Faith evaporating. "She's one of the best people I know."

"Is Mary another one?" Frank asked, remembering the pretty girl with the amber eyes he'd met at George's.

"Yes, absolutely. I'm very blessed with wonderful friends."

"I'd say they're blessed too."

Frank's eyes didn't waver and Lorelei didn't look away. She felt herself letting go and she didn't know if it was the whiskey or if it was the comfort and ease she found in Frank's presence. Maybe it was both. Whatever it was it made her scoot a bit closer to him. She wanted to take in his scent again and to feel the electricity that seemed to swirl between them. Frank didn't move, he appeared as relaxed and laidback as he had all evening as he watched Lorelei lean toward him. He kept perfectly still for he wanted the night to be on her terms even though he desperately longed to call the shots.

Lorelei carefully laid her hand on one of his, and they each felt the fire in that simple touch.

"Would you like to go somewhere and have a drink?" Frank asked, his voice low and deep.

"I can't drive. I've had too much."

"Ride with me."

Lorelei moved her hand to Frank's forearm. It was strong and muscular, like a baseball player's arm. The feel of his skin was tantalizing.

"Okay."

"I'm afraid it's the Harley, though. Are you all right getting your hair messed up by a helmet?"

Lorelei laughed delightedly. "You don't know me very well."

Frank stood, bringing Lorelei up with him. "I'll take that as a yes."

They walked out into the cool evening weather and Frank led her to his black and chrome Road King. He shrugged out of his leather jacket, put it around her shoulders and then lifted his helmet off the handlebars. "Put this on, young lady, it's the law."

Lorelei stood on the sidewalk in her beautiful blue dress and fashionable heels with poise and elegance as she shrugged into the leather jacket, which was much too big for her. She squashed the helmet down over her golden curls and looked up at him, her green eyes shining. Detective Frank Williams thought he'd never seen a woman look as adorably captivating as Lorelei Harper did in that moment. The odd, conflicting apparel made her look both adventurous and vulnerable, like a young woman tasting the not so long-ago freedom of girlhood.

Frank resisted the urge to take Lorelei in his arms and instead straddled his motorcycle and held out his hand to her. Lorelei took it and expertly hopped on behind him, tucking her dress around her legs and leaning comfortably back against the sissy bar. She's done this before, Frank thought, and he wondered if there was anything this amazing woman couldn't handle. Probably not.

"Where would you like to go?" Frank asked, starting the bike. The Harley rumbled contentedly, making the telltale "pop-pop" sound followed by a pause, only to be repeated over and over as they idled.

Lorelei felt the power of the motorcycle as it vibrated underneath her and a surge of happiness ran through her at the thought of riding it under the moon in carefree abandon. She laughed and said, "Wouldn't it be funny if we found out which hotel Faith is at and we banged on her door and interrupted her romantic evening? She deserves a little payback."

Frank coughed in mock modesty. "You know detectives have ways of finding things out, don't you?"

Lorelei's eyes widened impishly. "Could you... trace Jesse's car or something?"

Frank pulled out his cell phone. "Leave it to me."

"This is so much fun!" Lorelei said, practically bouncing on the back seat in excitement.

And in that moment Frank knew he'd do anything for the woman beside him. Anything at all.

Frank and Lorelei pulled up to the Manchester Hyatt, a beautiful forty story structure right on the water overlooking Coronado Island.

Lorelei reluctantly left the motorcycle and removed her helmet. She handed it to Frank and then fluffed up her curls. Most of them bounced right back into perfection, but a few stubbornly remained squished and mashed to the back of her head. Her dress skirt was rumpled and her cheeks were rosy from riding through the cool night air. As Frank dismounted, he regarded the woman before him with unmasked admiration. She was neither prissy, nor conceited. She had the confidence of a beautiful woman, but one who wasn't afraid to muss her appearance in the name of fun. As they had ridden along the coast, Lorelei deftly dealt with stops and starts and turns as naturally as if she'd been born to ride motorcycles. She was never stiff and never fought the bike- she shifted and swayed with it, sensing Frank's driving style early on. She relaxed into the curves of the road and didn't need to hold on since she had such a sense of how the bike was carrying them, yet she still placed her hands on either side of Frank's hips.

"Would you like to wear the jacket inside?" Frank was asking solicitously.

Lorelei started to say no but stopped herself. She had enjoyed being so close to Frank during the ride, feeling his solid body in front of hers; breathing in his heady, masculine scent. She'd felt safe and protected in his leather jacket, as though he were enveloping her somehow, keeping her warm and secure. She knew the jacket looked silly over her dazzling dress, but she wasn't ready to give it back, especially now that they were no longer pressed so close together.

"I'd like to keep it on, if that's okay?" Lorelei said, turning the collar up around her neck.

Frank seemed pleased. "Of course. Let's get you inside and out of the breeze." He placed a strong arm around her waist and led her toward the huge glass doors where a bellman waited to usher them in. Frank had lost his earlier reservations about not touching Lorelei. She had, after all, held on to him during the ride even though she clearly hadn't needed to.

They walked into the elegantly decorated hotel lobby of ornate furniture, beautiful artwork and a gargantuan chandelier dripping with crystals. There was a noticeable but gentle buzz as hotel staff glided around, greeting guests, taking their bags and suitcases, or giving directions to local points of interest.

Lorelei looked around admiringly. She'd never been to the Manchester and its ambiance was perfectly suited to her tastes - swanky, immaculate, and crackling with the energy of traveling business professionals and cheerful vacationers.

Frank moved his arm from around Lorelei and placed a hand on the small of her back. "Well, what room do you think Faith and Jesse are in?"

Lorelei looked at him blankly. "I didn't even think of a room number!" What had she been *thinking*? Well, some sort of mischievous all-in-fun revenge on Faith, for one. And for two, she liked Detective Frank Williams and had wanted to spend more time with him. In fact, as they stood there, close together, she took in his stocky, muscular body, close-cropped sandy hair and kind blue eyes, and felt the pull of chemistry sizzle between them like lightning. The spark ignited when his expression changed and he drew closer to her, his hands suddenly on either side of her face.

"She walks in beauty, like the night," Frank whispered softly, "of cloudless climes and starry skies…"

Lorelei closed her eyes, drinking in the poetic words, the deep baritone of his voice.

"Lord Byron," she breathed.

"You're enchanting, Lorelei Harper," Frank said, running his thumb across her lips. She shivered, for it had felt like the gentlest of kisses. When she opened her eyes, Frank was watching her, his desire apparent yet controlled. "Since we're not going to find your friends, let's go have a drink on the rooftop lounge," he said, letting go of her. "I'd really love to get to know you better. Would that be all right?"

Lorelei smiled, her face still tingling from his touch. What had Faith said earlier before she'd breezed out of Wyland's like a naughty cupid? Oh yes… "Make tonight all about you. Have fun. Let go." Maybe that's exactly what she was doing tonight. And she wasn't ready for the evening to end. She put her arm through Frank's and nodded decisively. "I'll have a dirty martini, Detective Williams. But since you bought me one at George's the night we met you must allow me to buy your drink tonight."

Frank instinctively flexed his bicep when he felt Lorelei place her small hand on his arm. He'd agree to anything to keep this beautiful girl by his side. "Deal," he said, and they walked across the expansive lobby toward a bank of elevators. As they rounded an immense hallway decorated with marble columns and plush carpeting, they heard a woman shriek and then giggle from somewhere across the corridor. All of a sudden Jesse and Faith sprang into view from the adjoining hallway. They were laughing hysterically, hands clasped and fingers intertwined, aware of no one but each other. Faith tripped ever so slightly and Jesse swooped down and tossed her over his shoulder, carrying her into a waiting elevator. As the doors began to shut on them, Jesse smacked Faith's rear end and she squealed in delight.

Frank and Lorelei stopped dead in their tracks, and when the elevator doors closed completely they looked at each other in surprise and then erupted in laughter.

"What luck!" Lorelei said excitedly. "Let's find out what floor they're going to!"

Frank ran up to the elevator and watched the digital floor counter above it. "They're getting off on twenty-five," he called back.

Like mischievous fun-loving teenagers, Frank and Lorelei darted into the next elevator to open its doors. They exchanged impish grins as Frank punched floor twenty-five. The doors closed and Lorelei took Frank's hand as they launched upward.

CHAPTER 16

*M*ary drove to Holokai's Hideaway, a popular espresso hut hidden amongst thick leafy green trees. Several tables, chairs and sofas were scattered around the alcove, books and magazines were stacked on cabinets, and the rich scent of freshly ground coffee beans hung tantalizingly in the air. Soft Hawaiian music drifted in from the tiny office in the back, playing in concert with the ocean waves lapping outside. Even on a Saturday night, the hut was busy, mostly young couples grabbing an after dinner caffeine fix before they embarked on an evening of dancing or bar hopping. Behind the counter stood Holokai, a big, stocky man always ready with a bright smile and the day's brew.

Roger burst through the plants and trees and bounded up to the coffee hut, placing his big paws on the counter. He gave a happy "Woof!" and waited expectantly.

Holokai disappeared into the back for a moment and returned with a dishtowel in one hand and a small slab of Spam in the other.

"Aloha kolohe!" Holokai said to Roger, tossing the faux meat to him.

Roger swallowed the Spam whole and gave Holokai an appreciative slobbery kiss.

"Pua'a!" Holokai groused distastefully, wiping drool from his face with the towel.

Mary came through the trees and shook her finger at Roger. "You were supposed to wait until I got out of the Jeep," she scolded.

"Nani!" Holokai exclaimed, smiling hugely at Mary. "E komomai!"

Roger jumped up on an unoccupied sofa and laid his head on the arm. He passed a bit of gas and it made a slight squeaking sound. He turned and looked at his rear end, confused.

Mary blushed. "Boxers," she said by way of apology.

"How are you, Nani?" Holokai asked. "The usual? Owen working tonight?"

"Fine. Yes and yes." Mary responded, smiling as Holokai enveloped her in a giant bear hug.

"Would you like one of my malasadas to go with your cappuccino? I just made a fresh batch an hour ago."

Mary lowered her eyes. "No, thank you."

"But you have not had one in so long! You love them! You used to eat them all the time. Come on. On the house!"

"No, I can't, but thank you so much, Holokai. I'm trying to watch what I eat."

Holokai let loose with a string of what sounded like Hawaiian curse words. "You need your strength for hapai. You too skinny," he observed, shaking his head.

Mary left cash on the counter and went to sit next to Roger as Holokai started banging around his small kitchen preparing her cappuccino. He brought it out to her with a sugared malasada on the saucer next to the coffee cup. He pointed at the delicious pastry authoritatively. "Coconut haupia inside. You eat."

"Thanks, Holokai," Mary said as she pulled out her journal from her knapsack.

Holokai nodded to her, then issued another "Pua'a!" to Roger before returning to his post.

Mary took a tentative sip of her cappuccino and then set it on the coffee table in front of her, deliberately avoiding contact with the tempting malasada. She had just turned to the first blank page of her journal to write her mother when her phone chirped with a new email from Lorelei. She tapped to open it, her eyes widening as she began to read.

From: Lorelei Harper / L.Harper@empireandmalkininc.com
To: Mary Crossfield / Mary@rogersleashbrigade.com
Subject: WE NEED TO GET A DRINK!

Mary,

I am emailing you from Wyland's, where I have fallen victim to our duplicitous friend Faith. If I don't hear back from you, I can only assume you were in on her scheme.

In case you *don't* know what's going on, she called the other day asking if she and I could meet, just the two of us. She said she needed advice only I could give her, which made me suspicious from the outset, but she was fairly convincing. I walked into Wyland's tonight- looking stunning by the way in that blue dress I bought at the boutique in Del Mar last year– and seated at the table were Faith and Jesse and *Detective Frank Williams*. No poetry or flowers this time, because Frank didn't have a clue I would be here. Faith had told him that Jesse was doing research for a crime novel he's writing. Which was a complete lie, of course, because what attorney with four children and a nutty wife has time to *also* write a book. HAVE YOU EVER?!

A few minutes later, Faith's phone rang and *allegedly* one of her tiny savages had fallen in the house. You should have seen her! What a performance! Then she and Jesse just hightailed it out of here, leaving me and Frank alone together.

You. Me. Pannikin's. Tomorrow. Okay?

Love you.
Lorelei Harper
Commission Accountant II, Brokerage Revenue Division
EMPIRE & MALKIN, INC.
200 Market Place I San Diego, CA I 92101
619-555-9222 (direct)
www.empireandmalkininc.com

Bonjour Mama,

My thoughts and emotions are jumbled today so I'm not exactly sure where to start this letter. I think that's why I came to the coffee shop to write you. I just had to get out of the house - and away from all things Owen - to clear my head.

Last night Owen told me he's leaving again soon, this time for some kind of training mission. He's been so attentive and romantic lately, and he hasn't mentioned the baby once since we had that awful fight, so I'm kind of wondering how long he's known about this departure and if that means his efforts have been...manipulative. I feel terrible even thinking that. And I also feel terrible because, in a way, I'm relieved he's going to be gone. I won't have to tiptoe around the elephant in the room: whether I can or will or even want *to get pregnant.*

I know I need to talk to Dad about all of this- I've kept him in the dark regarding my struggles with Owen and the baby because I don't want him to be upset with Owen, and because I think he's looking forward to becoming a grandfather. But that's not really fair to Daddy. He's never kept secrets from me, so why then, would I keep any from him? He's always been a transparent parent. And maybe having a heart to heart with him will bring me some measure of peace. He always gives good advice and is an excellent listener.

I'm a bit hesitant to even write these next words but, Mama, you're the only one I can confide in. Remember how I met Thomas McQuillan for dinner? I'm so embarrassed to admit this, but I can't stop thinking about him. I long to be in his presence again, to experience the force of his broody nature in regard to his writing. I want to feel his intense hazel eyes prying into my thoughts and moving over my body. I want to ask him questions about being an author, to find out what makes his creative mind tick. I also want to know, but would never ask, why he hasn't been able to publish anything for so long. What happened to cause his block?

I keep remembering the way he argued with me about Voltaire, how he called me an exasperating woman. It was as if he was taunting me, provoking me, trying to lead me in some sort of verbal dance to see how I'd react. Our sparring at the end of dinner was like playing with fire, for I simultaneously felt baited and yet distinctly aroused. A few erotic thoughts of Thomas have crossed my mind over the last couple of days (unbidden of course) and I've had to stubbornly chase them off. Thank goodness no one can read my mind. And then a few nights ago I dreamt Thomas made love to me- not in the way Owen and I make love, but in a very carnal, almost primal devouring of one another, body and souls. It was raw and messy and even indecent. I woke up in a cold sweat, my body humming with desire. The dream had been so real, so... sexy... and unlike anything I've ever experienced. I longed to return to the dream even though I knew it was wrong. And all the while, Owen slept next to me, lightly snoring, completely unaware that I lay beside him, burning for another man.

As the memory of being wrapped passionately around Thomas faded, shame crept in and filled Mary with guilt. Abruptly, she shut her journal. Had that dream just been an innocent unconscious fantasy brought on by celebrity admiration, or was it the first step down a dangerous path? Mary wasn't sure. All she knew was that nobody could solve her marital problems – not her imaginary mother and certainly not Thomas McQuillan.

CHAPTER 17

⸺

*F*rank and Lorelei stepped off the elevator at floor twenty-five and looked around in bewilderment. There were no halls lined with hotel room doors, no carpeted corridors leading to suites, no bright ceiling lights helping guests to find their room numbers. Instead, Frank and Lorelei found themselves standing in a huge, dimly lit foyer. Tiny pin lights dotted the ceiling above them like little stars against a dark, velvety sky. Numerous candles stood daintily in tiled alcoves along the walls, their flames dancing and swaying as though they were all listening to the same sensual song. Hushed voices, tinkling glasses and soft music drifted toward Frank and Lorelei from open wooden double doors at the end of the foyer. There was no one around; they were completely alone in the dusky, luxurious room.

Before she could register where exactly they were, Lorelei felt Frank's warm, seductive breath on her neck as he whispered, "I felt her presence, by its spell of might, stoop o'er me from above; the calm, majestic presence of the Night, as of the one I love."

Lorelei closed her eyes, her skin prickling with sensation as Frank's body drew closer to hers. She remembered Henry Wadsworth Longfellow from college but hadn't thought much of his writings back then. Now, however, hearing the poet's words spoken aloud by a flesh and blood man she was attracted to, Lorelei was drawn into the lyrical beauty of the verses. She continued the poem from memory: "...I heard the sounds of sorrow and delight, the manifold, soft chimes, that fill the haunted chambers of the Night, like some old poet's rhymes."

Frank watched Lorelei closely as the words of the poem dripped like honey from her full lips. When she finished, her eyes still closed, Frank gently reached out and lightly, provocatively, trailed his fingers down Lorelei's neck to her collar bone. The shocking pleasure of her silky skin burned his hand and her eyelids fluttered open in desire. Frank's touch was like a sea of flames and Lorelei leaned into him with a sigh of incandescent pleasure.

"Excuse me, but do you have reservations?" an elderly gentleman asked, materializing out of nowhere. He was dressed impeccably in a black tuxedo and shiny black shoes.

Embarrassed at having been caught in such a vulnerable moment, Lorelei stepped back from Frank and pulled the leather jacket tight around her torso.

"Actually, we got off on the wrong floor," Frank said easily. "But we'd love a drink if you have room in there." He gestured toward the big open double doors, where the sounds of muffled nightlife drifted out to them.

The distinguished man looked down his nose at Frank. "Are you guests here at the Hyatt? This lounge is strictly for Manchester habitué."

"Yes," Lorelei said firmly, gathering her wits about her. "Yes, we are. We're staying in one of the honeymoon suites." She took Frank's hand and pressed it against her cheek. "We just got married yesterday."

The gentleman raised a grey bushy eyebrow skeptically, then nodded and ushered them through the doors. Frank and Lorelei looked around in amazement, for they had entered into a very lavish cocktail lounge. A huge brass bar with two bartenders dominated one end of the room and at the other end was a small raised stage with a beautiful blonde singing jazz and playing piano. Female servers dressed in

French maid outfits glided through the room, carrying trendy cocktails to the obviously wealthy patrons.

Tufted couches, plush oversized chairs and elegant barstools littered the gorgeous Versailles parquet flooring, and miniature glass tables were sprinkled throughout.

The tuxedoed man led Frank and Lorelei to a stylish white loveseat in a darkened corner. "Congratulations on your wedding," he said, his respectful bow belied by his dubious tone.

"Did he just give me the side eye?" Lorelei demanded, laughing as the gentleman walked stiffly away.

Frank held her left hand in his own, kissed her ring finger and explained, "No diamond."

The instant she felt Frank's lips on her skin, Lorelei's blood went hot and her body ignited with shocking heat- heat she hadn't felt since... She looked at Frank inquisitively, trying to analyze his face, his movements, the depth of his eyes. Why was he having this effect on her? What was it about him?

Frank gazed back at Lorelei with an open expression that was neither guarded nor defensive. He wanted to know what was going through that perceptive mind of hers, but didn't feel free to ask without possibly compromising the connection they'd enjoyed all evening. Lorelei would share her carefully guarded thoughts on her own terms- if she wanted to. It wasn't just Lorelei's mind Frank wanted to get to know better... he was having a very hard time not pulling her roughly toward him until the full length of her warm body was pressed against his. He wanted to kiss her passionately and deeply, to feel her melt into him. He'd been about to place his lips on hers in the foyer but was now glad that their elderly host had interrupted. The last thing Frank wanted to do was to make any fast moves on this glamorous girl who had exuded nothing but kindness to him all evening. He'd do anything to see her again- including holding back any sophomoric advances that could be considered disrespectful. He imagined Lorelei

Harper most likely had to fend off admiring men on the daily. He wasn't going to be one of them.

Frank turned Lorelei around so that her back was to him and he slowly removed his leather jacket, sliding it off her shoulders and gently slipping it from her arms. Evocative thoughts of removing her dress as well taunted him and he imagined it pooling at her feet in blue waves so that he could worship her unclothed body the way he so desperately wanted to. Not rushed and fast, but with care and skill and meticulous fervency.

Shaking his head slightly, trying to ward off the passionate thoughts roiling through his mind, Frank threw his jacket on the arm of the white sofa and turned Lorelei back to face him. Her eyes were so very green, so very intense.

Just then, a peal of raucous laughter by the bar cut through the lounge, briefly drowning out the blonde jazz singer's voice.

Lorelei whipped her head around and sure enough, sitting at the bar a few feet away, were Faith and Jesse. Their legs were swinging freely from barstools and Jesse's arm was around Faith's waist, his hand resting on her bottom. Faith was holding a red fizzy drink with multiple maraschino cherries, and she was looking up at Jesse with adoring eyes.

Frank pulled Lorelei down onto the overstuffed couch and she nestled into his side, a vantage point that was within earshot but hidden from view. As they watched Faith and Jesse in amusement, Lorelei tried not to think about the heat of Frank's body against hers.

"You know, I don't think I've ever seen a married couple get along so well," Frank said.

"Those two were made for each other," Lorelei smiled in agreement. "They melt my cynical old heart and make me want to believe there is such a thing as soulmates."

Frank let the comment slide. Interesting.

They watched as Jesse picked up his full beer glass, and when he began to drink they could hear Faith chanting, "Chug! Chug! Chug!

Chug!" And Jesse did- draining the pint and slamming it on the bar in triumph.

Faith clapped her hands excitedly. "Another!" she called to one of the bartenders.

Jesse smiled lovingly at his wife, grabbed her shoulders and kissed her soundly. Faith threw her arms around Jesse's neck and kissed him back enthusiastically, without any reservations and oblivious to the disapproving looks of several patrons.

Frank watched them with a slight twinge of jealousy. He hadn't known a love like that in his own marriage; his ex-wife had never given herself to him so wholly- either in public or in private. He shifted slightly and Lorelei snuggled up closer to his side. He wondered what it would be like to kiss Lorelei the way Jesse was kissing Faith... with such carefree abandon. Before those thoughts could take over, he forcefully chased them off and tried to change the direction of his thinking pattern. He looked away from Jesse and Faith and instead focused on the singer on stage. She had long, thick blonde hair and her eyes were fashionably veiled with tenebrous, black rimmed eyeglasses. Her full lips were highlighted with a natural gloss that picked up the lights as she sang, and her shapely legs languidly stretched out under the piano as her stiletto heeled shoes pumped the peddles every so often. Her voice was as smooth as Irish cream, and the rise and fall of her breathy mezzo-soprano timbre flowed with the richness of melted chocolate.

Frank felt himself relax under the blanket of soothing jazz and, as he watched the blonde singer, recognition crept in. "Isn't that Lola Boudreaux?" he asked Lorelei.

"I don't know," Lorelei said, squinting at the pretty singer. "Who is Lola Boudreaux?"

"She's from America, but she sings a lot of really great French jazz. I'm pretty sure that's her."

"Is jazz your favorite genre?"

"I love all music," Frank said with feeling. "Anything. All of it."

Lorelei smiled. "And poetry. I don't imagine many cops can quote Longfellow and Byron…"

"That's a safe assumption. But really music is just poetry with a beat, right? Besides, I see a lot of – well, let's just say 'unpleasantness' in my work - and I've found that things of beauty keep me balanced, keep me from becoming too jaded. Sound crazy?"

"Actually, that makes perfect sense," Lorelei replied. "Can you sing?"

"Yes."

"Play an instrument?"

"Guitar."

"I'd love to hear you some time."

Frank smiled at what sounded like the possibility of another date. "I'd like that. Do you have a favorite song?"

Lorelei thought about it. "Not really. My music tastes are kind of eccentric. I like anything that either makes me want to dance or touches my heart somehow."

Frank picked up her hand and began to softly caress her fingers. "That means you have a true appreciation for rhythm."

"I like things that move me," Lorelei agreed coquettishly, her fingers tingling at his touch.

A server walked up to them, an exotically gorgeous African American girl in her early twenties. The French maid outfit hugged her curvaceous body and showed off all her attributes. She was round in all the right places, her skin glowing, her dark hair long and lustrous.

"My name is Amaya," she said in a mellow British accent, "and I'll be taking care of you this evening. What would you like to drink, loves?"

"Dirty martini, straight up, extra olives," Lorelei said.

"Just an ale for me. Whatever you have on tap."

"Stone Ruination double IPA. Is that all right, mate?"

"That's fine."

Lorelei didn't like the way the server was looking at Frank. The girl was polished and professional, but there was something in her doe brown eyes that seemed very, very interested in Detective Frank Williams. And why not? Lorelei asked herself. He was a ruggedly handsome man who offered a heady combination of openness and total self-control. And his long-sleeved shirt and tie did nothing to hide the fact that he was thick with muscle.

"I'll be back," said Amaya and Lorelei couldn't help but notice she had ramped up her sashaying walk as she glided away. Frilled white knickers peeked out at them from under her short black skirt and her fishnet hose had a sexy line running down the backs of her thighs and calves. Lorelei cast a sideways glance at Frank and was pleased to see that he wasn't watching their attractive waitress saunter off; instead he was looking at Lola Boudreaux.

"She has a phenomenal voice," he said admiringly.

Lorelei nodded. "This song is very romantic."

Frank turned to Lorelei, cupped the back of her head and ran his thumb over her soft cheek. "What a beautiful night this has turned out to be."

The moment was frozen in time, the couple lost in one another's eyes, their hearts pounding. Lorelei wanted Frank to kiss her. She wanted to know what his lips would feel like on hers, how her body would respond as he pulled her closer to his own with what she was sure would be expert, capable hands.

Frank saw the raw emotion flicker across Lorelei's beautiful features. Her eyes beseeched his, and in that moment he lost all of his earlier control. He leaned in and brushed his lips against Lorelei's and the touch was so shocking, so intense, that they jumped apart, staring at one another in confusion. Lorelei caressed her bottom lip and looked at Frank in wonder.

"What just happened?" Frank asked, breathing heavily.

Lorelei giggled and it was the most magical sound. "I think we have too much electricity between us."

"Or it could be because that couch has a lot of static," said a dry, British voice. Amaya set Frank's beer down in front of him and said to Lorelei, "Your martini will be ready shortly." Then, before they could even say thank you, she walked away with a swish of her small skirt.

A sudden shriek of merriment stopped all conversation in the lounge, startling people into silence. Lola Boudreaux actually turned from her piano and looked over at the bar to where Jesse and Faith sat.

Lorelei and Frank grinned at one another, then Frank casually put his arm along the back of the couch. Lorelei leaned into his side once again and let her head rest on his shoulder. They watched Faith and Jesse across the room, trying to hear all that was being said.

Jesse was holding Faith's red fizzy drink and was fishing out one of the maraschino cherries.

"What do you think that is?" Frank asked, pointing at the dark pink concoction.

"Probably a Shirley Temple," Lorelei guessed.

Jesse held one of the cherries up by its long stem and dangled it suggestively over Faith.

Faith opened her mouth and Jesse popped the cherry inside, stem and all. He looked at his wristwatch, pointed at Faith and said, "Go!"

After twenty seconds had passed, Faith pulled the cherry out of her mouth, its stem tied in a perfect knot.

"That's my girl!" cried Jesse. "Damn, you've got a talented tongue."

"Oh, Jesse…" Faith gushed, her face wreathed in smiles.

"But I already knew that." He winked at her knowingly and she flirtatiously undid the top button of his shirt. He cocked his head to one side invitingly and slid off his bar stool. Lorelei thought they were finally going to their room to express their affection in private but instead Jesse led Faith to a dark niche on the left side of the stage. The two began to slow dance in perfect symmetry. Their bodies fit like two precisely molded puzzle pieces created to lock in place, no space between their edges and every curve and contour complimented by the curves and contours of the other.

Suddenly, Lola Boudreaux's soulful voice grew louder until it filled the lounge. The music swept in and around Frank and Lorelei, the words seductive, the piano filling their senses with a symphony of enticing sounds. They leaned into one another again, and this time Frank cursed all his reservations and let his appetite take over. He pulled Lorelei to his chest aggressively, every one of his muscles flexed and tense, his hands tangled in her golden curls, his tongue desperately searching for hers.

Lorelei's entire body went limp. She'd never felt like this, never felt like such putty in a man's hands. Frank dominated her with his mouth and she was powerless to stop herself from responding. Without thinking, without being able to analyze and categorize what was happening, she let herself go and succumbed willingly to Frank's movements. She kissed him back with a passion she didn't know she possessed and he moaned in response, crushing her to him, his mouth moving to her neck, his lips tender as they trailed upward. He gently nibbled and sucked her delicate earlobe and she gasped at the sensation.

"Sorry to interrupt," broke in a British voice that didn't sound sorry at all. Amaya set Lorelei's drink in front of her and gave the couple an appraising look. Her gaze lingered on Frank and she lowered her eyes to his lips. She started to say something but then turned and walked away. This time Amaya didn't sashay.

Frank tried to control his ragged breathing and Lorelei noticed his hands were shaking slightly as he straightened his tie. She leaned away from him and took a big swallow of her martini, hoping to calm the intense feelings pounding through her veins. It was then, her mind still reeling, that she realized she was in a hotel alone with Detective Frank Williams- and she didn't even have her car to escape to. Surely Frank wouldn't suggest... No, he wouldn't. He was a gentleman. But then... what if she *wanted* him to keep touching her...

No, she told herself, absolutely not. Just because he's really nice, and… well, very sexy… doesn't mean…

There was one surefire way to kill the mood, to take the evening from sensual to chaste.

Lorelei took another mouthful of her martini and said, "Can I ask you a question?"

Frank sat back, trying to relax his body, to coax it away from the precipice of hunger. He'd had a taste of Lorelei Harper and he wanted more. But this was not the time or the place. He would not send this evening down a path either of them would regret.

"Anything," he said seriously. "You can ask me anything."

Lorelei drained her martini and took a deep breath. "Have you been married before?"

"Yes."

"For how long?"

"Eleven years."

"Do you have children?"

"One son. His name is Devon and he's eight years old."

"May I ask why you divorced?"

Frank's eyes grew sad. "Bridgette couldn't handle being the wife of a cop. It was hard on her."

Lorelei placed a sympathetic hand on his leg. "I'm sorry."

"It's okay, it's in the past. Actually, Faith was asking me all the same questions before you arrived at Wyland's."

Lorelei rolled her eyes.

Frank smiled. "She might be meddlesome, but it's quite clear she loves you like a sister. She said she could never live without your friendship."

"You two have become quite chummy."

Frank took Lorelei's hand and kissed the back of it, just as he had the night they'd met at George's. "You're something special, Lorelei Mildred Harper," he said with a wicked smile.

"She told you my middle name!" Lorelei said testily, but her indignation died out when Frank pulled her closer.

He ran a finger lightly down Lorelei's bare arm and goosebumps appeared as he continued to stroke her silky skin. It excited him to know his touch was having such an effect.

"Would you like to know what else Faith and I talked about?" Frank asked huskily, his lips barely an inch from Lorelei's.

"There's no telling what Faith brought up," Lorelei whispered distractedly, unable to think for the feel of his touch and the warmth of his closeness. "That girl is pure mischief."

"Actually, she told me to ask you a question," Frank said, affectionately brushing a wayward blonde curl from Lorelei's forehead. "Who is Connor?"

Lorelei froze. Her whole body turned to ice and her green eyes hardened glacially. "What did you just say?"

Alarm bells began ringing in Frank's head and he blanched at the look on Lorelei's face. "I'm sorry. I hope that wasn't too personal a question. Faith had told me you might want to talk about someone named Connor tonight- she said she thought it might help you 'let go' of something you've needed to."

Lorelei pulled away from Frank, her body rigid with fury, her mind spinning in a vortex of angry confusion. "Faith told you to ask me about *Connor*?"

Frank tried to remain relaxed and composed but those alarms inside his head were getting louder and shriller with each passing second. He forced his tone to remain calm. "Yes. I didn't mean to pry. I don't know who Connor is- she didn't tell me. Please, forget I said anything. From what I know of Faith she was just trying to help in some way because she loves you."

Lorelei had never felt so betrayed. Why was Faith doing this? Why was she butting in more than usual? How would Faith feel if the tables were turned? Would she want someone poking about in *her* business? Lorelei didn't know which feeling was stronger - the pain or the outrage; both ripped at her heart and brought hot tears to her eyes.

"How could you?" Lorelei wanted to yell at her friend. *"How could you?!"*

But when Lorelei looked over to the dark corner where Faith and Jesse had been dancing she saw that they were gone.

CHAPTER 18

*T*homas McQuillan sat hunched over his keyboard, shoulders tensed, brow furrowed, as he pounded out word after word of narrative. He wrote until the firestorm of creativity began to cool. As his inspiration slowed so did his keystrokes and he became aware of the profound silence all around him. Solitude was good for the artistic soul, but it also made for a very lonely existence. He'd written many times in such a flurry of excitement, catching ideas and dialogue and storylines right out of the air like a man netting butterflies. But when the frenzy was over, the flood of enthusiasm drying out and dying as he came up for air, it was sometimes jarring to realize there was no one around. No one to share the triumphs of his exhausted, yet satiated imagination with. No one to companionably laugh with or pour a drink for. No one to rub his tired shoulders and congratulate him on a well-written page or a finished chapter. And most of the time that was exactly the way he wanted it.

He leaned back in his chair, his eyes roaming idly around the study. Of all the rooms in his sprawling Rancho Santa Fe home, this one was his favorite. Just north of downtown San Diego, Rancho Santa Fe delicately stretched over the inland hills about five miles east of the ocean. It was a small and extremely wealthy area that offered very private luxury homes and exclusive estates hidden behind iron gates. There were no streetlights, no sidewalks, no signs along the well-tended roads. Thousands of eucalyptus trees dotted the countryside, along with orchards and wildflowers. Thomas owned several acres on the highest elevation, his home isolated and concealed. On the second floor, where his study, bedroom and game room were located, he could see the ocean on the horizon. Sunsets were particularly gorgeous, and oftentimes he would stand on his balcony, a gin rickey in hand, and watch the orange glow fall gently into the sea. He thought he'd seen the green flash once, but it had been so quick that he was never sure it wasn't his imagination.

He looked back down at his laptop, once an instrument of joy and passion, now often his enemy. Sometimes he wondered if it wasn't his hunger for writing that had evaporated, but rather his tolerance for all that came with it. He had been happy living the life of a novelist, though like most people he was always dreaming of reaching that next rung on the ladder – the fame, the fortune, the acknowledgement of his creative genius. And then one day it happened. A miracle. Everyone, it seemed, had read *Souls in Collision* and had been forever changed by it – whatever that meant. They all suddenly wanted to know what Thomas McQuillan had to say about... well, *everything*. At first he basked in it, was drunk on it; he couldn't get enough. He didn't remember exactly when the fame turned from a blessing to a curse. All he knew was that his life – enviable though it was – was no longer his own. It belonged to the paparazzi, the social climbers and the disreputable Hollywood characters seeking to slash his work to shreds in the name of box office dollars. Budding "novelists" stopped him on the streets or in restaurants, wanting to know how they could be published and if he would help them. Could he just read the first chapter of their book and send it to his editor with a kind word? Would he give his opinion on their prose and offer constructive criticism? It was exhausting.

And women... that had been an entirely different type of intrusion on his space. At the peak of his celebrity, women threw themselves at Thomas, all thinking they would be the one to lay claim to his California good looks, his considerable charm, and of course, his wealth. He couldn't go anywhere without a woman approaching him, trying to touch him, thrusting her phone number- or even herself- into his hands. He had, during that time period, decided to date only famous women because they understood the need for privacy from the public. Models and actresses wanted anonymity in their dating lives just as he did. Dating women from the general public was out of the question- they only wanted to be seen with him- to impress their friends or up their status or see their photographs in a glossy magazine even if they were only identified as "Unknown brunette/blonde/redheaded bombshell steps out with author Thomas McQuillan."

Then there was the one woman who he could never forget.

Production had just begun on the *Souls in Collision* movie, and Thomas, who was hired and paid an exorbitant income to be an onsite consultant, was soaring toward the height of his celebrity. He'd had a delightful romance with the lead actress, a woman so renowned and so stunning she couldn't go anywhere without being instantly recognized and fawned over. Thomas had never been in close range of anyone so absolutely perfect. He'd been nervous, almost scared to touch her, as though he wasn't good enough, pure enough, important enough. But Gemma Hamilton had made the first move. The twenty-five-year old actress was instantly attracted to Thomas' inconspicuous, easygoing California surfer persona. She asked Thomas about his writing process and quizzed him about his childhood and soon they were chatting away like old friends. Gemma had invited Thomas back to her room and there they had learned more about each other–physically and emotionally. By that time Thomas had been with more women than he could count, while Gemma, for all her notoriety, had only slept with three men. Those three men had, apparently, not been very skilled in the bedroom, for Thomas had introduced Gemma to a myriad of new experiences that left the young starlet begging for more.

When *Souls in Collision* wrapped, Gemma left for Australia, where she was filming her next role. There was no talk of continuing their relationship - it was what it was and it had been beautiful while it lasted. Gemma wanted a family and Thomas had made it clear from the beginning that children were not in his plan. He'd helped raise six siblings and had done his duty. The rest of his life was his and he wanted no part in rearing the next generation. Gemma had understood, but their relationship held a bittersweet note because they knew it was over before it ever really started. But for seven months, while filming on location in Wales, they had spent every available moment together and their nights were filled with cheerful laughter, companionable conversation... and a lot of nudity. Indeed, Gemma's sweet disposition touched something deep within Thomas and when he held her soft body against his own, he felt as though all was right with the world. He almost gave up his resolve to forever be a bachelor. Almost.

Knowing they had no future didn't make it any easier. When the time came, they said their tearful goodbyes in Gemma's hotel room, under a pile of warm blankets while cold snowflakes gently fell outside. Their kisses were tender, every touch nostalgic and poignant. They clung to one another fiercely, knowing it was the last time they'd hear each other's heartbeats, taste each other's lips, watch each other soar to the heavens. Thomas tried to memorize Gemma's graceful movements, her adorable idiosyncrasies, the way she would hold her breath when he ran his hand up her thigh... the glow of love emanating from her eyes.

The following year saw Thomas McQuillan win an Oscar for Best Screenplay and Gemma Hamilton for Best Actress. As Gemma went up on stage to accept her award, Thomas felt his stomach twist for it was very apparent that during their time apart Gemma had fulfilled her dream of starting a family. She was noticeably pregnant. A month later she married producer Dick Rimmel and few months after that she gave birth to a beautiful baby boy.

Thomas had sent flowers and a congratulatory note to Dick and Gemma and Gemma had replied a few weeks later with the simple sentence: "I miss you."

Back in his office, Thomas pulled himself forward to the present. Thoughts of Gemma did him no favors. His only focus had to be his latest work, a first-person narrative on the introspective ruminations of his protagonist, and one he feared might be bordering on the self-indulgent. He leaned back in his leather chair and reread the last few sentences he'd written:

> *"None of it makes sense to me. But then life is full of mysteries, isn't it? We never really know what's happening in another person's inner thoughts, or how they truly feel about someone or something. We only know what people choose to tell us about themselves and even those reveals can be untruths born of deceptive insecurity."*

He closed his laptop and decided that, self-indulgent or not, he was way too cynical for someone in his early forties. Then again, cynicism had its own reward: the less you allowed yourself to trust, the less you set yourself up for being duped. Thomas had seen enough shadiness amongst the rich and famous to last a lifetime. He much preferred to spend his days and nights far from the glamour and glitz of Los Angeles and Manhattan; he fiercely clung to his privacy, enjoying the relative anonymity of being able to freely move about in San Diego, where he blended in easily with the hundreds of other surfers roaming the coast. It was a sweet freedom that he held very dear. And he was extremely protective of it.

An exuberant bark cut through the silence, confirming that his writing session had indeed come to an end. Already annoyed, Thomas braced himself for the onslaught.

Voltaire came rushing into the study, his sturdy squat body shooting straight for Thomas on impossibly fast, stubby legs. Voltaire snorted loudly like a pig, an adorable sound to most but which Thomas found incredibly irritating. He reached down to pet Voltaire, but the blue

French Bulldog made a leap for his hand midair, completely ecstatic at any attention from his owner.

"Down, Voltaire!" Thomas commanded, but the sound of his voice only excited the dog more. Voltaire began panting and barking, jumping nonstop and trying to bite Thomas' hand in doggie delirium.

"Stop it! You are the most annoying beast!" Thomas said and not-so-gently nudged Voltaire aside with his foot; when that didn't work he shoved him with his leg. It wasn't a kick exactly, although the idea of punting him across the room was certainly tempting. Thomas smiled wickedly as he thought of gleefully pitching the little furry tank right out the window. But it was a hollow fantasy; he would never harm an animal.

Frustrated, Voltaire oinked loudly, leapt into the air and bit into Thomas' jeans.

"Son of a…" Thomas plucked Voltaire off his leg, tossed him out of his study and slammed the door. The dog threw his body against the closed door over and over, barking indignantly as though he were completely offended at such treatment.

"HELGA!!!!" Thomas bellowed, and a minute later he heard his housekeeper's footsteps hurriedly coming down the hall.

"Volpee, stygg pojke," he heard Helga say in her thick Swedish accent, "calm down and come vith me. You clean kitchen vith Helga now."

Voltaire's barking ceased, but the snorting grew louder as he focused on the plump older woman trying to coax him away from the door. His grey eyes reflected suspicion, for he was an intelligent dog and one that insisted on getting his own way.

Helga made a grab for Voltaire and he excitedly catapulted himself at her, bounced off her leg and ran down the hallway, barking madly. He wanted to be chased, one of his favorite games.

"I do not have time fer da running, Volpee. I must cook dinner. Volpee! Come here to Helga!"

Thomas leaned against the door and relaxed as he heard Helga move down the hall as quickly as her heavy legs would take her. Voltaire's barking grew fainter as he scampered off to another part of the house. Thomas knew it wasn't fair to saddle Helga with the responsibility of caring for Voltaire, but he didn't know what else to do. He certainly couldn't control the dog. Well, neither could Helga. He knew she was at her wit's end, for her cleaning and cooking were most times left unattended while she raced around after Voltaire trying to keep him occupied and out of Thomas' hair. Something needed to be done.

For the hundredth time that week, Thomas' thoughts ran to Mary Crossfield. He didn't know what he'd expected when he set up the meeting – was there a stereotypical "pet nanny"? – but it certainly wasn't the sweet and very lovely woman who had sat across from him at The Marine Room. How rare to see a smile without pretense, to hear words with no hidden motive. Mary appeared on every front to be fresh and pure as a daisy. Something perverse in him had wanted to test her gentleness, to push at her and see just how amiable she actually was. He'd been surprised to discover she had a little spark in her. The way her amber eyes had flashed and her back straightened when she was indignant. The way her skin flushed when he had called her exasperating. He'd liked having that kind of effect on a woman. The women he'd been dating for well over a decade were all completely self-possessed and unflappable. Mary Crossfield appeared to be putty in his hands, but not without offering a little fight first. For some reason this had quickened his pulse, piqued his interest immensely, and when she'd stood up and crossed the restaurant, he'd followed her every movement with his sharp hazel eyes.

He remembered her quick announcement of "I'm married!" and wondered what her husband was like. Was he as sincere and as unaffected as his wife? Somehow Thomas doubted it. Though she didn't speak of it, Thomas sensed Mary was protective of her marriage, and perhaps just as guarded with her personal life as he was with his own. Other than her experience with animals, she had not spoken about herself at all. What did she like to do in her spare time? What were her interests? She gave no indication of offering him special treatment just because he was a celebrity- the very opposite, in fact - as she was unwilling to drop her other clients for him. He liked that. It showed integrity and loyalty. Two things many people were either born without or had exchanged for personal gain.

Pushing Mary Crossfield from his mind, Thomas tentatively opened his study door and poked his head out. Voltaire was definitely gone. He breathed a sigh of relief and headed for his game room. Shooting a little pool would relax him and then maybe he would call Katya and see if she'd like to meet him at Mille Fleurs for a late dinner… and a nightcap at his place afterward. He and Katya had seen each other off and on over the past five years or so, meeting up whenever she was back in town from a photo shoot or a runway gig. The long-legged Russian beauty was fierce, independent and liked to discuss anything and everything American- from politics to religion to literature. Her accent was thick and, for Thomas, very sexy, especially when she was three drinks in and ready for a night of passion. The way she murmured his name when they made love drove him nothing short of wild. But, in the morning, Katya was always back to her cool, poised self, throwing him a kiss and a brisk "Dosevedanya!"as she breezed out the door. Their arrangement was perfect; each craved privacy and neither wanted long-term love. But whereas Thomas' disdain for commitment was a result of world-weariness, Katya's was born of blind ambition. At only twenty-five, she seemed to have already lived a full life; she had travelled the world countless times, gracing runways and magazine covers with her beautiful face and lean, angular body. But Katya, who had long ago lost any little girl naivety- if she'd ever had it at all – knew her modelling days were numbered. With an eye toward an equally glorious future, she had already begun taking acting courses, dance classes and voice lessons so that she could break into the American movie scene.

When he reached the game room, Thomas poured himself a stiff drink, then turned on a classic rock station and racked up the billiard balls. He had just bent over the pool table, focusing all of his intense concentration on the cue ball, lining up his shot with perfect precision, when he heard a crash from down the hall. A colorful profusion of Swedish curse words followed and then Voltaire barked angrily.

Thomas threw his pool cue on the floor and kicked at a nearby chair. He was going to have to do something about that annoying antichrist of a dog. Aggravated, he picked up his drink and walked out onto the patio. His property stretched before him, its pastoral beauty sweeping across a lengthy plateau until it gracefully dipped down the side of the mountain. Beyond the lush greenery, he could see the ocean in the distance, lapping lazily against the shore. He was too far away to hear the waves, but the sight of the water offered tranquility and contentment. In the calmness of the moment, he decided he would reach out to Mary Crossfield. He had to do something about Voltaire and sweet, kind Mary seemed like the answer.

The last traces of his irritability vanishing, Thomas resolved that he wouldn't demand Mary be on call as he had before; instead, he would insist she work for him part-time, on a daily basis. He would make it well worth her while. She didn't seem interested in money, but there had to be something else she wanted, something he could offer. He thought back to that indiscreet diatribe he'd gone off on about his writer's block at The Marine Room and how Mary had leaned in, intent on every word he said. Perhaps she was an aspiring author? But, no, she had not asked for advice, or asked him to read any of her work. Any writer worth their salt would have jumped at the chance to question him about *Souls in Collison*. Mary hadn't mentioned his novel at all. Perhaps she hadn't even read it.

Thomas walked back into his game room, picked the cue up off the floor and set it on the pool table. He went to his study and sat down to write Mary Crossfield, considering how he would word his email. What could he possibly offer to lure her away from her other clients? He closed his eyes and saw her wholesome, guileless face and admitted to himself that she was very pretty. Not sophisticated and confident like the women he was used to, but genuine and lovely. And married. Mary wasn't the sort of girl he was attracted to so there were no worries on that front.

Poising his fingers over the keyboard, he pictured Mary Crossfield's expressive amber eyes and began to type a letter to her; not a professional one full of business jargon and pompous demands, but a simple missive born of his heart. Mary wouldn't be bought, that much she had made clear, but an idea was forming in Thomas' mind, and he had a pretty good idea of how to go about winning her over, and giving her no choice but to work for him.

CHAPTER 19

⌐‿⌐

*L*orelei sat in one of the twenty-four black leather office chairs gathered around the wood and chrome conference table of Empire & Malkin's executive boardroom, her shapely legs crossed, back perfectly straight, and an annoyed expression on her face. It was Monday and she was waiting impatiently for Edmond Davies, the office operations manager, to make his appearance for their three p.m. meeting.

It was three-twenty.

Lorelei drummed her French manicured nails on the table, her lips thinning as she thought about tomorrow's deadlines. She really needed to be back in her office preparing broker payroll instead of sitting around waiting for the quirky, disorganized manager. Edmond might outrank her, but he was one of the least professional people she'd ever known. *Mary's dopey dog Roger would be a better leader,* she thought wryly.

Unfortunately, Edmond was here to stay, his position secured by a longtime friendship with the regional director. Edmond was educated, armed to the teeth with all the right credentials and degrees, and he was charming when he wanted to be. Lorelei was sure Edmond had breezed right through his lengthy interview process – in his case a formality - by turning on the "boys club" charisma with the all-male mucky-mucks in New York. Indeed, he got along splendidly with the brokers as well as all of upper management. If New York had any idea that Edmond was hardly ever in the office, that he abused his expense account and that he took long, liquid lunches then they weren't letting on. Lorelei knew that when an office was profitable, New York turned a blind eye - and San Diego had consistently been in the black for years. There would be no investigation into Edmond's poor management style unless someone within San Diego reported him to HR. And that wasn't going to happen because no one wanted to risk retaliation and possible job loss.

Lorelei sighed and looked at her watch. As long as Edmond stayed out of her hair and let her do her job, she couldn't care less about his unreliable and shady professional conduct. Besides, she'd be on a plane to Manhattan as soon as Margaret retired and then Lorelei would never have to look at Edmond's balding, pudgy head again.

Simone poked her head in the door. "Faith Dobbs is on the phone for you. Do you want to take it while you're waiting for Mr. Three Hairs?"

At the mention of Faith's name, Lorelei's heart plummeted and then began to pound with slow- burning anger. Faith had been blowing up her cell phone since Sunday morning, leaving voicemails and countless texts.

"Please tell Mrs. Dobbs I do not take personal calls at work."

Simone's big eyes widened at Lorelei's tone. "Okay…" She started to close the door.

"Wait!" Lorelei called.

Simone poked her head back in. "Yes?"

Lorelei paused for a moment, her anger subsiding into pain. "Please also tell Mrs. Dobbs to stop calling me altogether. Tell her... I don't want to talk to her for a while."

Simone looked uncomfortable with this task, but she nodded and gently clicked the door shut.

Lorelei closed her eyes and wondered what was motivating Faith to be so meddlesome lately. They'd been friends for well over ten years and this was the first time Lorelei had felt played or manipulated by her fun-loving friend. It wasn't so much that Faith had set Lorelei up with Frank on the sly, although that needed to be discussed in very serious not-to-happen-again terms; no, it was the mention of Connor. That was confidential sacred ground between girlfriends. Faith was right in that Lorelei needed to deal with the pain of losing Connor, but it had to be in her own time, not Faith's. Connor's betrayal was still so fresh- even after all these years- that the wounds had simply become a part of who Lorelei was. The emotional lacerations had left her bleeding, and instead of letting time heal them, she had just accepted the pain and allowed it to color her life, her decisions, her character. She wondered if perhaps the psychological bruises people carried with them became part of their identity. Maybe that's what had happened to her- maybe it wasn't just a broken heart she mourned, but a loss of the innocent girl she'd once been. Harboring the pain kept her from acknowledging love could find its way back in. It was easier to keep commitment and men at a distance, and concentrate instead on her successful career.

Lorelei straightened the statistical papers in front of her, took a sip of bottled water and pushed her personal problems aside. She stood and walked over to the windows to look out at the panoramic view of San Diego Bay and Coronado Island. The small peninsula leisurely floated in the shimmering ocean, sunshine dappling its sandy beaches. It had been too long since Lorelei had taken the ferry over to the island- she must set aside a day to do that. Perhaps Mary would join her- they could shop along the old-fashioned tree lined streets, hop the trendy wine bars, catch some rays on the beach before sunset, and finish off with a lovely dinner at Chez Loma. Lorelei's brow furrowed slightly. She hadn't heard from Mary since Saturday. Two days was a long time for them to go without any contact.

Lorelei refocused her thoughts to this evening's dinner plans with Niles. He had texted her after her Sunday morning hike on El Cajon Mountain, where she tried, unsuccessfully, to work off her resentment from the night before. It had taken almost two hours of rigorous climbing, and a lot of self-talk, for Lorelei to come to terms with the fact that Frank was not at fault. He hadn't known, couldn't have known, who Connor was. He'd trustingly followed Faith's advice, assuming the effervescent redhead would never hurt her beloved friend with a mere question.

The hike up and down the mountain was eleven miles, and by the time Lorelei had finished, her mind was a bit clearer. She had just slid behind the wheel of her Lexus when her cell phone chirped with Niles' text. Smart, impressively successful and very handsome, Niles Donovan was a broker at The Hillard Company, a competitive firm. Since meeting a few years earlier at a convention, Niles and Lorelei had gone out several times- nothing serious, only slight chemistry. There had been a bit of casual romance, a few laughs and a lot of shared inside jokes about the commercial real estate industry. Niles was easy to be with, good company and non-threatening. He was very involved with his ever-expanding client base and so had little time to pursue any kind of long-term relationship with a woman. When Niles felt like going out on one of his rare free evenings, he always asked Lorelei to join him- he was proud to be seen with such a glamorous and beautiful woman and he felt relaxed in the knowledge that Lorelei would never, ever want a serious relationship with him.

Lorelei had texted Niles back that she would meet him wherever he chose, knowing it would be somewhere exorbitantly expensive, always his treat. She wanted a night out on the town- to forget what happened on Saturday evening. Well… she didn't want to forget that *entire* evening. A shiver went through her as she remembered Frank's touches, his fiery kisses, his strong arms. She should really apologize to Frank for not speaking to him on the ride home, and for her curt dismissal. He'd left a message the next day asking if she would like him to take her to Wyland's to pick up her car, but she hadn't bothered calling him back and had, instead, taken a taxi.

The boardroom door slammed open and Edmond Davies crookedly walked in and plopped his pear-shaped form down in a chair across from Lorelei.

"Mr. Davies," Lorelei said, raising an eyebrow.

Edmond grinned sloppily and loosened his tie a bit. "Is it hot in here?" he asked, looking around.

"No," Lorelei said coolly. "Now, if we can just get started…"

But he wasn't paying attention. "Simon? Simmons? Simone!" Edmond was fumbling with the intercom in the middle of the big conference table. "Simone! *Simone*!"

"Yes, Mr. Davies?"

"Hi Simone!"

"Hi," Simone sounded wary.

Lorelei sighed deeply and tapped her foot.

"Simone?" Edmond warbled in a sing-songy voice. "Can you please bring me some coffee?"

"Cream and sugar?"

"Yup." Edmond hung up and flashed Lorelei a toothy grin.

The air conditioning kicked on, and the breeze from the vents stirred up the few lonely hairs on top of Edmond's mostly bald head.

Lorelei cleared her throat. "If we could start our meeting now, I'd really appreciate it. I have deadlines and-"

"Sure!" Edmond said benevolently, like he was granting her the wish of a lifetime. He spread his arms wide. "Let's chat."

"Thank you. I need your signature on the forecast for August's pipeline. I estimate we're on target for five million, and with LevTrust closing in September, projected revenue for the quarter should finish at twenty-two million."

"Geez, that's a lot of cash!"

Lorelei's lip curled. He was very tipsy. Again.

"Revenue recognition is not based on cash received, Mr. Davies," she said slowly. "Remember?"

He looked confused. "Then what is it based on?"

"Commissionable booked transactions."

"Huh?"

Simone walked in and set Edmond's coffee in front of him. "Can I get you anything?" she asked Lorelei, a note of sympathy in her voice.

Lorelei shook her head. "No, thank you, I'm fine."

Edmond Davies hiccupped and sipped his coffee, looking as though he hadn't a care in the world. The air conditioning blew his few hairs about some more and Simone watched them, fascinated.

"Is there something else, Simone?" Lorelei asked.

"Um... well, yes..." Simone shifted uncomfortably, her voice just above a whisper. "I gave Faith your message and she started crying. I thought you should know."

Lorelei was deeply concerned. Faith rarely cried. For the first time it occurred to Lorelei that Faith had no idea why Lorelei didn't want to talk to her. Unless Faith had called Frank to ask him... Or maybe Faith would call Mary now to find out if Mary knew...? Mary would freak if she thought her two best friends weren't speaking. Damnit. Lorelei didn't have time for all of this.

"Okay, thanks, Simone." Lorelei tried again. "Mr. Davies, if you would please sign the August estimate, we can all get back to work."

He squinted at the paperwork, his hands shaking slightly, making the pages rattle a bit while he read them. "Why aren't you counting the entire Dallas commission?"

"We discussed this before. SAB-101 states that contingent commissions cannot be recognized. The Dallas deal had an earning contingency."

Edmond looked blank. "You mean a termination right?"

Lorelei gritted her teeth. "Yes, most times that is the case for an earning contingency."

"I'll sign this estimate, but..." Edmond made a big show of being magnanimous, as though he were doing Lorelei a favor.

The air conditioning switched off and, disappointed, Simone left the room.

Edmond ended his signature with a flourish and clumsily stood up. As he tucked his pen back inside his suit jacket pocket, he winked at Lorelei and said, "I had lunch with Milton today."

That explains the drinking, Lorelei thought. Milton was one of the top-ranking brokers in New York and a notorious partier. "Why is Milton here in San Diego?"

"Golf. Good weather. San Diego has good weather for golf." Edmond hesitated and then began to giggle. "San Diego has good weather for everything."

Lorelei gathered her papers together and stood. "I'll just be getting back to my office."

"Wait! I have gossip!" Edmond said giddily, just as Simone poked her head back in the door.

"Mary Crossfield is on the phone for you, Lorelei. I wouldn't have interrupted but she's crying and she said it's urgent." Simone lowered her voice slightly. "Something about a doctor appointment."

Lorelei's heart squeezed. What doctor appointment? "Tell her I'll be right there." But before Lorelei could rush from the room Edmond Davies said in a loud, inebriated whisper, "Don't you want to know the gossip first? Margaret gave her notice."

Lorelei stopped short. "Are you sure? She's finally retiring?"

"Yes! Milton let it slip. I don't know what the company will do without Margaret - she's been in that position for years."

Don't I know it, thought Lorelei snarkily. She let the reality of Margaret's retirement sink in. Lorelei knew without a doubt New York would promote her in less than a month. Manhattan was within her reach! This was what she'd been waiting for, longing for, fantasizing about for so very long. Exhilaration bubbled inside her.

"Don't get that look in your eye, Miss Lorelei Harper," Edmond said, wagging his finger. "You know you can't replace Margaret."

Lorelei narrowed her green eyes. "What do you mean?"

"Why, we need you here, of course!" He paused for effect. "You didn't think I'd let you go, did you?"

Lorelei felt the color draining from her face. This could not be happening. She looked at Edmond Davies, wondering if this joke of a manager could really stand between her and what should be her new position. There had to be some way to fight him without tarnishing her good name with insubordination. Besides, New York would have something to say if he stood in the way. Wouldn't they?

Lorelei swallowed her tumultuous emotions and excused herself. "I need to take my call. Can we talk about this later?"

"Talk about you being the star employee of San Diego? And San Diego ONLY? Absolutely."

Lorelei was just about out the door when Edmond called after her, his voice cheerfully unconcerned, "Forget about New York, Lorelei Harper! You're not going anywhere!"

CHAPTER 20

*M*itch leaned back in his leather chair and rubbed his eyes. He'd been reviewing the geotechnical survey report from the lab for the Flagstaff lots and was slightly concerned about the groundwater levels and the subsurface data. Though it wouldn't increase the cost of development too much, he found himself wishing, as he often did, that his father was there to discuss the business with him.

He looked up at the ceiling of his home office and thought of the man who had taught him anything and everything about construction. Mitch remembered swinging a hammer with his old man, the two of them working in perfect tandem- and in total silence. Mitch's father had been all work and no play, for he'd had a family to feed and not much more than two pennies to rub together.

Every day after school, on weekends and during the summers, from the time Mitch was seven years old until he went to college, he apprenticed under his father, learning all he could about the building industry. Academic excellence was also expected, and after graduating high school as class valedictorian, Mitch easily won a full ride scholarship to Arizona State University, from which he emerged six years later with his Master of Science in Construction Management, *summa cum laude.* It was the first time Mitch had ever seen his father cry.

Mitch's siblings, Claude and Georgette, had also been beaming with pride on his graduation day. Claude especially had always known Mitch would be a success- no matter what he did with that incredible tenacity of his. Claude had never been jealous of his twin's achievements, nor his close relationship with their father. There was always enough love to go around the Morrison home, even if it wasn't shared through words and affection. The love was almost its own entity, another person sharing their house, bonding the five of them together in a ribbon of familial respect and devotion.

Aside from their looks, the twin brothers couldn't have been more different. Whereas Mitch had always loved working with his hands, being in the outdoors and creating structures and buildings, Claude, from his earliest days, preferred artistic pursuits. As soon as he was old enough, he began babysitting neighborhood children to finance his growing collection of paintbrushes, canvases, oils and watercolors. Claude was a visceral, intuitive artist whose talent and flair grew exponentially with each new composition he created. Friends and family marveled in his ability and as the years passed, word spread about the young virtuoso. By the time Claude was in high school he began receiving commissions for portraits and landscapes, and he let his schoolwork slide, maintaining a C average just to get by. He wanted only to be on the drop cloth in his room, a brush in hand. Art was both his escape and his reason for waking every morning, and now he was making money doing what he loved. History and math books were shoved aside and replaced by those on artistic style and technique. He went to any art show that came through Phoenix, laboriously studying each painting with ardent and inquisitive eyes. He graduated high school with relief and by then had saved up enough money from his commissions to travel to Cornwall. There in England, he studied under artist Margo Maeckelberghe whose studio, Carn Cottage, was located on the ridge atop the moors between Penzance and Zennor. Claude spent hours in that studio under Margo's tutelage, learning as much as he could as fast as he could.

For her part, Margo was pleased with her gifted student and his natural genius for color, and for two years Claude flourished under her apprenticeship. He sold many of his paintings and, before settling too comfortably into a Cornish artist's life, he left for Rome and Paris and Barcelona. In his letters home, Claude wrote eloquently of gazing upon the architecture of those beautiful cities, reveling in the colors of their sunsets, listening to the melodic flow of their languages, and above all, seeking out interesting and anomalous faces to paint.

Mitch and Claude missed each other terribly while Claude was abroad and the brothers kept in touch by phone as much as possible. Mitch chatted about all he was learning in college, the parties he went to, the girls he dated. Claude spoke of the music he'd fallen in love with in France, the colors of the sky in Spain, the intricacy of the sculptures in Italy. The twins took an avid interest in each other' lives and reveled in one another's successes. Even more than brothers, they were best friends and confidants.

Up until a month after their thirtieth birthday.

It was 1986 in the Black Hills of Jerome, Arizona, where Claude had just finished spending a lovely afternoon and a few bottles of wine discussing portraiture with fellow artist Jimmie Grest. Jimmie and Claude had met years earlier while standing in line for coffee near the Galleria degli Uffizi in Tuscany. They began chatting and discovered they were both budding artists from America. Claude was impressed with Jimmie's deep insight and keen eye for the abstract. The two became fast friends and had kept in touch over the years, so when Jimmie had called one day to say he'd be in Jerome, Claude dropped everything to meet him. They'd parted ways later that afternoon with a hug and a promise to get together again. Claude had felt a little tipsy but didn't think for a minute he wouldn't be able to navigate the two-hour drive through the desert and back to Mitch's house, where he was staying for a few months.

As Claude wound his way down through the Black Hills, he became lost in thought remembering a quote Jimmie had shared with him. It was from the early 1500s and had been said by Count Balthazar to famous painter Raphael after receiving the latter's portrait of his wife:

"Your image… alone can lighten my cares," the Count had declared. "That image is my delight; I direct my smiles to it, it is my joy."

"Those are the words every artist wants to hear of their work," Jimmie had said to Claude, his eyes shining. "To know your creation brings gladness of soul to another."

Claude was smiling as he drove down a particularly steep hill. There was nothing like talking about art with a fellow painter, someone who understood his passion. Claude stepped on the gas as he navigated the incredibly curvy, twisty road leading out of the Black Hills. He cruised across Highway 89 at the speed limit, but slowed to let a merging semi truck in. A jackrabbit darted out from the side of the road and ran in front of Claude's car. Without thinking, he slammed on the brakes to avoid running the small animal over and the vehicle behind him smashed into his back end. The impact sent Claude's car rocketing into the slowly moving semi, and in that starkly brief moment in time, without warning, without getting to say goodbye to anyone, without feeling the comfort and joy of holding a paint brush one last time, Claude's life ended in a flash of metal against metal, steel against steel.

"It was so quick that it would have been painless," Mitch's mother sobbingly repeated to Mitch over and over that night, as though saying the words would somehow bring the elusive comfort she so desperately wanted to feel.

Mitch didn't know if she was trying to convince him or herself.

In the days, weeks, months, after Claude's death, Mitch did everything he could to avoid the excruciating pain of losing his best friend. He buried himself in work, seeking distraction from the sorrow he couldn't escape, and when he wasn't working, he was allowing women to sidetrack his attention, indulging in the pleasures of physical gratification. But nothing could assuage the pain he felt, nothing could divert him from the grief he carried.

Until that fateful day Helene showed up on his doorstep with baby Mary. When he'd looked down into Marion Grace's perfect, tiny face for first time, he knew he was meant to be her daddy. Surely God had given Mitch this defenseless, beautiful being to treasure and take care of so that he could rejoice again in a life that hadn't had any hope or meaning since Claude's death. When Helene handed Mary over to Mitch she had no idea she was literally passing on to him his reason to feel alive again. And as Mitch held the small baby in his strong arms, a powerful feeling of unconditional love washed over him and he promised Helene then and there, without hesitation, that he would always be there for Mary; he would forever love and cherish the little girl with all his heart and soul.

Back in Mitch's office, the land line rang, pulling him abruptly to the present. Mitch pushed aside the report and reached past his coffee mug to pick up the old office phone.

"Morrison Home Builders," he said, hoping it was the Flagstaff engineering geologist with further information on flood prediction.

"Hi. It's Owen."

Mitch sat bolt upright, his heart beating a fast rhythm. His son-in-law never called. "Is Mary okay?"

"Yes. Yes, she's fine, sir."

Mitch's breathing slowed and he let out a long sigh. "Thank God."

"I'm sorry to scare you." Owen's commanding, confident voice held an unusual hint of trepidation.

"No problem at all. How are you? How's the promotion?"

"Good, sir, it won't be much longer now until it's official. But I'm sure Mary has talked to you about that."

Mitch's brow furrowed ever so slightly.

Owen cleared his throat. "Actually, that's sort of the reason I was calling. You and Mary are so close and I know she tells you everything and…"

There was a slight pause. Mitch leaned back in his chair, his eyes narrowing in suspicion. What exactly was going on between Owen and Mary? He knew something was up, but he was still waiting for Mary to tell him. Mitch wasn't sure why his daughter was holding back- they had always had an extremely open and loving relationship. His guess was she didn't want to burden him, but this in and of itself was puzzling, given how she had always confided in him in the past.

Mitch wondered if he should tell Owen that he hadn't talked to Mary recently and that whatever Owen wanted to say should be shelved, but his curiosity got the better of him. What was so important that his daughter's husband was making this out-of-the-blue call? Mitch was well aware that he intimidated Owen, so whatever it was must be immensely important. A small prick of conscience almost made Mitch end the call at that moment, but concern for his daughter won out.

"What is it, Owen?" Mitch demanded. "Tell me right now."

"It's about the baby..."

Tears sprang to Mitch's eyes and his whole body softened with emotion. "Mary's pregnant? My little girl is pregnant?" Mitch smiled, awestruck, and he looked at the framed picture of Claude on his desk. "I'm going to be a grandpa," he said wonderingly to his brother's beaming, paint-smudged face.

Owen backtracked. "No! I mean, no... Mary's not pregnant, sir, she's not..."

"What?" Mitch blinked.

"I didn't... I didn't mean to insinuate that..."

Elation immediately turned to confusion. "What the hell are you talking about? So Mary's *not* pregnant?"

"No, she's not. We haven't been able to conceive, sir. It's been almost a year and Mary still isn't-"

Mitch cut him off. "Wait..." he said with an edge to his voice, "Why are you telling me this?"

"Well, we are having some communication problems. As you know, Mary isn't sure she even wants to be a mother and..."

All the air went out of Mitch's lungs and he closed his eyes in understanding. *That's* why his daughter hadn't reached out to him.

She was afraid of letting him down, of telling him he might not ever have grandchildren. She didn't want to disappoint her daddy. Mitch felt a surge of love for his selfless little girl and with it a pang of remorse that she hadn't been able to confide in him. He hoped she'd been able to talk to Lorelei about her feelings and wasn't bottling them up. Mitch was seized by a sudden desire to throttle his son-in-law but decided to keep his provocation in check until he learned all he could. Mitch suspected Mary's reticence most likely had something to do with Helene's abandonment, but he wanted to make sure he knew all the facts before he reached out to his daughter.

"Why doesn't Mary want to have children?" Mitch asked.

The brief pause must have made Owen nervous. "I shouldn't have called. I'm sorry to have bothered you, sir. I just assumed Mary would have told you everything that's been going on and I thought between you and me we could... convince her what is best for the family, for us... for her..." His voice trailed off, unsure.

Son of a bitch. Mitch's hand went to the heavy paperweight from his desk, his fingers itching to throw it. Instead he took a deep breath and with barely concealed menace asked, "You wanted to talk to me about my daughter behind her back?"

"No! I mean, yes. I mean... It has always been assumed we would have children and I would pass on the Crossfield name and when I married Mary I knew she would be the perfect wife and that she would be a wonderful mother one day. You see, Mary has always been in agreement with everything in our relationship- until now. But this... this choice she is making... her being unsure about whether she wants to have kids or not... it's just not like her, sir."

"Because she's thinking of herself for once?"

"Because she's not thinking of what's best for us." Owen cleared his throat. "Don't you want to be a grandpa, sir?"

Mitch felt like his head was going to explode. He pounded his meaty fist on the desk. "How DARE you try to manipulate me!"

Owen began to lose some of his timidity. This was so unfair! What had he done to deserve a possibly childless marriage? Nothing! Nothing at all. He wasn't to blame here. "It is not my fault your daughter changed her mind about something that is of paramount importance in my life! This wouldn't even be an issue if she had become pregnant right after we discussed starting a family- it would have been too late for her to change her mind."

Mitch wanted to jump in his car and drive straight to San Diego, but he was unclear whether his true motivation was to knock Owen out or to sit down with Mary and have a much-needed heart to heart.

"Owen," Mitch said slowly, deliberately, "Mary is not a pawn in your family's little lineage game. She is a person with hopes and dreams and a mind of her own."

"I'm aware of that, sir, but this is one issue that can't be compromised on." Owen's impatience began to unravel and words spilled out one after the other. "My parents expect children of me. I can't let them down. I'm the only one! Surely you understand that since Mary is an only child too. Surely you can comprehend the amount of pressure I'm under. My mother calls all the time- ALL THE TIME- wanting to know if Mary is pregnant and I keep having to tell her no. I keep having to disappoint her, week after week, month after month. Do you know what a failure that makes me feel like? Please, sir, please talk to Mary and help her to see that having a family is the next logical step for us. She adores you and she listens to everything you say. Your word is gold in her eyes."

Mitch cracked his knuckles and wondered what it would feel like to put a fist through Owen's perfectly handsome face. "I will do no such thing."

Owen's voice changed when he realized Mitch wouldn't help Mary see the light of how her future should unfold. "Well, then, sir," Owen said, his voice steely, "at least tell me this: is Mary's inability to conceive genetic? Helene obviously didn't have any issues, but did her sisters or her aunts? Are there any female problems on that side that could have been passed on? I'd like to get Mary into the doctor as soon as possible for testing and it would be helpful to know any background information on the family in terms of infertility."

Mitch was too infuriated to speak.

Owen took the silence to mean he'd said something that missed the mark. He hesitated for only a moment and then ventured, "Sir, Helene was a real person, wasn't she? She wasn't someone you just made up to cover Mary's mother's true identity? I need to know the-"

With a roar of rage, Mitch slammed the phone down, ripped the cord from the wall and threw the whole thing over his desk with such force that the handset and receiver crashed through a window.

The deafening sound of shattering glass pierced the still air and Mitch wondered if what he was really hearing was the sound of his heart breaking for his little girl.

CHAPTER 21

*G*eorgette stood before the full-length mirror in her bedroom, critiquing the flowy tangerine dress she had bought the day before. Not bad, she thought, twisting this way and that, admiring her trim waistline and the elegant turn of her head. Her short, feathered hair glinted with beautiful silver hues and her dark green eyes were just as bright as when she was a young girl. Sure, she was covered in soft wrinkles - she was seventy-three years old for heaven's sake! - but they had done nothing to mar her vivacious spirit. And being in her seventies had certainly not curbed Georgette's penchant for romance.

George had loved Francesca since she'd first laid eyes on the rambunctious Italian well over forty years earlier. It had been 1976 and thirty-one-year-old Georgette was at a farmer's market in downtown Phoenix. She was reaching for a bouquet of particularly stunning sunflowers when she heard a woman shouting across the street. Heads began to turn as shoppers with baskets of fruit and vegetables and breads stopped what they were doing and focused their attention on the screeching voice. A dog began barking erratically and a man was yelling at the shouting woman. Georgette carefully returned the sunflowers to their water bucket and stepped out from under the market canopy to get a closer look.

A small, olive-skinned woman who looked to be in her late thirties was trying to wrangle a beagle away from a middle-aged bearded man.

"Let go of him!" she shouted in the man's face, her subtle Italian accent lilting in anger.

"He's mine! What is wrong with you?!" he yelled back at her. "Stop trying to take my dog!"

"I saw you hit him!"

"He's MY dog! I can hit him if I want!"

The small, wiry woman suddenly let go of the beagle and threw herself at the man like a crazed flying squirrel. Astonished, he lost his balance and fell backward, and she landed on top of him, knocking the breath from his body with a loud "WHOOSH!" She pushed a finger up under his nose and snarled malevolently, "You don't hit animals, mister!"; then she pressed a knee into his crotch and pushed herself to a standing position using dead weight. The man screamed in pain and rolled on to his side.

"You crushed my nuts, lady!" he wailed.

"You're damn right I did, *stupido*!" said the Italian. "I'm taking your dog. You try to get him back and I'll squash your tiny *pisello*." She grabbed the beagle and held it close. It stopped barking and licked her face. "You live with me now," she told it and walked away.

"You bitch!" the man called after her, enraged but still unable to stand up.

The small woman turned around and said, "Chiudere il becco, bischero," so threateningly that the man quieted, his eyes full of fury and the rest of him whimpering in pain.

Georgette crossed the street, walked up to the Italian and introduced herself. "That was a very noble thing you did."

"I'm Francesca Maria Benedetta Fogagnolo. Nice to meet you," the woman said pleasantly. Then her tone turned savage. "And that man over there is a *bastardo*!" She whipped around to glare at him, shook her fist in the air and shrieked, "And he will find his privates ground up in a meat grinder if he ever comes near this dog again!"

"Okay," Georgette said, putting a calming arm around both incensed Italian and bewildered beagle. "Let's get you out of here."

The women walked two blocks to O'Malley's Pub and sat on the patio. Francesca lit a cigarette while they waited for their beers and the beagle happily laid at her feet, enjoying the beauty of the fall day and the gentle rise and fall of the ladies' voices as they got to know one another over the next few hours.

Georgette was instantly attracted to the feisty woman across the table from her. Francesca was the opposite of George in every way- both in looks and in temperament. George was tall, almost regal in movement and stature, while Francesca was short, stocky and full of quick, energetic gestures. George was relaxed, slow to speak and slow to take action so she could allow her sharp mind to process whatever it was she was seeing and hearing. Francesca was full of barely contained enthusiasm; passion and words tumbled from her pouty lips faster than her mind could keep up with. Georgette's voice was warm and soothing while Francesca's inflection was deep, sultry and intense.

Georgette wondered if it was a case of opposites attracting and nothing more. She kept a safe distance from Francesca, leaning back in her chair, one arm folded across her middle while the other held her glass of ale. She regarded Francesca with eyes that betrayed nothing. A child of the 1950s, Georgette had learned very early on that one did not step outside the strict social mores deigned appropriate by church and state. Certainly, she knew she was never to reveal – even to those closest to her - that she liked women.

It wasn't that Georgette didn't like men - far from it! A tomboy through and through, she'd spent most of her childhood in the rough and tumble world of boys, wrestling with them, playing kickball, football or fishing down at the creek, oftentimes besting them with her skill and agility. That all changed in high school, however, when Georgette grew into a statuesque, very attractive young lady. Suddenly, boys were constantly asking her to dances, following her around the halls between classes, begging her to spend time with them during lunch hour. Frequently, she found little love notes shoved through the slats of her locker. Embarrassed, she would tear them up and throw them away.

At the same time, she began to notice her own growing feelings about other girls. Georgette kept such thoughts to herself, assuming there was something wrong with her. None of her girlfriends ever talked about liking other women– indeed, they were all completely boy-crazy. Certainly she hadn't met any other females who felt the way she did. Or if she had, they weren't talking about it either.

Yet despite this painful isolation, Georgette was above all a pragmatist. She might not be able to express her feelings for women, but neither would she marry a man knowing he could never satisfy the romantic side of her nature. She simply settled into life as a single woman. And it was a full, happy life- her friends were legion, her career as a molecular biologist was challenging and rewarding, even more so after she earned her PhD in genetics. She was also an avid golfer, and when she wasn't working she could often be found on the course at the country club of which she was a member.

But everything changed that afternoon at O'Malley's Pub. As Francesca chatted happily about her childhood in Italy and her teenage years in America, Georgette found herself hanging on every interesting word, her heart beating a little faster, a charmed smile touching her lips. The small, hot-blooded Italian woman was so much fun to be with; a petite spitfire who didn't care about social norms, in America or anywhere else. Francesca seemed to abide by no one's rules but her own. As they finished their third round of beers, Francesca invited Georgette to her home. She called it a "villa" and said it was within walking distance, which was good since both of them were fairly tipsy.

As the women walked up a flowered path, the beagle trotting cheerfully behind them, Georgette had her first glimpse of Francesca's house. It left her breathless, for the place was indeed a villa- sprawling and beautiful and immensely welcoming. It basked languidly in the Arizona sun, surrounded by cactus and mesquite trees, a large stone fountain cozily spilling water down its columns off to the right and a garden of vegetables off to the left. Francesca explained that the house had been in her family for years. After her parents passed away, Francesca's siblings had all departed for Italy but Francesca chose to stay in America, content to live alone in the home that held her parents' prized possessions and so many loving familial memories. Francesca's parents had been comfortably wealthy so Francesca didn't need to work for a living; she, instead, spent her days caring for friends, running errands for the elderly, and cooking vast amounts of mouthwatering Italian dishes to serve at her tremendously popular dinner parties.

As Francesca led Georgette into the foyer, George was immediately transported to another place and time. It seemed all of Italy was in the villa- from the tempting smell of garlic and butter in the air, to the Italian white lilies in jugs and vases scattered about, to the bottles of wine seductively squatting on countertops and side tables, just waiting to be opened and drunk. Georgette admired the paintings on the walls, the stone flooring, the antique furniture. She stood in the middle of the great room and felt completely at home, like the villa had simply opened its arms and enveloped her in a warm, fragrant hug.

Francesca set out a bowl of water for the beagle and then uncorked a bottle of red wine. She gathered up a few items from her refrigerator and carelessly arranged them on a giant lemon-colored plate. Georgette's mouth watered at the sight of the cheeses, the grapes, the salami and the Italian herbed bread slices.

Francesca held out a glass of wine to George and then said, a sparkle in her dark eyes, "Bella!"

Georgette flushed for she knew *bella* meant beautiful. As she sipped the wine, her eyes roamed around the walls of the house, its allure captivating.

Francesca sat down on a very puffy, cushiony couch and she patted the seat next to her. "Please?" she asked Georgette.

George sat, careful to not get too close to Francesca. The woman was having an intoxicating effect on her and she was trying to keep her complicated thoughts prudently masked.

It didn't work.

"You're not very good about hiding your feelings," Francesca said, examining George's calculated expression with interest.

George waved her hand and laughed nervously. "Whatever do you mean?"

Francesca leaned forward and took George's wine from her. She set the glass on a low table in front of them and placed a small hand on George's knee. Georgette sucked in her breath, for the touch was like molten lava running up her thigh.

"That's what I thought," said Francesca. She slowly moved closer until her face was scarcely inches from Georgette's. "I know you better than you think," she said in that sultry voice. "You are not the only one to feel the way you do."

"I don't know what you're talking about," Georgette said, her voice was coming out in short, sporadic breaths.

Francesca smiled, her eyes compassionate. "It is not wrong, Georgie, for women to love each other. It is the way some of us were born. That's nature. Surely you know that, with your education in the sciences?"

"Yes, but…" Georgette swallowed. No one had ever called her Georgie before. No woman had ever seen through her. No woman had ever looked at her the way Francesca was. Their faces were so close, their bodies almost touching. George thought she might faint from the erotic emotions coursing through her.

Francesca reached out and pushed a small silky lock of Georgette's hair away from her cheek. "You are the most beautiful creature I have ever seen," Francesca said. "Don't be afraid. I will not hurt you."

Georgette blushed, her normally reserved composure falling to pieces. "But I have never… I don't know how to…"

Francesca's voice turned velvety, her Italian accent sexily pronounced. "I will show you. I want to show you. Let me love you, Georgie. Let me show you paradise."

For three days the women remained sequestered in the villa. Georgette had never known such physical pleasure could exist. Francesca was a master musician, playing George's body like it was the most exquisite instrument she'd ever laid hands on. And Georgette was a fast learner; she quickly began to let go of her self-imposed restraint and she gave as much ecstasy as she received, taking Francesca to libidinous heights the lusty Italian said she'd never been to before.

After those three days, Georgette and Francesca were inseparable, and a few months later, deeply in love, Georgette moved into Francesca's villa. Georgette's family, and the couple's friends, assumed the two women were roommates, spinster pals who had found platonic companionship. But behind closed doors, the villa protected the women, listened to all their secrets and held them tight to its bosom. There were no bad days, no hard times, no sadness for ten years. A decade of bliss.

Until that fateful night in 1986. That's when Georgette had gotten the call. Claude was dead. Her baby brother gone forever. If anyone could have understood her lifestyle and loved her without judgement, it would have been tenderhearted Claude. But she'd never told him, never told anyone, and faced with his death she realized she'd kept the best part of herself from him. He would never know her true heart, the joy she felt, the way her life had been turned upside down and then made right by Francesca. Georgette, unable to stop sobbing, took to her bed and didn't leave it for five days. Hour after hour, Francesca tried to comfort her dear Georgie, never leaving her side except to help her to the bathroom or to bring her water. Georgette refused any food and she became weak with crying. She clung to Francesca, allowing herself to be rocked back and forth like a child, Francesca's voice softly uttering words of love, sometimes just singing broken verses of Italian song.

Slowly and lovingly, Francesca nursed her sweet Georgette back to the world of the living.

After a month's absence, Georgette returned to work and she and Francesca entered into a new phase of their relationship. It was Claude's death that made George face the truth of her life- a life she no longer wanted to hide. She told all her friends, all of her family, that she and Francesca were not only lovers, but committed to one another on every level. Francesca and George's friends embraced the couple, accepted their situation and loved them all the more for their honesty. George's parents acknowledged the news with gruff acceptance and very few words. Mitch had just chuckled, slapped Georgette on the back in camaraderie, and said, "I don't blame you, sis. Women are deliciously tantalizing, aren't they?"

Francesca, happy to be free from the confines of living a double life, became more outgoing, eccentric, and fun-loving than ever. She lost any sense of filter and her days were filled with silly antics, small adventures and lots of laughter. One day George came home from work to discover a pygmy goat in the kitchen. Francesca explained she'd found him in Guadalupe trotting down a dirt road and looking forlorn and lonely. She had quickly pulled over, stuffed him into her small car and named him Steve. Georgette was adamant that Francesca had stolen the goat from some poor farmer, but Francesca only said, "If someone really owned Steve then they should have taken better care of him and not let him run amok."

During his weeklong stay, Steve ate part of a couch, three of Georgette's dresses and her briefcase, a carton of Francesca's cigarettes and two cassette tapes, one of which was Tony's Bennett's Greatest Hits, George's favorite. When George declared that their houseguest had worn out his welcome, Francesca hung up "Goat Found" signs all over Guadalupe. The women received sixteen calls, all claiming the missing goat was theirs. Francesca, astounded at the obvious larcenous intentions of the adoption hopefuls, told all of them off in Italian, squashed Steve into her car once again and handed him over to an animal sanctuary in Buckeye where he peacefully lived out his days with a featherless chicken, a deformed cow and a three-legged cat named Schrodinger.

Francesca and George lived exciting, fulfilling lives, for they never tired of doing things for others and they never, ever grew bored of one another. As the months passed, George's pain over losing her little brother lessened ever so slightly, but mostly she was numb and operating on autopilot. Work challenged her mind, and Francesca, with her liveliness and constant shenanigans, kept George laughing. But it wasn't until Mitch showed up at their door one day with a blanketed bundle that Georgette began to truly heal from her loss.

George had held baby Mary in her arms and listened to Mitch's story of Helene. Francesca, having stubbed out her cigarette as soon as she saw the infant, leaned forward to catch every word Mitch spoke. As he talked, his voice became low and scratchy, his tears barely in check. Georgette and Francesca exchanged glances and knew, without speaking, that they would do whatever they could to help Mitch raise his new daughter.

"We're here for you," Georgette had said. "We'll always be here for you and Mary."

"Please," Mitch begged them, "please don't ever tell Mary the truth."

The women had promised, and Mitch, relieved to have the support of his sister and her partner, relaxed at last. He smiled for the first time since Claude's death. Francesca got up, opened a bottle of wine and the three adults toasted to Mary's long life and prosperity. As they talked and drank and laughed in the sunny living room of the villa, life began to take on new meaning and new purpose for Francesca and Georgette. They now had parental-type responsibilities and, while those responsibilities were not full-time, the aunties took their roles very seriously.

Francesca promptly gave up smoking and put her beloved villa up for sale. She and Georgette bought a smaller home in Tempe, closer to Mitch's house. When the couple moved in they child-proofed every nook and cranny and made one of the bedrooms into Mary's very own so that she would know their house was her house too. Over the years

Mary spent many days and many nights in the Tempe home, watching movies with her aunties, learning how to cook from Francesca, lounging by the pool reading with Georgette, helping with little chores, or simply sitting at the big kitchen table doing crafts by herself while listening to strains of Italian opera wafting in from the CD player in the living room.

With her father actively expanding his custom home business, Mary found herself with her aunties regularly when she wasn't in school. Morrison Home Builders was becoming one of the most in-demand contractors in the Valley and Mitch was on top of the world- reveling not only in his commercial success, but also adoring every aspect of being a father.

Georgette often wondered if Mary knew the impact she'd had on her and Mitch's lives, that her arrival had been the only balm strong enough to mend their broken hearts after losing Claude.

The front door slammed, making Georgette jump and bringing her back to the present. Francesca's footsteps sounded in the hall and her voice carried into the bedroom.

"I'm home, pussycat! Guess what? I shot the silhouette man right in the nards! Isn't that funny?"

Francesca barged into the room, her grey hair spiked out around her head, her wrinkled face weathered and craggy and beaming with impish delight.

She stopped short when she saw Georgette in the new beautiful tangerine dress. Francesca's dark eyes swept over the willowy body of her lover.

"Oh, Georgie, my love. Sei bellisima."

As Georgette turned from the mirror to look at Francesca all she could see was the small, sultry Italian girl from so long ago who had once said in her sexy accent, "Let me love you, Georgie. Let me show you paradise."

And so she had.

CHAPTER 22

From: Thomas McQuillan / T.McQuillan@ThomasMcQuillan.com
To: Mary Crossfield / Mary@rogersleashbrigade.com
Subject: My Sincerest Apologies

Dear Mary,

I want to thank you for taking time out of your busy schedule to listen to my concerns regarding Voltaire. As you probably gleaned from our conversation, he has caused quite a bit of upheaval for me.

I also want to apologize to you for my assumptions with regard to your clients. In fact, I admire your loyalty to them and your - dare I say, harsh rejection? -of my suggestion that you drop them and work exclusively for me. Please know that as demanding or insensitive as it may have seemed, it was meant as a compliment.

You had mentioned that you wondered why I even have a dog when I don't appear to like him. That was a valid point. I may not have strong affection for Voltaire, but I did love his previous owner - my Grandma Molly.

For as long as I can remember, my grandmother had wanted a French Bulldog, but my grandfather always had one reason or another for not getting one. It was one of the few things they disagreed upon. You see, my grandparents were one of those hopelessly annoying couples who hold hands and kiss in public, who laugh at each other's jokes even when they're not funny, who connect on every level-spiritually, conversationally, mentally, emotionally. I've never seen that kind of beautiful, poetic love anywhere else.

Seven months ago, they celebrated their sixtieth wedding anniversary and my extended family (and there are a lot of us!) rented the Alcott Mansion in Temecula for the weekend. On the night of the big anniversary party my grandfather stood up and gave the most impressive speech I've ever heard. He then toasted my grandmother with all the love and promise of a newlywed. After he kissed her, he clapped his hands and a maid came rushing in with a large box that had a giant silvery bow on top of it. She handed the box to Grandma Molly.

Grandpa Bob smiled adoringly at her. "As Voltaire once said, 'The husband who decides to surprise his wife is often very much surprised himself.'"

Grandma Molly was ecstatic when she pulled the top off the box and lifted out a tiny, blue Frenchie! She looked at my grandpa with such happiness and gratitude that, literally, there wasn't a dry eye in the place.

My grandparents named the puppy Voltaire and they doted on him like he was a little emperor. He was pampered and spoiled and loved, and his antics brought them nothing but joy.

As it turns out, Grandpa Bob had another reason for gifting Grandma Molly with Voltaire. He had found out about the cancer a few weeks before their anniversary but kept it a secret because he wanted the celebration to be perfect. What was the point, when the doctors said there was nothing they could do? Two months after Voltaire joined their household, Grandpa Bob quietly left it.

Instead of turning to Voltaire for companionship and love as my grandpa had envisioned, my grandma collapsed in Grandpa Bob's old recliner, refusing to move or speak and declining any food or drink. We called an ambulance on the third day and she died in the hospital, heartbroken and bereaved, two weeks later.

I am the oldest of six and my siblings all have children. Voltaire is not good with kids, so none of my brothers or sisters wanted to risk their children being bitten. My parents didn't want to take Voltaire since their fourteen grandchildren are constantly in and out of their house. That left me... childless and with plenty of room for a spoiled rotten puppy who'd had his world ripped apart by losing both of his beloved owners. None of us wanted to adopt Voltaire out- we felt he should remain in the family out of respect for my grandparents.

And that, in a nutshell, is my predicament. I really didn't want Voltaire in my life and, yes, he makes me crazy, but we are forced to live together and we do try to get along. Voltaire had a rough start to his young life and I know little to nothing about canines so we sort of just muddle through. The one thing Voltaire and I have in common is that we both loved Grandma Molly, and, I think, we both wish we could have made a difference somehow in bringing her back from the brink.

I didn't want Voltaire, and he damn sure didn't want me. We both suffer our grief in different ways. I know Voltaire acts out because he is confused and sad and maybe a little angry. I guess I am too. So perhaps he and I have more in common than I thought.

I know it is too much to ask of you to watch him full-time, but I am hoping you can maybe clear longer intervals in your schedule for us, preferably at least six hours a day, five days a week. Should you accept my offer you will be well compensated for your time, at three times your normal rate. You will have the gate code and key to the estate, as well as a bedroom in the east wing should you ever need a place to rest. Of course you are welcome to make use of the pool (Voltaire loves to swim) and the jacuzzi, as well as the theatre in the basement. Helga, my housekeeper, lives on the property and she will be able to assist you with anything you might need.

If this does not convince you, perhaps I can sweeten the pot even further. That night at dinner I was watching your face while I spoke of my writer's block. You have very expressive eyes and there was something in them that my intuition picked up on. Could you be a budding writer? I ask because if you are, I would like to offer my services to you in the form of authorship coaching and mentoring. I'm not a teacher by any means, but I would welcome the opportunity to answer any of your questions and to help you with character sketches, plot outlines or storyboarding. I could be way off in my assumptions here, but I don't think so. I believe somewhere within your mind and soul, Mary Crossfield, there is a writer waiting to emerge. Let me bring her forth. I'd like to.

Am I attempting to bribe you? Yes, I am. I believe your calming presence will help Voltaire, and I can tell (and Willow assures me) that you are a trustworthy person.

Please let me know if this arrangement is agreeable. I have attached a confidentiality contract for your perusal.

Life is full of surprises. I am a practical man, but also an artist- this leaves my psyche hovering somewhere between idealism and realism. So from my idealist side I will tell you this: I believe our meeting is kismet and has purpose. We both need something from one another and I'm willing to compromise on the logistics if you are.

With warm regards,
Thomas

⌒

From: Georgette Morrison / g.morrison@novagenetics.com
To: Mary Crossfield / Mary@rogersleashbrigade.com
Subject: George & Pauline

Mary, my dear…

How are you, sweet girl? I miss you so and hope to see you soon. Aunt Franny sends her love along with lots of hugs and kisses.

A few weeks ago I found an old letter your great-grandfather wrote to your great-grandmother. He penned it in the early 1900s and it was the last letter he wrote to her before he proposed.

I know you love romance and the written word so next time I see you I will deliver the letter into your safe keeping. I would send it via mail, but I don't want to chance it getting lost. In the meantime, I've typed it out below for you to read.

I hope you are having an excellent week. Please tell Owen hi from us and give Roger lots of scratches behind his ears from his Great-Auntie George.

I love you,
Aunt Georgette

Picacho, New Mexico
September 9, 1908
Miss Pauline Hulbert,

I sure wish you was here for I am having a time. I will be up Sunday and hope to find the same sweet Pauline as ever and know I will. I don't believe anything that anybody tells me- if I did I would be the unhappiest boy in the world, but I believe you and not some at the news carrier. Don't know if you can read this or not. I am trying to cook dinner and write all at the same time and in a hurry also. I have got a good one on you and I think I shall hurrah you a little Sunday. I will not tell you now but will Sunday- it must be so for the most truthful man in the country told it.

All I wanted was just to let you know that I was all ok and just the same as your ever loving...

Geo

CHAPTER 23

*L*orelei removed her reading glasses and rubbed her temples. The Pickard Venture commission was almost ready for processing, but it was trickier than she thought. Blend and extends could be extremely difficult to calculate. She rolled her shoulders and tried to clear her head. Maybe she should go to the ground floor café and order a pomegranate smoothie. The walk would do her good and the healthy beverage would give her a little pick me up.

As Lorelei pushed back from her desk a gentle knock sounded on her office door. "Come in!" she said, tucking the confidential papers on her desk away in a manila folder.

Tatum, a junior broker on the Sagura Team, poked her head in. "Do you have a minute?"

Lorelei smiled. "Absolutely."

Tentatively, Tatum came in and clicked the door shut behind her. Lorelei was immediately on alert. Most junior brokers didn't need to have private meetings; their commissions were already decided upon at set rates when they signed hiring contracts with their team.

Tatum sat on the edge of one of the two chairs across from Lorelei's desk. She was dressed impeccably in a cream suit with a lime green silk blouse underneath. Her dark hair was pulled back in a loose chignon and her light, pastel makeup was subtle. Tatum was being groomed for a promotion to senior broker by Heath Sagura himself, and she was a quick study. She was currently working on her confidence in front of the team's mostly male landlord clientele, but her sleek good-looks and unassuming manner kept her at the forefront of many a meeting. The landlords liked her fresh proposals and new ideas. Heath Sagura, Lorelei knew, occasionally rewarded Tatum out of his own pocket, padding her commissions under the table for a job well done. Lorelei would have preferred not to have been privy to this information as it was a clear violation of tax laws, but as far as she knew it didn't happen too often and reporting such behavior to HR was more hassle than it was worth. She knew Niles did the same thing with his junior brokers whenever they kicked in new business or negotiated a fat lease agreement, so it was one of those "don't ask, don't tell" situations that seemed to pop up in the commercial real estate world more often than not.

Tatum cleared her throat and clasped her hands together so tightly her knuckles turned white.

Lorelei's green eyes widened in concern. Clearly, whatever was about to be said needed to be handled delicately.

"Would you like some water?" Lorelei asked, turning to her credenza where she always kept a carafe of ice water and a few glasses.

"No, I'm... I don't need anything to drink. Thank you, though." Tatum gave a wobbly smile of appreciation and then looked down at her hands.

Lorelei sat back in her chair and crossed her legs. She tried to put the young girl at ease. "I heard you did a great job with the Bradshaw closing. Apparently the owner was a bit difficult? Sagura said he's never been so glad to see a sale agreement get signed. I heard he took the team to Mastro's for a very expensive celebration dinner."

Tatum nodded. "It was really great of him. And that evening was a lot of fun. And... yes, the owner was, um... temperamental."

Lorelei laughed. "Well, I'm glad that's all behind you. Now..." Lorelei leaned forward slightly, her voice low and calm, her expression concerned. "What can I help you with?"

"It's actually…" Tatum twisted her hands together. "It's actually not about commissions."

Lorelei's brow furrowed. "Is this personal?"

"No. I mean, yes. I mean…"

"It's okay, take your time. I'm just going to check my email while we're sitting here and you can start talking whenever you feel comfortable, all right? No rush."

Tatum looked at Lorelei gratefully and shifted in her seat nervously.

Simone rang through to Lorelei's phone. "Margaret's on the line, Lor."

"Please tell her I'll call her later."

"Will do. She sounds kind of weird."

"I don't know what that means. Please hold all my calls until further notice."

"It means she doesn't sound bossy and condescending like she normally does. Like it's weird because she sounds like a normal person."

If Tatum hadn't been in the room Lorelei would have chuckled, but instead she said, "I understand. No more interruptions though, okay?"

"Got it."

Lorelei saw the red DND button light up on her phone. Good. She went back to her email, mindlessly scrolling through it while she waited patiently for Tatum to start talking.

A full minute passed and then Lorelei heard a sniffle. Lorelei reached up and plucked a tissue box off a shelf to the side of her desk. She pushed it gently across to Tatum. "You know," she said, "I'm kind of thirsty. I know you said you didn't want one, but I'm just going to pour you a glass of water when I pour mine."

Tatum pulled a kleenex from the box and dabbed at her nose. "Okay."

When Lorelei sat back down, both of them with water glasses in hand, Tatum took a shaky breath and said, "I think I need to file a sexual harassment complaint with HR."

Lorelei's eyes narrowed. She knew the brokers were prone to flirting, especially with the younger girls in the office, but… harassment? Tatum had been with the company for almost a year now. Had Sagura crossed a line? Perhaps the night of the celebratory dinner when there was, assumedly, alcohol being consumed…?

"Tatum," Lorelei said kindly, "I want to help you with this, I really do. You know the company has zero tolerance for any kind of inappropriate behavior. But I am not your manager, I'm an accountant. I handle budgets and finance and payroll, not employee relations. You need to talk to Edmond; as our operations manager, he is the one to govern anything having to do with non-adherence to policy."

Tears ran down Tatum's cheeks. "But I can't talk to Mr. Davies," she wailed. "I can't! I came to you because I knew you would understand. I knew you would help me." Her voice rose higher and became more desperate with each word.

"Okay, Tatum. Take a deep breath, all right? Deep breath. Again. Good. Let's start from the beginning. Why don't you take a sip of water first?"

Tatum wiped at her eyes and took a big gulp from her glass. "I know you're not the one to handle these kinds of things. I know that. But everyone here looks up to you and I know they come to you with all kinds of stuff when Mr. Davies isn't here. You never betray confidences. Everyone respects and trusts you." Tatum let out a shuddering sigh. "I wish YOU were our manager and not-"

"Tatum, I cannot file a complaint with HR on your behalf because I do not have a supervisory title. I want to help, but aside from being a sounding board there is little I can do."

"He… he… groped me, Lor!" Tatum's voice cracked. "We were passing each other in the hall and I think he had been drinking at lunch or something and he was asking me about my weekend plans and then he said my boyfriend seemed like a real tool at the Christmas party last year. He said, 'That little twerp isn't good enough for you. Or should I say, not *man* enough.' Then he hugged me and when he pulled away he ran his hand down my back and squeezed my butt. I didn't know what to do!"

Lorelei could feel her blood begin to boil. She would have never guessed Heath Sagura could act in such a manner. He had always been completely professional and above board... and deeply in love with this wife of ten years. And drinking? Sagura had never even been tipsy at an event. Something wasn't adding up.

"Tatum, was this the first time? Has he touched you inappropriately before?"

A fresh wave of tears started. "Yes! I should have said something sooner but I kept thinking it would be the last time. And he was always so apologetic after it happened. Or the next day."

"How many times has this occurred?" Lorelei demanded. She was trying to keep her temper in check but she could feel the blush of anger creeping up her chest and neck. How DARE Sagura take advantage of this sweet and very hard-working junior broker? How DARE he?

"I think like... four or five maybe."

Lorelei mentally counted to ten. Being upset would not help the situation. She looked at Tatum earnestly. "We really need to involve Edmond in this. I will set up the meeting with him and I will sit by you the whole time. Sagura needs to be reported immediately."

Tatum looked bewildered, her tears ceasing for a moment. "Heath? No, not Heath. Heath is amazing. He would *never* do anything like that!"

Lorelei felt such relief that the air went out of her lungs. She'd known Sagura a long time and couldn't believe she had misread him so completely. But if it wasn't him...?

"It was Mr. Davies, Lor," Tatum said, answering her silent question. "It's Mr. Davies."

Lorelei felt the blood drain from her face.

"That's why I came to you," Tatum explained. "Help me, Lorelei. Please? I don't know who else to go to."

"Of course," Lorelei said reassuringly, thinking fast. "Let me make a phone call. I will not betray your confidence. This is your story to tell and yours alone. It took great courage for you to come to me. I'm advising you to work from home until this is resolved. HR will launch an investigation after the complaint is filed and you need to be safe from any kind of retaliation."

Tatum's eyes shone with gratitude. "Oh, thank you so much, Lorelei. Thank you! Thank you!" She blew her nose noisily and chugged the rest of her ice water. "I feel so much better. This has been weighing on me. I didn't want to complain… I don't want to lose my job…"

"You did the right thing by telling someone. Where is Edmond right now?"

"He went into his office after he…"

"Did he see you come in here?"

"No, Lor. No one saw me come in."

"Good. Go home right now. Everything's going to be fine. Pack up your things and I'll talk to Heath for you. I'll tell him you have a family emergency and you needed to leave right away. When you're feeling better give him a call tonight and let him know you'll be working from home for the next few days."

"Thank you. Thank you so much." Tatum stood and took a deep breath. She cleared her throat and said, "I'm sorry I was so unprofessional by crying."

"You are a human being, not a robot," Lorelei said, giving the girl an encouraging smile. "In fact, you should be proud of yourself for speaking up and not allowing Mr. Davies' abhorrent behavior to continue."

Tatum slipped out of Lorelei's office, and when the door clicked shut behind her, Lorelei slammed her fist on her desk. That bastard! Edmond Davies was, by far, the most incompetent person she'd ever worked with and now it seemed he was a handsy, predatory creeper as well. Lorelei's mind went into overdrive as she weighed her options.

How on earth was she going to maneuver this very sticky situation so that Tatum felt safe in sharing her story with HR without fearing backlash?

Moreover, how could she help her in a way that did not overstep? Lorelei was quite literally not in a position to assist an employee with such a delicate predicament and she had to be careful in order to protect herself. She also had another reason to make sure she herself kept behind the scenes: Edmond's comments forbidding her from taking over Margaret's job.

No. Best not to go there. Her New York aspirations would have to wait. Tatum was more important.

With a hardened glint in her beautiful green eyes, Lorelei picked up the phone. Edmond Davies was about to have his ass nailed to the wall.

CHAPTER 24

Katya stood poised on the edge of Thomas' diving board, her slender, perfectly toned body taut with concentration. She was completely nude, wearing only a severe expression on her beautiful face. She bounced once and leapt into the air, her lithe, six-foot frame arching, the crystal blue water barely splashing as she broke the surface and swam to the other side of the pool. Swimming laps was only part of the rigorous exercise routine which, coupled with an extremely strict diet, kept her body spare and angular, without an ounce of softness.

Katya was on her fifteenth lap when she heard barking in the distance. Damnit! It was that obnoxious dog Thomas had adopted several months back. Katya didn't understand why Thomas' family hadn't just dropped the annoying mongrel at the pound after... after... *someone* (who was it?) had died. Katya couldn't remember who had passed away. Thomas' aunt? Grandfather? Oh well, it didn't matter. All she knew was that it was irritating having Voltaire around. Once, Katya had left the front gate open hoping the dog would run off, but Voltaire had merely roamed Thomas' outlying courtyard area and pottied on all of Helga's tulips. A few hours later the flowers perished, having succumbed to a horrific acidic death. Helga had been beside herself, kneeling in the dirt and clutching the withered plants to her plump chest. "Lord Baby Jesus, why haf you curse me with dis Volpee who ruin Helga's pretty posies? Dat dog is the divil himself."

A loud splash brought Katya's head from the water and she glanced over to where the cascading rock waterfall gushed and burbled at the end of the pool. Sure enough, Voltaire had leapt off one of the boulders and his grey head bobbed on the surface as he eagerly doggie paddled toward her.

"Go away!" Katya yelled at him as she swam in the other direction.

Voltaire began barking excitedly, making a beeline toward her. They were going to play his favorite game, and there was nothing he enjoyed more than chasing someone- whether it was on land or in the water.

Helga came out from the side of the house, her thick soled rubber shoes squishing through the immaculate grass and onto the pool decking.

"Volpee, stygg pojke!!!" she said sternly to the swimming dog. "Get out of da vater!" She clapped her pudgy hands together loudly. "Now, Volpee! You come here to Helga!"

Katya reached the pool stairs and gracefully climbed out, squeezing water from her long, thick hair.

Helga averted her eyes from Katya's naked body, a slight blush on her round cheeks. Helga had known Katya for five years, ever since the Russian beauty had begun dating (if *that's* what the young people called it) Thomas, but even after all that time Helga could not get used to how free Katya was physically. The girl was brazen and confident. Helga wondered if Katya had ever experienced a moment of uncertainty or insecurity in her short, successful life. Probably not.

Voltaire made it to the pool stairs and launched himself out of the water. He barreled toward Katya, his thick body wriggling, his short hair sopping wet and shooting droplets into the air around him.

Katya took several steps sideways and then angled her body so that the shallow end of the pool was behind her. She held her hands out to Voltaire and cooed, "Good boy! Come here! Come on!"

Voltaire ramped up his oinking noises excitedly, his feet flying as fast as they could.

Helga looked on in confusion. Never had Katya EVER called Voltaire. As far as Helga knew, Katya hadn't even touched the dog or said anything nice about him- or to him. Perplexed, she watched as Voltaire rushed head-on toward Katya.

Thomas came out from the house and began walking toward them. Neither Voltaire nor Katya saw Thomas as the gap narrowed between girl and dog; they had eyes only on each other.

Just as Voltaire zeroed in on Katya, his tongue hanging out, a silly smile lacing his lips, Katya jumped out of the way, and Voltaire, confused and unable to stop, rocketed through the air, banged his head on the side of the pool and let out a painful yip before plunging into the blue water.

Katya laughed, a cruel smirk rippling her pretty mouth. "Stupid dog!" she said to the bubbling water where Voltaire had just sunk.

"Katya!" Thomas said, shocked.

Katya whipped around in surprise, but her expression didn't alter.

Helga soundlessly joined the couple on the edge of the decking and she peered into the pool. "Volpee?" she implored, her soft face concerned. "Volpee? You come out of da vater now to Helga. Volpee?"

The bubbles stopped breaking at the surface and, alarmed, Thomas jumped into the pool fully clothed. His head disappeared from view for a moment and he came back up with a sputtering Voltaire. Carefully, Thomas climbed from the water and laid Voltaire on a nearby lounge chair. The dog coughed a few times and then licked Thomas' cheek as though to say, *Right, thanks for rescuing me, mate, but I had it all under control. Really.*

Helga came bustling over, picking up Voltaire and squashing him to her chest in a giant, loving hug. "I light fire fer you now and den I cook. Would you like some pork chop, my alskling?" She walked quickly toward the house, holding Voltaire like a newborn baby.

Thomas turned on Katya. "That was horrible. He could have been seriously injured."

Katya shrugged one shoulder. "Whatever. He's fine."

"I didn't even know you were here."

"Your office door was shut so I didn't want to interrupt in case you were writing. I don't know why you won't let me read your work. Are you still only two chapters in?"

Thomas clenched his jaw. He should have never told Katya how *not* far along he was with the novel. As he looked at her his agitation grew – he felt intruded upon. He'd given Katya a key to the house and the gate code long ago, but it had been more of a courtesy gesture rather than an open invitation. The access had come in handy on more than one occasion when she'd flown back into town on the redeye and she came to him directly from the airport. On those nights, Thomas slept peacefully, knowing the sexy supermodel would crawl into bed with him when she arrived- there was no need for him to get up and release the locked gate or open the door. But today was different- Katya hadn't ever just shown up uninvited. It was the first time she'd broken Thomas' unspoken rule.

Katya smiled at Thomas, tilting her head to one side. "I have exciting news. Don't you want to know why I'm here?"

Thomas sighed. Not really.

He said, "I need to go inside and change out of these wet clothes."

Katya reached out and began unbuttoning Thomas' shirt. "Why don't you take them off here?"

Thomas grabbed her hands and stilled them on his chest. "Stop it. You know we are not alone. And you need to stop being naked in front of Helga- it makes her uncomfortable."

Katya rolled her eyes. "So what? She's only the help."

Thomas shook his head. The girl was impossible sometimes. He picked up a jade green beach towel from one of the deck chairs and wrapped it around Katya so that she was covered. When he was done, she pressed her slender body up against his and he could feel the hardness of her physique through the towel and his clothes. Just like her personality, he thought - hard.

"I want you," Katya purred in his ear. "We can do it in your bedroom with the door shut since you're such a prude."

Thomas felt his temper begin to flare. Katya had shown up unannounced, used his pool, embarrassed his housekeeper, attempted... well, to *murder* his dog and now she wanted him to perform on command? He pushed her away and turned to walk back into the house.

"Not now, Kat. I'm not in the mood."

"The hell you're not!" she said, dropping the towel and sidestepping around him. She took his hands and put them on her body. "I know you, Thomas McQuillan. I know what you like, and I know how you like it." She kissed him deeply, seductively, her mouth expertly caressing and biting Thomas' lips until his body began to respond against hers. "Take me upstairs," she demanded, pulling back to look into his hazel eyes. When she saw desire reflected back at her she felt sleek and satisfied.

The couple made their way through the huge house and up toward Thomas' bedroom. He paused in the hallway and then pushed Katya toward the game room. After they entered, he shut the big wooden door and switched on the radio. AC/DC's "Highway to Hell" blared out from the speakers. *Perfect*, Thomas thought caustically, as he turned to Katya, who stood aloof and imperious, waiting for him to come to her and please her.

Katya smiled at him wantonly, her slender body beginning to move rhythmically with the harsh beats of the song. She ran her graceful hands through her long hair, closed her eyes and let her lips part alluringly.

Thomas watched her, knowing he would never turn her away. They were too good together. He wanted her just as much now as he had five years ago when he'd first laid eyes on her. No, maybe he wanted her *more* now... they knew each other's bodies so well that he could bring her pleasure over and over, every time, in every way. He loved the fact that she was willing to try anything. She'd never told him no and she'd never failed to send him over the edge into oblivion.

The memories of their past trysts made Thomas' whole body go rigid with lust. He stripped off his wet clothes and strode over to where she stood, still swaying to the pounding music. He grabbed her roughly and pulled her across the room to the pool table. "Get up," he said gruffly.

Katya slowly, sexily climbed onto the expensively carved cherry wood billiards table. She lay back on the green wool of the playing surface, her luxurious hair spilling all around.

"No," Thomas said, swiftly joining her on top of the table. "On all fours." He flipped Katya over in one quick motion so that she was on her stomach. He pulled at her hips until she was on her knees and he groaned when she sensuously backed up into him and they became one.

Katya allowed Thomas to have his way with her, enjoying the deep sensations he expertly sent quivering through her body. She could never get enough of this man. He knew exactly how to catapult a woman straight to the heavens with his mouth, his hands, his...

Katya's eyelashes fluttered and she gasped as a thousand electrical currents shot through her. She screamed Thomas' name, her body convulsing in spasms of pleasure. Unable to hold her weight any longer, her arms gave out and her face hit the green wool of the pool table. She lay, limp and breathless, for only a moment before Thomas harshly pulled away, turned her over to face him and took her again, his hands forceful and unrelenting in their pursuit and... oh, so very, very capable. Her back arched and she clawed at him, the pressure somewhere deep inside building so fast she couldn't control it.

Thomas watched her, his face set, his eyes indifferent, as Katya fought and lost the battle to keep her climax at bay. Lightning and thunder crossed her beautiful face as she succumbed to the storm of ecstasy, and when she had stopped crying out, the clouds of passion peacefully floating past, she whimpered senseless words, incoherent with euphoria. Thomas, ragged and shaking, his restraint stretched to the breaking point, gave Katya no rest. He aggressively pulled her arms up over her head and pinned them there so that she was unable to move. He had done his part and pleased his lover; now it was his turn. Without regard or thought to the girl trapped underneath him, he savagely took his pleasure from her body.

When Thomas collapsed on top of her, finally spent, it occurred to him that the pool table beneath them was much like Katya- hard and unforgiving and rough. Their relationship was raw sexual attraction - two skilled lovers who found release and solace in one another – nothing more. Even now, locked in the most intimate of embraces, their hearts weren't involved at all. This private arrangement, such as it was, was perfect for both of them because neither wanted more.

"Now," Thomas said curtly, as he pulled himself up on his elbows, "just so we're straight, don't ever come over here unannounced again. Tell me your news, Kat, and then go. I need to write."

Katya smiled demurely, her shrewd eyes taunting him. "Ah, yes, you must return to your tormented author existence." She ran her hands down his muscled back, feeling the fresh scratch marks she'd left only moments before. Purring with contentment and satisfaction, she said, "I auditioned for a small role in *Syndicate Protocol* and I got the part."

"Congratulations," Thomas said, and he meant it, for he knew how much Katya longed to break into Hollywood's film industry. "Who's the director?"

Katya averted her eyes. "John Bhear."

"Bhear? Don't know him. And the producer?"

"I'm not sure."

Thomas' sharp hazel eyes swept her face. She was hiding something. "Tell me the rest, Kat."

"That's all I came to say. I knew you'd be happy for me."

He rolled off of her and she grabbed his hand before he could leave the pool table.

"I'm not done with you, Thomas McQuillan."

"Oh, but I am done with you."

"For now."

He nodded. "For now."

CHAPTER 25

Thunder boomed loudly overhead and the lights in Mitch's house flickered several times. Dust and dirt pounded the outside walls and pelted the windows. Summer cicadas ramped up their buzzing, vibrating their tymbals in maddening cacophony as sand and silt billowed across the desert floor. It was growing darker; the sky a bizarre, brownish color as the wall of dust, known as a haboob, began to block the sun.

As Mitch and Bertie turned to look out of the dining room windows, lightning flashed brilliantly and a huge crack of thunder shook the house. Harsh winds battered the large mesquite trees out back and tumbleweeds bounded across the desert floor like unraveling yarn balls.

"I think we're going to lose power soon," Mitch said as they finished dinner and started on dessert. "Hopefully it won't stay off too long or it's going to get very hot and unpleasant in here."

"You really should get a generator," Bertie said absently as she dipped a finger into her chocolate mousse. She licked it off and her brown eyes went wide. "This is delicious!" She picked up her spoon for another taste, but Mitch grabbed it out of her hand.

"Don't, Collins." His eyes didn't leave her lips. "Use your finger again."

She did. But this time she was slow about it, purposeful, seductive... titillating.

Mitch groaned in despair. "I wanted to have a serious conversation tonight. I want to get to know you better… to learn about your past, your… your… hopes and dreams… your…" He was rapidly losing any train of thought.

The tip of Bertie's pink tongue swirled around the top of her finger as she lapped up the remaining chocolate from it. She gave Mitch a cheeky smile. "So let's talk. What would you like to know?"

"Um…"

"My life is pretty uncomplicated and fairly boring, Morrison. Let's talk about you instead." She took her spoon back from him. "Have you talked to Mary lately?"

Mitch, disappointed about Bertie using a utensil, shook his head to clear it and focused on thoughts of his daughter instead. "Not since I called her after I got off the phone with Owen."

"Have you heard from Owen again?"

Mitch's eyes took on a ferocious glow. "No."

"Maybe you should call Mary tomorrow. Just to make sure she's okay."

"It's more than that Collins. I don't want to just know she is all right. I want to *make* everything all right. But Mary is an adult. Her life is her life and there is a fine line between being there for her and being intrusive." He sighed. "It seems so long since Mary and I *really* talked. I knew something was wrong- but I had no idea the issues ran as deep as they did until I spoke to Owen. I know he loves Mary, and I know he's under a lot of pressure from his parents. I…I used to trust him." Mitch rubbed his thumb across his chin. "He's changed a lot. Or maybe he hasn't. Maybe I've misread him all along and it's always been about him, his family and his career."

"Do you think their marriage will be okay?"

Mitch looked out the window. Large raindrops were starting to splatter on the desert floor and on his wrap-around porch. The wall of dust was moving on and a microburst was about to follow. "I don't know. Mary was upset Owen called me, but not entirely surprised.

She said he's been obsessed the past few weeks about her not being pregnant. I think she was more hurt by it than anything. Seems it was just one more thing he's done lately that's made her feel... well, unloved. He's going to need to lay off this baby idea if he wants things to work out with Mary."

The rain outside began to patter insistently on the roof and a streak of nearby lightning lit the dining room with a flash of white radiance. Mitch gazed out at the storm, a sad expression on his face.

"You're a good father, Morrison," Bertie said quietly.

Mitch turned to her, his amber eyes conflicted. "I hope I've been. Maybe I've protected her too much. She's so innocent, so untouched by the difficulties of life. She went straight from under my protection to being under Owen's. She's never stood on her own two feet, never felt the taste of independence. I guess I was glad for that in a lot of ways- I never wanted her heart to know pain or suffering or betrayal."

"That's not realistic…" Bertie said lightly.

Mitch's landline rang and they both jumped at the intrusion into their thoughtful conversation.

"Don't you need to answer that?" Bertie asked when Mitch made no move toward the phone.

"Nah. Let the machine get it."

Bertie laughed. "The *machine*? You have an answering machine?"

"I'm old school, Collins."

After four rings, they heard Mitch's pre-recorded deep voice: "You have reached Morrison Home Builders. Leave a message and we'll call you back."

The machine beeped, followed by a pause and a crackling on the line. "Allô?" a female voice with a heavy French accent said. "Allô? Iz Mary Morrison there, pleaze? Allô?"

Mitch bounded to his feet and crossed the room, snatching up the phone. "Hello? This is Mitchell Morrison. No, Mary is not here." A pause. "How did you get this number?" A long silence followed and then Mitch sat down heavily on a chair, listening intently to whatever was being relayed on the other end of the line. He uttered an, "Uh-huh," a couple of times and once asked for clarification. The caller spoke broken English. Mitch knew no French.

"I understand," said Mitch after a few minutes. "Yes. Yes, I have the same address." He was quiet for moment. "I will make sure she gets it. Okay. Thank you." He hung up the phone.

Bertie stood and went to him. She placed a small hand on his shoulder. "Is everything okay?"

"That was Helene's sister." Mitch turned somber eyes to Bertie's lovely face. "Helene passed away yesterday."

CHAPTER 26

*L*orelei was curled up on her soft red couch, her feet tucked up underneath her. She'd had a long day at the office and was more than ready for a lovely dinner with Niles at Barclay Prime and whatever came after. But first, business.

"I wanted to talk to you about a possible move to Hillard," Lorelei said to Niles.

He cocked his eyebrow curiously. "Really?"

Niles Donovan stood at Lorelei's immense metal and wood bar pouring two glasses of chardonnay into sparkling opaque goblets. His suit coat was draped over one of Lorelei's three wooden bar stools and he had rolled up his dress sleeves and unknotted his tie leaving it hanging around his neck in casual refinement. Niles was devastatingly handsome, the quintessential rich businessman, intelligent, sophisticated and charming. He was a confident man, yet he allowed himself to show slight vulnerability whenever it worked to his advantage. He was top broker at The Hillard Company, where he consistently grossed over ten million in sales each year. He loved his work, the thrill and excitement of negotiations. He also loved his freedom and independence which was why, outside of property tours and boardrooms, his only interest in women revolved solely around Lorelei Harper. She was smart, breathtakingly beautiful and she had no desire whatsoever to rope him into a commitment.

Niles and Lorelei were extremely compatible, great friends and superb lovers. Niles had no intention of letting Lorelei move to Manhattan for he wanted her no further than San Diego. He was thrilled when she had called to say she wanted to discuss possible opportunities at Hillard. She didn't confide particulars in him, but he sensed there was an unethical management issue at Empire & Malkin and Lorelei was somehow embroiled in it. Good. It saved him time trying to figure out how to keep her from moving away whenever the opportunity presented itself, which given Lorelei's business acumen, would probably be sooner than later.

Niles re-corked the chardonnay and made his way to where Lorelei sat on the couch looking enticingly provocative even in her conservative business suit. He set the glasses of wine on the stylishly modern coffee table and held out a hand to help her up.

"Why don't you go change into something more comfortable?" he suggested as she stood.

Lorelei looked up at Niles for he was several inches taller than her. He was trim and fit, his shoulders broad, his face completely clean shaven. His dark, wavy hair was perfectly coiffed and his solid jawline signaled the auspicious combination of masculinity and stubbornness. He bent his head to kiss her full lips and she leaned into him. Her heart fluttered but it was a calming feeling, a sense of comfort and companionship. Niles was a proficiently savvy lover and he had a temptingly virile body, but Lorelei felt no passion, only the restful trust she'd placed in him long ago.

As Niles parted Lorelei's lips with his own she responded as naturally as if they'd been together all their lives. Yet she couldn't help but recall Detective Frank Williams' delectable kisses and how they'd sent little shocks of electricity all through her being. She remembered the way his hands had felt buried in her hair and how seductive the warmth of his breath was on her neck. Disturbed, she hastily pulled away from Niles and picked up her wine glass.

"What time are our reservations?" she asked, taking a sip of chardonnay.

"Seven."

Lorelei moved toward the small circular staircase leading up to her huge loft bedroom. "I won't be long."

"No rush," Niles said, sinking down onto the couch and opening *The New York Times*.

Lorelei was halfway up the stairs when she turned to look back at Niles. He was the picture of relaxation with his arm along the back of the sofa and his right ankle crossed over his left leg. He held *The Times* at eye level while he scanned content for news worthy of his attention. He was completely at home in Lorelei's condo since he'd spent many evenings and weekends there. He knew where everything was kept from the silverware in the kitchen to the clean fluffy towels in the linen closet upstairs.

Niles was emotionally safe. He wasn't going to hurt Lorelei. And he fit perfectly into her well-ordered life.

Lorelei continued up the stairs as she thought about these things.

Safe.

Unable to cause harm or heartbreak.

So unlike Connor.

Lorelei reached her elegant bedroom and set the glass of chardonnay on the dresser before slowly removing her business suit and silk blouse. Standing alone in the middle of her room, against her better judgement, she grudgingly allowed herself to think about Connor. He had been so full of life, so full of love, so full of intensity. Everything about him had drawn her in, consumed every part of her being. She'd lost herself in Connor O'Cassidy, the irresistible musician she'd given her heart and soul to over ten years ago. They'd been so happy, so in love, so very young.

After three years of blissful coupledom, Connor's small-town band, Crash Corpse, hit it big. It all started with a song they had written called "Nice Deadly Lady," a morbidly romantic tune that began to receive playtime on local radio stations. A short few months later, Joey Gerson of Greenlight Records signed Crash Corpse after watching them perform at a cramped venue in Oceanside. Gerson was impressed with how every single person in the overflowing audience sang along to the band's songs word for word.

Greenlight opened significant doors, creating mass marketing opportunities, and within the year Crash Corpse had risen from local talent to national fame. Connor O'Cassidy was on top of the world recording, touring and writing fresh, cutting edge music. And the more time and energy he put into the band, the less he put into his relationship with Lorelei Harper. Connor's phone calls became more infrequent, his visits increasingly sporadic, and Lorelei knew that what they had once shared would never revive. With steel resolve and a shattered heart, she told him it was over and he had cried and held her close, murmuring that he was sorry, so very sorry. But the next day she saw his picture in the paper, his arm around a curvy brunette as they smiled at one another and walked into a bistro in LA.

Lorelei had spent more than a few nights crying herself to sleep. She'd really thought Connor was her soulmate and she'd loved him with everything in her, given him the best of who she was. And it hadn't been enough. What she offered him couldn't compare to the temptation of fame, and the perks that came along with it. Lorelei wasn't the type to wallow, and she certainly didn't let her self-esteem take a hit, but if there's one thing she prided herself on, it was making sure any weak spots didn't get a second chance at revealing themselves. After six days of grieving, she locked her heart up tight and vowed never to let a man inside again. And she hadn't. Work came first and it always would, unless her family or friends needed her. Men were allowed into her circle if they were intelligent, kind and independent… but most importantly, if they did not appear to pose any sort of threat to her carefully guarded heart.

Men had come and men had gone, but she'd never let any of them emotionally close enough to hurt her. The ones who had stimulated her mind, made her laugh and offered intimacy without passion were worthy of a few dates, perhaps even several. But there was always a cutoff point. Except with Niles. He was different. Perhaps because their relationship was so incredibly symbiotic, in that neither felt the pressure of commitment. But for Lorelei it was more than that- she also needn't fear the vulnerability of falling for him. His touches brought pleasure, but they never made her shiver, never gave her goosebumps, never caused her to lose control.

And then... Detective Frank Williams had come along the other night, slipping in under her highly attuned radar and making her feel things she hadn't felt since Connor. And, if she were being honest with herself, Frank elicited sensations that she'd never actually experienced with Connor. There was something about the steadfast, considerate detective that knocked on Lorelei's soul and asked to be let in. And it terrified her.

That fear was why she had not returned any of his calls or texts. Yes, she had had a wonderful evening with him but now was the time to draw the line. She knew whatever chemistry was between them would end up burning her in the end. Connor had taught her that.

Niles was safe.

Frank was not.

Lorelei moved into her walk-in closet and chose a flowy, violet dress with cream-colored ribbon trimmings. It gracefully swirled around her voluptuous figure, the material soft as gossamer, the ribbons winding their way around her small waist and cascading over the back of her skirt. She looked like a sexy garden nymph, full of magic and sunlight and softness.

As Lorelei checked her reflection in the mirror, she pushed all thoughts of Connor and Detective Frank Williams from her mind. Better to focus on the life she could control, not the feelings she couldn't. She'd have a lovely dinner with Niles tonight and there would be amusing, intelligent conversation because he was charming and exceedingly bright and well-rounded. Afterward they would probably have a nightcap back at his place and they would make love, a warm, affectionate, satisfying endeavor that would leave both of them satiated. But Lorelei knew, in the locked-up recesses of her heart, that the pain of desire still lurked, hungrily crying out for more.

She floated down the stairs carrying a pair of dainty strappy heels the same color as the ribbon on her dress. She'd left her dress open in the back since Niles was there to help her with the long, difficult zipper that ran the length of the bodice.

As she reached the bottom step she noticed that he wasn't on the couch. "Niles, where are you? Can you please zip me up?"

There was a long pause and then Niles called back, "I don't think we're going out tonight, Lor."

Frank stopped on the sidewalk for a moment and looked up at the beautifully elegant thirty-story high rise before him. It seemed fitting that Lorelei would reside there. The modern architecture and swanky building design made the sky scraper both inviting and desirably recherché. It occurred to Frank, once again, that Lorelei Harper was totally out of his league.

He quickly shook off this depressing thought and made his way up to the blue entrance carpet. A uniformed bellman guarded a prodigious glass front door and eyed Frank's approach somewhat suspiciously.

"Hello, sir," said the doorman. "Beautiful day out."

Frank nodded and smiled. "That's why we live here, right?"

"Indeed, sir." He waited.

Frank scratched his head and put a hand on his hip. When Faith had called him she made him promise he would go to Lorelei's condo and try to talk to her. Tearfully, Faith had given Frank her best friends address and begged him to make Lorelei understand she hadn't meant to hurt her.

"I'm so dumb," Faith had cried, her voice rising in agitation. "So stupid! I should *not* have told you about Connor."

Frank tried to calm her down. "But you didn't. You didn't tell me who he is or anything about him. It's okay, Faith. It's okay. You didn't do anything wrong. We'll fix this, all right? From what I know of Lorelei, she's a very fair person. And what I do know, without a doubt, is that she loves you."

Faith sniffed. "I love her too. I love her so much..." her voice trailed off in a wail that launched a fresh round of tears. "You don't understand, Frank! She's the only family I've got. I knew her before Jesse and before Mary and before I had my babies..."

"Listen, if it makes you feel any better, she's not returning my calls or texts either. I'm sure she's just overloaded with work. Accountants have lots of deadlines, right?"

"I guess so." Faith let out a long, wobbly sigh and then took a deep breath. "Can you go to her condo? Check on her? Make sure she's okay?" A sob escaped. "Make sure she doesn't hate me and she knows I'm so, so sorry? Please? Oh, please, Frank! I can't get in her building unless they call up to her first and what if she said no and then I would be standing outside on the sidewalk just... just... *rejected*... and I can't even throw rocks at her window to get her attention because she's on the twenty-eighth floor and *I can't throw that high*. But you're... you could get in because you're a detective, right? Right? Oh, please..."

At the end of their call, Frank hadn't been able to refuse kindhearted Faith. He also didn't *want* to refuse her because it gave him a reason to see Lorelei again. He hadn't been able to stop thinking about her, his mind recalling every moment of their evening together- the tilt of her head when she listened to him, her witty, perceptive conversation, the way she embodied strength of character with compassionate sentiment. Even if Lorelei didn't care to pursue any kind of romantic relationship with him, Frank hoped she would at least let him take her out for an occasional dinner, or even just drinks. Brief snapshots of time with Lorelei would be better than no time at all.

The bellman watched Frank warily and then his gaze fell on Frank's waistband. There, nestled next to Frank's holstered gun, was his shiny badge.

"Oh," said the bellman nervously, "I didn't realize... I apologize, officer. Please," he swung the door wide, "come in. Welcome to Park Place. You'll find Gretchen at the desk to your right. She's our concierge and she'll be able to help you with whatever you need."

Frank gave a friendly nod and offered his hand. "Appreciate that. Thank you."

The bellman shook hands. "Name's Mikey. You need anything at all, just let me know." His voice lowered in concern. "Is everything okay, officer? My residents are safe? There's not... there wasn't a crime reported?"

Frank clapped Mikey on the back. "Nothing to worry about. I'm just here to... interview someone."

"Oh!" Mikey was eager to help. "Do you know which unit to go to?"

"2819-A"

Mikey whistled. "Lorelei Harper." He smiled, his eyes twinkling with affectionate warmth. "She's a real lady, Miss Harper. Very kind to all the staff. Everyone here loves her." He winked conspiratorially. "Not too hard on the eyes either."

Frank laughed. "No, she's not."

Mikey ushered Frank inside and closed the door behind him. The lobby was beautifully decorated, the ceilings high and lofty, the flooring an opulent limestone. There was a wide, graceful staircase to the left and a baby grand piano against the floor to ceiling windows overlooking Harbor Drive.

Frank knew Lorelei would be home; Faith had said her best friend always relaxed for an hour after work to let herself unwind before any evening activities. The thought made Frank's heart race because he knew he'd be standing in front of her in just a few minutes. He crossed the lobby and stopped in front of a humongous ornate mirror. He ran his hands over his cropped sandy hair. He was wearing jeans, a casual button down shirt and a sport coat and, as he stared at his reflection, he had a sudden pang of insecurity. Lorelei hadn't reached out to him, meaning she wasn't interested. So what the hell was he doing here? If she wanted to see him again she would have returned his calls. But, the thing was, Frank just couldn't let go of the chemistry he'd felt with Lorelei. He couldn't believe it hadn't meant anything. Certainly Lorelei experienced the same magnetism because he'd seen it in her expressive green eyes, felt it in her luscious kisses.

Okay, so he wasn't sleek and sophisticated like the guys she was probably used to dating. He didn't look successful or wealthy. His speech wasn't cultured. His bank account was hardly overflowing. Frank was rough and tumble. He was a cop, he was muscular, he was a protector, a fighter and a blue collar worker. Shaking his head, Frank turned from the mirror and headed toward the front entrance. It had been a mistake to come here.

But then he remembered Faith's tearful pleas and he stopped. He'd made a promise.

Purposefully, before he could turn around again, he strode toward the elevator bank. Silencing the self-doubt coursing through his veins and pounding in his mind, he stepped out onto floor twenty-eight and wound his way down the hallways until he stood in front of unit 2819-A. Before he could talk himself out of it, he knocked on the door.

Footsteps sounded, the door swung wide and Frank came face to face with what appeared to be a Giorgio Armani model. "Can I help you?" the man asked politely.

Disconcerted, Frank was about to say, "I'm sorry, I have the wrong place," but Lorelei's voice drifted out to them from within the condo, "Niles, where are you? Can you please zip me up?"

Frank felt his heart plummet and he looked accusingly at the handsomest man on the planet. This guy was exactly who Lorelei should be dating, but somehow the reality of that galled him. It wasn't fair. Frank wanted to be the guy who seemed perfectly at home in her condo, confidently opening the door to strangers. But most of all, Frank just wanted to be the guy who got to talk to her, listen to her laughter and feel her arms around him. As these thoughts churned through his mind, he felt his defenses go up and he resorted to the safest, most secure place he knew where to speak from.

Pulling his badge from his waistband, Frank said commandingly, "Detective Williams. I'm here to see Miss. Lorelei Harper. *Now.*"

The Armani guy's jaw dropped, then he turned and called behind him, "I don't think we're going out tonight, Lor."

CHAPTER 27

⌒

Bonjour Mama,

I wonder what you are doing right now. Are you in France with your family? Or did you stay in America? Or maybe you moved on to another country? Did you ever marry? Have other children? Grandchildren? Do I have half-brothers and sisters somewhere? Nieces and nephews? I'm curious to know if I look like them, but then I think probably not because I'm a carbon copy of my dad. Well, the feminine version, anyway. He and I have the exact same amber eyes and super long eyelashes, same complexion, same facial features and same cheekbones. Whenever we're in public together people always know we're father and daughter. But according to him, my height and petite frame come from you.

He also says I also inherited your artistic nature, although mine lies in the written word rather than the paintbrush. How I wish I could see one of your paintings! Dad said you were very talented with oils and that your charcoal sketches were amazing. It bothers me that you left nothing of yourself behind for me. It's almost as if you never existed.

As you can see, I've been thinking a lot about family lately, probably because it's become such an issue between me and Owen. To be honest with you, I don't even want to try to get pregnant anymore. Sometimes I feel angry with him for the way he's pressuring me, but mostly it's just sadness. I don't want to be a bad person, Mama. I don't want to fight with Owen and I don't want to tell him no, especially about this. But it is especially about this that I HAVE to say no- at least for now. Bringing a baby into the world is a huge responsibility. I don't know if I'm ready for that. Owen says it doesn't matter- that when the baby comes then all the maternal feelings will come too. He said the baby and I will instantly bond and I will forget all about my doubts. He talks with such confidence that I really want to believe him. But what I honestly want is for all of these problems to go away. It's not so much that I don't want to deal with them, I just don't know how.

I didn't even tell Owen that Daddy called me the other night, for surely he would take whatever I said as accusatory. Daddy was furious, and he has every right to be, so I had to play down my own emotions in order to coax him out of his anger. I even told him I wasn't surprised that Owen called him, but truthfully, I was shocked. Then again, it seems everything about Owen's behavior shocks me these days. He's even been curt with Roger- yelling at him for something silly one moment and then playing ball with him the next. I've wondered if he's maybe nervous about the training mission, but that doesn't even make sense since its perfectly safe. It's not like he's going into combat.

I hate to say Owen forced me to go to a fertility specialist because that's not true- I went because he didn't seem to give me much of a choice. If I didn't go, it would be yet another fight, and I definitely didn't want that. Besides, maybe the doctor would say I'm unable to have children; then Owen would drop the whole idea and we could go back to being the loving couple we used to be. Or would we? I wonder if Owen will be upset with me if I can't physically have children. What if the option were taken away from him entirely- and not by my choice? Would he blame me?

The appointment lasted about an hour. Dr. Rygert was polite and no-nonsense; definitely not the warm and fuzzy type. She was in her thirties, very fashionable and attractive, and she had long, pretty hair and big round glasses that made her look immensely intellectual. There were framed photographs of babies on her office walls and huge leather-bound books perfectly arranged on a massive bookcase. After *the formality of introductions, she began asking me a lot of questions-some of them things I've only ever discussed with Owen or Lorelei in private. But most of the inquiries weren't so personal, thankfully. She asked how long Owen and I have been trying for a baby, if he or I smoke or drink, if we're tracking my ovulation, if any members of our families suffer from infertility and what each of us do for a living.*

When I said I was a dog-walker Dr. Rygert looked over her glasses at me and said, "Oh. How... interesting."

My cheeks felt hot and I picked at my running shorts in embarrassment (I hadn't had time to change since I came directly from Willow's house after walking Patchouli). Dr. Rygert probably only deals with women like herself – highly educated and highly successful. I certainly felt like an out of place anomaly in her very high-end, richly decorated medical building.

After answering all of Dr. Rygert's questions, a nurse drew my blood and gave me a urine test and then she put me in a small dark room and made me completely undress with only a small hospital gown to cover myself. A few minutes later Dr. Rygert gave me an uncomfortable pelvic exam and then she explained I would need to have an internal ultrasound. When I saw the wand which was meant to go inside of me I was a little afraid, which I know is silly, but even so, I asked if Owen could come in and hold my hand. She said no, that it would only take a few minutes and I should just relax. She was not very gentle about whatever it was she was looking for (she said something about inspecting my ovaries and uterus for irregularities). I bit my lip and stayed as still as I could the whole time. When she was finished she handed me a washcloth to clean with, then left without saying anything further.

I cried in that dark room. I felt very alone, and rather violated; not so much physically, but mentally. I was so confused about everything (my emotions, Owen, a possible pregnancy, becoming a mother...) and I just really didn't want to be there. It dawned on me that these are the types of moments most women must long for their mother; to have a mother's arms to run into for comfort and sympathy. I did sort of wish for you, even though I have Aunt Georgette and Aunt Francesca back home, and then I felt guilty for even wanting you when I have them and that made me cry even more. Eventually, I took a deep breath, got dressed and went to join Owen in a small private waiting room. I curled into a chair next to him, tears still drying on my cheeks, and didn't say anything. He patted my knee and nervously joked that at least I didn't have to do what he was about to do. I wasn't sure what he meant until Dr. Rygert came in with a plastic jar marked "Crossfield, Owen -Semen Analysis." Wide-eyed, I brushed the tears off my face and grabbed his hand as he got up.

"Do you want me to come with you?" I asked him.

"No," he said, suddenly cold, as if I were doubting his masculinity, then he walked down an adjoining hallway with Dr. Rygert right behind him. I craned my neck to see where they were going. She opened a door and ushered him inside. They both disappeared for a moment and I assumed Dr. Rygert was giving Owen instructions (how awful it was to have a beautiful woman telling my husband what to do regarding something so intimate!). I felt sick to my stomach when she came out of the room, shutting the door gently behind her. She called to a nurse and though she lowered her voice I heard her say, "Give him twenty minutes. His wife is in the waiting room; can you please check on her? She's a bit emotional."

The nurse, different from the one who had drawn my blood, was a plump, kindly woman named June and she did come in to see me about five minutes later while I was thumbing through a magazine. She sat down next to me, a box of tissues in one hand and a mug of hot tea in the other. The mug had little pink and blue pacifiers painted on it with the words "Already in my heart, someday in my arms" written across the middle.

Nurse June handed me the tea and said, "It's chamomile. Good for the uterus." She then patted my stomach encouragingly, and though it was more a maternal gesture than an intrusive one, I started crying all over again.

I waited for what seemed like forever and finally Owen came back into the waiting room. He seemed tense and stressed and he barely looked at me when he said, "I spoke with Dr. Rygert and she's going to make an exception for us and rush all of our test results since I'm shipping out soon."

At the front desk area Nurse June smiled at us. "Can you both come in for the follow-up Wednesday at ten?"

"Yes," Owen said right away.

"Is that okay with you, Mrs. Crossfield?" Nurse June asked me pointedly after shooting Owen a quick, annoyed look.

"Yes," I said, "I think so." I felt Owen's eyes boring into me and added, "I'll make sure to rearrange my client schedule."

"We'll be here," Owen assured Nurse June. "And the payment for today has been taken care of, correct?"

"Yes. Ellen Crossfield called in earlier with her credit card number. She instructed us to keep it on file for all future appointments and testing."

I couldn't believe my ears. My in-laws KNEW about this? And they were footing the bill for... I suddenly felt a wave of nausea so strong that I reached out for the desk and steadied myself. Of course Charles and Ellen were involved in this. Of course my extremely private moments were their business because, above all else, they wanted a grandchild to carry on the Crossfield name. Why, oh why, had this never occurred to me when Owen and I got married? I thought back... because we were young and Owen wasn't the same controlling person he is now. Because we never really discussed having children- it had always just been assumed we would one day. When did the stakes suddenly get so high? When Charles and Ellen realized I might not be able to have a baby? Or did Owen tell them I'm having second thoughts?

Once we were outside in the parking lot standing by the Jeep, Owen said, "Look, Mare, I'm sorry. I'm sorry about all of this I..." he ran his hands through his dark hair and he looked so sad, and so tortured, that I reached for him in a rush of compassion. He pulled me against his chest and whispered in my ear, "I'm sorry... I'm so, so sorry."

I clung to him because I didn't know what else to do. We stood like that for a long time and I made an effort to push aside my doubts and fears. After a bit I felt Owen shudder and his breath catch, and I realized he was trying not to cry. I wanted to pull back, to look into his face, but he kept me pinned against him.

"Owen, are you okay?"

"I love you, Mary. I love you so much."

"I know you do. I know."

"No matter what happens, you know I love you, right?"

"Yes, of course..." I was becoming alarmed.

But then his spine stiffened under my hands and I knew he was switching gears. Owen was back in command.

"I'll see you at home in a couple of hours?" he asked, and we stepped apart. I searched his eyes for traces of tears or vulnerability. There was none.

I lied. I told him I had two dogs to walk, that I would see him at home later. I wanted time to think and I couldn't do that with him around. I don't ever remember feeling that way before. Given the choice, I have always preferred Owen's company over my own. But standing in that parking lot, I knew I longed to be anywhere else- anywhere at all, as long as it was away from Owen. So much so that I lied.

I never lie.

Flashbacks of the past couple of months washed over me... Owen telling me how to dress, what to eat and what not to eat, demanding the times and days of my cycle, making love to me and then talking about the baby during or right afterward. I wanted to scream. I wanted to run and be free and... then what? What did I really want? What was happening to my marriage? Our marriage? What had happened to us?

Owen kissed me gently on the lips and instead of my heart picking up speed it just thumped with a dull dread. I knew what was on his mind.

"I'll make dinner so we can eat as soon as you get home," he said, moving his hand up my thigh slightly.

"Okay."

"And afterward," his hand went a little higher, "we can go to bed early..." The tips of his fingers suggestively pulled at the hem of my shorts. His lips were on mine again and he kissed me hungrily, not with desire, but as though this was what was required to bring me to a place of passion. I kissed him back, waiting for the love I knew I felt for him to catch fire and burn my body as it normally does, but my emotions froze cold and nothing was igniting.

"I should go," I said, breaking away and swinging into the Jeep, gripping the steering wheel so hard my knuckles turned white.

Owen's eyes were hopeful. "See you soon, and then we'll -"

But I backed out of the parking spot before he finished. I didn't want to hear it. I didn't want to hear any more about sex or the baby or the fact that those two things have become completely intertwined in his mind. When did making love cease to become about pleasure for him? Instead, it seems to be just a means to an end. To him, what he had done by himself in that room at the doctor's was probably no different than what we do together. Perhaps the intimacy I crave doesn't exist between us anymore. I thought things were better that night we went to The Marine Room, but it turns out that was just the calm before the storm.

I drove to Seaport Village and parked outside of the Upstart Crow – the bookstore where Lorelei and I met five years ago. The Upstart Crow represents the beginning of the best friendship I've ever known, and as I stared out my windshield at the red brick building with the big black crow and the little iron coffee tables out front, I felt comforted. How Lorelei made me laugh that day! And how awed I was by her glamour and self-confidence. Over time I learned what a caring person she is, so protective of her loved ones and very, very strong. I know I can go to Lorelei with anything. If you met her, Mama, you would like her- I know you would because everyone likes Lorelei.

As I sat there remembering that day, I realized that my relationship with Lorelei has been a bit one-sided over the past few months; most of our conversations have been about me and my problems. It's just that Lorelei is so in control of her life, so successful in every way, that it's sometimes hard to imagine her having any problems at all. She knows what she wants and she knows how to get it. No one dictates Lorelei's fate except Lorelei. Maybe that's why I lean so hard on her- because I want to be like her.

I picked up my cell and dialed Lorelei's direct line at Empire & Malkin. She didn't answer so I rang the main number. A nice girl named Simone said she would tell Lorelei I was on the phone- Simone sounded very sympathetic, probably because I was crying again. As I was listening to the hold music, I wondered what I was going to do about that evening. If I told Owen I didn't want to make love he would be angry. If I gave in, I would lose another piece of myself.

I know that the heart is stretchy and it can swell with love and wonderment and magic, but I also know it can close up tight, squashing its very defenseless parts inside steel walls of caution in order to brace against pain. How easily I let my heart run away from me when I fell in love with Owen all of those years ago, but now, especially after today, I can feel myself shutting Owen out even though it's not necessarily what I want.

I listened to Empire & Malkin's hold music for a couple of minutes and then hung up. I really shouldn't have been bothering Lorelei at work. I had been thoughtless to ring her- interrupting her deadlines with my personal problems. She was busy chasing her ambitions just as I should be busy chasing mine.

I remembered Thomas McQuillan's email and I wiped my tears away as I recalled his words (they touched me so deeply that I'd memorized them): "I believe somewhere within your mind and soul, Mary Crossfield, there is a writer waiting to emerge. Let me bring her forth. I'd like to."

And, oh, how I want him to. How I long to bask in the presence of a successful author and learn all I can from him. My identity has been caught up in Owen for so long that I have let my creative side fail. Yes, Lorelei has been wonderful to discuss books and literature and poetry with, but I want more. I want to dive into Thomas' thoughts and have him teach me nuance and subtext and style and... and I want to see if I have what it takes to do the one thing I've loved doing since I was a little girl. I started a short story last week just to flex my writing muscles and it felt so good to put proverbial pen to proverbial paper as my fingers flew across the keyboard of my laptop. My mind was alive with imagination and for those moments I wasn't Mary the Wife or Mary the Dog-Walker or Mary the Girl Who Can't Conceive. I was Mary the Writer.

I did go home and make love to Owen that night. I shut my heart up tight and went through all of the motions. He never questioned- or noticed- my lack of response. He took his pleasure (or should I say, did his baby due diligence) and afterward he went into the living room and watched baseball with Roger.

Owen is leaving on his training mission soon, and I'll do everything I can to make him happy until then. After all, I love my husband. But when Owen is gone, and I'm alone, I'm going to start doing things for my own personal growth and on my own terms. I know what you're thinking- it's easy for me to say that since Owen isn't going to be around. I suppose you're right, Mama, but I've got to figure things out before he gets back. By then I hope to be done with my soul searching, ready to stand up to him about what I really want out of life.

In the meantime, I think Thomas McQuillan is the key to unlocking my literary castle in the air. I'm going to take him up on his offer.

CHAPTER 28

A s Katya drove away from Thomas' house, she replayed the events of the day. She was over the moon that her dream of becoming a Hollywood actress was beginning to unfold. She had known Thomas would be happy for her, but there was just one teeny, tiny problem. In a desperate moment of greedy tenaciousness, she'd told the director, John Bhear, that she and Thomas McQuillan were in a loving, committed relationship, and that Thomas was almost finished with the first draft of his next novel. Katya had shared these tasty and wholly untrue morsels with wide, innocent eyes, knowing the information would ultimately instigate a juicy PR frenzy surrounding *Syndicate Protocol*.

And she'd been right.

John Bhear, who had thought Katya's looks were perfect for the role of Bethie Howatch, was rather unimpressed with her weak acting skills during closed auditions. On the other hand, she did have a certain presence and her fame as a model could generate some interest in the film. He watched her with critical eyes, noting that she was, at the very least, comfortable and relaxed in front of an audience and a camera.

He'd have to think about it.

John Bhear, at only thirty-one years old, was directing his first full-length feature film. He was both ebullient and nervous about being placed in the director's chair and it was imperative that his debut movie be a box office smash. It helped, obviously, that Republic Pictures had signed hunky megastar Keith Chadwick as the leading man. Keith would definitely draw the crowds, but John wanted audiences to feel an emotional connection with his movie, not just be entertained.

John cut Katya off mid-sentence as she was spouting a dramatic line on stage.

"Thank you!" he called from his seat in the audience. "We'll be in touch."

Instead of walking into the wings like the other hopefuls, Katya gracefully glided down the steps and approached John Bhear where he was sitting by himself, apart from the crew. The casting agents, camera operator and director's assistants watched her warily and then went back to squabbling with each other about an actor who had great vocal delivery but a horribly goofy laugh.

John was taken aback by the tall, beautiful Russian who walked right up to him with such poise and self-possession. She hadn't an ounce of trepidation in her eyes even though she stood before the man responsible for deciding her acting fate in his movie.

Katya held out her hand, officially introducing herself. Without waiting for an invitation, she sat next to him, leaning her lissome body into his as though they were old friends sharing secrets. She asked about his family, his hobbies, his travels. It was obvious she had studied up on him, for she knew all the right questions to ask and she expounded on his answers with very astute, and clearly practiced, comments.

Admittedly, he was impressed with her demeanor. It was obvious she was driven and had passion for acting. But despite her agent's promises on the phone to him earlier that day, John was not convinced Katya had the chops to act the part.

"About my role..." Katya began, as though she'd already won it.

"My dear," said John, as kindly as he could, "I don't know if the part is right for you..."

But before he could say more, Katya began to chat about how happy her boyfriend would be when she told him about her acting debut. She said innocently, "You *do* know Thomas McQuillan, Mr. Bhear?"

For a moment John was dumbfounded. "Thomas McQuillan? You are dating the author *Thomas McQuillan*?" He hadn't heard *that* name in *ages*.

Katya managed to force a demure blush to her cheeks, lowering her eyelashes in mock modesty. "For the past five years. We're very much in love."

"I'll be damned," said John, scratching his head. Suddenly he became excited. "Is Thomas working on his next book by any chance? The world has been waiting for almost a decade."

Katya nodded enthusiastically. "Oh, yes! He's almost finished with the first draft. It's brilliant, Mr. Bhear, just brilliant."

"You've read it then?" he asked eagerly.

"Of course!" Katya gushed, pressing her hands to her heart. "I just know it's going to be bigger than *Souls in Collision.*"

"I'll be damned," John said again.

John had been just twenty years old when he'd seen *Souls in Collision* on the big screen, and the movie had left an indelible mark on the young and hopeful acting student. John was instantly obsessed with the famed director who had meticulously and ingenuously brought McQuillan's bestselling book to life, and he walked out of the theatre inspired and fizzling with creative restlessness. The following day, he went back and watched *Souls in Collision* two more times. And after that, he knew without a doubt, he wanted to be a director, *not* an actor. John felt a burning desire to take a book or a play or a screenplay and make all the words literally come alive. Imagination was a beautiful thing, but John wanted to take imagination and give it faces and voices and sweeping scenery and incredible sets. He left his acting classes and enrolled in film school, eagerly awaiting the next Thomas McQuillan book to become a movie. But after several years of publishing silence, it became clear that Thomas McQuillan was no longer writing. John, disappointed, figured McQuillan must have retired while he was at the very peak of his celebrity, choosing a life of ease and anonymity over fame and exploitation.

But now…

John Bhear wanted the exclusive movie rights to Thomas' new manuscript so badly he could taste it. And it appeared that Katya, whose lovely face flowered with the blush of a girl in love, was the key. Giving her the part would no doubt bring McQuillan within reach. Besides, if John secretly leaked to the press the exciting news that not only was Thomas McQuillan dating well-known supermodel Katya, but he was also about to publish his next bestseller, it would create a media sensation, and tons of publicity, surrounding *Syndicate Protocol*. It only took a split second for John to make up his mind, his heart beating a steady drum of exhilaration. His movie was going to become the talk of Hollywood. John stood up abruptly and announced to everyone that Katya Vetrov would take on the role of Bethie Howatch.

And Thomas McQuillan, whether he wanted to or not, was about to return to the spotlight.

CHAPTER 29

    *L*orelei stood transfixed at the bottom of her small, circular staircase, watching as Detective Frank Williams strode purposely into her living room.

Niles trailed behind him, his brow furrowed in concern. "Lor, this is-"

"She knows who I am," Frank said gruffly, his eyes riveted to her face.

"Listen, is there some sort of trouble? I'm sure we can work this out, officer..." Niles brought all of his charm to the forefront. "Why don't you sit down and I'll get you a cold drink. Iced tea? Lemonade?"

Frank turned around and looked at Niles so threateningly that the well-dressed businessman physically recoiled.

"I need to speak to Miss Harper in private," Frank said, nudging Lorelei toward the first step.

Niles held up his palms in a show of acquiescence. He sat on the red sofa and picked up his newspaper, his forehead still creased with worry. Deciding calmness was the best avenue to take he said disarmingly, "If you need anything, Lor, I'll be right here. Just call down to me, and I'll come up."

"That won't be necessary," Frank replied, urging Lorelei up the stairs. As he followed her, he saw, to both his horror and delight, that her dress was completely open in the back. His mind plunged into chaos as he watched the silky softness of her skin sway gracefully with each step.

As soon as they reached the second floor, Lorelei turned on Frank, furious. "How dare you come into my house and order me around!"

Frank sheepishly met Lorelei's fierce gaze and then quickly looked away. It was then that he realized the entire upper level was a giant loft bedroom. The décor was a delicate balance of elegance and comfort. And the bed... the bed was enormously round and covered with the most sumptuous, luxurious red comforter Frank had ever seen. A canopy hovered over the circular shape, just below the ceiling, draped in a delicate, gauzy fabric that cascaded cozily and intimately around the bed, secluding it from the outside world.

In a daze, Frank looked from the bed to Lorelei and then back to the bed again. He was an idiot. He'd burst into her condo unannounced and uninvited where she was apparently entertaining some sort of love interest. He'd acted like an overbearing, macho cop and dragged her off, half-dressed to her bedroom. And now... now she was looking at him angrily and he had no excuse whatsoever for his behavior.

Lorelei, still waiting for an answer, put her hands on her hips and glared at him with those brilliant green eyes. "Well?" she said. "Why are you here? What do you want, Detective?"

You... Frank longed to say. *You. On this bed. You. Without that dress. You. Because I haven't been able to stop thinking about how much fun I had the other night. You. Because I know you feel the electricity between us just as much as I do. You. Just you, Lorelei Harper...*

But Frank said none of that. Instead, he turned away, ran his hands over his short, cropped hair and sighed. He pulled himself together. He was here for Faith, the sweet girl who had begged him on the phone to fix things between her and Lorelei. Things that were technically his fault. It was he who had brought up Connor and ruined the evening that had been going so well. Frank wanted to straighten everything out. He wanted to take Lorelei on another date. He wanted Faith and Lorelei to be friends again. And he wanted that guy downstairs to go away and never come back.

Frank took a deep breath and turned to the beautiful woman before him. "Hey, I'm sorry. This isn't how I planned for this to go…"

"I'll repeat," Lorelei said succinctly, *"why are you here?"*

"For Faith."

Lorelei pointed at the stairs. "Out! Get out!!!"

"No!" Frank said. "No. Hang on. I came here because I wanted to apologize for what I said the other night." He paused. He was hesitant to even utter that one damnable word again. "I didn't know bringing a certain name up would ruin our perfect evening. I was having such a good time with you." Frank's voice deepened. "I enjoyed listening to you and learning about you. I didn't ever want the night to end. And I certainly didn't want the night to end the way it did. Can you forgive me? Please?"

As Frank talked, Lorelei could feel her heart slowly picking up speed. His voice was triggering the same sensations she'd felt during the evening they'd spent together. She vividly recalled the lines of poetry he'd whispered in her ear… the way his masculine scent had given her a strange feeling of both contentment and seductiveness… how he'd caressed the bare skin of her arm… the sensual kisses he'd brushed against her lips before passion took over and their embrace intensified…

Frank looked very vulnerable as he waited for her response. Vulnerable, yet… so very tough. His shirt was slightly rumpled and his muscles were almost too big for his sport coat, which was pulling at the seams a bit. There was a small hole in the left knee of his Levis and his large hands were strong and calloused. Frank's square jaw held an uneven five o'clock shadow, his eyes reflected a hint of impenetrability and his overall bearing was unpolished and rugged.

Lorelei felt physically and emotionally drawn to this man. This man who was the complete opposite of anyone she had ever dated, and certainly the opposite of Niles, who was currently waiting downstairs for her. Common sense took over. Of course Frank asking about Connor hadn't been his fault. She had already come to terms with that after her long hike. She could forgive Frank, but that didn't mean she should let him into her life. He was too tempting. Too alluring. There was something about Frank Williams that sent thrilling shivers through her body.

"You don't have any reason to ask for forgiveness, Frank. I should be the one to apologize. I'm sorry I ended our evening so abruptly." Her beautiful face softened, her green eyes veracious. "I had a wonderful time."

"I did too… and I'd like a repeat. Can you give me another chance, Lorelei?"

"I don't think that's a good idea." Lorelei moved away from him and leaned against her heavy vintage dresser, careful to keep her naked back hidden from view

Frank sighed and rubbed his chin. He looked up at the ceiling and then back at Lorelei. His eyes were tormented, his voice thick with tension. "Tell me you can't feel the attraction between us, Lorelei. Tell me those goosebumps I felt on your arm that night weren't because of me. Tell me…" he stepped closer to her, bridging the space between them, "you didn't feel safe in my arms and tell me my kisses meant nothing to you. Tell me, and I'll leave right now." Her lips were so close, so full and tantalizing. "Tell me…"

Lorelei leaned away, pressing herself against the dresser, crumpling the back of her pretty lavender dress. Her heart was racing so fast that her breath started coming in quick and shallow.

Frank didn't touch her. He wanted permission. He wanted consent.

There was a slight creaking noise on the stairs behind them and then Niles said, "Everything okay up here?" His question was directed at Lorelei, but his suspicious eyes were on Frank.

A silence fell over the room.

Then Frank turned and said, "Everything is fine. Go back downstairs."

Niles looked very offended. He was not used to being ordered around. And what exactly was going on anyway? This didn't look like a normal police visit. Not that Niles knew what a normal police visit looked like. But it certainly couldn't be like *this*...

Lorelei found her voice. "I'm fine. It's okay, Niles. Detective Williams will be leaving shortly."

Niles' eyes narrowed. "He'd better be."

Frank made a quick, jerky movement as though he were going to launch himself at Niles. The handsome businessman flinched in fright and then hurried back down the stairs.

Lorelei giggled. "That wasn't very nice. You scared him!"

Frank grinned, his eyes mischievous.

Lorelei relaxed her body a bit. "You really should go, Frank. Niles and I have dinner reservations."

"Why are you going out with that guy, Lor?"

She said nothing.

"Okay, I get that he's good-looking and probably successful, but... he doesn't seem like your type."

"Oh really? And what is my type?"

"Someone that can make your heart race..."

"And you think he can't?"

Frank crossed his arms. "Nope."

"You barely know me," Lorelei said, pushing past Frank to put some distance between them.

"Does that matter? When you know something's right, you can feel it. Doesn't that count?"

Lorelei turned away, her open dress forgotten. "No," she said, her voice barely above a whisper, "it doesn't count for anything."

Frank willed himself not to look at her seductively exposed skin. "Tell me why, Lor. Why do you think that?"

"Because sometimes, when two people think it's right, one person eventually doesn't anymore."

Frank chose his words very carefully. "Yes, that's true. That can happen."

"…and then the person who still thinks it's right is left with unreturned feelings."

"You're talking about long-term relationships here."

"…when someone falls out of love."

In that moment Frank knew who Connor was. Oh, not the person himself, but what he represented: a world of hurt and confusion and betrayal. It was beyond Frank how any man could possibly fall out of love with Lorelei Harper, but that was beside the point. Now he knew what he was up against. The very thing that drew Lorelei to Frank was the very thing that was scaring her off. The thought made his heart constrict and he fully looked at the gorgeous woman in front of him, her head bent, her dress and her heart open. Frank wanted to lovingly take her in his arms and kiss all her pain away. He wanted to make her see the beauty of love again. But there was only one way to do that, and it couldn't be physical. He would need to offer friendship and nothing more. Lorelei Harper was going to have to learn to trust again, to trust that the feelings of intimacy and passion were not enemies. The knowledge that she'd shut up her heart so tightly gave Frank some measure of satisfaction; it meant Mr. Wonderful downstairs couldn't send Lorelei to the heavens, for if he could, she wouldn't be with him. She was most likely only dating men who were safe.

Frank walked across the room and gently pulled Lorelei back against his broad chest. "Let me be your friend, Lor. Let me hang out with you- take you to concerts, on bike rides, hikes, picnics at the beach… whatever you want to do. Just so we can talk and laugh and get to know each other better. I like you as a person." Frank chuckled. "Yeah, you're gorgeous, but I can get over that and just pretend you're one of the guys."

Lorelei smiled and her body relaxed into his. "Really? One of the guys?"

"Sure. We'll burp after we eat and scratch ourselves in public. It'll be great."

Lorelei turned around to face him, her expression suddenly serious. "Why? Why would you want to just be my friend when we both know you want more?"

"Because I'd rather have you in my life on your terms than not at all."

Lorelei's green eyes misted. "I don't know what to say."

"Say yes."

"What if I want more than friendship and I get scared?"

"Let's try it. Ask me to kiss you."

Mesmerized by the longing in his eyes, and the arousal coursing through her body at his nearness, Lorelei said, "Okay. Please kiss me, Detective Williams."

Frank's lips drew nearer, then stopped just before hers. "Nope," he whispered.

Lorelei burst out laughing, then remembered Niles and put a hand over her mouth.

"I'm not here to scare you, Lor. I'm here because I like you. Just friends?"

"One of the guys?"

Frank nodded. "One of the guys. Don't ask me to kiss you again because I don't kiss dudes."

Lorelei touched her bottom lip thoughtfully. "Your kisses are… I've never felt so on fire when a man has kissed me before…"

Frank groaned loudly. "Oh god, DON'T say that. Do you want me to pick you up and make love to you on that sexy bed of yours right here and right now?"

Lorelei giggled. "Kind of."

Frank clutched at his head. "You're killing me!"

"Sorry." Lorelei put out her hand. "Friends?"

Frank looked at her, his eyes blazing. "Friends. I want you to trust me."

They shook hands on it and then Frank said. "Now, the real reason I'm here…"

Lorelei dropped his hand. "I know… Faith. I just don't want to talk to her yet."

"She's sorry, Lor. She didn't even tell me who Connor was. She's just worried about you." And now Frank knew why. "I think she sees life as one big fairytale."

"Because it turned out to be a fairytale for *her*…"

"Yes. And she wants you to meet your Prince Charming because she thinks that will make you endlessly happy."

"I am happy. There has to be more to it than that."

"There is." Frank sighed. "She doesn't want you to move away."

Lorelei's eyes widened. "And if I fall in love and marry someone in San Diego I won't ever leave her…"

"She mentioned something about you moving to Manhattan. She's afraid of losing you."

Lorelei sat heavily on the edge of her bed. It all made sense now. Other than Jesse and the kids, Faith didn't have any family. Her family was Mary and Lorelei. Of course she was worried about Lorelei moving far away. She should have thought of this…

"Thank you, Frank. I understand now. I'll talk to her. In fact, I'll go over to her house this evening…" Lorelei's voice trailed off uncertainly as she thought of her dinner plans at Barclay Prime.

As though on cue, Niles' footsteps sounded on the stairwell and he poked his head into the loft. "Lor, we should really go… we'll be late for our reservations."

Frank, his voice hardening with authority, turned around slowly to look at Niles. "Miss Harper isn't going anywhere with you tonight. I need to take her to the station for further questioning."

Niles' face went red. "What is this about? What right do you have to barge in here and then haul her off -?"

Frank reached behind him and Niles, startled, put up his hands. "Hey, man, no need to use force."

"I'm not going to pull my gun on you, moron," Frank said, yanking a pair of handcuffs from his waistband. "But I'm afraid Ms. Harper will need to be restrained during transport."

Niles visibly paled. Whatever was happening at Empire & Malkin was way more serious than he'd thought. What had Lorelei gotten herself into? Whatever it was, he didn't want any part of it; Niles had a reputation to protect, a client base who needed to believe he was ethically and morally unsullied.

"Okay," Niles said, "I understand. I'm just going to go. You're all right, Lorelei?" He didn't wait for an answer. "I'll call you later." He bolted down the stairs and out the front door.

"Wow, he's so chivalrous," Frank said.

"He's a good guy. Probably worried about his reputation."

"You know what I'm worried about?"

Lorelei smiled flirtatiously. "What?"

"That I'm standing over the most gorgeous woman I've ever laid eyes on and that woman is half-dressed and sitting on an incredibly inviting bed."

"Tempted, are you?"

"I have handcuffs." Frank teased, dangling them suggestively by one finger.

Lorelei laughed delightedly and Frank gave her a slow, easy smile.

It was going to be very, very hard for Frank to keep his emotions in check around Lorelei Harper. But the affection he felt for her, and the knowledge that her heart needed trust, not lust, cooled and banked his fire and he returned the handcuffs to the back of his waistband.

Frank held out his hand to help her from the bed, then turned her around and zipped up the back of her dress. Her silky curls brushed his fingers and he longed to touch his lips to the soft column of her neck. Suppressing every screaming, excited nerve in his body, he circled her back to face him. "It's going to be real tough being friends with you, Lor. But let's start by grabbing a beer and then I'll take you over to Faith's."

"Is that what guys do? Drink beer for dinner?"

"Yup. And maybe we can pick up a couple of hot chicks while we're at the bar."

"I was meant to be dining at a lovely restaurant this evening…"

"Well, you're a dude now so I'm afraid onion rings are gonna have to suffice."

Lorelei laughed, and then, "Frank?"

"Yes?"

"Thank you."

"For what?"

"For knowing what I need from a man without my having to say it."

CHAPTER 30

*G*eorgette was packing her suitcase when Francesca came bounding into the bedroom wearing skin-tight pleather pants, a black satin tank top and four-inch stiletto heels. She teetered to the left slightly, a big smile on her painted red lips, her short grey hair spiked playfully around her head.

"Look at the pants I got for our trip!" Francesca said, strutting past the armoire, hands on hips.

George laughed. "Those are great! You'll be the sexiest thing in…"

Francesca cupped her ear. "Where?"

"No! Stop trying to get it out of me- our destination is a surprise."

"Humph." Francesca wobbled over to the full-length mirror and wiggled her butt a bit to see the effect. "Not bad for an eighty-one-year old."

George smiled. "You're the most beautiful woman I've ever known."

"And you to me, sweetheart." Francesca tapped her chin thoughtfully with a gnarled finger. "You know, we can't be going TOO far since we're driving, not flying. Colorado? New Mexico? Texas? Now, Texas would be fun because of all them cowboys out there carrying guns. They're my people, you know."

"Franny, I really don't like you being so into this gun thing. I mean, I don't mind that you're taking classes and all, but -"

Francesca struck a tough guy pose and curled her lip. "You got nothin' to worry about, dollface," she snarled, "not with me around to protect you." Quick as a flash, she pulled her gun from the waistband of her pants and pointed it at the toilet in their adjoining bathroom. "Hands up, perp! I've got you in my sights!"

The phone began to ring.

"That's probably my backup," Francesca called over her shoulder.

Georgette rolled her eyes. "Hello?" she said, picking up the receiver.

Mitch's voice came over the line, cheerless and low. "Hey, sis."

"Hey yourself. Are you okay?"

Francesca turned around at the tone and tucked her gun back into her pants. She joined Georgette and the two women sat on the edge of their bed, heads bent close together as they listened to Mitch tell them about his conversation with Helene's sister.

When Mitch was done George said softly, "Helene dead- I can't believe it. What sad news. She was a lovely person."

"Babette is having some of Helene's things mailed to my house for Mary." Mitch sounded hesitant.

"And you haven't decided what to tell Mary…" Georgette guessed.

There was a pause. "Right."

"Mitch, she deserves to know the truth and now seems like a good time to tell her everything. Mary will be glad to have something of Helene's. Will there be at least one of her paintings?"

"I would imagine. Babette mentioned a journal, a few silk scarves, some old photos and a bit of cash. Helene had nothing to her name. You know she was never interested in money."

Francesca nodded. "Lived like a gypsy, that one."

"She was only sixty years old," Mitch said. "Still so young."

"You bet your bippy that's young!" Francesca said, smacking her pleather-clad thigh.

"How did it happen?" Georgette was full of sympathy. "Did Babette tell you?"

"Helene committed suicide."

"Oh darling! Do you want me? Where are you? I can jump in the car right now."

"I'm fine, George, really. I haven't seen Helene in... well, it's been since she left Mary with me, so thirty-two years. It's not like we've been close all this time. I feel very bad for Babette."

"Yes. You and I both know what it's like to lose a sibling."

Mitch sighed heavily. "I don't think I can talk about Claude right now."

"Of course." George let a silent moment pass. "You need to tell Mary."

"No."

"Then how are you going to explain Helene's things to her?"

Francesca patted Georgette's back. "He isn't going to give them to Mary, honey."

Georgette was shocked. "He wouldn't do that! Mitch! You wouldn't do that?"

There was a long pause, which ended with Francesca saying, "See?"

Mitch's voice was low and full of concerned purpose. "I cannot, and will not, tell Mary about the death of a mother she never knew. What would be the purpose in that?"

"Don't you think we all deserve to know where we come from?" Georgette asked quietly.

"Do we?" Mitch countered. "Does knowing where we come from change anything about who we really are? Mary's parentage doesn't matter, George, because she is who she is in the here and now and nothing can alter that. I won't hurt her for no reason."

"I come from Italy," Francesca said. "Knowing my Italian heritage means everything to me- it's part of who I am."

"Are you saying you would be a different person if you didn't know where you were born and what your mother was like?" Mitch asked.

"Yes," Francesca said with gusto. "Yes, absolutely."

Mitch's temper flared. "And if I tell Mary all about the past- a past she wasn't even alive for- you think that will change her for the better? No! It will only upset her. *What is the point*?"

Georgette's voice became stern. "The point is that she deserves to have her mother's things, Mitchell. You owe her that at the very least."

"She is my child and I will do as I see fit."

"That's the problem. Mary is *not* a child. Stop treating her like one."

"Why don't YOU stop treating ME like one!" Mitch roared at his sister. And with that, he hung up the phone.

Thomas McQuillan took a sip of the gin rickey in his hand and gazed out over the balcony of his upstairs game room. The air was sunny and warm and an ocean breeze gently ruffled his shoulder-length sandy hair. An image of Gemma on the beaches of Wales floated through his mind. She was running toward him, laughing, her smile lighting up his heart. He remembered catching her, pressing her close, burying his face in her fragrant hair. Holding her had brought him such peace. Draining his gin rickey, he shook his head and tried to dismiss memories of the past. It was useless to think about what could have been. He had never regretted his decision to not have children, but every once in a while a prick of pain would touch his heart and he knew it was because he missed Gemma's sweet-natured kindness. He wondered if that was part of the reason he was inclined to trust Mary Crossfield so readily. Mary and Gemma had similar dispositions and they both emanated an innocence that the world hadn't been able to taint.

Thomas wandered back inside to his game room, running his hand along the pool table as he passed it. Katya was coming over tonight. The thought of her instantly made his hand clench. He was sure she was hiding something and he was going to pry it out of her by way of copious amounts of booze and mind-blowing sex. In the meantime, he would check his email again. He still hadn't heard from Mary- was it possible she was turning down his offer by way of simply neglecting to reply? He pictured her artless face with its smattering of freckles and it somehow merged in his mind with Gemma's honest eyes and ingenuous smile. The effect caused his heart to skip a beat and he wondered why he hadn't thought of the similarities between the women before. Not so much in their physical appearance, but in their pure, unaffected temperaments.

He'd been lying to himself about not feeling attracted to Mary at The Marine Room. Or maybe his subconscious hadn't filled his conscious in on the fact that he very much saw in Mary what he missed about Gemma. He felt a sudden rush of relief that Mary *hadn't* acknowledged his request to nanny Voltaire. It was probably better for everyone involved if Thomas never saw Mary Crossfield again. He'd find someone else to keep The Frenchie Angel of Darkness busy. The problem was finding someone confidential and trustworthy. Maybe Helga had a relative who liked dogs and wanted a bit of extra cash.

In the meantime, Thomas had some killer cocktails to make. He went downstairs into a small wood-paneled room lined with shelves of liquor. A large table made of glass and stone squatted comfortably in the middle of the thick, rich wall-to-wall carpeting. Thomas pulled a fat ceramic pitcher off a shelf and began pouring libations into it, along with juice and a few ice cubes from the mini freezer. As he stirred the sweet-smelling aperitif, he thought of Katya, and he knew that after a few glasses of his booze-laden concoction coupled with a marathon lovemaking session, she was going to confess whatever it was she wasn't telling him. His writer's intuition knew she was up to something. And it had to do with him.

CHAPTER 31

⌒

Faith and Jesse's house was nestled in a large grove of sycamore trees in the little city of Poway just outside of San Diego. The area was countrified and had a small-town feel. Lots of wildlife sprang up unannounced and it hadn't surprised Lorelei when Faith had said on the phone a few weeks ago that raccoons were living in her backyard.

Lorelei was glad Frank was with her. She enjoyed his calm, reassuring company immensely and, truth be told, she was slightly nervous about talking with Faith. Not because she thought their friendship was on the line but because Lorelei now understood why Faith was acting the way she was and it made Lorelei feel very guilty. She should have known, should have understood.

A very young, very exuberant Faith had happened upon Lorelei right after she'd broken up with Connor all those years ago. Lorelei was at Embarcadero Park, staring across the bay and watching sailboats float peacefully by. She had tears on her cheeks as she thought of her lost love now in the arms of some brunette tramp in Los Angeles. Or maybe he was with a blonde tramp now. Or maybe he was with all kinds of tramps at the same time. Who knew? Famous bands were notorious for their promiscuous behavior, right? And why not? What man could resist women throwing themselves at their feet?

Lorelei pulled a tissue from her purse and was daintily blowing her nose when a tall, lanky redheaded girl in her late teens came out of nowhere, crashing into her and sending them both sprawling onto the grass.

"OH MY GOSH!!! I didn't see you!!!" squealed the redhead in despair. "Are you okay?" She clumsily got to her feet and put her hands on either side of Lorelei's face. "AHHHHHHH!!! You're crying! I've hurt you! I'm so sorry! Can you get up? Let me help you!" She pulled at Lorelei's arm, awkwardly stepping on her knee in the process.

Lorelei shoved the girl away and grunted in pain. "I'm fine. My head is just a little sore. What were you doing anyway?"

Faith picked a candy apple up off the ground, grass pieces sticking out of the caramel. "I wasn't paying attention to where I was walking because I was eating this. It's soooo good!" Faith gestured toward a cart with a bright red umbrella parked on the edge of a dock. "They're selling them over there." She began trying to pluck the grass out of her treat.

"Yuck! Don't eat that. Just go buy another one."

Faith colored slightly. "Oh, they are expensive. I only had enough for this one."

Lorelei stared. "What do you mean? How much are they?"

"Six dollars."

"That's not exp-" Lorelei stopped herself. The girl before her was not dressed nicely. Her clothes were too big for her slender frame and the colors, which had once been vibrant, were faded and dull.

Faith took a bite of apple and moaned in delirium. "Soooo good! Please have some." She shoved the gooey mess toward Lorelei.

"You know what? Why don't I treat you to a new one? *Sans* grass."

"You don't have to do that," Faith said, but her eyes lit up at the prospect.

Lorelei bought two candy apples and the girls sat at a picnic table and chatted. Faith was easy to talk to and Lorelei immediately liked the effervescent redhead. They joked and laughed and then told one another of their hopes for the future. Faith said she was going to meet her Prince Charming one day and they would have lots of children and she would live happily ever after. Lorelei said she would work her way up in the ranks of a corporation until she became chief financial officer and then the sky would be the limit. And eventually, after the girls had finished their apples and shared their dreams, Lorelei quietly confided in Faith about Connor, and somehow when she said what had happened out loud, it didn't seem as awful as it felt. Her heart still hurt beyond repair, but the more she talked, the more she could see how relationships didn't have to be helpless. One could choose a partner based on set, analytical criteria that didn't involve vulnerability. One needn't ever get hurt again.

Faith listened in sympathy while Lorelei spoke, but her eyes grew fierce when Lorelei allowed a few tears to fall.

"If I ever meet Connor O'Cassidy," she screeched, "I will punch his junk! You are *such* a nice person. And... I'm not hitting on you or anything, but you are like TOTALLY gorgeous. Connor is a fool *AND* a jerk! He doesn't deserve you and you're better off without him."

Lorelei found out Faith was a coffee barista in Solana Beach at a place called Holokai's.

"You should come in some time! I can give you a coffee on the house. It wouldn't be stealing because I get a free one during every shift I work so you'd just be drinking mine."

Lorelei smiled. "That would be nice. And what do you do when you're not working?"

"I volunteer at Saint Patrick's Home for Children."

"The orphanage?" Lorelei's face grew serious.

Faith laughed, a silvery, tinkling sound. "They're not called orphanages anymore, Lor. And don't look so sad. It's a wonderful place. I was very happy growing up there."

"You... you were... you are...?"

"Yes. A lady found me in a women's bathroom at a second-hand store when I was just a few days old. She took me to a police station and they brought me to Saint Patrick's."

Lorelei's eyes misted. "So... you don't have any relatives?"

"Well, I guess I do. I mean, I suppose somewhere out there I have a mom and a dad and maybe some siblings. But my real family were all the kids I grew up with. I loved them so much and I liked helping take care of them. I used to rock some of them to sleep and they would come to me when they were sad or needed a hug. A lot of them wanted me to kiss their booboos or help them with their homework. I started to realize over time that your real family doesn't necessarily have to be blood- your real family is who you choose. But those kids are leading lives of their own now."

Faith cast her eyes downward and a rare look of sadness crossed her face. "It's just me. I was never any good at school so scholarships weren't an option. I'm lucky Holokai hired me right out of high school. He taught me how to make cappuccinos and lattes and he lets me keep all the jar tips which is really sweet. And I've met some very nice customers, but it's kind of hard to make friends who don't already have lives- families- of their own. Holidays are really difficult." Suddenly she looked up, the bright smile back, her eyes sparkling with excitement. "But you know what, Lor? One day I'm going to meet my Prince Charming. He's going to sweep me off my feet and I'm going to have sex and we're going to have tons of cute chubby babies."

Lorelei laughed. "You're going to have sex...? Don't tell me you're a virgin?"

Faith looked rapturous. "Yes! I'm waiting for Mr. Right. I want my first time to be with the man I love."

Lorelei sighed. "You know the odds of that are like slim to none, right? Do you not recall my JUST telling you about how the 'love of my life' walked out on me?"

"Oh," Faith reassured, "Connor wasn't the love of your life, Lor. Your Prince Charming would never walk out on you."

Lorelei rolled her eyes. "Do tell. And how are we supposed to know if a man is really our soulmate or not?"

Faith smiled serenely. "Because you will feel whole. Like you've only been half a person all your life until you met him. And you'll burn for him just as he burns for you- when you touch there will be fire and electricity. And you'll feel emotionally safe with him, like free to be yourself. You'll always have each other's backs and you'll never run out of things to laugh about, even in the rough times."

"Wow. That all sounds great." Lorelei shook her head. "Too bad it's not real."

"Oh, but it is!" Faith said emphatically, bobbing her head up and down, her red hair blowing in the ocean breeze. "And I know it's going to happen for both of us!"

Lorelei smiled at the girl and thought how sweet she was despite the background of her circumstances. Lorelei guiltily considered her own privileged upbringing, her successful, loving parents and her innate acceptance of a prosperous life filled with very little worry and very little struggle. She was currently enjoying her second year at the university and she knew once she graduated, the world would be her oyster. Lorelei had never taken the gifts she had been given for granted, but she'd certainly never looked at her life through the eyes of someone without stability, security or the safety net of parents. How had Faith managed to hold on to the optimism of life while enduring very little, if any, loving support?

Over the next several months, the two girls saw each other frequently and grew to love one another as fiercely as sisters. Lorelei welcomed Faith into her circle of college friends and brought her home on holidays and school breaks. Faith adored Lorelei and was heartbreakingly grateful to find a new family who welcomed, loved and accepted her.

And then one day, a year or so later, Faith called Lorelei and shrieked into the phone, "I MET HIM! I MET HIM!!!"

"Who?" Lorelei demanded. "Stop squealing! I think you blew out my eardrum…"

"My Prince Charming! Oh, Lor, his name is Jesse and he just graduated from law school and he came into Holokai's today and ordered a black coffee and I was so nervous because I knew, I KNEW, it was him because I touched his hand when he gave me change and it was like my whole body caught fire. He's *the one*, Lor! He's the one who's going to make me burn!"

"I don't think you can know that after one meeting. Which was, by the way, just a man coming in to buy a coffee at a local coffee shop."

"Oh no," Faith disagreed knowingly. "He's my Mr. Right."

And sure enough, it turned out he was. Day after day, week after week, Jesse continued to frequent Holokai's until one day he worked up enough nerve to ask out the vivacious redhead behind the counter. They dated for only a short time before Jesse popped the question and he never batted an eyelash when Faith proclaimed that she wanted to wait until they were married before she gave herself to him fully.

Lorelei never forgot the phone call she received the morning after Faith's wedding day.

"OH MY GOSH, LOR!" Faith screamed. "I LOVE SEX! I LOVE IT! IT'S SO MUCH FUN! And Jesse is AMAZING! And we've done it like six times even though it kind of hurt the first time. And he does this crazy thing with his tongue and … he's so sexy and patient and he gives me goosebumps… and when he holds me after we make love I feel so safe. Lor, I feel whole now. He's my other half."

Lorelei had smiled, beyond happy. Maybe fairytales *did* happen. Only time would tell. Marriages were often fun and exciting at first and then real life kicked in and sex and passion and playfulness fell by the wayside as the monotony of bills and jobs and responsibilities demanded priority.

Lorelei wanted to believe in the happily ever after for Faith because if anyone deserved a lifetime of love, it was her best friend.

When Faith came back from her honeymoon, and she and Lorelei were eating candy apples on the bay, Faith said, "Even though I found my other half, part of my heart will always belong to you, Lor. Even when I have my own family one day, and I love them with all that's in me, you were my family first. You took me in and loved me and gave me the security and the friendship and the support I needed. I'll always need you. Always."

⌒‿

Frank parked his truck and looked at the adorable house in front of him. It was very old and rather haphazard, as though the farmers of the past who had lived in it slapped on additional rooms in drunken whims. Bright flowers and patches of green grass poked up through the river rock scattered in the driveway and big sycamore trees surrounded the house protectively as though the branches were arms of comfort. Frilly curtains hung in all the windows and a large, crooked chimney rose from one side of the roof. A chicken ran by the front door, a little boy in overalls right behind it in hot pursuit.

"Chicken!" the boy yelled excitedly. "Chicken, come here! Hi, chicken! Where are you from? I won't eat you! Come back!"

A teenage girl trailed after them, her hair, her clothing and her combat boots all black as night. She wore a spiked dog collar around her thin white neck. "Hank!" she called. "Don't touch that chicken! No chicken! Hank! I said NO CHICKEN!"

Frank looked at Lorelei and she laughed. "Never a dull moment here."

They climbed from the truck and Frank consciously kept his hand away from Lorelei's waist and the small of her back as they walked toward the house. Friends, he told himself sternly, we're just friends.

Lorelei knocked on the door and within a few moments it swung open to reveal Faith's daughter Madison. Her long hair was in pigtails and she was wearing a small checked apron.

"Auntie Lor!" she said excitedly, grabbing one of Lorelei's hands to pull her inside. "I didn't know you were coming over!"

Before Lorelei could respond, a shriek of epic proportions sounded from the back of the house and then Faith was running top speed through the living room. She propelled herself into Lorelei's arms, wrapping herself around her friend.

"LOR!" she wept into Lorelei's golden curls. "Oh, Lor! I'm so sorry! I'm so stupid! I love you! I would never hurt you. I'm so sorry!"

Frank stepped back, his eyes damp. He'd never seen anyone show love so wholly and so completely. Faith cried as though her heart were breaking, her body wracked in sobs.

"I thought I lost you..." Faith wailed. "I thought you were never going to speak to me again... I thought you hated me..."

Lorelei pulled an arm free and stroked Faith's unruly red hair. "Shhhh... I'm here. You'll never lose me. We'll always be friends."

Faith pulled back, her eyes wild and pleading, her face streaked with tears. "You forgive me?"

Lorelei smiled. "No. There is nothing to forgive. *You* need to forgive *me*. I overreacted and I'm sorry." She glanced at Frank affectionately. "And I'm glad you called Detective Williams and asked him to come over to my place."

Faith sniffed in amazement. "Really?"

Lorelei nodded. "Really."

Faith's eyes moved excitedly from Frank to Lorelei. "So you guys were alone at the condo?"

"Fay..." Lorelei gave her a look of warning.

"DID YOU HAVE SEX!?!?"

Frank coughed, stifling a chuckle.

Lorelei put her hands on her hips. "Niles was there too."

Faith's eyes were round as saucers. "Really? That's SO kinky! I need details! Madison, go outside with Hank and Wicky or upstairs with Joel and Scotty. Mommy and Auntie Lor have to have adult girl talk."

"Noooooo!" Madison wailed. "That's not fair! I want to hear too! What does kinky mean?"

Lorelei rolled her eyes. "You can stay here, Maddy. Detective Williams and I are just friends."

Faith frowned. *"Friends?"* she said it as though it were a filthy word.

"Yes," said Lorelei firmly.

"Yes," echoed Frank.

"If they're just friends," asked Madison suspiciously of her mother, "then why does Detective Williams keep looking at Auntie Lor like he wants to kiss her?"

Faith shrieked with laughter, her tears forgotten. She put her arm around Lorelei and said, "Come into the kitchen, you guys. Maddy is making cookies."

"Faith, you and I really need to talk for just a minute. Maddy, will you take Detective Williams into the kitchen and pour him a glass of milk?"

"Okay, Auntie Lor." Madison grabbed Frank's hand and said, "Can you skip?"

And it turned out he could. Lorelei watched the big, muscular detective skip across the room hand in hand with little Maddy and felt her carefully guarded heart slowly turn over.

"He's your other half, Lor," Faith whispered, "I can see it in your eyes."

"I've been down that road before, Fay…."

"You have *not* been down that road before. Connor wasn't your Mr. Right!"

"Then why did he *feel* like my Mr. Right?"

"I don't know. Maybe he was a smooth talker. Maybe you were too young. Maybe you were confused about what your Prince Charming is really supposed to be like. Your true other half would *never* walk away from you, no matter what. You and Connor were never a whole." Faith's eyes welled up with tears. "I hate him!" she cried passionately. "I hate Connor for hurting you and I hate him for jading you into thinking true love doesn't exist!"

"What if it doesn't?"

"But it DOES! Look at me and Jesse!"

"You and Jesse are the exception, Fay, not the rule. Fairytale love isn't real, but somehow it became real for you." She hugged her friend. "It couldn't have happened to a more deserving person. But, listen, I'm not here to talk about fairytales. I'm here to talk about us."

Faith went very still. "Okay..."

"You know it has always been in my plan to move away - to spread my wings and fly to wherever my career takes me. You knew that when we met and nothing's changed."

Faith crossed her arms and looked down at her scuffed sneakers. "Please don't leave me, Lor," she said, clearly on the verge of tears again. "You're my sister."

Lorelei reached out and cupped Faith's cheek. "Just because we live in different cities doesn't mean we stop being sisters. I'll always be here for you no matter how many miles separate us."

Faith swiped at her running nose, her voice rising, her eyes haunted. "You don't understand! You don't understand what it's like to not belong to a family. You don't know what it's like to know you were thrown away in a random bathroom by someone who didn't love you enough to keep you. You don't know what it's like to wonder why you were rejected when you didn't do anything wrong other than be born. You don't know what it's like to be alone on holidays or not know your actual birthdate or not have anyone come to school for you on parent-teacher conference days." She grabbed at Lorelei desperately, dropping her head onto Lorelei's shoulder, her tears spilling down Lorelei's back. "You don't know what it's like to know that your best friend, the girl you love like a sister, has always planned to leave you behind, just as you were left behind as an infant. You can't abandon me, Lor. You just can't! I'm so sorry. I know it's so much to ask."

Lorelei held her friend as she cried, not knowing what to say or how to say it.

"Don't leave me..." Faith took a deep, shaky breath, her plea filled with hurt and pain, "... don't leave me like they did..."

CHAPTER 32

"I'd like to get everyone together tonight," Owen said in between bites of kale and quinoa. He and Mary were having lunch on the patio at Hooligan's Healthy Hut. Roger lay at their feet, having lost interest in the food when he realized it was only a godforsaken meal of lettuce and vegetables with nary a morsel of cow, chicken or fish in sight. He'd made his displeasure known with a whine of disapproval, but both Owen and Mary seemed to be lost in their own thoughts which, presumably, had nothing to do with the current non-meat situation.

Mary looked down at her salad bowl and picked at the greenery. What she wouldn't give for a big plate of French fries.

"I'm thinking the eight of us," Owen continued, "Horse, Corinne, Tex, Ricki, Jambo, Happy… and all the kids of course."

Mary was listless. She felt listless. She identified with the lettuce in front of her which also seemed to lack life and energy. Owen had continually been bringing up the baby the past few days. Over and over and over. She still wasn't pregnant. They were making love regularly, but it was passionless. They'd returned to see Dr. Rygert and both of their initial test results had come back normal. Owen gave another sample and further testing had been scheduled. Mary was tired, she was sore and she was emotionally raw from being poked and prodded into having a baby that she wasn't even sure she wanted.

Owen said, "How about we have everyone over to our place? If you could prepare a nice meal and your chocolate soufflé I'd appreciate it."

Roger looked up at Owen and blinked as if to say, "You're kidding, right?"

"Or we could all go to George's or Wyland's?" Mary suggested. "That would be so much easier. But, Owen, this is everyone's last evening together- I'm sure they all just want to be at home; alone with their families."

"You're probably right. It was just an idea. I should have thought of it earlier." Owen looked disappointed. "It's just that it... would have been nice to have the gang together one last time before we ship out tomorrow."

"You never told me where you're going. Where's the training mission?"

"Not completely sure. Orders will come down once we board the carrier."

"That's unusual, isn't it?"

Owen sipped his iced tea casually. "Not really."

Mary's brow furrowed. Something wasn't right. She scanned Owen's face but saw nothing out of the ordinary there. He appeared relaxed and at ease and he looked incredibly handsome in his khakis and dark brown polo shirt. Mary was wearing her usual attire of running shorts and sweatshirt. Not exactly fashionable, but she'd come directly from walking an adorable Old English Sheepdog named Mr. Fluffer Muffin. She wondered if Owen was unhappy with the way she was dressed. At least he hadn't said anything about her appearance, so there was that to be grateful for. It was a rare occasion these days that he didn't find cause to criticize her for something.

Mary's cell phone rang, snapping her out of her thoughts.

"Hello?"

"Mary, this is Jason. Listen, Charlotte told me you gave her your notice. Is it true you're letting all of your clients go?"

Mary stole a quick glance at Owen. She hadn't told him she'd given up all of her customers except Nancy Harris and Willow Starflower. And she most definitely hadn't told him about Thomas' offer. She had just emailed her acceptance to him this morning and hadn't heard back yet. Probably because he was absorbed in his writing. Maybe he wouldn't even respond for a few days.

"Um, yes…" Mary hedged. "That's right."

"But why? We really need you. Can we do something to work this out?"

"I would really love that, but… I have a very… demanding client coming on board and I'm unable to maintain my current schedule to accommodate him."

Owen looked at Mary inquisitively, one of his brows raised.

"So you're basically ditching all of us for someone better?" Jason asked bluntly.

"No!" Mary said, appalled. "No, it's not like that!"

"Well it certainly sounds like that." Jason snapped. "Your new client must be very special – and by special I mean *rich* - for you to throw away your loyal clientele."

"Jason, please…"

"Don't worry about it. Sorry I bothered you."

Mary stared at the phone in her hand. Jason had hung up.

"What was that about?" Owen asked suspiciously. "Wait a minute – is this 'demanding client' that guy you met at The Marine Room?"

Mary sighed. "Yes. He's hired me to work six hours a day and he's paying me triple my normal rate."

Owen leaned back in his chair and crossed his arms. "Really? That's interesting. And why would he do that?"

"He has trust issues. I think he knows I won't gossip about him because Willow told him such nice things. He thought the extra cash would help convince me to work for him." And coaching sessions too, Mary added silently. They were the real draw, not the money. But, *oh,* she felt horribly guilty about dismissing her clients!

"If he knew you at all he would know he doesn't have to shell out cash to keep you quiet- you're the most ethical person I've ever known. What is he afraid you'll tell people?"

Mary sighed. "Where he lives. *Who he is.* Maybe what he's working on..." She'd fall over dead with delirium if he let her read his manuscript.

Owen looked at his wife, a touch of jealousy flashing in his blue eyes. "How old is this guy? Should I be worried, Mare?"

"No."

Yes. Yes, you should.

Mary had had another dream about Thomas McQuillan the night before. It was much like the other ones she'd been having about him, but sexier, more romantic. In this dream Thomas was reading to her while they snuggled together in a king-sized bed filled with feathery white pillows. Mary was entranced by the sound of Thomas' voice, her mind enthralled by the beautiful words that fell from his lips. She had become so lost in the absolute comfort of being in his arms that when he stopped reading and placed his mouth over hers, she responded without hesitation or inhibition. As their kiss deepened, Thomas' hands roamed over her body, searching, exploring, lighting every part of her on fire. He tore off the blue nightie she was wearing, ripping it open at the front and leaving her bare and exposed. Picking her up off the bed, he set her on a writing desk and she wrapped her legs around his waist, gripping his thighs with her hands.

"You're mine after this, Mary," Thomas said, his voice thick with emotion.

"Yes," she whimpered.

"There's no turning back."

"Yes." A bit stronger.

"Do you want to give yourself to me?"

"I do. So much." It was a confession and a demand all at once.

Thomas possessively growled her name and was inside her so quickly that she lost her breath in a brilliant haze of wonder and desire and pain and relief. He trembled slightly when they became one and he buried his hands in Mary's hair, twisting it around his fingers and pulling on it until her head was tilted back. She saw the passion raging in his eyes, the sheer depth of his desire, and she instinctively knew he had no playbook moves, no rules of engagement- Thomas McQuillan was raw and real and unfettered. He began to move inside her, kissing her voraciously, as if both his mouth and his body wanted to devour her whole.

He whispered breathlessly into her ear. "You're my muse and you're mine."

"I'm yours. Only yours."

It was strange, but something reminded her that she had said those exact words to Owen. But had she? As the unbidden thought of Owen broke through the arousal of her dream, Mary felt at war between her conscious and her subconscious. She fought the urge to wake up, could feel her physical body shift anxiously as though it too preferred fantasy over reality.

She'd woken up abruptly, disoriented at being precipitously torn from Thomas' arms. She looked around and saw that Owen was snoring beside her, flat on his back, his mouth hanging slightly open. Roger was on his doggie bed across the room, his back legs twitching as though he were chasing dream bunnies.

Mary, tears in her eyes, had curled on her side and hugged her knees to her chest. What was happening to her marriage? Thinking of Thomas in such a way was poison to her relationship with Owen. But somehow she couldn't completely stop the daydreams about Thomas' intense hazel eyes, his broody demeanor and that literary mind of his that had captured her through *Souls in Collision* all those years ago. Even when Mary could push her daydreams aside, Thomas seized her willing body in the stillness of the night through her sinfully eager, unconscious psyche.

Owen cleared his throat at Hooligan's and shifted in his chair, bringing Mary back to the present. "I'm sorry things have been kind of rough on you lately," he was saying, toying with his salad. "I feel like there's so much that still needs to be done before I leave."

"It's okay." Mary pulled her thoughts away from Thomas.

"I wonder if I should have left another sample with Dr. Rygert..." Owen mused aloud.

"They actually want you to wait seven days in between -"

"I know," Owen said in frustration, "but I don't have the luxury of time."

Roger whined, the hackles standing up on the back of his neck.

"What is it, boy?" Mary asked, looking around.

Owen's cell phone chirped and he answered it on the second ring.

"Hello?" He made a face at Mary. "Hi, Mother."

Mary leaned her chin on her hand. *Great.*

"Yes," Owen said into the phone. "Yes, everything is fine. Yes, she's with me."

Owen's eyebrows suddenly shot up and his intake of breath was so fast he choked.

Mary handed him a glass of water and mouthed, "Are you okay?"

Owen waved her off, coughing. He said into the phone very slowly, "Can you repeat that, Mother?" There was a long, palpably silent pause, Owen muttered something incoherent and then he hung up.

"What's going on?" Mary asked. "Are your parents all right?"

Owen looked away uneasily. "My mom just landed in San Diego. She decided to surprise us with a visit."

CHAPTER 33

Katya sauntered into Thomas' foyer wearing a slinky, skin-tight red dress that looked as if it had been meticulously painted over her figure by a master artist; it clung to every inch of her lean torso and left nothing to the imagination. Her makeup was bold and harsh, her cheekbones made more pronounced with artful shading and highlighting. Her false eyelashes were unbelievably long and they fluttered about on the edge of her lids like delicate drunken butterflies. Her hard mouth was drenched in a shade of crimson that complimented the red of her dress perfectly, and her thick hair spilled elegantly over her shoulders and down her back in long, loose waves.

Thomas walked out from the little room where he had mixed their drinks and when he saw Katya he stopped dead in his tracks.

"You look handsome," she said, and because he still hadn't moved, she glided to him and ran her hand across his stomach, then into the waist of his trousers.

Thomas clutched the two cocktails he was holding as Katya's touch sent flames licking up his legs. He took a deep breath to calm his rapidly beating heart and in so doing, inhaled her beautiful scent. It was deliciously musky with trace hints of vanilla- a sexily redolent combination that matched her carnal, hot-blooded temperament.

"I thought we were staying in tonight," Thomas said. He took his time passing his eyes appreciatively over Katya's firm body. "You look so glamorous." He tried to offer her one of the cocktails but she pushed his hand away.

"I made reservations for us at Jacopo's," she said. "My treat."

Thomas looked down at his casual attire. "I'm hardly dressed for a five-star, Kat." He set both drinks on a driftwood table close to the foyer's opening wall. "Helga prepared dinner for us, and then afterward I thought you and I could…" He reached out and touched the soft, red fabric encasing Katya's ribcage, seductively tracing the seams on either side.

"Yes-" Katya said, her voice breaking off as Thomas ran a hand down her hip and then pressed it into the small of her back. He drew her in close, his face mere inches from hers. She looked from his penetrating hazel eyes down to his warm lips and back to his eyes again. The man was subtly charismatic and she felt the familiar pull of his magnetism. Her body started to respond against his and for a split second she wanted to rethink her plan. But, no, she needed to follow through with it. Her budding movie career was at stake.

Thomas leaned in to kiss Katya's merlot colored lips, but she pulled back before he could mar her perfectly applied make-up.

"Come on," she said, her hand on his chest to keep him at bay. "Go get dressed. Jacket and tie required."

Thomas sighed, irritated with the change in plans. He supposed the logistics of where they ate mattered little; seduction would still take place afterward. He kissed her cheek, careful not to smudge the artwork, and then crossed the foyer to the sweeping curved staircase that led to the second floor.

Katya watched him leave with a pang of remorse. He was so handsome, so in control. It had taken every ounce of her willpower not shed her dress right there in the foyer and demand he please her. But there would be time enough for that after dinner. That is, if he wasn't too freaked out by what was about to happen.

Katya looked at her tiny platinum watch inlaid with diamonds and tapped her expensive red shoe impatiently. They had to be at the restaurant by seven so that by seven-forty-five they were in the middle of enjoying their dinner. They had to look settled and cozily romantic. Maybe they should feed one another. Steal a few kisses. Katya would keep one hand possessively on Thomas' knee throughout the evening. What else did couples in love do? Katya thought about some of the idiotic chick flicks she'd seen. They always seemed to be showing lovers staring deeply into one another's eyes, each listening intently to what the other was saying. She could certainly fake an interest in whatever Thomas wanted to talk about. After all, she was an actress now and could surely act the part of a smitten, doting girlfriend.

The problem was... in her own enigmatic way, she really did like Thomas. She didn't love him of course, but the strong attraction they shared meant a great deal to her. Katya hoped she wouldn't lose him over this. She wavered slightly at the thought of possible consequences, but she raised her chin and steeled herself for what was going to launch her into unmitigated stardom. She'd already made the deal, and tonight was the beginning of Thomas' return to the spotlight.

At eight p.m. the paparazzi would arrive at Jacopo's. They'd already been tipped off by an anonymous source that famous author Thomas McQuillan would be there with his long-time girlfriend, supermodel-turned-actress, Katya Vetrov. They were also informed that the couple was contemplating marriage, but Thomas was first putting the finishing touches on his new manuscript, which was slated for publication in September.

Katya was so consumed with her thoughts about the evening that she didn't notice Thomas descend the staircase looking like he had stepped out of a bad boy version of GQ. His vinyl grey, custom-fit Ermenegildo Zegna suit was tailored precisely to his exact measurements and both the design and cut of the material showed off his trim, muscular physique. He wore a white dress shirt and a deep ebony tie and his sandy shoulder-length hair was tamed, parted down the middle and tucked seductively behind his ears.

As he strode confidently across the entryway to where Katya stood, he adjusted the cufflinks at his wrists and said, his voice enticingly deep, "I'm ready."

Katya turned and lost her breath for a moment as she took in the debonair and suave man in front of her. She reached out and ran her hand over the stubble along his cheek and chin, loving the feel of his rough five o'clock shadow. Thomas clenched his jaw at her touch and she saw the spark of desire imbue his hazel eyes.

"You look positively sinful," Katya said appreciatively. "Like a sophisticated rebel."

Thomas looked at her so intently that his gaze was almost tangible. "Let's stay here. Come upstairs with me." He reached for the cocktails still sitting on the driftwood table.

Before Katya could respond, Helga came bustling into the foyer. "You eat dinner now, yah?" She stopped when she saw how elegant they both looked. "Underbara!" she exclaimed, clapping her chubby hands together. "Beautiful!" With maternal affection, she reached out and straightened Thomas' tie and patted down his jacket collar, neither of which required her ministrations, but brought comfort to her motherly soul. Katya rolled her eyes in annoyance.

Barking sounded from the back of the house and Helga turned and yelled, "Volpee! Quiet, stygg pojke! Helga come back soon!" In a normal voice she said to Thomas, "I have kept him locked in da kitchen vith me so he would not bother you fer your dinner date."

"We're going out," Katya said, waving a slender hand dismissively.

Helga's face fell. "I did not need to cook?"

Thomas put a hand on Helga's shoulder. "Our plans changed last minute, but I promise I will eat your delicious supper tomorrow. I appreciate the time you spent making the meal," he smiled charmingly, "but I appreciate your keeping Voltaire away from me all afternoon even more."

Helga nodded. "Okay, Thomas, okay. I clean up da dinner and haf it fer you tomorrow. You haf a good time tonight. I take care of Volpee."

"Thank you, Helga. And, listen, I got an email earlier from Mary Crossfield, the pet nanny. She's coming over tomorrow morning to meet Voltaire. She'll be able to keep him out of your hair for quite a bit of the daytime from now on."

"Oh, thank you, Lord baby Jesus!" Helga exclaimed, clasping her hands together and looking up at the ceiling in rapture. "Ohhhh... dis is such good news!"

Katya's cat-like eyes narrowed. "*Who* is Mary Crossfield?"

"The pet nanny," Thomas repeated.

"Why didn't I know about this?" Katya asked imperiously.

Thomas stared at her, puzzled. "Why would you care, Kat?"

"What's that supposed to mean?"

"Do you like Voltaire? Do you reside here with us? Do you have any say in my life, my business or my daily habits?"

Helga made a weird sound that sounded like a snort, then quickly looked down at her white-laced nurse's shoes.

Katya pouted. "That was uncalled for."

Thomas sighed, his insides twisting. Ever since he'd received Mary's acceptance letter, he'd been filled with trepidation. He obviously couldn't turn her down after having done everything in his power to convince her to work for him. He told himself that the similarities between Mary and Gemma were due to his overactive, bloated imagination. Yes, he would always miss Gemma, but that needn't seep into other areas of his life. Besides, he probably wouldn't see much of Mary anyway. She would be watching Voltaire in another part of the house while he, peacefully, and without interruption, worked on his novel. Oh, his novel. The one that was barely off the ground because every time he wrote a few pages, he wound up deleting them from his hard drive. Just the thought of his unfinished work left him angry. But that didn't mean he had call to take any of it out on Katya.

"I'm sorry," Thomas said, taking her hand. "We can talk more about it over dinner."

"She isn't going to board with Helga, is she?" Katya asked irritably.

"No, no. She has her own home. She'll only be at the estate six hours a day while I'm writing."

"I see," Katya replied, but she looked anything but understanding.

"Good, because I don't have da room in my quarters," Helga put in. "My space has many t'ings from my home country in it."

"Lots of candy dishes filled with Swedish fish?" Katya smirked.

"Stop being such a bitch," Thomas said. "What is it with you?"

"We're going to be late for our reservations," Katya said impatiently, ignoring the rebuke.

Thomas turned to his housekeeper. "Helga, I'd like you to be in my study at nine tomorrow morning when I meet with Mary. After that, if you could show her around the place and make sure she knows where Voltaire's food, water, leash and toys are kept, I'd appreciate it. I told her to make full use of the pool, the game room and the theatre. You might also want to show her how the fireplace works. Make sure she knows where on the grounds Voltaire is allowed to roam."

"Of course. Helga vill be d'ere and I meet Mary Crossfield."

Thomas smiled. "And let's hope Voltaire is on his best behavior."

Helga laughed. "Volpee does not haf any good behavior."

"We need to go," Katya broke in, restlessly inching toward the massive front door.

"See you in the morning, Helga." Thomas said, turning and placing his arm around Katya's waist.

"In da morning. Good night."

As Thomas led Katya across his columned portico and down the wide stone steps to where her limousine idled patiently, he suddenly remembered he couldn't avoid Mary Crossfield. He had promised to be her writing coach – it was part of their agreement. How had he let that conveniently slip from his mind? He imagined the two of them, heads bent over whatever she was working on, discussing the beauty of language and the art of weaving words together to create imagery. He thought of teaching her how to tap into her deepest, darkest secrets so that she could feel their raw power and unleash them on a page destined to evoke emotion from her readers. He contemplated the depth of her compassion and wondered if she was as pure as she seemed. With a start, he knew he wanted to find out- and that realization was disquieting. He wanted to get to know Mary better, to discover what made her tick, perhaps see if she and Gemma really were alike. Thomas groaned inwardly, for his musings screamed intimacy in its highest form outside of the physical. Literary pursuits were always poignant and touching, and sharing those feelings with another person in such close proximity would certainly cause emotional friction. Especially when one of the persons was adorably innocent and feminine.

What had he done?

Katya curled up beside him as the limo wound its way through the dark streets of Rancho Santa Fe. She purred into his ear, "You will please me after dinner, Thomas, yes?" She pulled on his tie seductively and licked his bottom lip, careful not to smear her lipstick.

Roughly, he pushed her away. "Yes, Kat, I will please you. But you must please me first."

She adjusted her dress. "Whatever you want."

They rode the rest of the way to Jacopo's in silence, each lost in their own thoughts. As they stepped out of the limo and made their way into the fancy restaurant, Katya felt elated. Tonight she would be on every celebrity news site from Perez Hilton to TMZ.

And so would Thomas McQuillan.

CHAPTER 34

⁓

*M*itch awoke with a start, his fist clenching and unclenching the navy blue sheet covering his naked body. His eyes opened slowly, waiting for the pleasure of seeing Bertie next to him, her gorgeous figure in peaceful repose. As his vision cleared, his smile disappeared, for what he now thought of as "her" side of the bed contained no "her." For a moment, Mitch felt a weight press upon his chest like an anvil had set up squatter's rights on top of his heart. Bertie was gone; he now remembered this, and the knowledge dragged his normally cheerful disposition down a dark tunnel of dysphoria.

Mitch shook his head impatiently. This wasn't like him. Normally he awoke with tranquility and a zest for life, not this unfamiliar, unwelcome melancholy. He had spent nearly every day, and every night, with Bertie since their first date, and in that short, brilliant, exquisite time she had become a part of him. Mitch ached for Bertie constantly, wanted her by his side at all times. He loved her laughter, her witty banter, her intelligent remarks, her graciousness, the funny, but caring way she talked about her quirky authors… and, he realized now, her absence left a hole in his existence. He lay there thinking about all of the seductive ways she touched him with her hands, her mouth, her body. He'd never experienced such a highly physical connection with a woman before. Whenever he held her tightly, passion pounding through his veins, it was as natural as if they'd been making love together their whole lives, yet each time was as exhilarating as if it had been the very first.

Mitch had no doubt of the magic he shared with Bertie, for he had been enjoying the company of the opposite sex for years and *never* had one made him feel like this. Women had always been receptive to Mitch and were curiously fascinated with discussing, experiencing and indulging in new and fun explicit escapades with him. Complacency wasn't even a part of Mitch's vocabulary. Not since his university days, when he and Dale had overheard a man at The Boozy Turkey bemoaning the fact that his girlfriend had broken up with him. The man poured out his heart to the bartender, and anyone within unfortunate hearing distance, that "Tina Jo" had told him: "The first time you boinked me we were in bed for six hours! SIX HOURS, YOU SON OF A BITCH! What the hell happened?! After you figured out what gets my engine revved you did the SAME DAMN THING EVERY TIME. *EVERY TIME, DARYL*! Yeah, sure, you can crank my ignition switch and pop my chassis, but there's more than one way to insert and turn a freaking key! Sex with you the last few months is down to a half an hour and during that half an hour you do the SAME THING! THE SAME THING, *DARYL*!" And poor Daryl, after shouting this morose, yet eye-opening recap, had laid his head down on the bar and sobbed into his cocktail napkin. Mitch watched in sympathy while the man hiccupped in remorse and sniffled with inebriated indignation.

"Well," Dale had said, chugging his beer, "that was gross. Let's go play some pool."

As Mitch chalked the end of his cue stick, he thought about what the man at the bar had said. Tina Jo, it seemed, broke up with Daryl because the man had grown complacent in the bedroom. Maybe that extended to complacency in other areas of their relationship?

Mitch beat Dale at several games of eight-ball that night, his mind half on pocketing stripes and half on what females wanted from men. Mitch loved women and quite naturally wanted to please them and so he spent the next few weeks asking his female friends a lot of questions. To his surprise, they were happy and eager to talk about their views on romance. They seemed genuinely delighted to discuss not only their own version of an idyllic fairytale but also the feminine longings they held close and dear. Mitch was an excellent listener and he identified a common theme – women had an instinctual need for passion and infatuation. A woman wanted to feel appreciated and desired, to be able to flirt and play sexy. Romance somehow equaled newness and surprise; and it always, always required a man's absolute focus and attention.

Mitch put these new discoveries into practice when he began dating several of the sorority sisters at Kappa Delta Phi. The result was astonishing, for word spread amongst the female college population that the tall, muscular construction student was, in fact, a quixotic Romeo, and Mitch suddenly found himself in high demand. He was a loving young man and he never abused the attention lavished on him. He graciously valued each girl he was with respectfully, affectionately and without pretense. He'd always been a gentleman both in public and in private and that, despite his aversion to commitment, brought females into his circle near and far.

But of all the women Mitch had been with over the years, none had pulled at his heartstrings as Bertie did. When Mitch was with Bertie, he felt whole and totally alive. He felt as though his soul had found a home.

Shifting his naked body under the navy sheet, he stared at the empty side of the bed, wishing Bertie were there now. He longed to stroke her hair and tell her how beautiful she was. He wanted to watch her dark eyes light up and hear her husky voice moan his name... "Touch me like that again, Morrison. Yes. Right there. Don't stop. Oh, Mitch... Mitch..."

He groaned and rolled over on his back. A whole week. A whole week without Bertie. She had flown to Florida for a three-day writer's conference and by the time she returned to Arizona he would already be in San Diego. Although Mitch could not wait to see his daughter, and was very much looking forward to the time they would spend together, he knew part of him would be silently missing his Bertie.

Mitch flung back the sheet and stood up. Enough! He was not given to flights of fancy and, although Bertie was indeed a special woman, he had a very full life with much to do. There was no sense in wasting time moping about for a gorgeous woman. He sighed deeply. A gorgeous woman who had become an integral part of his life. Who was he kidding? He had fallen and he'd fallen *hard*.

He pulled on a pair of boxers and padded into the kitchen. A small screen TV sat companionably on the large island, and he switched it on and changed the channel to local news. He grabbed two coffee mugs, hesitated, and then testily put one back. That was a new domestic habit he'd developed rather quickly. Shaking his head, he poured himself a cup of coffee and was walking, mug in hand, through his living room, when the doorbell rang. He started toward the entryway when he realized he was only wearing boxers. "Just a minute!" he called and went to his bedroom to pull on a pair of shorts and the t-shirt he'd been wearing last night. It had Bertie's scent on it and his pulse quickened. The doorbell rang again and Mitch went back to the entryway and yanked the door open. A young man in his very late teens stood there with a clipboard.

"I have a delivery for Mitchell Morrison," the boy said. "That you?"

Mitch took the proffered clipboard and signed his name. "Yup."

The boy jerked his pen at a small trailer hooked to a large white truck behind him. "It's all in there. Okay, if I bring it inside, mister? Or do you want it on the porch?"

"Just set it in that corner of the living room." Mitch pointed at an alcove behind one of his leather couches.

"Nice house you got," the kid offered. Then he went down the porch steps and opened the back end of the trailer. Mitch craned his neck to look inside and saw a few boxes and three large frames covered with cloth.

Helene's personal effects had arrived.

CHAPTER 35

⟋⟍

"*I* heard a new joke," Francesca said, rubbing her hands together in glee as she and Georgette slowly drove down Pima Street in the tiny desert town of Gila Bend. "A naked priest, a Klingon and a wombat walk into an Australian prison…"

"NO!" Georgette said firmly, gripping the steering wheel of her Mercedes tightly. "I've heard you tell that one before and I don't care to hear it again."

"When did you hear it?"

"At the Granger's party a few weeks ago. You told it after doing five shots of tequila, remember?"

Francesca looked thoughtful. "Actually, no."

"Well, you were quite drunk. I'm not surprised."

"The Granger's throw bitchin' parties," Francesca said, pulling a bejeweled hand mirror from her huge, bottomless purse and examining her reflection. "I'm thinking about getting part of my head shaved before their next one." She tugged the hair above her right ear back. "What do you think?"

Georgette sighed. "Francesca, you are eighty-one years old…"

"Good lord, you're right! I'd better do it quick before I'm dead."

Georgette rolled her eyes and turned on to the Interstate 8 ramp.

"I can't wait to get to San Diego," Francesca said excitedly.

"How did you know? This was supposed to be a surprise trip!"

"I hacked into your email. Saw the reservation for the Hotel Del."

"Francesca Maria Benedetta Fogagnolo!!!"

Francesca shrugged. "What?"

Georgette's cell phone rang, diverting her from further exasperation. She smiled when she saw it was Mitch.

"Hey, sis. Sounds like you're driving. Do you want to call me back?"

"No, it's fine. We're on the boring stretch now between Gila Bend and Dateland."

"Dateland? Are you heading to San Diego?"

"Yes, just for a weekend getaway."

"So you'll be there while I'm with Mary? That's great! Can we get together?"

"That's what I was hoping for. And, listen, Mitch, I'm really sorry about the other day. You were right- I overstepped my boundaries. I do treat you like a child sometimes when it comes to Mary."

"I'm sorry too. That's actually part of the reason I'm calling. I wanted to apologize for hanging up on you. I lost my temper."

"No worries. How is Bertie?"

Mitch grunted in displeasure. "Out of town."

"You poor thing. You sound a bit miserable."

"I miss her. I miss her face and her laugh and I miss holding her…"

Georgette smiled. "This one is different, Mitchell."

"So it seems."

"Have you finally met your match?"

"Is there such a thing?"

Georgette looked lovingly over at Francesca. "Yes. Yes, there is."

Mitch paused for a moment and then, "Helene's things are here, George."

"Oh, my dear boy."

"There's a journal. She only wrote in it once a month, sometimes once a year, but it goes all the way back to her childhood."

"Did you… have you… been reading it?"

"Yes." Mitch cleared his throat. "Did you know she was planning her wedding after she found out she was pregnant with Mary?"

"What?"

"She had a dress and everything."

"She never said anything…"

"Nor to me."

"But I didn't know things were that serious…"

"Apparently they were to her."

"That poor girl."

"I should have been better to her, George. I should have…"

"Regret does not serve us, Mitchell. You were very good to Helene when she brought Mary to you. The circumstances were… not ideal. There's no blame to be handed out and you certainly have no business assigning any guilt to yourself. And in the end, Mary could not have been blessed with a better father."

Mitch was quiet for a moment. "Thanks for that, George. Means a lot."

"Did Helene… did she say in the journal before… why she…"

"Why she ended her life?"

"Yes." Georgette could feel tears prick her eyes.

Mitch's voice cracked. "Her last entry was two weeks ago. All it said was that after three decades she just couldn't bear to live with a broken heart anymore."

CHAPTER 36

*O*wen opened the front door and hugged his rigid, well-dressed mother. They embraced awkwardly; affection had never been Ellen Crossfield's strong suit.

"Darling," she said, patting him stiffly on the back.

Owen watched a sleek, black car pull away from the curb. "I'm glad you had a safe trip." He forced his voice to sound casual. "How long are you staying?"

She waved an elegant, bejeweled hand. "Oh, just until Sunday."

"The day after I ship out."

"Yes. So can I come in? You're not going to make me stand out here all night, are you?"

Owen moved back. "Of course. I'm sorry. I'm still… surprised that you're, uh… here in San Diego."

"Well, I thought it might be a good idea for me to have a talk with Mary in person. She and I will have a nice little *tete-a-tete*, woman to woman, about her future as a mother. I love giving advice and I'm very good at it. And I imagine she'll appreciate any input I have since she doesn't have a mother of her own."

Owen shut his eyes in dread and closed the door as Ellen stepped over the threshold and into the entryway.

Roger trotted cheerfully down the hallway to greet the visitor, but he halted in his tracks when he saw Ellen Crossfield. She tried to smile at the dopey dog, but her face didn't look natural. Roger let out a low growl and then turned and walked away.

"Do you know," Ellen said to her son, "that there is a woman prowling around your neighborhood? I saw her a few streets down. I think you should call the authorities."

"Was she old and wrinkly? Hiding in foliage?"

"Why, yes!"

"That's just Imogen, head of our HOA. She's a bit nosy, but she's harmless. Didn't you see her last time you were here?

Ellen thought for a moment. "I don't remember anyone so unattractive. I honestly thought she was a huge bat."

Owen laughed. "Why don't you make yourself comfortable in the living room, Mother. Would you like hot tea?"

"Please. And where is Mary?"

"Upstairs changing out of her work clothes."

Ellen sniffed. "Oh, yes, the animal business."

"Listen, Mom, I don't know how much time Mary will be able to give you this weekend. She's got a new client coming on board tomorrow and her father is flying in for a few days."

Ellen's eyes lit up and a coquettish lilt crept into her cultured voice. "Mitch will be here?"

Ew.

"I'll be right back," Owen said, escaping the room in search of hot tea... and his wife.

Mary was on the phone in her bedroom when she heard the doorbell ring. She inwardly groaned. Owen's mother had arrived.

On the other end of the line, Faith chirped away about their plans during Mitch's visit.

"Yes, sure, Dad and I can hang out tomorrow night." Mary said, her voice dropping as she listened for sounds downstairs. "Aunt George and

Aunt Franny are coming too. Yes, they're in town, they're staying at the Del. Yes, it's great. Yes, Owen leaves around noontime." There was a pause. "No, I haven't spoken with Lei in the past few days. I think she's pretty busy at work." Another pause. "She isn't going to New York any time soon, Fay. That Margaret lady is still there. I know… I know… I can't bear to think of her leaving either…, Oh Faith! Why are you crying? Are you okay? No, no… don't worry, Lei isn't moving away yet…" Mary turned around and saw Owen standing in their bedroom doorway. "Listen, Faith, I have to go. Are you sure you're all right?"

Owen strode forward and sat on the edge of their bed.

"Ok, Fay. I love you too. See you tomorrow."

"Going out with the girls?" Owen asked as Mary hung up the phone.

"Yes. They always worry about me when you're gone."

"Don't want you to be alone on the first day?"

"Well, I won't be- Daddy will be here and…" Mary cautiously ventured, "your mother is here…"

"She goes home in two days."

Mary couldn't conceal her relief. "Really? Oh good, that's not too long. Did she say why she's here? I mean, was there a reason for her coming out unexpected? And by herself?"

Owen wiggled his eyebrows. "Maybe she's hoping she has a chance with your dad."

Mary giggled. "That's so gross!"

"Actually… there is a reason. And I hate to tell you but you need to be prepared."

"Okay…"

"She wants to talk with you about being a mom. I imagine it will be about how she thinks you should act as the mother of a Crossfield progeny."

Mary plopped down next to her husband. "Owen…"

He put his arm around her. "I am so sorry. I think you just have to take whatever she says with a grain of salt. Don't let her get to you."

Mary sighed. "Did she ask why I'm not pregnant yet?"

"No." Owen took a deep breath. "But I'm sure that will come up. Especially since she's paying for fertility testing and treatments."

Mary pulled away and stood up. "I don't want to talk about any of this. Particularly with her."

"I know." Owen held his head in his hands.

"And Daddy is going to be here and I don't want her around. I have been looking forward to spending time with him…"

"I know," Owen said again, his voice miserable. "I'm so sorry, Mare."

Mary pulled off her running shorts and her sweatshirt and kicked off her sneakers. "I have a busy day tomorrow what with meeting my new Frenchie client in the morning and then you leaving in the afternoon and going out with the girls and Daddy in the evening. Maybe Ellen and I can talk on Sunday before she leaves. I will give her no more than two hours."

Owen looked up, his blue eyes troubled. "I'm sure she'll understand. She can't expect you to be available on a moment's notice."

Mary stared at her husband. He looked so tortured, and not just about his mother, though she was certainly reason enough. Maybe this training mission was going to be very complex and strenuous. She walked over to him only wearing her sports bra and underwear. Owen watched her move across the room and for a moment she thought she saw his eyes dampen.

When she was close he put his hands on her hips and looked up at her earnestly, his voice shaking. "You are the most beautiful woman in the world. Never forget that. Never forget how much I love you. You have made me so happy, Mary. So happy." And then he pulled her to him until his head rested on her stomach. She held him there, stroking his back with warm, soothing hands. His arms went around her waist and Mary nostalgically flashed back to the night Owen proposed. She'd held him this exact same way after she said yes. Back then, she had felt excitement and happiness and afterward they had made love – slow and sweet – in anticipation of their new life together.

Owen seemed to be having the same memory for he pulled back and looked at Mary with so much love in his face that she gasped softly.

"Please," Owen begged, "please let me make love to you right here and right now. Not for any other reason than because I want to give you pleasure. Please Mary, please…" He stood and pressed his lips to his wife's. Not hurriedly or in an obligatory way, there was nothing in his kiss that was urgent or demanding this time. His hands roamed down over Mary's body while his lips seductively captured hers over and over in a mesmerizing cadence of sensuality and exploration.

Mary's arms involuntarily went around Owen's neck and she responded to his kisses without thinking. Lost in a time warp between past and present, she realized the Owen who was loving her right now was the Owen she had married. This wasn't Owen the pilot or Owen the wannabe father. This was the Owen that loved and adored her. Before she could tell herself to harden her heart, Owen picked her up and placed her gently on the bed. "Be right back," he said and went to their bedroom door. "Mom," he called out loudly, "I have an urgent call from AirSec I have to take. I'll be downstairs in a bit." Owen shut and locked the door and began removing his clothing as he walked toward where his wife lay, her eyes heavy with desire, her honey hair spread out around her. When he was completely naked, he saw Mary suck in her breath as she looked down at his physical longing. She began to writhe on the bed in anticipation.

Owen bent over her, slowly removing her underthings and dropping them on the floor. "I want you, Marion Grace Crossfield. I've always wanted you. You and only you…"

For the next half an hour the couple found themselves drowning in the passion of their love. They kissed and touched and laughed and moaned and sighed in fervid pleasure. Owen caressed Mary as if it were the last time he'd ever stroke her silky skin. He pressed her against him as though memorizing inch by perceptible inch how their bodies fit and molded together. He watched her climaxes as though permanently etching every expression and every sound in his mind. And later, when they lay still and satiated, the silence almost palpable, Owen said with gravid feeling, "Thank you for loving me."

Mary turned to her husband, her eyes full of tears. "I've missed you so much. Now that you're back, you're leaving tomorrow."

With a groan of despair, Owen took his wife in his arms and held her as if he never wanted to let her go.

Ellen Crossfield looked at her expensive watch and tapped her Manolo Blahnik heel. Owen had been on his phone call for almost forty-five minutes. She did so hope he would come back downstairs soon. It was a colossal waste of time to just sit in someone's living room.

She started to get up, but Owen's big black drooling Boxer came over and sat in front of her, blocking her path.

Ellen nudged at Roger with the toe of her shoe. "Move along, dog."

Roger didn't bat an eyelash.

"Move!" And Ellen poked her pointy heel right into Roger's rear end. Roger responded by letting loose with a loud, juicy fart.

"Oh!" said Ellen, covering her nose. "Oh! OH! You disgusting animal! What do they *feed* you?" She began pawing frantically through her purse. She pulled out a dainty handkerchief and held it to her mouth.

Roger jumped up on the couch next to her and placed his big head in her lap.

"My Prada skirt!" Ellen screeched, shoving at Roger's face to no avail. "You uncivilized beast!"

After a few minutes of struggle, Ellen gave up. Roger had fallen asleep on her legs. She looked around in despair and her eyes fell on a television remote control just within reach on the coffee table. Straining, she leaned forward, her fingertips grazing the black device. After several tries she was finally able to retrieve it and she turned on the television. There was nothing really on, nothing worth her time anyway. A few reruns, some game shows, local news. She stopped on a celebrity gossip program because they were talking about the latest fashion trend for women in their thirties. Ellen was of the belief that as long as one was conservatively fashionable, one need not dress one's age.

A parade of beautiful actresses, all under forty, filled the screen and Ellen settled back and lost herself in one of her favorite pastimes-critiquing other women. Good heavens, some of them had no clue how to dress! Didn't these celebrities pay people to attire them tastefully? And some of the make-up trends! Was looking like a painted harlot with shimmer highlights all the rage right now? What were these women thinking?

The show switched over to rough video footage of a restaurant. Through a bay window, a couple could be seen eating together at a cozy table and the woman, beautifully attired in a red (was it Halston?) dress had her hand on the man's knee while they chatted animatedly. The man had longish sandy hair and rough stubble on his handsome face. Ellen leaned in a bit… she knew those two people, but from where? The woman was a model, surely, for she had that boyishly svelte body that was so popular on the runways. And the man… he was clearly some sort of wealthy surfer. His suit was perfectly tailored. Ellen squinted. She was positive it was an Ermenegildo Zegna.

A voiceover came on. "And we're now going live to Rancho Santa Fe, California. Have you been wondering what happened to Thomas McQuillan, bestselling author of *Souls in Collision?* Well, we have the exclusive scoop on his newest release as well as all the dirt on his hot and sexy romance with Russian supermodel, Katya. Stay tuned."

Owen kissed his wife's closed eyes, then her nose and then her plump, pliable lips. She stretched luxuriously against him and he ran his hands down the length of her supple body.

"I need to go downstairs," Owen said regretfully. "Stay up here if you like. The car will be back to pick Mom up in an hour. And then after she leaves…"

Mary smiled lazily. "It would be rude for me not to come down and at least say hi…"

"You look like a fallen angel," Owen said, tracing the flush of her skin. He kissed her thoroughly, leaving her head spinning, her mind a glorious kaleidoscope of colorful prisms. "I'll be back in an hour."

"Okay."

"Why don't you sleep for a bit? I'll wake you up when I come back." His tone became both serious and sad. "I can't… I don't… Mary… I just want to hold you all night…"

"Owen, what's wrong? You're acting so different. You… are you nervous about this mission tomorrow?"

At the mention of the mission something seemed to snap within Owen. He disentangled himself from Mary and left the bed. "No. Of course not. Why would you say that? It's just a training exercise." His blue eyes took on the familiar hardness she had grown accustomed to. Owen the pilot was back at the controls.

Mary, confused at the sudden change, sat up. "I'll get dressed and then come downstairs to say hello to Ellen. I need to be polite."

Owen shrugged. "I can just tell her you're not feeling well." He pulled on his clothes and then stared at his wife for a moment, all traces of vulnerability gone. When her eyes filled with tears, he turned quickly away, walked to the bedroom door and shut it behind him.

Mary watched her husband leave and she felt something deep inside splinter. She couldn't do this anymore. She didn't want to. She dressed slowly, taking her time, methodically putting clothes on as though each movement was somehow bringing her closer to resolve. She was glad Owen would be gone tomorrow. And maybe, just maybe, when he returned, she wouldn't be there waiting.

CHAPTER 37

22 February 1986

The weather is most gorgeous here in Arizona; very mild and sunny, perfect for picnics or hiking large dirty hills that the locals think of as mountains. I'm only staying in the desert for a few more days and then I'll hitch a ride to Los Angeles. One of the other artists staying at the hostel I'm rooming in might give me a ride, which would be perfect. I've saved for so long for this trip and I'm trying to make every penny count.

Anyway, the reason for this entry is that I just met the most intriguing man while I was at a tiny coffee shop in Tempe.

I was sitting at a corner table desperately missing everyone back home and trying not to cry into my une noisette (the espresso was adequate, but not like I'm used to), when a very handsome man walked in. I couldn't help but notice him because there was something striking about the way he moved that drew my artistic eye. I forgot all about feeling lonely and wondered if I were to paint this man, what colors would I use to represent his distinctive look? While I was scrutinizing his demeanor (and thinking I'd probably combine purple and yellow to portray the lines of his confident bearing), he seemed to sense my staring and turned to look at me.

I was completely knocked off guard by his eyes because they were the most compelling and unusual color I've ever seen! Not brown, not copper or golden... I would describe them as translucent resin- the deepest of ambers. If for no other reason (and believe me, there were plenty) than the desire to try and recreate that color on canvas, I stood up and approached him. I couldn't help myself. I don't know what got into me. I was completely drawn to him.

I started babbling- telling him my name is Helene and that I am traveling on an art sabbatical and that I live in Paris with my family whom I'm missing deeply. I said that my trip has been very rewarding because I've seen many works of art across America that have been inspiring. And I told him after I leave The States I will be going to Italy for a few weeks.

He watched me as I talked, his eyes never leaving my face, and I started to blush at how forward I was being. He didn't seem to notice and appeared interested in everything I had to say and after he ordered his coffee, we sat at my table and talked for almost an hour.

We chatted back and forth like best friends who hadn't seen one another in months. He told me about his life growing up in Phoenix with his parents and his twin brother and his older sister. His family all sound very nice. He asked about my paintings, my travels, my hopes and dreams. He was so attentive and caring that I nearly threw myself into his arms, but instead I excused myself to the ladies' room and gave myself a stern talking to.

Mirrors don't lie, and my reflection wasn't exactly complimentary. My long light brown hair was wavy and tousled and caught up in a pretty blue scarf I'd seen at a street festival back home. I hadn't any makeup on as usual and my outfit - mon dieu! The flowy skirt and peasant top were comfortable but hopelessly out of fashion.

"Helene," I scolded into the mirror, "don't act like a fool. That man is not interested in you – he is just being kind because you are lonely." But even as I said the words, I knew they weren't true. The man at the table was interested in me, I could see it in those incredible eyes. Maybe he likes French women who look like artsy, unconventional bohemians? Or perhaps it had something to do with what Jacques had

said to me right before we broke up: "Helene, your beauty is raw and real and it turns conquering macho men into desperate boys begging for approval. But the sexiest part is- you have no idea how exquisitely tempting you are."

Even now, thinking of that makes me blush. Jacques could be so dramatic. I'm glad we ended our romance but were able to stay friends. Whatever it was that he was talking about, whatever it is that causes men to approach me (and Jacques to break up with me out of jealousy), I suppose it was the reason I'd had such a lovely time at the coffee shop with... you know, he never did tell me his name.

He asked me out when I got back to our table from the ladies' room and of course I said yes. I felt just as attracted to him as he was to me. We are meeting tonight for a late dinner. He said he's taking me somewhere that serves spicy, southwest food so that I can try the true culinary flavors of Arizona.

I'm so excited to see him again. But I leave for Los Angeles in two weeks so I will NOT get attached. If anything happens past dinner it will only be a fling. A fun and casual fling with a handsome American.

Thank heavens Papa taught me English when I was a little girl.

"I miss you so much, Collins," Mitch moaned into his cell phone. He was standing by his gate at Sky Harbor Airport, waiting for his plane to begin boarding. All around him, fellow travelers were bustling about grabbing coffees and making last-minute phone calls or trips to the restroom.

"I miss you too, Morrison," Bertie said, her southern accent husky with feeling.

"I'm sorry to bother you while you're at the conference. I just needed to hear your -"

"Actually, I'm on a fifteen-minute break so this is perfect timing."

Mitch ran a large hand over his face. The sound of Bertie's voice caused all manner of sensual memories to surface. He forced his mind to stay present. "How's it going there?"

"Great. I've made some good contacts." She paused. "The evenings are pretty lonely though…"

"I'm glad to hear that. Hate to think of you spending your nights with some whimsical poet or tragic novelist."

Bertie laughed. "No chance. After you, Morrison, every other man pales in comparison."

Mitch's voice deepened, "I can't wait to hold you again."

"Three more days. And after that I blocked off my schedule until the following Sunday. I won't leave your side until you head for Flagstaff."

"God, I love you."

There was a long, profound silence. Other than his family, Mitch had never said those words to a woman before, yet they'd just slipped out as naturally as if he'd been saying them to Roberta Collins his whole life. Of course Mitch loved- his mother, Georgette and Mary – and had told them so often - but a woman he'd dated? No way. He'd never come close to loving any of the females he'd been with. Sure, he'd been captivated by some of them, enamored with a few, definitely in lust with more than he could count, but *in love*? Absolutely not. Mitch gripped the phone tighter. It was true. He loved the woman at the other end of the line. So very, very much.

Bertie was silent.

As they each sat clutching their cell phones on opposite sides of the country, neither uttered a sound. It was as if time hung suspended, the world swinging on a pendulum of an uncertain certainty. And then, quietly, Bertie softly whispered, "I love you too."

7 March 1986

I'm in love. I know I'm in love because I can't stop thinking about him. I want to be with him all the time and when we're apart my stomach gets all tied up in knots and it's hard to breathe.

I know I've only known him for less than two weeks, but there's something mystical between us. Something... I haven't felt like this before. I've never wanted a man so badly. And not just sexually. I love the way his American accent sounds and I love what he talks about. Everything he says is fascinating. And he's strong and confident and so very compassionate. I know... I sound like an awful, lovesick teenager. I hate to even write such romantic drivel, but I can't help how I feel, and besides, this is my private journal- it's not like anyone is ever going to read this.

But he's not perfect- I know that, even though I'm totally infatuated. We had a little tiff a few days ago and I'd gone into a full-blown temper and I was so mad that I couldn't speak English and yelled at him in French. He stared at me as though I was crazy and when I finished he said, "That was the sexiest thing I've ever seen. I kind of like it when you're angry. Scream at me some more."

And I said tartly, "C'estinacceptable, monsieur! You are a bad boy!"

He came at me so fast I had no time to think. He picked me up in his arms and sat on a chair, placing me in his lap. Slowly, carefully, he undid the yellow silk I had my hair tied up in and he ran his fingers through my hair over and over until I calmed down. He said, "I'm sorry. I'm sorry for upsetting you." I started to speak again, my temper growing hot at the thought of his earlier words, but when I opened my mouth, he covered it with his own and I forgot all about being mad. He kissed me for so long I became dizzy and then he pulled my blouse over my head and buried his face between my breasts (I still haven't been able to get myself to wear brassieres every day like the American women do). We made love together right on that chair and it was the sweetest moment of my life.

The thing he'd said that had upset me so badly was that he would never settle down. He wasn't cut out to be a "one-woman man." I told him that was stupid and the most ridiculous thing I'd ever heard. He chuckled and told me he was allowed to have opinions about his own life. It was then that I realized he was telling me that whatever was happening between us was not going to end in permanency. Oh, the unfairness! I'd told myself the day I met him that this would just be a fling, but... that was before I realized how much I would feel for him. I want to give him my heart but clearly he doesn't want it.

What we share is transient for him.

But, for me, it's forever. I know it is. I can feel it in my bones. Somehow we're connected on a spiritual level. I don't know how or why or what will come from it, but he and I, by design, have a purpose in this life. A beautiful, perfect purpose.

I leave for Los Angeles in two days and then I will never see him again. He is fine with that. I want to die.

In the meantime, he said we will make the most of the next forty-eight hours by spending every moment together. He has rented a small cabin two hours away in the cool of the faraway real mountains by Christopher Creek. Part of me thinks this is a bad idea because I know I will only grow closer to him and it will be harder to say goodbye. But the other part of me wants to grab every minute I can with both hands and to hell with the emotional ramifications. Besides, it's entirely possible that when I'm back in France, this time with him will only be a fond memory, a blip on the radar screen of my life and nothing more.

No. Be realistic, Helene. You know better; you can feel it in your soul.

Oh god, I'm so in love. So absolutely in love.

I can't wait to spend the next few days with him... laughing and chatting and making love over and over and over. I said earlier that I want to give him my heart, but that he doesn't want it. Well, I'm going to give it to him anyway.

And damn the consequences.

CHAPTER 38

⁓

"How did they know?" Thomas demanded of Katya as he paced back and forth before the stone fireplace in his bedroom. He yanked at his ebony tie and ripped it off, hurling it across the room.

Katya willed tears into her eyes, blinking rapidly. "I don't know! That was just so strange. I mean, we've never been trailed by paparazzi before."

"Not about us, Kat, about my book. How in the hell did they know I am writing another book?"

Katya contemplatively sat on a black oversized boudoir chair and shook her head in wonder, her perfectly made up eyes crinkled in confusion. "Well, it's been awhile since *Souls in Collision* came out. Maybe they just assumed…?"

Thomas spun on her. "No way. They had details. Don't you remember them asking what date in September it was going to be available to the public? Why would they have a particular month?"

Katya shook her head, bewildered. "So bizarre…"

"No one has paid any attention to me in several years. Why now? Why?! I've been so happy in my privacy; so glad to be left alone."

Katya removed her red stilettos and set them carefully next to the chair. "But are you really happy, Thomas? You haven't been able to write anything for so long. It's been, what, ten years? The manuscript you're working on now- the one you won't let me read- aren't you only two chapters in because you keep ripping up pages? Or deleting them, or whatever."

Enraged, Thomas yelled, "That is none of your goddamn business!"

Katya stood, her temper flaring. "Then make it my business! Why do you keep things from me? You've never let me in. I don't know what you're thinking or what you're doing or what you want." Her voice lowered acidly. "Except I know exactly what you want when it comes to pleasure, Thomas McQuillan. Because that's the only thing you share with me!"

"We're not a couple, Kat! You don't care about me. You've never cared about me. You like that I can show you a good time and that's it."

"That's not true!"

Thomas sighed. "Yes, it is. We're together for mutual satisfaction. When have you ever said, 'I care for you, Thomas' instead of 'Please me, Thomas'?"

Katya stared at him. "Do you want me to say I care for you?"

"No, of course not." Thomas ran a hand through his sandy hair and went to stand at the huge picture window looking out over his property. In the far distance he could see the twinkling lights of Encinitas. "We're together because we get along, because we're both private people and because we have this crazy physical attraction. But that's all."

Katya felt a strange stirring in the pit of her stomach. It hurt to hear him be so factually definitive about their relationship. She *did* care for him in her own way. Why couldn't he see that? It wasn't her fault she didn't know how to properly love a man. She'd never known much affection in her life. Her parents were cold and distant and she had eagerly left Russia at fifteen, doing anything and everything to work her way to America where she knew fame and fortune surely awaited a beautiful, unscrupulous girl. Men had swiveled in and out of her young life, men who used her and who she used in return. Thomas was the first man she had known who showed genuine kindness and character.

"I think that if I could love a man then I would love you, Thomas," Katya said awkwardly. Expressing real emotion was so much harder than faking it.

Thomas laughed, a mocking laugh, deep in his throat. He didn't even turn around. "Yeah, sure," he said sarcastically. "You'd trade your soul and mine to get what you want."

"No..." Katya came across the room. "I..."

Thomas did turn then. He grabbed Katya by the shoulders and shook her slightly. "What is it you aren't telling me? I know you've been keeping something from me. What is it, Kat?"

"I don't know what you're talking about..."

"Yes, you do!" Thomas released her and picked up a scotch decanter on the small whiskey rack by his big screen TV. "I was going to seduce you tonight. Get you drunk. Make you tell me..." He poured a liberal amount of Macallan into a glass tumbler and tossed it down his throat. "My writer's intuition is never wrong."

Katya's head began to pound; she had known this evening was going to be hard for Thomas, but, honestly, tonight's little publicity stunt hadn't done him any real harm. So the public was now expecting a book? So what? Maybe that would drive him, yes, motivate him, to finish his novel. She wondered if baiting him might galvanize him into action; make him see that what had happened was actually good for his career.

"Tell me," she said with cold provocation, "do you still have writer's intuition even though you can't write, and when you do write you say it's trash? Do you still have writer's intuition even though you haven't published anything in a decade? Don't true literary geniuses say writer's block is bullshit anyway?"

Thomas' hands shook as he poured himself another scotch. Rage filled him. "It was you," he said, his voice ominously low. "It was *you* who talked to the press, wasn't it? Get out of my house."

"Oh, don't be silly," Katya began, but her voice held a tremor of uncertainty.

"Who promised you what, Kat? Who did you whore yourself out to so that you could climb a rung on the ladder of exploitation?"

"I don't know what you're talking about..."

Thomas slammed the decanter down and turned to face her, his blood pumping hot. "Yes, you do! Don't lie to me! We've never lied to each other! In five years, Kat, we've been nothing but honest. Brutally honest about what we want."

Katya closed the gap between them and clutched at his jacket lapels, forcing him to look into her eyes. "I want *you*, Thomas. I've always been honest about that."

"You want me for your own purposes." He pried her fingers from his suit and swallowed a mouthful of scotch.

"Why are you even with me then?" Katya yelled in frustration.

Thomas refilled his tumbler. He'd had plenty to drink at dinner and imbibing now was only making him more emotional. "Because I use you for my own pleasures just as you use me." He raised the glass to her in a mock toast. "You get what you give, darlin'."

"Fuck you," said Katya.

"I believe I already asked you to leave. Get out, Kat."

"No. I'm not leaving without a proper goodbye." Katya played the only trump card in her deck. She didn't want to lose Thomas McQuillan. For more than one reason. She pulled her dress over her head and stood completely nude in front of him. Her breasts were so small that she rarely wore a bra and she hadn't even bothered with a thong since her dress was so tight.

Thomas' eyes raked down over the naked body of his lover and despite his anger he felt his own body begin to respond. The contradiction made him furious.

"Get out!" he shouted into Katya's face. "Get out! I never want to see you again!"

"But I want to see you again, Thomas," Katya purred, and in one slick movement she had his suit pants and boxers around his ankles.

She tilted her head to one side. "It looks like *you* have lied to *me*. Your body quite clearly wants to see me again even if you don't."

All the fight left Thomas and his shoulders drooped. What had his life become? Sure, he had money. Sure, he had success. But love had continued to elude him. Gemma was gone, out of reach; happily married and with a brood of children. And his first love, writing, seemed to be gone as well. Aside from his email to Mary Crossfield, he hadn't written a heartfelt sentence in ages. He was a failure at everything that mattered to him. A failure at love.

Katya's devious eyes swept over Thomas' face. He was very intoxicated. She'd have him eating out of the palm of her hand in an hour's time. Everything would be forgiven and forgotten tomorrow morning. All she had to do was comfort him the only way she knew how. Slowly, carefully, she unbuttoned Thomas' dress shirt and ran her hands over his chest. He sucked in his breath as she moved closer, letting her hips touch his. Gently, she flicked her tongue across his neck and then whispered, "Let me please you, Thomas. I want you to know how much I care for you..." she reached down and he gasped at the sensation of her cool fingers closing over him, holding him, stroking him.

Katya slipped the rest of Thomas' clothes off and then led him to his king-sized bed, which was elevated above the rest of the room on a dark wood dais. A large mirror on the wall behind it afforded Katya the distinct pleasure of seeing Thomas' athletic body from another angle. She always appreciated the view.

Caught somewhere between inebriation and anger, Thomas realized that what he really felt deep inside was loneliness. The thought startled him and he let his mind wander as Katya laid him back on his bed and began kissing her way down his chest. Of course, a writer's life was lonely, for one could only truly tap into creativity when one was in solitude. But outside of that, Thomas had his friends, his family... he hardly lived a life of isolation. But maybe what he was missing was a companion- someone who truly understood his soul. But he'd had that. And he'd let her go.

Katya's calculating lips moved past Thomas' stomach and she trailed her manipulative tongue further down, licking her way to making amends. Thomas groaned in response, his pelvis shifting. He felt for Katya's soft hair and placed his big hands on her head, arching his body for more contact. "Yes..." he murmured fervently, and Katya knew she had him right where she wanted him. He moaned again, "Yes, please..."

Katya shrewdly smiled to herself. He was begging.

Thomas let go of Katya and gripped the black bedspread beneath them, writhing and gasping as she pulled out every technique in her wanton bag of tricks. His mind was a snake pit of turmoil and lust, his body drowning in the waves of eroticism Katya cunningly plunged him into over and over, gently, harshly, methodically and then faster and faster... her lips, her tongue, her hands working together as one. He cried out, racked with spasms of release and then he lay quiet, spent, his fingers relaxing around the crumpled sections of the bedspread he'd been twisting.

Kissing her way up his torso, Katya laid her head on Thomas' chest contentedly. It was the first time she'd ever pleased him without demanding to be pleased herself; yet instead of feeling hollow and unsatisfied, she felt peaceful, elated at having given pleasure without expecting anything in return. Perhaps this was the start of learning how to care for Thomas McQuillan. She could learn. She could.

She pulled a soft throw over them from the foot of the bed, tucking it around Thomas and then she placed her hand on his stubbled cheek. "Go to sleep. I'll be right here when you wake up."

Thomas' lips were moving and Katya strained to catch what he was saying, longing to hear the sweet words of gratitude he was whispering for her. She knew no one could please Thomas McQuillan as she could. Her heart went cold just thinking about any other woman being with him. She mustn't screw this up. Somehow, some way, she needed to be able to hold on to him, not just because she needed his return to celebrity to help her career, but because she really did care for him.

Thomas' arms tightened around Katya and he mumbled gratefully, "That felt so good. Thank you... I'm sorry... I think I've had too much to drink... I'm so tired..."

"Shhhhh..." Katya said, kissing his neck.

"I love you," Thomas mumbled, half asleep.

In the shocking silence that followed Katya eventually whispered, "What did you just say?"

"I said I love you, Gemma... I'll never love anyone but you..."

His voice trailed off in a snore and Katya, for the first time in her adult life, began to cry.

CHAPTER 39

*M*ary drove her Jeep slowly through the tree lined streets of Rancho Santa Fe. The roads were narrow and impeccably cared for. There were no potholes or debris in this neighborhood of pristine, rolling terrain. Mary admired the countryside, the citrus and eucalyptus trees, the very expensive cars she passed. She drove by an opulent golf course, a tennis club, an equestrian center and multiple hiking trails winding their way up into the hills. She knew the area was affluent, but it was altogether different seeing the large gates and sweeping driveways in person. Most of the homes were hidden from view on large properties rife with privacy foliage. She was both nervous and excited to step foot on Thomas McQuillan's estate. She was also nervous and excited to see Thomas McQuillan himself.

The night before, when Mary had come downstairs to say hello to her mother-in-law, she had been shocked to see Thomas and a supermodel having dinner together on a celebrity television show. Aside from a quick greeting and a kiss on Ellen's cold cheek, Mary had been glued to the screen, drinking in every detail.

The model, a tall, thin, beautiful girl, sat cozily close to Thomas, and Mary instinctively knew the couple had been together for a long time. The way they made eye contact, shared laughter, touched…

Mary felt a hot sensation of jealousy burn through her when Katya leaned in and kissed Thomas on the cheek. Thomas had smiled but drew back slightly in surprise, as though that kiss was unusual, a gesture of kindness he wasn't used to. Katya's hand moved up from Thomas' knee onto his thigh and Mary saw him shift and give Katya a white-hot gaze of raw desire before returning to his dessert. The show announcer talked of Thomas' new, upcoming book, set to be released in September. Mary was surprised, for she remembered Thomas talking of writer's block and his struggles with having lost his muse when they were at The Marine Room. Had he somehow shed the cloak of despair shrouding his creativity? And, even if he had, was a few months enough time to publish his next work of art?

After several moments, Thomas and Katya had stood, their desserts finished. They walked casually out of the restaurant and reporters rushed them immediately. Katya was perfectly poised and polite, posing for pictures and answering all questions in a friendly, sanguine manner. Thomas, on the other hand, looked ready to lay flat anyone who got close to him and he gave no responses and no comments. His face was hard set in anger and his broody hazel eyes flashed in confounded hostility.

Mary heard the paparazzi ask Thomas about the book he was writing. They wanted to know what date in September it would hit store shelves and be available for download. Mary saw his face go white with rage and embarrassment and that's when he grabbed Katya's arm and shoved her toward the opened back door of their limousine. The interesting thing to Mary was that Katya didn't seem to mind the rough treatment at all. In fact, it looked like she quite enjoyed it, for she turned her cat-like eyes on Thomas and gave him a slow, sultry smile.

Mary wanted to cry. She wanted to be sick. She was so ashamed of the dreams she'd been having about Thomas- dreams that implied someone like Thomas would be interested in someone ordinary like her. Of course Thomas McQuillan would be with a breathtakingly gorgeous supermodel like Katya. Katya with her statuesque body poured into the skin-tight red dress she was wearing, her long magnificent legs slender and elegant, her hair and make-up professionally done. She had not one blemish, not one wrinkle and not one freckle anywhere to be seen. She moved with grace and confidence and she and Thomas looked well together; like they belonged together. Two perfectly chiseled people carved from the same majestic stone.

Mary made small talk with Ellen, even though her private, inner thoughts were flying all over the place. Mary must have said the right things because her mother-in-law seemed pleased with all of her responses. She knew she had agreed to see Ellen on Sunday morning for brunch, but that was the only part of their conversation she could remember.

Owen had barely said a word, his eyes still hard, his mouth set. Mary couldn't quite grasp how he had just made love to her with such sentiment, such devotion, less than an hour ago. He seemed almost angry with himself about what had transpired upstairs. He had kept his distance from Mary even after Ellen left.

They went to bed without speaking to one another but during the middle of the night, Mary had woken up when she heard Owen talking in his sleep. It sounded like he was saying, "My wife, my wife, my wife…" He muttered the refrain over and over and over until he began to shout it. Mary frantically called his name and drew him toward her.

"Wake up, Owen! Wake up! Owen! Owen, please!"

"My wife! MY WIFE! MARY! MARY!"

"Shhhhh… I'm right here. Shhhhh…"

Owen had finally woken up fully and he clung to Mary as though he couldn't bear to ever let her go. When her alarm went off in the morning she'd had to extricate herself from his arms and he'd moaned and rolled over, his hair in disarray, his body tense even in sleep. Something was definitely wrong, but what it was, Mary didn't have a clue. Why had he closed himself off to her? What was going through his mind?

She showered and dressed as quietly as possible, piling her light brown hair on top of her head in a messy bun and applying just a touch of lip gloss, and a few swipes of mascara to her long lashes.

Pulling her thoughts to the present, Mary turned down a long private street and idled the Jeep outside of an immense, locked gate. She saw a profusion of gorgeous tulips behind the iron bars on either side of the driveway. Someone had taken great care to plant and cultivate the exquisite flowers. She'd have to keep Voltaire away from those. A dog of his energy level would most likely plow through them like a bull in a china shop.

Mary pressed a large, green button on the keypad and a friendly voice said through the speaker, "Dis is Mary Crossfield, yes?"

"Yes," said Mary, butterflies in her stomach. She was so nervous!

"Helga buzz you t'rough."

The gate swung wide and Mary followed the gently curving driveway through Thomas' beautiful grounds. She looked around in pleasure, for the grass was a dazzling green- the kind you want to run through and throw yourself down in on a sunny day. A small brook ran along a rocky bank in the distance and Mary longed to go dip her toes in it, to listen to the sound of it burbling and babbling.

As Thomas' house came in to view Mary's eyes grew wide. Actually, *house* wasn't the right word. It was a stately manor of brown stone, three stories high, with ivy crawling its walls. Huge, friendly windows were flung open, welcoming and inviting. Mary stopped the Jeep under a columned portico and a plump woman in a white uniform hurried down the wide stone steps.

"I'm Helga," she said as soon as Mary climbed from the Jeep.

Mary smiled. "Pleased to meet you. Mary Crossfield."

Helga clapped her pudgy hands together in excitement. "Helga is so glad you're here, Mary Crossfield." And in a rush of gratitude she reached out and enveloped Mary in a warm and motherly hug. "You take care of Volpee for Helga vile Helga does her verk. Ohhhhh... I'm so happy you're here."

Mary's face was squashed into Helga's substantial bosom and it was hard to speak. She patted the housekeeper's back in acknowledgement and when Helga finally released her she said, "Thank you. I'm glad to be here."

"You meet Volpee later," Helga said hastily. "Ve don't vant to scare you off first t'ing." She laughed good-naturedly. "I kid, of course. Come vith me."

Mary followed Helga into the foyer and looked around with undisguised interest. Being in the home of a famous author she had admired for years was an overwhelming assault on her senses. She found herself trying to take everything in at once- the masculine décor, the neoteric architecture, the fresh clean smells, the cool ocean breezes blowing in through open windows... everything was exactly how she would have pictured it if someone had asked her to imagine what Thomas McQuillan's house looked like.

Mary trailed after Helga as they walked through the massive house, her eyes roaming over every wall, every piece of furniture, every knickknack and book until they arrived at a very large kitchen.

Helga pointed to a stool next to a gigantic island. "Sit. I bake pastry for breakfast. Dey almost done. I gif you one."

Mary was about to say no out of habit but then she remembered Owen was leaving today. He'd be away for a few months and she would be free. Free to eat whatever she wanted. Free to enjoy the foods she'd missed so much over the past several months. Free to let her waistline get a little bigger. Free to not have to worry about eating unhealthy in case it hurt the non-existent baby. Mary sniffed the air appreciatively, for the kitchen was redolent with the scrumptious aromas of made-from-scratch baking. Even if she gained a little weight over the next month or so she would have time to diet it off before Owen returned home.

"Yes," said Mary decidedly. "Yes, please, I would love a pastry."

"Oh! Helga is so happy! I make butterkaka for Mr. Thomas. You like da cinnamon, Mary Crossfield?"

"What is butterkaka?"

"It is a Svedish cinnamon bun cake with almond paste und vanilla custard."

Mary almost fell off her stool. "That sounds *so* good." She bit her lip in anticipation. "It's been just ages since I've had more than a few bites of any kind of pastry or dessert or, well, bread or sugar..."

Helga nodded sagely. "I know dis. I know dis because you are too skinny for your bones. You let Helga cook for you when you are here in da house and I fatten you up."

Mary laughed. "I don't think that's a good idea."

"V'hy?"

"Oh, my husband wouldn't like it."

Helga puffed her chest out and her face turned pink. "Well, if dat isn't da dumbest t'ing I ever heard! You listen to Helga, Mary Cross-field, you eat whatever da helvete you vant!" She patted Mary's hand vigorously for emphasis.

When the cinnamon buns came out of the oven their overpowering fragrance wafted over to Mary and her mouth began to water.

Helga waved a puffy royal blue potholder over the pan and said, "Dees just cool off fer a minute and den Helga serve you. I know dat you were supposed to meet vith Mr. Thomas dis morning first, but he is..." her voice trailed off uncertainly as she searched for the right words, "... he had a rough evening and vas not feeling so vell so Helga vill bring you up to his study a bit later."

"I understand." Mary thought about the furious look on Thomas' face when he stepped out of the restaurant last night. Was he inundated with calls from agents, directors and publishers anxious to profit from his return to the public eye? His fans would be coming out of the woodwork clamoring to buy his new release - surely he would be constantly peppered with requests for interviews and appearances. And he was dating the supermodel Katya- the media would be all over that as well, asking for every salacious detail about their relationship.

Helga put a large cake bun on a plate and set it in front of Mary along with a napkin, a silver fork and a chilled, frothy glass of milk.

"Please, eat with me," Mary said. "You can tell me about Voltaire while we enjoy your butterkaka."

Helga looked pleased. "Okay, I eat vith you, Mary Crossfield." She got another plate and sat across from Mary companionably.

The two women began chatting as naturally as if they'd known each other for years. Mary was interested to learn about Helga's life in Sweden and what brought her to America. Helga was fascinated by Mary's childhood in the hot desert with no siblings and no mother. They talked about Voltaire and Helga had Mary laughing at descriptions of his antics. With no guilt whatsoever, they each took another cinnamon cake bun and continued their friendly conversation.

Mary had almost forgotten where she was. She was so relaxed and having such a nice visit with Helga. Her mouth was in complete and utter ecstasy as she savored each bite of butterkaka slowly and with great appreciation.

"Oh Helga, I can't tell you how good this tastes," Mary said, closing her eyes and taking the last bite of her second bun. "It melts in your mouth... it's so..." she tried to think of the appropriate descriptive word but all that came out was a guttural moan of pure delectation.

Helga laughed, delighted, and Mary laughed too because she knew she was making a fool of herself over food.

"How professional," cut in a snarky voice. "Is this how you conduct first-time meetings with new clients?"

Mary stopped giggling. A piece of butterkaka fell out of her mouth as she gaped in astonishment at the famous fashion supermodel Katya Vetrov.

Helga's smile disappeared. "Good morning, Miss Katya. Can Helga get you coffee?"

"Yes." Katya sniffed the air contemptuously. "God, it smells like calories in here." She turned her cat-like eyes on Mary. "So *you're* the pet nanny."

Mary had never in all her life felt so completely gauche and awkward. Katya was dressed only in a man's button-down shirt, which, because of her tall height, barely came below her panty line. She had removed the perfect make-up Mary had seen on the TV last night and her hair was rumpled, sexily spilling down her back in long, messy curls. The unkempt look only intensified Katya's beauty- she looked like a seductive harlot who knew what the boundaries were and wasn't afraid to cross them. Her eyes were shrewd and highly intelligent and her demeanor radiated an aggressive confidence that abided no emotionalism whatsoever.

Instead of waiting for an answer, Katya grabbed the coffee mug out of Helga's offered hands and said, "I'm here quite often, pet nanny, so you'd better get used to seeing me around. I don't need to introduce myself since the look on your face clearly says you know who I am."

Helga looked thoughtful. "Maybe she look at you like dat because you not wear da clothes on your bottom haf."

Katya rolled her eyes, but before she could utter a word of retort, Thomas strolled into the kitchen in search of coffee. He was dressed casually in surfer shorts and a light blue t-shirt. His hair was still wet from his shower and he had small purple smudges of tiredness under his intense hazel eyes.

Helga's face lit up. "Thomas! I make butterkaka for you. I get you a plate. And Mary Crossfield is here. Helga likes her very much."

Katya laughed derisively. "I wouldn't eat anything with the word 'caca' in it."

Thomas poured himself a cup of coffee. "Shut up, Kat," he said without looking at her. He brought his coffee over to where Mary was sitting and said, "Welcome. Good to have you here. I'm sorry we're getting a late start today." He flickered his eyes at Katya. "And sorry some of us are half-dressed."

Mary hardly knew what to say. She was so overwhelmed and she felt so out of place. Katya was obviously not a nice person and Thomas looked... well, Thomas looked so handsome and so laid-back that vivid images from her dreams flashed through her mind, taunting her, tempting her, playing with her feelings which were in a heightened state already. In desperation, she looked down instead of at Thomas or Katya but all she saw was Thomas' hand wrapped around his coffee mug and the sight of his fingers reminded her of the night she'd dreamt he had run them all over her body. An embarrassed flush began to color her cheeks at the memory and she wanted nothing more than to run from the room. This was a mistake. She shouldn't be here. Who did she think she was? She wasn't classy enough or, quite clearly, worldly enough to be in the company of celebrities.

Thomas sat down on a stool next to Mary and Helga put a plate with two cinnamon buns in front of him.

Mary groaned inwardly. This was bad. He was so close she could feel his body heat.

"I vas going to bring Mary to your study in a vile," Helga was saying to Thomas.

"It's okay. I felt better after my shower so I came down. We can just talk here. I'm sorry I wasn't ready for our nine o'clock meeting." He shot Katya a look of pure venom. "It was a shitty night."

Katya smirked. "Once we got into your bedroom it wasn't."

Mary felt Thomas stiffen next to her. "Kat, please leave. I have business to discuss with Mary."

Katya hopped up on a kitchen counter, swinging her long, tanned legs in complacency. "I'd like to listen in." She narrowed her eyes at Mary. "After all, I'm here quite often."

There was a warning in there somewhere but Mary had no idea why. She stole a quick glance at Thomas and saw he was watching her.

"Yes," Thomas said to Mary, "Katya is quite involved with the care of Voltaire. In fact, she sometimes comes to the house just to play with him and take him on walks. Her favorite part of the day is when they cuddle together."

Katya sipped at her coffee and flipped her tousled hair over her shoulder. "I am about as good with Voltaire as Thomas is at writing his current…" Her long fingers curled in air quotes. "…*book*."

Thomas turned white with fury. "You know what?" he said to Mary in a very controlled voice. "*Now* would be a great time for you to meet Voltaire." He looked at Helga. "Is he in his garden pen out back?"

"Yes. Helga put him out t'ere a half hour ago so he vill vant to come in soon." She addressed Mary. "If you do not do vat Volpee vants den he dig out of da pen after t'irty minutes."

"Since you're not dressed, Kat, you stay inside," Thomas said over his shoulder, leading Mary from the kitchen.

"Dat not stop her…" Helga muttered, turning toward her dishes.

Mary followed Thomas across the room, every nerve in her body alive and at attention. He brushed against her arm as they walked and she flinched as though scalded. Her eyes flew to his face in embarrassment, but if he'd noticed he didn't let on. He kept up a steady stream of chatter about Voltaire and Mary tried to concentrate on the words coming out of his mouth, not just on his mouth.

Katya watched them walk out of the kitchen together, her sharp eyes missing nothing. She'd seen Mary jump when Thomas touched her. And she'd seen the way Mary looked up at him with very round, very adoring eyes. There was something pure about Mary Crossfield, something sweet and innocent. Mary wasn't a beautiful girl by industry standards. Pretty enough, striking eyes, but very ordinary. But for some reason Katya felt uneasy about the girl being here. Maybe because Mary was her complete opposite. But that meant she'd have no sexual prowess at all so she was hardly a threat. Katya shook her head. Why was she even thinking this way? Thomas wouldn't be tempted by some pet nanny who looked like the girl next door and appeared to have no more street smarts than a nun.

Katya leapt off the counter, leaving her coffee mug for Helga to pick up and wash. She headed for the main staircase, unbuttoning Thomas' shirt as she went. Mary Crossfield should be the least of her concerns. Especially after last night.

Katya knew exactly who Gemma Hamilton was, although Thomas hadn't told her many details of their brief affair. Katya had met Gemma a few times at red carpet events and once during Fashion Week in New York. She'd found the actress to be friendly and wholesome, her dimples cloyingly cherubic. Gemma had offered to show Katya pictures of her children, but quickly changed the subject when she saw Katya's look of revulsion.

Katya had no idea whatsoever why Thomas loved that woman. Especially after all this time. She hoped that it was just the alcohol talking last night giving him weird ideas, but maybe he really did still harbor some feelings of affection for the actress.

Well, there was only one way to take care of the situation. Thomas needed to be free from any other woman except Katya. She'd never cried over a man before, and last night would be the last time. Thomas belonged to her and her alone. There was too much at stake now that she realized she really and truly cared for Thomas- and that her budding movie career depended on their relationship being public.

Katya flopped down on Thomas' bed and reached for her cell phone. She dialed her personal assistant and when Gregory breathlessly answered Katya said, "Get me in touch with Gemma Hamilton, pronto. See if she's still in L.A. and set up a lunch. She and I need to talk."

CHAPTER 40

⌒

Bonjour Mama,

I know it's been a while since I wrote, but I've been making notes on what I want my novel to be about. I've been spending every spare moment scribbling down ideas and playing with possible storylines. While it feels so good to write and create, I'm filled with a lot of self-doubt. I construct several paragraphs and then read them and they're not very good. I rework everything and then it's even more awful. I don't understand! I mean, how can I love doing something but be so bad at it??? Did you ever feel that way when you were painting?

Speaking of self-doubt, I met with Thomas McQuillan this morning to go over my duties for Voltaire and I don't think I've ever felt so nervous and inadequate. Do you know who Katya Vetrov is? If you don't, she's a supermodel and she and Thomas are dating. I met her this morning and she is SO pretty- like naturally beautiful. She has the most gorgeous, smooth complexion and luxurious, thick hair that looks super soft. But she's sort of mean. Actually, she seems a lot mean. I was kind of scared of her. I hope I don't run into her very often when I'm there.

I also met Thomas' housekeeper, Helga, who is very kind and let me eat some of her freshly baked cinnamon bun cake. Then Thomas took me outside to show me the grounds (he said Helga was supposed to do it but he wanted to get out of the house) and he was way more easygoing with me today than he was during our dinner at The Marine

Room. He seemed genuinely interested in talking with me and before we went to Voltaire's pen he led me down a pathway between the trees to a small pond surrounded by blue meadow sage. We sat on a bench overlooking the water and Thomas talked a lot about his family and Voltaire. He didn't speak of his book or of Katya or of the fact that he was on a celebrity gossip show last night looking absolutely livid. He was giving off an open, casual vibe, but I know from our dinner together that he is very private person so I kept a million questions to myself and tried to just concentrate on what he was saying. I enjoyed listening to him and lost a lot of my nervousness because I was so enthralled with his stories, especially about the love his grandparents had for each other. Despite the fact that I was relaxing a bit, I was still very conscious of his physicality. We were not touching, but were very close on the bench because it was a rather small, stubby wooden thing. Thomas didn't really look at me while he was speaking - he mostly stared out over the still pond.

The meadow sage was blooming in brilliant blues, and monarchs hopped and skittered over the flowers, their wings opening and closing, revealing the intricate orange and black artistry painted across their backs. It was so peaceful being there with him and had you asked me just a month ago if I'd ever imagine I'd be sitting in idyllic scenery, sharing a bench and beautiful conversation with Thomas McQuillan, I would have said you were absolutely mad.

Just as I was thinking we'd been out there for quite some time and should go check on Voltaire before he dug out of his pen, Thomas turned to me and said, "I didn't realize you have freckles until I saw you outside in the sun."

I touched my nose self-consciously and looked up at him. Those hazel eyes of his seemed to have fathomless depth and I found myself unable to say anything as we stared at each other.

He smiled sadly and said, "I used to know someone who had freckles on her nose just like yours."

For lack of anything else that came to mind I said, "I must have gotten them from my mom because Dad doesn't have any."

He looked interested. "You don't know if your mother has freckles?"

I shook my head and told him about you. About what little I know of your love affair with Dad and how you are French and a painter. I told him I wasn't sure if you are here in The States, or in Paris.

He was intrigued. "But don't you want to find her?"

I said that you must not want to be found or else you would've reached out to me by now and I respected that. I told him how I had a wonderful upbringing and he let me chatter on about Daddy and Aunt Georgette and Aunt Francesca. He asked about growing up in Arizona and he wanted to know how I got into the pet nanny business. Of course that led into my inability to put down roots anywhere long term because of the military and now because of Owen's job at AirSec. I told him my work, like my life, has been rather transitory.

Thomas said, "You didn't tell me at dinner what your husband does for a living. So he's in the service."

I explained that Owen used to be a Navy fighter pilot but now works for a defense contractor. Thomas was highly impressed.

"I'd ask you to tell him I'm grateful for his service, but I assume–per our confidentiality agreement–he doesn't know I've hired you."

"I haven't told anyone, Thomas." It was strange saying his name in such an intimate setting. I liked the way it rolled off my tongue. I immediately felt guilty so I started talking about Owen, telling Thomas my husband was leaving on a work trip and wouldn't be back for a few months.

"But don't you know exactly when he's returning?" he asked.

"No, this training mission seems very vague."

Thomas asked about the situation in the Middle East heating up. "Owen isn't heading that way, is he?"

I said I didn't know and Thomas said we would rush our meeting a little faster so I could get home.

"Why?" I asked.

He seemed surprised. "So you can be with your husband before he leaves."

It was then that I felt truly awful. I stared out over the pond at the property beyond. There were lots of trees and grass and foliage, and Thomas' acreage spans a big hill so there are great views all around. I should have been home with Owen but somehow it didn't really matter. If I were home he would just be wanting to try to make a baby again. One last time before he ships out. Not because he loves me or because he's going to miss me but because he has some duty to fulfill. The thought made me tear up and I looked up at the brilliant blue sky to try to keep myself in check. Crying on the job wouldn't do at all. Maybe Katya is right and I AM unprofessional.

"Hey," Thomas said, "I didn't mean to upset you. Did I say something wrong?"

I was deeply touched that he seemed concerned. I assured him I was fine, that my allergies must be acting up. We stood and he took me to meet Voltaire. What a cutie pie he is, Mama! He looks like a grey potato with a Winston Churchill face. Because of his smashed-in nose he constantly snorts and wheezes and the more excited he gets the louder he grunts. He's terrible about jumping up on people and has no manners whatsoever. Thomas was completely over the whole situation. He leashed Voltaire and then handed him over to me irritably saying, "He is the worst dog!"

We walked back to the house and Voltaire was horrible on his leash. He pulled this way and that, choked himself and peed on his own leg because he was too impatient to finish watering a tree before returning to the path. I'm going to have my hands full with him, but I think - I'm pretty sure - he just needs regular exercise and lots of love. I can definitely give him those things during my six hours a day starting next week, but the rest of the time...

I said to Thomas, "I think Voltaire needs more attention than he's getting."

"Oh really?" said the testy Thomas I remember from The Marine Room. "Then I suppose it's a good thing I've hired you. I'm sure you'll take care of that for me."

"What about YOU?" I countered. "When do you take time out to play with him?" I bit my lips. It's not my place to judge.

A silence followed and then Thomas ventured, "You have a very soft heart for animals, don't you?"

I nodded.

"It's a gift. Not everyone has that."

I stopped walking and looked up at him. "What a nice thing to say."

He stopped too and he turned so that we were almost touching. In the bright sunlight his eyes looked green rather than hazel and they seemed insightfully extraordinary as though he could see my thoughts and read them. I was so conscious of everything about him that when his gaze drifted to my lips, I lost my breath in a rush of nervous entice-ment. Shaken, I abruptly turned and started walking again, Voltaire leading the way. I told myself not to be embarrassed, for surely Thomas knows he has an effect on women. Especially average girls like me.

I didn't see him again after we entered the kitchen because Helga continued with a tour of the house. She showed me the fireplace in the living room, the game room upstairs (Thomas has a really nice pool table that Dad and Dale would love), the home theatre and a small guest room tucked away in a back corner of the third level that Helga said is mine for as long as I'm employed. It's a truly adorable space with a double bed swathed in blankets and throw pillows, a tiny antique desk and chair and a small window overlooking the pond Thomas and I had sat next to. I'm sure I'll never use the room, but Helga said to think of it as my office.

"If you verk for a company den you haf someplace to put your stuff, yes? Same t'ing."

It's not the same thing at all, but I didn't argue.

I asked Helga where Voltaire sleeps at night and she said with her in her quarters.

"Sometimes Thomas comes home late or has company. It's better dat Voltaire rest vith me."

I wondered if by "company" Helga meant Katya.

I think as long as I'm giving Voltaire one hundred percent of my attention while I'm there we're going to get along great. He's not at all a bad dog; he's just lonely and untrained. Helga does the best she can, but she has job duties she needs to tend to and she can't be doting on him all hours of the day.

Anyway, I got home earlier than expected from Thomas' place and Roger was sniffing me all over, from head to toe. He does this every time I meet a new client. I wonder if he feels cheated on?

Owen isn't home, which is weird. He didn't have any plans this morning. I called his cell phone but it's switched off. I guess I should be glad he's not here because now I've had a chance to write you, which is a better pastime than Owen wanting to... Oh, Mama! We made love last night and I thought the Owen I married was back, but then he disappeared again. I don't know what's worse- being married to Dr. Jekyll and Mr. Hyde, or just Mr. Hyde. Okay, I know that's a little extreme, Owen has certainly not ever been cruel or violent, it's just that... would you think I was a terrible person if I told you that lately, sometimes, I really think I want to end my marriage? Not only do Owen and I want different things, like whether to have a baby or not, but he doesn't really listen to me anymore - my needs, my desires... I don't think I'm a needy person. It's just that I miss the connection he and I used to have. When we used to talk endlessly and laugh all the time and spend hours in bed. I wanted to be with him all the time, to share everything with him, and now... now I would rather be alone. I'm so lonely even when we're in the same room. I still love him. I really do. But not in the same way. I guess I'm just so lost, so confused.

I often wonder how you felt about Dad. I know you weren't together that long, but did you love him? Or maybe there wasn't enough time?

I guess I'd like to at least think you and Dad had strong feelings for each other. That's just the romantic in me, but I do so hope there was great affection between you. That my being conceived wasn't just simply an accident and nothing more.

I just heard Owen come in downstairs. I'll write more later.

P.S. Speaking of Dad, I pick him up at the airport in three hours. I'm so excited to see him!

---

23 April 1986

The two days in the cabin were absolute bliss. I cannot adequately describe how romantic and beautiful the lovemaking was. I know I will never experience anything like it again. Ever.

Those forty-eight hours only convinced me that I am deeply in love. I gave him my heart and he took it. He held it tight as though it were dear, but when we said goodbye he gave it back. He wished me luck. He did not ask me to keep in touch, he did not say he would write. I cried, I pleaded, I told him I would never love another. He smiled and kissed me on the forehead and said I would in due time.

"You are too beautiful to be alone," he assured me.

I told him I would rather be alone than be with any other man but him.

He said I would change my mind when I met the right person.

I asked him if he believed in soulmates and he said no.

I told him he is mine, but he didn't believe me.

When we hugged I clung to him, trying to memorize everything about the man I love- I buried my face in his neck and inhaled his scent, I ran my hands over his back, loving the feel of his muscular body, I searched his eyes, touched his lips, asked him to say "Helene" over and over so that I could etch in my heart the sound of his deep voice caressing the syllables of my name. I kissed him deeply, languidly, taking my time savoring him, knowing it would be the last time I'd know the taste of his passion.

I never made it to Italy. I decided to come straight home to France from America. I couldn't stop crying after I said good-bye. I still cry. I'm crying as I write this.

And I'm also crying because I just got home from the doctor.

I'm pregnant.

⌒‿

"Owen! Where were you?" Mary came downstairs to find her husband rummaging around in the refrigerator.

He jumped as though she'd struck him and he stiffly turned around. He had a beer in one hand and his blue eyes were troubled.

"You never drink before noon," Mary said. "Are you okay?"

Owen popped open the can and swallowed several gulps. "I'm fine."

Mary's brow furrowed. "You don't look fine. You look..." She had never seen him like this before. His clothes were rumpled and his hair, although combed down, seemed somehow out of place and his hands were shaking. She moved toward him and he backed up, flinching slightly.

"I'm just going to go upstairs and take a shower," he said, downing the rest of his beer and tossing the can in the recycle bin.

"You haven't showered yet today?"

"I did, yes, but, I... feel like I should have another one." He shifted as far away from her as he could and moved toward the stairs. "I'll be back down in a few."

Roger got up from his doggie bed in the corner and started to follow Owen upstairs. On the third step, Roger caught a whiff of something and he shoved his black nose into Owen's left pant leg. Heavy sniffing ensued.

"Owen, where were you this morning while I was gone?"

But Owen had already raced up the stairs before Mary could see all the shades of absolute guilt that colored his face.

CHAPTER 41

25 May 1986

I finally worked up enough nerve to call him. I told him I was pregnant.

He was shocked. He asked if I was okay. If I needed anything. Money?

I said I just needed him.

There was a very long silence.

He told me he had never expected to be a father. He took a deep breath and said he is a responsible man and he would do anything and everything for the baby. He said he would love the baby and take care of it.

I said, "Would you love and take care of me too?"

"We've already talked about this, Helene."

"But I love you so much. I love you enough for both of us."

"That's not the way it works…"

"Can I come to America?"

He said, "Of course. Would you like to have the baby here instead of in Paris?"

I said, "I want to be with you."

"You know I'm not ready for a commitment. But I'm here for our child. Always."

I lost my temper and yelled at him in French. I slammed down the phone and I screamed his name in misery and cried until I couldn't cry anymore.

~

Bonjour Mama,

I just got home from saying good-bye to Owen.

You know what happened? I realized it isn't being a pilot that changed Owen. I think I've known that all along... I was just looking for something to blame, and his career was a convenient scapegoat.

I saw Horse and Corinne clinging to each other. They were hugging like best friends and kissing like lovers. She said she would miss him even though they'd only be separated a few months and he said her soul lived in his heart and he would be thinking of her all the time. I saw him wipe tears from her cheeks and then hold her tenderly against his chest.

Owen stiffly patted me on the back while chastely giving me a peck on the lips. His expression was distracted and he wouldn't look me in the eye. He walked away without looking back and I knew then that I'd lost him.

Or maybe it's him that's lost me.

~

"Daddy!" Mary flung herself into her father's arms as soon as he disembarked from his plane.

"Little one!" Mitch said, catching his daughter and holding her tightly in a big bear hug.

"I'm so glad you're here."

"I'm glad I'm here too." Relieved might have been a better word, Mitch thought, as he held Mary close. He felt an overwhelming sense of comfort being able to see with his own eyes how his little girl was doing. He pulled away and searched her face for traces of stress or exhaustion, but he found only her sweet nature reflecting back at him.

"Are you okay?" he had to ask. As a parent he knew he wasn't always going to get a complete answer to this most common of inquiries, but he was savvy at discerning whether the reply was truthful, placating or a pacifying half-truth.

Mary looked down before responding.

Ah, thought Mitch, the first sign of a veiled response.

"I'm fine, Dad." Her voice wavered slightly.

Mitch pulled Mary into another hug. "Glad to hear it, baby," was all he said.

But he knew she wasn't fine at all.

Thomas raked his hands back through his sandy hair and leaned against the balcony railing outside of his upstairs game room. He looked out over the eucalyptus trees dotting his sloping property and reveled in the serenity of the view. Only the sounds of the wind rustling through the leaves and the occasional cry of a seagull pierced the cool, damp air blowing around him. The sun seemed to smile upon Thomas McQuillan, warming his skin and highlighting the golden hairs along his forearms, touching his face with friendly rays of solicitude.

Katya came up from behind and wrapped her arms around Thomas' waist. She leaned her cheek against his back and sighed. "Is the pet nanny gone?"

Thomas turned around to find Katya still dressed in his shirt from the night before, except now it was unbuttoned in the front so her entire smooth, tanned torso was visible.

"Kat, we need to talk."

Katya looked down. "I know."

"I'm still so angry with you about last night." In a barely controlled voice, Thomas went on to explain he was livid the paparazzi had been involved with their evening out, but what particularly infuriated him beyond all comprehension was that she had talked to the press regarding his supposedly almost-finished novel.

When he finished, three fat crocodile tears slowly coursed down Katya's cheeks and she clumsily brushed them away with uncharacteristic childishness. She said she'd had a moment of weakness when she'd seen that the part in *Syndicate Protocol* was within reach. She admitted she had made a deal with the director, John Bhear, but assured Thomas that last night's arrangement had been a one-time incident. She apologized profusely and said she hadn't meant any harm.

"But, Kat, you broke my trust. You know that my privacy is paramount and you not only betrayed that aspect, but, more importantly, you shared false information concerning my current writing situation. You had no right whatsoever to gossip about where I'm at with my book- true or not."

Katya nodded in agreement, her lips trembling. "You're right. I'm so, so sorry, Thomas." She embraced him imploringly, her face buried in his neck.

Thomas held her, confused by her abnormally passive behavior. Could she really be sorry? Did she honestly care for him? Or was all of this just an act? He pulled back from her and tried to read her thoughts. She bit her lip and her eyelashes fluttered, as though she were nervous about feeling so vulnerable.

Expecting an aggressive full-court press to go to bed, Thomas was surprised at the demeanor of this new, docile Katya.

She reached up and tenderly held his face in her hands. "I care for you, Thomas McQuillan," she said, her cheeks wet with remorseful tears. "Please forgive me. Please."

Thomas saw a flicker of deceit flash in her cat-like eyes and instinctively something snapped inside of him. He brought Katya hard against his chest, kissing her deeply, letting his hands roam over her body. He didn't let go until she was shaking, clinging to him in desire.

Meek and amenable, Katya let Thomas lead her from the balcony into the game room. "Where would you like me?" she asked, acquiescent and eager to please.

Thomas removed his shirt from her naked body and turned her around so that her back was to him. He pressed her up against the wall so she couldn't move and couldn't see him, and he whispered in her ear, "What are you really up to, Katya?" He ran his palms down her rib cage and across her hips and she shivered in response. He let his hands drop below her stomach. "Tell me," he said gruffly, possessively capturing the most feminine part of her.

"Nothing," Katya whimpered.

"I don't believe you." He pushed into her from behind, letting her feel the excitement of his body through his clothing. She was pinioned between Thomas and the wall, his strong arms on either side of her and his hands caught up in her most secret of places. He began a rhythmic kneading, expertly massaging and manipulating her sensitive, velvety contours. Skillfully, he brought her to the edge of her endurance over and over, stopping just before she burst into the incendiary combustion of pleasure. Katya began to plead with Thomas for release, her brow covered in sweat, her chest heaving with gasps of unfulfilled need.

"No," Thomas said harshly. "Not until you tell me what you've been saying about me behind my back."

"Please," Katya moaned, "please…"

Thomas let go of her. "Look at me, Kat."

Slowly, she turned around, her breathing ragged, her face a mixture of arousal and regret.

"I don't trust you anymore," Thomas said simply.

"No! Thomas, no! I'm sorry! I'm so, so sorry!" she reached for him, but he pushed her hands away and crossed his arms.

"I didn't mean to hurt you." She looked down at her bare feet. "I've worked really hard my whole life to get to where I am. You know I want to be an actress and I couldn't pass up this opportunity.

All John Bhear wanted was the movie rights to your next novel and some publicity for *Syndicate Protocol.*"

"That's it? You swear? How am I supposed to keep you in my life if I'm worried you're going to betray me?"

Katya wrapped her arms around Thomas' waist. "It won't happen again. I promise. I'm so, so sorry."

"How sorry are you?"

"What do you mean?"

Thomas picked Katya up and carried her across the room to a low-backed bar stool. He set her down and kneeled in front of her, placing her legs over his shoulders.

"I mean," he said, "I don't believe you feel guilty for hurting me."

"I do feel guilty… I do…" Her voice had taken on a pleading tone he had never heard before. "Don't stop this time, Thomas, please…"

Thomas gripped her inner thighs with his hands, pushing her legs against her chest as he nuzzled into the ripeness of her private, delicate skin with his mouth. His lips and tongue explored her silken smoothness, stroking and inflaming her into a frenzy of desire. She reached down and pulled at his hair and then passionately raked her fingernails across his back in a fit of voracious urgency.

Thomas released one of her legs and reached inside of her, never breaking contact with his mouth. Katya went still and quiet and he knew her body was about to catch fire and convulse. He waited until the very brink of her tumble into torrential eruption and then quickly, torturously, he pulled back, leaving her alone and feeble on the precipice of what would have been wild and cataclysmic rapture.

Thomas stood up, his hazel eyes opaque with enmity. Coldly, he addressed the quivering, powerless girl in front of him.

"Get out of my house, Katya, and don't ever come back. I will *never* forgive you for using me."

Without a backward glance, Thomas walked from the room, slamming the door behind him.

CHAPTER 42

*L*orelei paced up and down in her bedroom, her thoughts focused, her intelligent mind methodically working through the current complications in her life. She was very good at neatly storing difficult situations in metaphorical boxes, spiritedly delving into them one at a time at her own convenience and on her own schedule. She would open a box, pull out the problem contained inside, work it through and dispatch it out of her consciousness by shipping the box off to its resolved destination. Sometimes she would have to do this several times over a select period of time, depending on the enormity of the predicament, but she was always able to keep each complication separate from the others, and most definitely separate from impacting her personal life.

But somehow, her present dilemmas seemed to be bleeding over into one another's boxes. First and foremost, Faith's tearful plea that Lorelei never leave San Diego was almost more than Lorelei could bear. Her heart had ached as she'd stood there holding her friend, murmuring words of assurance while desperately trying to come to grips with what an eventual move would do to Faith's sweet and gentle spirit. For now, New York was quite possibly out of the question anyway, what with the sexual harassment investigation about to commence. After consulting with a very well-respected, very pricey employment attorney, Lorelei had decided to buck Empire & Malkin's subordination structure and reach out to Joe Thompson, vice president of human resources, directly. Joe, surprised by an unmediated call from an employee, wanted to know why Lorelei hadn't contacted Nadine Clawson, San Diego's regional HR director.

"Because she is a long-time friend of Edmond's, sir," Lorelei had said. "I believe if I reported to her what has been occurring in this office, she wouldn't be able to evaluate the situation fairly- and I'm wary of retaliation. The safest avenue for me career-wise has been to keep silent, but I can't do that anymore. Not after what an employee told me. Now, I'll understand if you need to place me on probation during the inquest, but I'm going to say my piece."

Joe was defensive. "Retaliation is against company policy, Miss Harper, surely you are aware of that."

"I am aware that human resources exists not for the protection of the employees but to protect the company from being sued by the employees."

"What is that supposed to mean?" Joe blundered.

"It means I've talked to an attorney and I know my rights. You will record our conversation when I officially file my complaint during our interview. I have copies of all the documents I've found incriminating Edmond for dishonest abuse of his expense accounts. When you speak to the employee who wishes to file a sexual harassment claim you will allow me to be in the room with her at all times. And when all of this is finished, and Edmond Davies is fired, I will be promoted to the commission analyst position in New York within the month."

"Well!"

"I assure you I am not being disrespectful or insubordinate. I love this company and it has always been my plan to work my way up through the ranks to an executive financial position. When your assistants do their research on me, Joe, they will find not one blemish on my record. I am ethical, hardworking and the best commission accountant in the commercial real estate industry."

"I feel like you're the one running the show here, Miss Harper." Joe's tone became condescending. "You *have* seen an organizational chart, haven't you? Commission accountant comes in way below vice president. Are you sure you want to speak to me this way?"

"With all due respect, you're not my direct supervisor. I realize your position is preeminent, but I need to look out for myself and for the employee Edmond Davies harassed. This situation has nothing to do with titles. Edmond's corrupt and improper behavior *will* come to an end or I will involve my attorney and file a charge with the EEOC. I want this handled with utmost impartiality."

"Are you threatening me?"

"Of course not! Threatening you would be just as wrong as... retaliation."

Joe cleared his throat. "I'll have my secretary be in touch to schedule a conference call. In the meantime, please send me all relevant documents in your possession. Good day, Miss Harper."

Abruptly he clicked off the line and Lorelei had leaned back in her office chair and let out a long sigh. Although she felt confident, it was quite possible the entire predicament could blow up in her face. She needed to really start considering options. Niles had assured her that a position was waiting for her at Hillard. And there was The Avett Group- they'd been trying to recruit Lorelei for several months. Avett was a last resort, for though they had promised to double her current salary, they were a smaller broker house and therefore unable to offer her the career growth she desired. The thought of moving to a stagnant position flew in the face of everything she believed in, but even Lorelei couldn't deny that a safety net was nothing to sneeze at.

Niles had called earlier to see how she was and he asked tentatively about what line of questioning she'd been required to answer at the police station. She tried to be as vague as possible, not wanting to reveal Frank's real reason for coming over to her condo, and also wanting to protect the sensitive situation she'd gotten herself tangled up in at Empire & Malkin.

"Is there anything... illegal going on?" Niles had asked.

"No, nothing like that."

"So… what you're involved in is all above board?"

"Yes, of course. Niles, how long have you known me? Do you really think I would dirty my hands?"

"No." There was a slight pause. "It's just that… if cops are asking you questions then…"

"There's nothing to worry about now. That's all taken care of."

"No more enquiries?"

"No more enquiries."

Niles heaved a great sigh of relief. "That's fantastic, Lor. So can I buy you dinner Saturday night?"

"I'm sorry, but I already have plans. I'll be with Faith and Mary. Mitch is in town and we're taking him out."

"Maybe I could meet up with you guys? Will you be at Club Cobalt?"

Lorelei laughed. "If we can get in. Last I heard they're being very picky about who's allowed behind the ropes."

Niles voice sounded puffed up and important. "Don't you worry about it. I'll make a call. Just give them my name at the door."

"That's sweet. I appreciate it."

"And I'll see you inside when you get there."

Oh.

She'd walked right into that.

And then Faith had called this morning. She sounded happy and excited, her voice three octaves higher than normal. "LOR!!! I CAN'T WAIT TO GO OUT WITH YOU AND MARY AND MITCH TONIGHT!!! It's going to be so fun! I made dinner reservations for us at Salty Shark."

"Thank you for doing that."

"Sure thing! It'll be so good to see Mary. I hope she's okay. I worry about her with Owen gone."

"I know… and I've had so much happening at work that I haven't talked to her lately. It'll be nice to catch up. And great to see Mitch."

"Ohhhh," Faith squealed, "I can't wait to dance with him! That man is SO sexy!" Then she continued in a casual afterthought, "Oh, and, Lor, I invited Frank to hang out with us all evening."

"No! Fay, Niles will be at the club. That's not a good idea."

Faith let out an adorable peal of laughter. "You and Frank are just *friends* so why would either of you care if the guy you occasionally date is there or not? See you at Sharky's at seven!"

Back in her bedroom, Lorelei brought all of these thoughts to a close and stopped pacing. She stored each problem into its appropriate mental box. One was labeled "Faith & Not Moving", one was simply named "Mary", one was "Frank and Feelings", one was "Work – NY & HR", one was "Niles – Possible New Position" and the one she tried to never touch, the one that remained unresolved year after year, was labeled "Connor O'Cassidy – Scars."

Objectively closing all of the boxes she had opened and shelving them for the time being, Lorelei moved toward her closet and began sorting through dresses to see what she would wear tonight. She almost chose a pink strapless cocktail dress that showed off her shapely legs and elegant shoulders, but then she remembered Frank's declaration that he would view her as a guy from now on in the name of friendship. With a mischievous sparkle in her green eyes, Lorelei reached way back in her wardrobe and retrieved a swanky red pant suit.

As she held it against her voluptuous frame and regarded herself in the full length mirror, she remembered the way she'd felt when Detective Frank Williams had kissed her on the couch in the hotel lounge. Her skin heated as she recalled the sparks he'd ignited, how excited her body had become knowing he desired her just as much as she desired him. When Frank held her in his strong arms it was as though time stood still and all that existed in the world was their movements, their sighs, Lorelei's racing heartbeat, Frank's masculine scent and the swirling magic of attraction that flowed in and around them.

A memory of Connor uninvitingly floated across Lorelei's consciousness, blotting out the image of Frank. Connor was standing in the surf, his hand outstretched. "Come on," he called, "get in the water with me!" She had run up to him, her eyes shining with love and happiness. "It's too cold to go in," she'd said, laughing as a wave lapped against her ankles and chilled her skin. "I'll keep you warm," Connor had promised, his hands on either side of her face. "I love you, Lorelei Harper." And he had kissed her with such feeling and vulnerability that she had no doubt in her mind that their names had to be written in the stars. "I love you too," she professed and he said, "I'll never let you go. Ever."

But he had. Only a short year later. He'd walked away without a fight.

Lorelei threw the red suit over a chair and sat down on the edge of her bed. Is this how Faith was feeling? Discarded and expendable? Wasn't abandonment the same, no matter if the person moving on was a best friend, a lover or a parent? Rejection was rejection, plain and simple. And it was so much worse to be rejected after one had been loved because then the entire past could only be a lie. If Connor had truly loved Lorelei he would have never left. If Faith's parents had truly loved Faith they would have never deserted her. If Mary's mother had really loved Mary she would have never walked out of her life and left Mitch to raise their daughter on his own. So didn't it stand to reason that if Lorelei truly loved Faith then she wouldn't move away? If not for any other reason than because Faith had begged her not to. After all, the two women were bound by the bonds of friendship- a connection oftentimes stronger and more powerful than those between spouses. Could Lorelei really turn her back on her best friend because Faith's request was too high of a price to pay? Was Lorelei being too selfish? Or was Faith? Surely Lorelei could pursue her career passions within San Diego. Or, if she really wanted to broaden her corporate prospects she could commute to L.A. Did Faith even realize she was trying to clip Lorelei's wings? And if she did know, was Faith's pain more important than Lorelei's goals and dreams?

Shoving aside all of these questions, Lorelei sighed. She had just packed up her metaphorical dilemma boxes and here she was opening the Faith one. And, she admitted, the Frank one. And… the Connor one had seen the light of day briefly as well, although it most certainly had not been deliberate.

Lorelei was never one to feel overwhelmed. Rather, she fed off of stress, deadlines and problem solving. She was the one everyone counted on, both at work and in her personal life. The only issue with being the rock was that sometimes she wanted to be the one who leaned on another for support. But she was fearful to do so because she didn't want to burden those she loved. It crossed her mind that Frank would be the perfect person to rely on- someone she could confide in, and trust to have good judgement. Maybe tonight at the club, when everyone was dancing, she would buy Frank a drink and the two of them could have a private chat in a corner of the bar, friend to friend. She pictured Frank's eyes searching hers while she talked- he would concentrate on what she was saying, truly trying to understand her feelings and then offering sound advice. He would say he appreciated her trusting him and he would offer to listen any time she needed him. Then they would move on to more lighthearted banter. She would ask about his detective work and about his son, Devon. She would ask him to take her on another motorcycle ride and she would remind him that he had said he would play his guitar for her some time.

Caught up in this comforting daydream of what she hoped would transpire tonight, Lorelei completely forgot Niles would be there too. Niles, who was used to holding Lorelei's hand, slipping his arm around her waist, kissing her lightly on the cheek, the lips, whispering words of adoration in her ear… Niles was bound to do all those things in front of Detective Frank Williams.

CHAPTER 43

⌒

19 September 1986

There isn't one moment of one day that I don't feel like a total and absolute fool. Looking back, of course, I can see the red flags taunting me, thrilling me, waving my heart into the bullring. And like any headstrong woman with a mind for romance, I willingly allowed that heart to be trampled, stomped on and horned to the ground. I think there was a part of my mind that thought I was grown up enough to handle falling for a man and then letting him go. That's what a mature woman of the world would do, yes? A secure, normal woman meets a man and if she likes him then they share a few laughs, have some great conversation, perhaps embark on a bit of delightful sex and then, when either feels like the relationship isn't going anywhere, they casually say "Au revoir," no hard feelings. The secure, normal woman would look back on her memories of the man fondly, even allowing a touch of nostalgia to bring a sweet smile to her lips.

But, oh no, not me, not Helene. I never held any of myself back. I never guarded my heart or built walls against my emotions. I let all of the desire and the affection and the infatuation that was inside of me spill out over onto him. I couldn't help it. And, honestly, I didn't want to help it. I've never half-lived my life.

I cry myself to sleep every night still. At bedtime I lay in the darkness and ache to see his amber eyes and feel the sensation of his large hands stroking my hair. I daydream of his smile, his sense of humor, his gentlemanly ways. I long for his kisses, his touch, the way the very essence of me came alive when I was next to him, his body close to mine, his breath on my neck and his arms holding me tight.

When this baby is born and he sees her (everyone tells me it's a girl because I've been carrying high and craving sweets like mad), I believe he will finally understand we are meant to be together. How could he not? We created a life, he and I, the most intimate bond a man and a woman can share.

I'm so sure of this that I'm going to begin planning our wedding. I can't wait to find the perfect dress. I wonder if he will want to marry here in Paris? Or maybe in America, close to his family? I know Papa and Maman will take care of the baby while we are honeymooning.

Ohhhhh... I can't hardly wait for this baby to be born so he and I can start our new life together.

I want all of him, all of the time.

Forever.

⌒‿

After Katya finally stormed out of his house, Thomas immediately called a gate company as well as a locksmith. He reset all of the alarm codes and scoured his bedroom to remove any and all traces of Katya Vetrov ever having been a visitor. Then he called Helga into his office.

"Katya is no longer welcome here," he told his housekeeper. "Make sure she never regains entrance, no matter what she says to you. Here are the new keys and a copy of the codes. Distribute them to the landscapers and the pool guy please." Thomas' eyes narrowed on Helga's mottled face. "Are you okay?"

Helga's lips thinned out. She bit the inside of her cheek and nodded her head.

Thomas smiled in understanding. "Ahhhh, okay, go ahead and let it out. I know you never liked her."

Helga expelled an astoundingly loud shriek and clapped her pudgy hands in pure joy. Jumping from foot to foot while looking toward the heavens, she exalted, "Oh baby Jesus, you answer Helga's prayers to send da evil vitch away from my sveet Thomas. T'ank you! T'ank you! Helga praise you!" Then, fearing she had been insensitive, she came around Thomas' desk. "Are you all right? Are you having pain in da heart?" She placed a warm, motherly hand on his chest.

Thomas patted Helga's hand. "Yes. But not from saying goodbye."

Helga straightened, crossing her plump arms over her mammoth bosom. "Vut does dat mean?"

"It means Katya hurt me very badly." Thomas sighed and leaned back in his office chair. "Have you ever had someone break your trust? Someone you've known for years?"

Helga's face smoothed in animosity, her eyes shooting fiery daggers. "Yes, Helga has had dis happen. Katya did dis to you? Dis is v'hy you vere on da television last night? V'hy people keep calling da house vanting to talk vith you?"

"That's right."

"I cannot believe she do dis to you!" Helga tried to say something else, but all that emerged was a scary progression of incensed Swedish words. Harumphing noisily, she grabbed the new keys and codes off his desk and stomped out of the den, shutting the door behind her and yelling down the hallway, "Shush dat barking, Volpee! Helga is coming!" Thomas could hear her muttering furiously to herself, but the only words he could decipher were "horrible" and "skinny shrew" before Helga's voice faded away in the distance.

Thomas stood up and wandered back to his game room. He poured himself a hefty gin rickey and took it outside on the balcony, leaning his arms on the railing and inhaling deep breaths of fresh sea air.

"I'm going to miss her," he said out loud. It felt good to say it. Cleansing. He would never tell a soul that he was sad to have said good-bye to Katya Vetrov, but there it was. They had, after all, shared five years of a mutually satisfying, if not slightly dysfunctional, companionship. Thomas had not slept with anyone else while Katya was in his life. Not out of deference to her, but because she assuaged his physical needs in spectacular fashion. Katya had the same desires and hungers, the same shunning of commitment, the same cynical view of love. Thomas knew Katya had been emotionally abused by men during her climb up the ladder of success, but while he felt a measure of compassion for what it must have been like for the young and beautiful girl, he also knew Katya, to some extent, had used those men in return. Thomas wondered how she could have switched off her feelings so easily but, the more he thought about it, the more he wondered if she was sensitive enough to even experience real pain. Certainly she was hard and rigid- in mind as well as body. Thomas had found her personality a welcome escape from Gemma's soft and delicate sweetness. Katya distracted him with a perverse strength and Thomas was all too glad to shed any painful reminders of Gemma both in conversation, and in the bedroom.

Thomas' cell phone rang in his pocket, startling him out of his thoughts. It was his agent, Lennie. Again.

"There. Is. No. Book," Thomas pronounced succinctly, answering without a hello. "Stop leaving me voicemails."

"Hey," said Lennie in a rush, trying to say as much as he could as fast as his mouth would let him, "so there's not a complete manuscript yet. So what? Take your time. When it's done we'll have all of Hollywood beating down your door."

"Too late," Thomas said darkly, thinking of all the calls he'd been fielding today.

Lennie chuckled. "Meet me, Tom," he said cajolingly. "We need to chat."

"No. There's nothing to talk about."

"Sure there is! Your future. I want to know about everything going on with you and how we can make it profitable."

"For you or for me?"

"For both of us, of course. Listen, I've got bottle service all lined up for us at Club Cobalt tonight in a private suite. Overlooks the dance floor and no one will even know you're there."

"Then why go?"

"Because the only women they let in that place are HOT. Be nice for you to have something to look at while you're drinking expensive champagne and chatting about the future with an old friend."

"Friend, huh?"

"Of course!" Lennie purred. "After all we went through with *Souls in Collision?* I've never seen a celebrity get so many endorsement offers and interview requests! And, geesh, the women! I'm not surprised you ended up with a supermodel. Katya Vetrov, eh?"

Thomas sighed loudly.

Lennie's tune changed. "None of my business I know. But I'll bet she's a real conceited bitch. Gave 'er her walking papers after the press fiasco did you?"

"I have to go, Lennie…"

"Sure you do! Hearts to break, books to write! I'll see you tonight."

"I don't think…"

"Great! Go through the side VIP entrance and give them my name. They'll take you up the back stairs to our suite. Later!"

Lennie hung up and Thomas tapped his phone on the railing in annoyance. He wasn't ready to get back in the publishing game yet. It was too soon. He didn't have enough written. Writing was riddled with pressure. Before, he'd had nothing to compete and compare against. Now, given *Souls in Collision's* astronomical success, the public would be panting for something extraordinarily brilliant. It would only make sense that Thomas' next work of art would be just as remarkable, if not better. The mere thought made Thomas break out into a cold sweat. He knew- knew he'd have to get past the perceived demands of his readers and just write for himself- but how could he do that when he was filled with insecurity? It wasn't like he'd written *Souls in Collision* in a mystical trance with magic ink. He'd simply penned the novel exactly the same way as he had penned his previous books- without thinking too much. Words, storylines and characters flowed out of Thomas instinctively and all the while he never thought twice about the plot or the prose. Writing and storytelling (two vastly different talents) came as naturally to him as breathing.

Thomas McQuillan was scared. Scared he'd already given away the best of himself both in literature and in love. And now... now with *Souls in Collision* and Gemma Hamilton behind him, maybe the rest of his life was just a wasteland of inadequacy.

He shook himself. No use traipsing down the road of self-pity. How had he gotten so morose?

Thank you, Katya.

Thomas drained his glass and went back inside. Crossing the game room and striding down the long hallway to his bedroom, he purposefully opened the double doors to his immense walk-in closet. Sifting through his wardrobe, Thomas came upon a dark blue suit with clean lines and a vintage cut. It was brand new and had just been tailored the week before. He'd never worn it. Perfect. He wanted nothing that reminded him of Katya. Just the thought of her brought a pang of remorse - anger with himself for not having discerned her duplicitous nature and sadness over the knowledge he wouldn't set eyes on her again. He would miss laughing at her acerbic wit, answering her questions about American literature, debating over politics and... he was going to miss the white-hot physical attraction they shared. But most of all, he suspected Katya's exit from his life was going to leave the door wide open for memories and reminders of Gemma to waltz right in. The entrance was no longer barred and protected by the distraction of a carnal, callous woman.

Thomas slipped into the suit and went to stand before the full-length mirror. He knotted a sleek, sophisticated tie at his neck, then gazed into his eyes. A tortured man stared back at him and he knew he was going to have to suffer the grief of losing Gemma. He couldn't keep burying his feelings, pretending he hadn't wounded and scarred himself by walking out of her life. He wondered if his determined retreat into self-protection had anything to do with his writer's block. That was a rather huge thought to process. Could one's unresolved anguish bleed over into their creative work? Stifling it, clotting it, tying it up in a huge red ribbon of uncompromising repression?

He was thinking too much.

A night out at Club Cobalt this evening would be just what he needed. It would certainly trump staying in and stewing over his failures. Maybe he would even allow Lennie to reach out to the publishing house.

Perhaps a forced deadline was just what he needed.

CHAPTER 44

The young uniformed valet opened Lorelei's car door and offered a white gloved hand to help her out. She stepped from her Lexus into the cool night air and as soon as the valet set eyes on her his jaw dropped and he stuttered, "Ha-have a lovely evening, miss."

Lorelei smiled and walked up the wide stone stairs leading up to The Salty Shark. The five-star restaurant was perched on the edge of Sunset Cliffs overlooking the sparkling blue waters of the Pacific. Sharky's served only the freshest of seafood and was known far and wide for their exceptionally creative and delicious fare.

A hostess opened one of the enormous glass double doors and Lorelei stepped into a pristine lobby decorated with high-end beach accoutrement and beautiful oceanic artwork. Windows, long and tall and wide, protected the guests from the high winds blowing up over the cliffs while also affording them panoramic views of the sea.

Lorelei strolled across the wood flooring, her high heels elegantly tapping their way to the small concierge desk where a tiny young woman in a formal grey skirt suit sat with a large, leather-bound scheduler in front of her.

"Good evening," said the girl. "Welcome to Sharky's." Her voice was as smooth as satin, her expression professionally deferential.

"Hello," Lorelei smiled. "Reservations are under Faith Dobbs."

The girl looked down at the list before her and in so doing noticed Lorelei's adorably clad feet. "Oh my goodness!" she exclaimed, all semblance of formality evaporating. "I love your shoes! Those are so cute!" She glanced back up at Lorelei. "And sexy. Wow. They look fantastic with that outfit too."

"Thank you," Lorelei said politely. "I ordered the shoes from Neiman's." Then in a confidential tone she added, "They were twenty percent off and I couldn't help myself."

"Oh," said the girl, bubbling over with female camaraderie, "I wouldn't have been able to either! Even if it set me back a few paychecks." Then suddenly her expression shuttered and she was once again the serious concierge. "Are you with the Dobbs party, sir?" she asked pleasantly.

"Reckon I am," said a deep male voice.

A big smile lit up Lorelei's face and she whirled around only to be caught up in a giant bear hug that left her breathless and laughing.

"Good to see you, young lady," said Mitch, settling her back on her feet. "You look as beautiful as ever."

"You clean up pretty nice yourself," Lorelei said, her green eyes appreciatively sweeping over his muscular build and well-cut suit.

Mary rushed forward from behind her father. "Lei! Oh, Lei, I've missed you. I know it's only been like five days since we last talked but it seems like forever!" Mary threw herself against Lorelei and the two girls clung to one another.

"I know. I'm so sorry, Mare. Things have been crazy at work." Lorelei pulled back. "Are you okay? You called the other day but hung up before I could get to the phone."

"Yes, I'm fine. I'm sorry I bothered you at work."

"You're never a bother, you know that." Lorelei searched her friends' eyes. "And you're not fine. I can tell."

Mary skittered a quick glance at her father and said guardedly, "No, really, I'm okay, Lei."

"Ah." Lorelei gave Mary another hug and whispered in her ear, "We'll chat later. Just you and me."

"Yes, please," Mary whispered back. Her tone held a note of desperation and Lorelei squeezed her friend tighter.

"Nice to meet you, sir," said a familiar male voice from behind the two girls and Lorelei felt an unexplainable shiver of restlessness skip down her spine. She let go of Mary and saw Detective Frank Williams shaking hands with Mitch. The two men sized each other up with one glance and apparently liked what they saw. Mitch clapped Frank on the back and said, "Nice to meet you too, son."

Then Frank turned and caught sight of Lorelei. Her heart stopped when she saw his face, for his eyes blatantly disclosed the intense emotion running through him. For a split second she glimpsed the true depth of his feelings and it was startling to see the powerful yearning passion that lurked there. Lorelei wanted to reach out and touch him, to see if she could physically absorb what was happening in his mind so she could enjoy the sensations too. She knew it was that enigmatic chemistry between them, the electrical charge in the air that occurred whenever they were in close proximity to one another. She stepped forward to give him a friendly hug, but he moved away abruptly and his features dulled into an indiscernible expression.

"Hi," Lorelei said uncertainly. When Frank didn't respond she smiled at him encouragingly and said, "You told me that I'm one of the guys now so I thought I'd dress like one." Slowly, she turned in a circle so he could thoroughly observe her outfit from head to toe. Lorelei fully expected him to give her an appreciative, conspiratorial wink at their shared inside joke.

But Frank's demeanor was not friendly in the least, instead it was ice cold, and Lorelei knew he had, for some unknown reason, retreated into cop mode.

"Very nice," he replied indifferently before turning his back on her to scrutinize one of the paintings behind him.

Frank stared hard at an oil on canvas portrayal of Cardiff Beach and willed his heated emotions to settle down. He concentrated on the swirls and strokes of light blues and yellows and peaches that all blurred together, the blotchy waves of the sea rising up to an orange sun. He could hear Lorelei, Mary and Mitch happily chattering away behind him and his shoulders stiffened. He was being ridiculous. He was a grown man! A detective! A father! He couldn't let a woman break him down. But this wasn't a conventional man-likes-woman situation. Frank wasn't free to play out his natural inclinations. He'd made that clear to both Lorelei and himself. They were friends, nothing more. He needed to deal with that because he'd made the rules. And he'd made the rules because he wanted her in his life. But the way she looked tonight...

Frank guessed she had decided to go for a semi-masculine look to play up his "you're one of the guys" comment with regard to their relationship. It was a very thoughtful, playful gesture, but the problem was Lorelei, who was the iconic voluptuous bombshell personified, had stripped all traces of her delicate glamour in favor of a faux machismo, and the unintentional result was exquisitely tantalizing and seductive. She had donned a skin-tight red pantsuit, the legs narrowing at her ankles in order to show off stylish tuxedo stilettos encasing her small feet. The shoes had quite their own personality with a column of black buttons running along a white strap on the arch of her foot and ending in a sassy black bowtie over the top of her toes. The lapels on her suit jacket were covered with the softest of red velvets and she wore no shirt underneath, allowing the open collar to slightly reveal the inner rounded swells of her breasts. Somehow the entire ensemble, which would most likely have looked tomboyishly chic on the classiest of women, only served to further glorify Lorelei's hourglass figure.

But it wasn't just what she was wearing, it was also the way she had groomed herself in a manner she must have assumed would give off an understated snub at femininity. Lorelei had worn no makeup whatsoever. Frank shook his head grimly for she had most likely assumed leaving her face unpainted would play down her ravishing loveliness. Instead, it had quite strikingly shown Frank the lusciousness of her naturally long lashes, the perfect arch of her brows, the sumptuous curve of her dewy lips and the porcelain elegance of her creamy skin. She had straightened her curls and slicked her hair back in a trendy, sleek look that made Frank fantasize about what she must look like in the shower every morning. And the freshness of her face without cosmetics… he envisioned waking up next to her raw beauty in the morning after a night of showing her the pleasure he so expertly wanted to give her.

Indeed, Lorelei's efforts had succeeded only in heightening Frank's barely contained lust. Fortunately, he'd caught himself before saying something he'd regret. He'd stoically disengaged from the present, just as he did so often when arriving at a crime scene. He removed all emotion from his disposition and bullied himself into mentally detaching from the circumstances. But it was hard. So hard, he'd had to turn away from Lorelei so that he could corral his tender thoughts and try to force them into taking a backseat to his needs.

No, Lorelei's "manly" look had the complete opposite effect on Frank. He knew she'd intended it to be a fun, amusing nod to their newfound friendship, but all he could do was stare miserably at the painting of the sea and desperately wish he could squash his feelings and be the man he knew she needed him to be tonight.

CHAPTER 45

Mitch looked at his watch and then at Lorelei. "It's seven-twenty. Should we go ahead and let them seat us? I don't want to lose our table, but maybe someone should check on Faith again?"

Lorelei pulled her cell phone out of her tiny black purse, muttering under her breath. Finding Faith's name in her contacts she rang through and got voicemail. "She's still not answering," Lorelei said, resigned. "Let's go ahead."

The concierge girl, overhearing, spoke up. "If you'll follow Angus, he will make sure you are all comfortable. We have a lovely table by the waterfall pond reserved for your evening."

"Oh," Mary said, her eyes lighting up, "do you still have the large koi?"

"We do."

Mitch reached over and ran a large hand over his daughter's hair. "You have always loved animals."

Mary smiled up at her father and two pairs of amber eyes met, mirroring identical love and affection.

A tall, dark man in a crisp uniform approached and said, "Good evening. I am Angus and I'll be taking care of you throughout your meal. If you'll just come with me."

Mitch and Mary started to walk away and before Frank could follow them Lorelei stepped in front of him, blocking his path.

"We'll be right there," Lorelei called to Mitch. And then she whirled on Frank, her emerald eyes flashing. "Okay, Detective, what's going on?"

Frank tried not to look at her. He wanted to go stare at the painting some more. The benign painting that didn't have sexy curves, or a vivacious laugh or pretty feet.

When he didn't answer, Lorelei lost her temper and, balling up one of her small hands, she punched him in the arm. It wasn't meant to be painful, only to get his attention, but the shock of her touch made Frank's bicep contract and he sucked in his breath. His hardened façade fell away and Lorelei glimpsed the simmering emotions he was trying to keep hidden.

"Oh," she said. They stood facing one other, both looking down at the hard wood floor beneath them. "I feel the same way," Lorelei admitted softly. "You look very handsome tonight."

Their eyes didn't meet. They didn't dare.

A scream of excitement cut through the air and Faith was on top of them in a swoop of effusive warmth and cheerfulness. She put one arm around each of them and dragged them into a group hug just as a mother hen would gather her baby chicks.

"Tonight is going to be so fun!" Faith said happily. "I'm going to eat every single piece of calamari in this restaurant." She let go of Frank and Lorelei and kissed each of them on the cheek. "I'm sorry I'm so late." She gestured at her blouse which was turned inside out. "Scotty had an accident on me and…"

"Would you like to be seated, ma'am?" Angus was back in the lobby and ready to escort the latecomer into the dining area. "I'll share our specials this evening with you while we walk to -"

"Yes!" Faith squealed eagerly. "Mitch and Mary are already inside?" Without waiting for an answer she said to Angus, "Can you put an order of calamari in for me right away? I'm so hungry I could eat a hundred wooly mammoths…" Her voice trailed off as she and Angus made their way together across the elegant dining room, but before Frank and Lorelei could resume their stilted conversation Faith's voice floated back to them when she laughingly shrieked, "That's so gross! That's what squid ink actually is?! Why would you put black mucus in a risotto dish?!"

Several diners turned to stare at the disheveled, ebullient redhead and Lorelei and Frank began to laugh. As their eyes met their levity subsided awkwardly and Frank said, "Come here. I can't stand not touching you." He reached out and drew Lorelei against his broad chest, resting his chin on top of her sleek hair, careful not to muss it. "I'm sorry," he whispered. "I'm sorry I'm not handling this well." He tightened his hold on her. She felt so good.

Lorelei pressed her cheek against Frank's suit jacket and inhaled his distinctive manly scent. She toyed with his tie and said, "I'd really like some of your time tonight. I've got a lot going on and… I could use a strong shoulder to cry on, so to speak."

Frank put Lorelei from him, stooping slightly to look straight into her eyes. "Are you all right?"

"Yes. Yes, of course. I didn't mean 'cry' like that. I'd just really like to ask your advice on a couple things." She looked up at him openly, honestly, trust written all over her beautiful face.

Frank was flattered. "Of course. Anything you need. I don't know if I'll have the answers you're looking for, but I'll be a listening ear at the very least."

"Thank you," Lorelei said simply, gratefully. "If it's all right with you maybe we can sneak away for a bit at the club. There are a few private tables in the back." She winked at him. "I'll buy you a drink. What's the going rate on your counseling services?"

"It's a four-drink minimum, but I'll take a dance instead."

"Deal," said Lorelei and they grinned at each other.

"By the way," Frank said, putting her hand through his arm as they walked toward the dining room, "if you were trying to look like a guy tonight you failed miserably."

Lorelei laughed. "I thought it would make you smile."

"It made me want you more than I did before." He glanced down at her teasingly. "So, thanks for that."

Lorelei's hand flew to her mouth in mock horror. "Are you saying you find me sexier as a man?"

Frank chuckled, low and deep. "Yeah, that's what I'm saying."

As Frank led Lorelei to their table in the back by the delicate indoor koi pond, he could feel every eye in the restaurant on the gorgeous girl beside him. He wondered if the people who were staring knew there was so much more to her than her outer beauty. She was kind, compassionate, a great friend to her girlfriends, a successful career woman… by any standards, she checked off every box on the ideal woman list. But no one was perfect, and he wondered what kind of faults Lorelei kept hidden from the world. Of course there was the biggest one- Connor; the name that shouldn't be mentioned, the blot of pain in her history that kept her from moving forward in the realm of love.

When they reached the table, Frank pulled Lorelei's chair out for her and took his place to her left. Faith was noisily chatting to Mitch and Mary about someone named Bertie and her eyes were round and bright with curiosity.

"So, like, you… you LOVE her?" Faith asked, her voice high with excitement.

Mary giggled and Mitch shifted in his seat. "Reckon I do."

"This is SOOO romantic," Faith sighed. "Lor, Mitch here met the love of his life."

"I didn't say *that*…" Mitch began.

"But I can see it in your eyes!" Faith said, her face dreamy.

Lorelei stared at Mitch. "Are you serious, big daddy? You fell for someone? The devil himself must be freezing his butt off! I want to know all the details!"

"Yes!" said Faith. "Tell us *everything*! She must be super-hot. You wouldn't be with just any chick. She's gotta be smart and funny and charming and…" she turned to Mary, "Just wow! I thought your dad was the ultimate unattainable bachelor!"

"Me too," Mary agreed, giving her dad a sweet smile. "We talked about her at Rudy's over lunch. Daddy's only known her a few weeks."

Faith nodded her head vigorously, her untamed red hair tumbling over her shoulders. "That's the way it was with me and Jesse. I just *knew*."

"I remember," Lorelei said with an affectionate smile. "He came into Holokai's one day and your life was never the same."

Faith's face lit up. "I knew it for sure when he touched my hand for the first time. I got all these crazy electrical currents running up my arm."

Frank cleared his throat and Lorelei looked away, the tension between them palpably obvious.

Mary stared down at the tablecloth, her eyes misting with tears. She remembered Owen's touches when they were first married and how she'd never felt so close to heaven. She wondered how Owen was doing tonight. Was he thinking of her? Did he miss her? She felt only a sense of relief that he was gone, and acknowledging that was distressing in and of itself. Had the love they shared ever been as pure and as idyllic as Faith and Jesse's? And if yes, then why had it been allowed to shrivel over time? If she and Owen could get it back, would she even want it? He had hurt her so much, over and over and over that her answer would probably be... no.

Mitch was watching his daughter closely, worry lines etching the corners of his eyes. Something was seriously wrong. And it was more than just about the non-existent baby.

A waiter came to the table interrupting everyone's thoughts. "My name is Brad and I'll be assisting Angus tonight." Poising elegant silver tongs over an equally elegant silver bowl he said, "Roquefort and almond sourdough rolls with St. Clair butter." He addressed Faith. "One for the lady?"

"Gosh, yes!" Faith said enthusiastically. "Can I have three?"

"Fay!" Lorelei admonished.

Brad looked uncomfortable. "Well, I only have one for each guest at the moment. But I could come back with more…"

Angus approached the table with a steaming platter of calamari.

"Ohhhh, heaven!" squealed Faith, nabbing one and shoving it into her mouth.

Lorelei dropped her head into her hand and Frank politely hid a smile behind his napkin.

"Would madam still like three rolls?" Brad asked.

"Yes!" Faith said emphatically. "I'm *so* hungry…"

Mary looked at her father across the table and explained, "Faith's pregnant, Daddy."

Mitch smiled. "Well, that's wonderful!" He picked up his wine glass and toasted Faith. "Congratulations, young lady. Dinner's on me tonight so you eat as much as you want."

Lorelei groaned. "Don't tell her that! You're essentially giving matches to a pyro in a fireworks tent."

Faith giggled. "It's not like I'm going to explode, Lor!"

"Is Jesse home with the kids tonight?" Mary asked.

"Good grief, no! Can you imagine? He's out with the guys. They're going to some dive bar downtown to drink beer and play darts. Wicky is at the house. She's spending the night since I don't know what time either of us will be home."

Frank settled back in his chair and swept the table with his eyes, enjoying the laughter and banter going on around him. Lorelei had such great friends. Which made him wonder why she would want to confide in *him* tonight? He looked at Mary, the endearing wholesome girl with freckles and troubled, guileless eyes. Not exactly someone you would want to dump your problems on; his practiced bloodhound senses told him she was very emotionally fragile. And Faith… well, Frank had seen firsthand how powerfully sensitive she'd been over the thought of Lorelei moving away. No, Faith wouldn't be someone Lorelei could go to for advice either- especially if it had to do with work, which Frank suspected it did.

But then that was the bigger question, wasn't it? How would Frank feel if Lorelei moved to New York?

Faith crammed an entire roll into her mouth and groaned in ecstasy. She mumbled something and a few crumbs fell out of her mouth and onto her plate.

Mary giggled and caught Lorelei's eye roll just as Faith inhaled, sputtered, and began choking.

Mitch leaned forward urgently. "Faith! Are you okay?"

Faith waved her hands in the air frantically.

Frank was off his seat in a nanosecond, his strong arms going around Faith's torso from behind as he hauled her from her chair.

Lorelei jumped to her feet, her hands balling into fists at her side. "Faith!" she demanded. "Spit it out! Look at me, Fay! Cough as hard as you can!"

Mitch's voice was commanding. "Faith, touch your throat if you want Frank to help you."

Faith patted her neck and Frank placed his fist under her rib cage and thrust inward and upward.

Mary began to cry as Faith's lips took on a bluish-purple color and Mitch yelled to Angus, "Call 9-1-1 NOW!"

Frank used the Heimlich Maneuver once more before taking the heel of his hand and giving Faith five swift, hard blows between her shoulder blades.

"The baby...please be gentle!" Mary begged, tears coursing down her cheeks.

Lorelei felt her body turn to ice as she stared at the scene unfolding before her. This wasn't happening. This couldn't be happening. "She's my sister..." she heard herself say out loud in what sounded like a terrified, helpless plea.

Faith's eyes began to roll back and Frank pulled her against his body once more with a strong, intense abdominal thrust. A large chunk of bread popped out of Faith's mouth and she sagged back against Frank, her face pale, her blouse rumpled and wrinkled.

Frank settled her back in her chair and kneeled beside her. "Are you okay? Can you feel anything else in your airway?"

"No." Her smile was wobbly as she threw her arms around his neck and said hoarsely, "Thank you. Thank you so much. I'm sorry. I'm really sorry."

Lorelei was kneeling on the other side of Faith. "You're really okay?" she asked, deep lines of concern creasing her forehead.

"Yes."

"You scared me." Lorelei took a deep breath. "That scared me."

Mary dashed tears from her cheeks with a cloth napkin. "Let's get Fay to the girl's room. Some cool water on her face will feel good and we'll turn her shirt right side out."

Faith looked down at herself and laughed weakly. "There's a stain on the other side from Scotty."

Frank and Lorelei helped Faith to her feet while Mitch went in search of Angus to tell him to cancel the ambulance.

Faith put her arm around Mary, while Lorelei turned to Frank, admiration in her eyes.

"Thank you, Detective," Lorelei said, her voice breaking. "Thank you for saving my best friend's life." And then she was in his arms and kissing him deeply, gratitude and affection on her lips, fire and passion in her touch. The sparks between them ignited and they became lost in their own world- the restaurant and all of its gawking patrons forgotten.

Mary stared at the couple, her mouth hanging open.

"See," said Faith, sighing romantically, "he's her soulmate. She just doesn't know it yet."

Mitch came back to their table just as Frank and Lorelei broke apart. Mary and Faith were slowly making their way through the dining area toward the ladies' room.

Frank cleared his throat. "Well, little lady," he said to Lorelei, brushing his knuckles against her soft, pink cheek. "I've never been thanked like that after an emergency before."

Lorelei's breath caught, her thoughts roiling, her heart hammering. She shouldn't have kissed him. She shouldn't be exposing herself to such vulnerability. She was going to get hurt again.

But Frank wasn't Connor.

Right?

No, she had been wrong to cross the line Frank had drawn. She had let a moment of sheer panic turn into a moment of sheer pleasure.

"I'm sorry," Lorelei whispered, great feeling in those two words.

"Hey," Frank said, his voice soft, "it's okay. These were extenuating circumstances. But don't let it happen again. Remember - I don't kiss dudes. I was just being nice."

Lorelei laughed. "I'll be back in a moment." She turned to Mitch. "I'm just going to join the girls. If you'll excuse me."

The men nodded, then took their respective seats at the table as the other diners around them finally stopped staring and went back to their meals. Frank and Mitch remained silent, their thoughts caught up in the shock of what had just happened. Each took a few calming swallows from their wine glasses before engaging in small talk.

"So, you're a contractor, sir?" Frank asked eventually.

"I am. Ever since I was a tyke. Runs in my family."

"Did you want Mary to go into the business? Follow in your footsteps?"

"No, I think my little girl was cut out to be a writer. She tends toward the arts." Mitch paused. "Like her mother."

"Most would consider construction to be an art," Frank offered.

Mitch looked pleased. "My father would have fallen into that category."

The men allowed several quiet moments to rest between them while they enjoyed their sauvignon blanc. Neither touched their bread, for the rolls now held a sinister aura despite their innocence.

"Have you ever been to Club Colbalt before?" Frank asked after a bit. "I hear it's very exclusive. Typically only A-listers get in. Rich folk. Celebs."

"This will be my first time," Mitch said conversationally and then he switched gears, his expression intense, cautionary. "Listen, son, I need to say this… if I'm not mistaken, the nice lady in the red suit thinks you're something pretty special." Mitch's voice was firm, his message loud and clear. "Lorelei Harper is a good girl. I don't want to see her get hurt."

"I understand, sir. I assure you I respect her highly and my intentions are aboveboard. But…" Frank cleared his throat, "we're just friends."

"Reckon I don't kiss any of my friends that way," Mitch said dryly.

"It's complicated…"

"Because of Niles?

Frank's defenses rose to the forefront.

Mitch smiled encouragingly. "Don't worry about him too much. Niles Donovan has prominence and money, but I've never seen Lorelei look at him the way she looks at you. If he tries to pull anything tonight just remember that."

Frank's eyes flashed to Mitch's face in alarm. "Niles is going to be at Club Cobalt?"

"That's how we're getting in. No one told you?"

CHAPTER 46

⌒

Katya Vetrov had never been so humiliated or so hurt in all her life. As she paced back and forth in her austere home, she raged both inwardly and outwardly. There was no one to hear her screams of indignation or her cries of remorse. One minute she was cursing Thomas McQuillan like a madwoman possessed and the next she was weeping loudly, her stomach in knots, her heart wrenching with dejected sorrow. Katya was on the verge of losing a battle in which she had no hope of winning. Thomas McQuillan was done with her- he'd made that perfectly clear with his vengefully erotic cat and mouse game.

"YOU BASTARD!!!" she shrieked into her lifeless living room. "I hate you! I hate you!!!!"

She kicked at a tall crystal Baccarat vase and it plunked over onto the lush carpeted floor with a dull thud. She kicked it again, hurting her toes in the process. Letting out a piercing howl of frustration that would have scared off any werewolf within hearing distance, she sank down onto the floor and covered her head with her hands. Rocking back and forth as she used to when she was a little girl, she desperately wished for the comfort of love; a love she had never known as a child and never earned as an adult.

"I'm sorry, Thomas," she whispered brokenly. "I'm so sorry..."

Her cell phone rang from across the room and she sprang to her feet, her heart in her throat. Maybe he was calling to apologize... to say he had just been in a bad mood earlier. Could she come over? He wanted to finish pleasing her. He was sorry. He would make it up to her…

But, no. It was Gregory, out of breath with excitement, happy to report he'd been in touch with Gemma Hamilton's people and had scored Katya an impromptu lunch meeting in Hollywood tomorrow. Katya checked her voice, making sure she belied no traces of histrionics.

"So soon?" she asked.

"She had a cancellation. Her assistant said she only has forty-five minutes, and I told her we'd be honored to take it."

Katya was galled. She hated kowtowing to celebrities. After all, she was a celebrity in her own right. Not nearly as famous as Gemma, but still… one day she would be. Once her movie career took off. In the meantime, hobnobbing with the A-listers was just part of the game. But, now… now she didn't need to see Gemma anymore; not since she wasn't at risk of losing Thomas. She'd already lost him. A horrific stabbing pain of loneliness shot through her. She'd lost him… she'd lost him… the words tumbled around in her chaotic mind over and over and over…

"Hello? Katya…?" Gregory sounded concerned. "Are you ok…? Did I lose you?"

Did I lose you? Maybe she hadn't lost Thomas- maybe *he* had lost *her.*

Katya's back straightened. Yes! HE had lost HER! Oh, and what a mistake he had made!

NO, a small voice inside her reprimanded, *you got what was coming to you; you betrayed his trust, you know you did.*

Gregory said, "I'm going to hang up and ring you back. We must have a bad connection…"

A bad connection. That's what her relationship with Thomas had been. A bad connection between two people who had different motives, different goals, different outlooks on life. Thomas was stuck, mired in his own insecurities and self-doubt; he was neither moving upward nor forward. Katya, on the other hand, was determined, driven and motivationally hell bent on getting what she wanted. Thomas was kind to people of lower class; Katya viewed them as irrelevant underlings with no value. Thomas was interested in others, curious about their pasts, their quirks, their passions; Katya could care less about others unless they could somehow be exploited to further her career.

Katya lifted her chin. She and Thomas had nothing in common other than their potent, uninhibited sexual appetites. And surely she could find that elsewhere. California was teeming with wealthy, handsome men who would welcome Katya Vetrov into their bedrooms. She could pick who she wanted and take her satisfaction where she pleased. That was far more powerful than allowing herself to care for one man. One man who had known the map of her body and where every treasure lay, ripe for his taking. And he'd used it against her in the end. Pirating his way across the sea of her desires, pillaging, ravaging, plundering until she had writhed and moaned to the end of the plank, ready to jump into the waters of paradise. It was then that he had pulled her back as his captive, yanking her from the edge of glory and humiliating her on that bar stool in his game room. She felt sick remembering the look of disgust on his face as he stared down at her, freeing her from any of the chains that bound them together, uttering words of painful retribution.

Self-righteous anger rose above the heartache of loss, and Katya knew she couldn't let Thomas get away with how he'd treated her. An evil smile flickered over her lips and her dark cat eyes flattened with spitefulness.

"I'm still here, Gregory," she said, her voice brittle and hard. "I'll meet Gemma tomorrow. Thanks for setting it up."

Katya threw the phone down and got up slowly, deliberately, a plan forming in her mind. Thomas McQuillan was about to pay for what he'd done to her. And, oh, vengeance was going to be sweet.

CHAPTER 47

*M*ary unlocked the front door to her townhouse and Roger came careening around the entryway corner at a dead run, flinging himself on his beloved mistress. When he saw Mitch, Frank and Faith behind her, he let out several delirious yips of excitement. But when his gaze fell on Lorelei he absolutely lost his mind. Barking in ecstasy, he launched himself straight at his One True Love, panting and drooling all over himself in a boyish display of teenage infatuation.

As Lorelei warded off the unsolicited canine ardor, Mitch whispered to Frank, "Looks like you've got additional competition."

Frank laughed weakly, complimented that a man like Mitch would see fit to tease him, but dreading the evening ahead where Niles awaited all rich and suave, teeming with charm and oozing success. Ugh.

"Are you sure you don't want to go to the hospital, Fay?" Mary was asking Faith. "I feel like you should get checked out…" she turned to Frank uncertainly.

"Highly advisable." Frank agreed. "Especially because of the pregnancy."

"But I feel fine!" Faith said brightly. "Honest! My throat is a bit scratchy and I'm a little sore where Frank punched me in the chest, but other than that I'm okay. Really!"

Frank winced. "I would appreciate it if you referred to what happened between us as 'the Heimlich Maneuver' or 'compression of your diaphragm.'"

Lorelei nudged Faith toward the stairs and said, "Let's get you changed into something appropriate for the club's dress code. Mitch said Aunt George and Aunt Francesca are going to meet us here instead of at Cobalt, so we should probably hurry this up a bit."

Faith turned to Mary. "I'm sorry to be borrowing something so last minute…"

"It's ok! I have a really pretty dress I wore to the AirSec ball earlier this year and I think it will fit you. The only thing is… it's a short skirt and you're so much taller than me. You'll have to keep your knees together when you sit down, and be careful not to bend over in front of anyone."

"I can do that!" Faith assured her cheerfully.

"As long as Jesse isn't around," put in Lorelei and the three girls dissolved into gales of laughter.

***

Georgette pulled her Mercedes into Owen and Mary's driveway and switched off the headlights.

Francesca leapt out of the car immediately. "I can't wait to see our girl!" she said excitedly. "I feel like it's been forever."

Georgette stepped from her vehicle, careful to keep her gorgeous dress from creasing. She felt like a gossamer princess swathed in fabric woven specifically for her by glittering fairy godmothers. The sales girl had told her she looked just like Helen Mirren in it.

A rustling noise came from the hedge to the right of the women and they both started in surprise.

"Who's there?" Francesca demanded.

Silence followed.

Francesca backed up into George protectively as though she were shielding her. She reached into her purse and started to pull something out. Alarmed, Georgette pushed Francesca from her.

"Please tell me you do NOT have your gun in there, Franny!"

"Damn straight I do. I have a right to protect me and mine."

"I cannot believe you! You *cannot* bring that thing out with you in public! First of all, California has strict gun laws and…"

"Yeah, yeah, blah, blah…"

Francesca eyeballed the bushes menacingly and, deciding there wasn't any danger, teetered off toward the front door in her high heels, her pleather pants making swishing sounds as her thighs brushed against one another.

Georgette sighed long and loud and then followed her partner up the driveway.

Francesca knocked on the door and it swung open a few moments later to reveal Mitch. He gazed at his sister-in-law in amusement. "Nice outfit, Fran."

Frank came into the entryway and his jaw dropped when he caught sight of the eighty-one year old in a halter top and skin tight pants.

Before Francesca could move aside to let Georgette into the house there was a slight movement just off the porch. Frank instantly tensed, his eyes sweeping the perimeter beyond.

"Excuse me, sir," he said to Mitch and moved past both him and Francesca. When Frank saw Georgette on the step he said encouragingly, "Why don't you go inside with the others, ma'am, and shut the door behind you."

Francesca was immediately on alert. "I knew I heard something," she said to Frank. "You a cop? You look like a cop. What kind of piece do you have on you?"

Frank looked down at the small wrinkled woman at his elbow. "Detective Frank Williams. Nice to meet you. Now please go into the house."

"Nice to meet you too. I'm Francesca Maria Benedetta Fogagnolo. And hell no! I'll be your back up."

A figure in black scooted behind the Mercedes and Francesca, darting in front of Frank and shoving him aside, pulled her gun from her purse and took aim. "HANDS IN THE AIR, PERP, OR I'LL BLOW YOUR BRAINS OUT!"

After emitting an ear splitting scream of terror, the figure ran off into the night leaving a small wet trail on the driveway.

"I think it peed its pants," Francesca said to Frank with a nod of disgust. "What a pansy."

Georgette came rushing from the doorway. "Franny! Oh my god! You could have been killed!"

In a commanding, but gentle voice Frank said, "Ma'am, I'm going to have to confiscate your weapon." When Francesca didn't pass it along to him he pried her fingers from the grip and cocked the slide back. Looking up in surprise, he ejected the bullet and said in disbelief, "You loaded the chamber?"

Francesca put her hands on her hips. "Well, duh. What's point of carrying a gun if it doesn't have ammo at the ready?"

"Francesca! Go in the house right now!" Georgette's face was white with fear and anger. She turned to Frank. "Officer, please don't send her to jail. She really doesn't mean any harm."

"Everyone, get inside," Mitch ordered, ushering them back through the doorway. After the women were seated on one of Mary's leather couches in the living room, Mitch said, "No need to worry. I think that was just Imogen St. Perux out there."

"Who's that?" Frank asked, releasing the magazine from Francesca's gun and pocketing the bullets.

"The nosy HOA president," Georgette said. She turned to Mitch, raising a shaking hand to her forehead. "Does Mary have any wine already opened? I could really use something to calm my nerves."

"What about the weed stuff?" Francesca asked. "Remember that time Owen had his flyboy buddies over here and they let us try some?"

A little cry escaped George's lips and she looked at Frank in distress. "She's not talking about marijuana, officer. My partner doesn't do drugs." She turned to Francesca. "You're going to give me a panic attack."

"It's only some vile alcohol that tastes like gasoline," Francesca informed Frank as she patted George's hand comfortingly.

"Jeremiah Weed bourbon?" Frank ventured.

Francesca snapped her fingers. "That's it! I got so drunk on it that I tried to make out with one of Owen's friends- I think his name was Horse. Big fella. Weed must have done some real weird stuff to my brain because I don't even *like* fellas. Sexually, I mean." Francesca's eyes brightened. "Say, speaking of sex, you guys want to hear a joke? A naked priest, a Klingon and a wombat walk into an Australian prison..."

Mitch said quickly to Georgette, "I'll be right back with your wine."

⌒〜

Upstairs, Mary pulled a pink tube dress from her closet. It was soft and shimmery with tiny white flowers dotting the bodice and a pretty bow at the waist. She brought it over to where Faith and Lorelei were sitting on the bed, chatting and giggling like sisters.

"Ohhh..." Lorelei said. "That is *so* you, Mary!"

"I'll say!" Faith chimed in. "Very innocent and feminine."

Lorelei scrutinized the length. "I'm afraid it's not going to look so innocent on you, Fay, with your height."

Faith stood up and took the dress from Mary, kissing her on the cheek. "I'll just go change. Thank you for letting me borrow it."

Faith disappeared into the master bath and Mary sat on the bed with Lorelei, careful not to wrinkle her white knit chiffon gown.

"Do you want to talk for a minute?" Lorelei asked gently.

Mary hung her head, then, tentatively, she said, "Lei... Owen really hurt me last night and I... I don't think I can find my way back to him again..."

Lorelei's eyes narrowed into malevolent slits of pure venom. "How did he hurt you?" The words came out harsh and succinct, as though each word was its own sentence.

"He was the real Owen last night for almost an hour. The Owen I married; the one I fell for when we were teenagers. We made love and it was like the old days, you know? He was so sweet and caring and he wasn't just touching me because he was going through the motions of trying to get me pregnant. He was thoughtful and considerate and..." she stopped, blushing shyly. "It was really nice."

"What happened afterward?"

"It was like something triggered him and he shut himself off from me. I'd say he became a different person but it wasn't like that at all. He just became the Owen he's been for the past few years. And I saw... I saw the difference between who he used to be and who he is now and they're such completely opposite people. It was a little scary, I guess, but, mostly it made me grieve for what used to be. I know that people change and marriages grow and expand to allow that, but..." Mary's eyes welled up with tears.

Lorelei reached over and held Mary's hand. "It's okay..."

"But how do I know what's right anymore? I mean, what is the unselfish thing to do? Do you let go of someone because your needs aren't being met? That doesn't seem fair. I made a commitment to Owen when we got married- for better or for *worse*."

Lorelei sighed. "I imagine you're asking the same questions every married person has probably asked themselves at some point. Be truthful with me, Mare- do you still love Owen?"

Mary nodded, her honey hair brushing against her bare arms. "Yes. Of course."

"Are you *in* love with him?"

There was a long silence and then, "I'm in love with the old Owen, but after last night... I don't think the old Owen is ever coming back." Mary bit her lip. "I'm also worried about tomorrow. Ellen is staying at The Del and I'm having brunch with her."

One of Lorelei's eyebrows lifted in distaste. "She's in town? And, no, you damn well don't *have* to have brunch with her. Don't go, Mary. That woman will do nothing but stress you out."

"I already said I would. It will be fine." She took a deep breath. "I'll be fine. I'm just a bit nervous is all."

"Take your dad with you."

A hint of a smile touched Mary's sad face. "I'm sure she'd love to see him, but, no, I think she wants to talk to me one-on-one."

"About why you haven't provided the Crossfield's an heir yet?"

"You make it sound so crass."

"Speaking of crass..." Lorelei chuckled as Faith walked back into the room.

Mary looked up and gasped. "Fay, you look breathtaking!"

"Like a virginal hooker," Lorelei added.

Faith turned in a circle so her friends could see the full effect of Mary's dress on her tall, slender body. Her lovely legs were long and gorgeous and, with the skirt being so very short, they were displayed almost in their entirety. The dress' big bow and small flowers gave Faith a fresh, ingénue persona which was a strange contrast with the possibility of a peep show down below.

"Do not trip, fall, bend or sit," Lorelei instructed, turning Faith around and steering her back toward Mary's bathroom. "And let's do something about your hair and make-up."

CHAPTER 48

A crowd of well-dressed attractive people surrounded Club Cobalt. They grouped themselves in clusters while waiting in roped off sections. Most were preening for each other, taking selfies or craning their necks to see if they could catch a glimpse of a celebrity or two. Although L.A. claimed the lion's share of famous California A-listers, San Diego attracted more than a few stars who found rest and relaxation in the laid-back beach city.

Mitch, Frank, Georgette, Lorelei, Mary and Faith were ushered inside Club Cobalt promptly after they gave Niles' name to security. Francesca, however, was made to wait outside, her hands indignantly planted on her hips, her spiky grey hair standing on end.

"I'm with them!" Francesca insisted, watching her family and friends disappearing inside the club.

"Ma'am, we have a dress code…"

"Oh, come on! I saw a paparazzi picture of J. LO wearing this exact outfit to Provocateur. If she can get into a ritzy Manhattan club wearing it then I can get into Club Cobalt."

Another security member joined them. "He'll be here in a minute to confirm."

"Who?" Francesca demanded.

"Niles Donovan."

The guards spoke to one another for a few moments, their voices too low for Francesca's hearing aids to pick up on. She saw them shoot her an amused side eye more than once. Eventually Niles came out. He looked incredibly debonair and sophisticated in a black sharkskin suit. He glanced at Francesca briefly and said to security, his face inscrutable, "If you gentlemen wouldn't mind letting her through tonight, I assure you she will obey the dress code next time." He then slipped each of them several hundred-dollar bills.

"Damn!" said Francesca. "I knew you had money, but..."

The inner ropes were lifted and Niles and Francesca entered the huge three story building. Soft blue lights cascaded down the walls and across the high ceilings. A mammoth dance floor sprawled in the middle of the enormous main room and private balconies were discreetly pressed up against high side walls. Francesca asked Niles what the balconies were for and he relayed that they were cozy hideaways for the rich and famous.

Gorgeous wait staff and sexy bartenders mixed and mingled with guests, their trendy uniforms custom-fit, their hair perfectly coiffed, their personalities dazzlingly outgoing and vivacious. A steady beat of techno music pulsated around Niles and Francesca as they made their way toward a small sectioned off area to the left of the dance floor. Mitch and Mary sat together on one royal blue couch while Lorelei and Frank lounged companionably on another. Faith stood to the side, longingly watching the people who were dancing. Georgette came rushing at Francesca, her arms outstretched.

"Thank goodness you finally got in!" she said, hugging her partner. "We sent Niles out there when security told us they stopped you at the door."

"You would not *believe* how much cash that man has in his pants!" Francesca said, pointing at Niles' trousers.

Mary giggled and caught Lorelei's eye.

Niles glared at Frank. "I see my seat was taken while I rescued a member of our party."

Frank stretched luxuriously, his arm going along the back of the couch behind Lorelei. "This is a comfortable seat too. Good of you to allow a man of the law to take a load off."

Niles crossed his arms. "You know, I'm still not clear on how you ended up invited, Detective. The only thing I know about you is that you were harassing my girlfriend in her condo..."

Frank smiled easily and cut him off. "She's not your girlfriend, Clark Kent. Get that through your pretty little head right now."

"Pretty?" Niles said, highly offended. "I'll have you know..."

"Far as I can see," Frank continued conversationally, "you left me alone with Lorelei in her bedroom and if she were *really* your girl, well, then, that wasn't a very gentlemanly thing of you to do. In fact, you didn't do one damn thing to make her feel like you had her back- unless your version of being a gentleman is running down the stairs like a scared rabbit."

"Why you..." Niles lunged at Frank, his eyes spitting fire.

Frank was on his feet in a second, his muscles tensed, his hands balled into fists.

Mitch stood abruptly and edged his way between the two men. "Frank," he said, placing a hand on the younger man's shoulder, "stop provoking him. Don't do this."

Niles eyeballed Frank over Mitch's shoulder. "I think it's time you left, Detective. I'm not sure what kind of places you're used to," he looked Frank up and down scornfully, "but this venue is for people of a certain echelon- an echelon I'm quite certain is beyond your prole-tariat imagination."

Lorelei sighed and stood up. "Okay, I think we've all witnessed enough testosterone for the evening." She turned to Niles and said firmly, "Frank is a servant of the law and that puts him in his own class, a class that is worthy of our respect and admiration. I do not want to hear you insult him again." Then she looked at Frank. "You are here as Niles' guest and I would appreciate you showing him some courtesy as our host." She paused. "Now, shake hands and stay away from each other for the rest of the evening."

Frank and Niles gave Lorelei quick glances of sheepishness and shook hands without making eye contact.

Faith pulled Mary from the other couch and then put her arm around Lorelei. "I know you both like Lor," she said to Frank and Niles, "because she's wonderful, but I'm afraid she belongs to me and Mary this evening." She gave each of the men a radiant smile. "Now, if you'll excuse us girls, we're going to the powder room to talk about you and what just happened. You boys behave until we get back."

Lennie whistled low and loud as he leaned over the railing of the private balcony he shared with Thomas. He'd had to pay dearly for the hidden suite on the second floor of Club Cobalt, but it had been worth it to get Thomas McQuillan in his clutches for a one-on-one meeting.

"Check out the babe in the red suit," Lennie said, nudging Thomas with his elbow. "Slicked back blonde hair, great body Man, Cobalt really attracts the crème de la crème."

Thomas glanced down disinterestedly at the girl Lennie pointed out and wondered what Katya was doing tonight. He waspishly contemplated the countless nights of celibacy that now stretched before him. Maybe he should just call her… He shook his head. No, absolutely not.

Then his eye caught sight of someone familiar. He leaned forward, squinting at the vast floor below. There were two other women with the blonde Lennie was wolfishly leering at. One of the girls was a very tall redhead who resembled a cute, newborn giraffe. But the other… the other girl was petite, slender, her honey hair spilling in beachy waves down her arms and her bare back. The dress she wore was long and white and it gathered in all the right places against the curves of her body. Thomas did a double-take. The pet nanny! What was the *pet nanny* doing here?

Lennie asked for another round of champagne from their pretty hostess and when she left he began to chat about publishing houses desperately panting after the next bestseller.

"The problem is…" Lennie said, "… they keep looking to the old tried and true authors. No editor wants to touch the slush piles because ninety-nine percent of the stories are crap. But sometimes you gotta weed through the bullshit to find a pearl, am I right?"

"That doesn't even make sense," Thomas said, his eyes following Mary Crossfield across the floor below.

"You're right. I've had too much to drink already. It was a bad analogy…. or is it an allegory? Apologue? Whatever you writers say… Anyway, what I'm trying to get at is that when you finish your novel you'll have The Big Five pounding on your door offering gargantuan, juicy advances and promising royalty percentages up the wazoo."

"Great," said Thomas distractedly. The white dress was mesmerizing the way it glided with the motion of Mary's feminine figure. Thomas was reminded of the night she'd walked away from him at The Marine Room, the soft yellow fabric she'd worn brushing against her temptingly attractive backside.

Lennie was still talking. "The world is your oyster, Tom. Finish your book and let's get you back where you belong. On top."

Mary and her two friends disappeared into a cluster of people. He wondered where she was headed. The rooftop patio with its fireplace and twinkling lights? The secluded bar area in the back with its darkened ambiance and tiny tables?

Thomas ignored Lennie while he scanned the floor patiently, waiting to catch sight of the lovely girl in white when she returned. White. The color of purity. He recalled a poem he'd read not so long ago that romantically proclaimed, "…white is the color of new beginnings… white… white… softness and light…" And then… Thomas remembered from childhood that old story of Alice who had chased the White Rabbit, following him down a hole into the mystical, distorted world of Wonderland. What was it the White Rabbit had said? Oh, yes! It was: "Oh, dear! Oh dear! I shall be late!"

Thomas sighed, his heart heavy.

Purity.

New beginnings.

Softness and light.

Was it too late?

What about Gemma?

Thomas knew he was drunk.

Mary pulled her cell phone from her small pink clutch and looked at the time. She was astonished to discover they'd been at the club for almost three hours already. She'd been having so much fun with everyone and was now alone, relishing a slight breather while her friends and family were otherwise occupied. She looked out over the dancefloor packed with laughing, exuberant people enjoying the freedom of a night out. Beautiful bodies were everywhere, high on excitement and the latest creations of Cobalt's mixologists. Champagne flowed, music blared, lights flashed, energy surged... it was complete sensory overload.

Georgette and Francesca had disappeared to the rooftop patio for cocktails and Faith was pulling Mitch onto the dance floor after shrieking, "OH MY GOSH THIS IS MY FAVORITE SONG RIGHT NOW!!!" for the tenth time. Niles had been accosted by three business associates who were using Club Cobalt as a networking opportunity. They wanted Niles' opinion (and insider savvy) on the mixed-use high rise going up for sale in the Central Business District. After trying to blow them off, Niles eventually got sucked into a heated debate on whether or not the building's yield and value-add potential would keep the buyer turning a lucrative tenant profit for many years. Frank, relieved to see Niles preoccupied, whisked Lorelei off to a hidden table in a dark corner.

Mary stood against a wall, half hidden by a fat leafy plant. As she sipped her dainty strawberry cocktail she felt a tiny prick of electricity at the back of her neck. Startled, she looked around but didn't see anything unusual. Goosebumps rose on her arms and she felt very, very shy all of a sudden.

Someone was watching her.

Thomas practically lolled off the balcony railing, his gaze so intense on Mary Crossfield that he almost forgot where he was and who he was with. For the past three hours he'd been busy tuning Lennie out so he could watch the way Mary's smooth, soft body moved under her white dress. His hazel eyes followed the sway of her hips, the curve of her thighs, the rise and fall of her chest, and all the while his heated imagination ran wild. Thomas' baser instincts told him Mary was a sensual person, one who knew of physical decadence. Yet... just below that wholesome surface of hers he detected a curious fissure of hidden desires and untapped talents.

Or maybe it was just the alcohol messing with his mind.

He looked over his shoulder to order another drink and saw Lennie tipsily hitting on their hostess. The man was a talented, fantastic agent, but a walking cliché.

Thomas went back to staring at Mary. His curiosity had cranked into overdrive when he observed her friends and family. They all seemed so loving, so close. He couldn't hear what any of them were saying of course, but he found their appearances and their actions to be very entertaining. There was an older lesbian couple - one woman was statuesque and classy while the other looked like Phyllis Diller dressed as a prostitute. There was a mature, very good-looking gentleman in a tailored suit. He was deeply tanned and he had large, calloused hands like those of a workman. Thomas knew he was Mary's father because he and Mary shared such similar features. There was another guy, younger, tougher, with close cropped hair who would sometimes stare daggers at an affluent gentleman in black Armani. The two men seemed to be purposely keeping out of each other's way. The blonde bombshell in red Lennie had spotted earlier stayed close to Mary, and the tall cute girl trying to pass off a tube top as a short dress giggled a lot and drank no alcohol whatsoever.

But the most touching observation was the way Mary and her father openly adored one another, their eyes sparkling with affection, their laughter genuine and spontaneous. The big man was clearly protective over his daughter and their bond seemed exceptionally close. Thomas surmised their relationship wasn't just representative of child and parent, but that they were good friends as well as kindred spirits. The sweetest display of the devotion between them was when Mary's father reached over more than once to stroke his daughter's long, honey hair, the gesture comforting and paternal.

Thomas was almost ashamed to be spying on Mary, who was, technically, his employee, but he was too intrigued to look away. What a cast of characters she had in her life! And there was so much love surrounding her... no wonder she appeared as fresh and as ingenuous as a child.

He leaned forward as much as he could, scrutinizing Mary's face. He could barely make out those adorable freckles sprinkled across her nose. Her eyes were clear and alert but Thomas sensed sadness somewhere within them. Maybe because she was missing her husband? The ex-Navy fighter pilot. Thomas wondered what he was like. Probably very tough. No nonsense. Extremely intelligent and dexterous. Capable, dependable. Thomas stared hard at Mary for several seconds and she rubbed the back of her neck as though something had touched her there. Then she shyly glanced around in such an innocently alluring way that a highly erotic thought shot through Thomas' imagination.

And just like that, creativity struck.

Oh, not because of Mary Crossfield herself, but perhaps because of what Mary Crossfield represented- kindness, softness, naivety... everything he'd been missing from the opposite sex for way too long. He'd been living a life he wasn't necessarily proud of, treading in the shallow end of satisfaction, shying away from swimming into the deep waters of what his heart really desired... compassion and understanding and sensitivity. But now with Katya gone...

"I know we've had a few," Lennie was saying, "and maybe even a few too many..." He slapped Thomas on the back, "But can we spend at least a few minutes talking about business?"

Thomas made up his mind in an instant. "You know what, Len? Draw up the contracts as soon as you can. I'll have my novel done in four weeks. I want it published in September, just like Katya told the press it would be."

Lennie sat bolt upright. "Are you serious?"

"Quite."

"But..."

"Just do it. I want everything signed by Monday. I'm tired of my own excuses. I'm tired of holding myself back. I'm tired of feeling like a failure. A forced deadline is my only escape."

"There's going to be press when word gets out..."

"I understand."

"And Hollywood will be desperate to get the rights..."

"Great. But, Len, make sure John Bhear is blackballed from bidding. That bastard will *never* get his hands on any of my scripts."

Lennie gave him a curious look, then shrugged. "Whatever you want, Tom, I'll take care of everything." He cleared his throat. "And I assume my previous percentage still holds?"

"Add three percent to your end."

Lennie couldn't believe his good fortune. What had gotten into Thomas McQuillan?

"And, Len," Thomas pointed below them to the side of the dance floor, "see that woman in the long white dress by the plant?"

Lennie squinted and then nodded. "Yes, I see her."

"Send her party three bottles of Boerl & Kroff. I'll pay you back."

"An anonymous gesture, I assume?"

"Yup. Thanks for an interesting evening. See you Monday."

As Thomas walked out of the suite and down the back stairs, Lennie leaned forward and peered intently at the girl in the white dress. Whoever she was, it seemed she was Thomas McQuillan's muse.

CHAPTER 49

⌒

"*I* don't understand why you're so upset, Niles. We're not exclusive. We've never been exclusive. You know I date other men." Lorelei was trying to be kind as she spoke with Niles in their bottle service area. "Besides, whatever you think is going on between Frank and me... isn't. We are friends and only friends."

Niles ran a hand through his thick, dark hair. "He doesn't look at you like a friend. But that's not the point. The point is you've never dated *in front* of me. Tonight you have brought a man to a place that I invited you and your friends to and that's not -"

Lorelei cut him off. "I didn't invite him this evening. Faith did. And you're right, I should have told you he'd be coming. But, honestly, Niles, Frank and I are just friends and you and I are *not* committed so you need to let this go."

Niles moved in closer, his arm going around Lorelei's waist. He nuzzled her ear and whispered, "But after the club, you're mine, right?" He slowly ran his hand down her back and pulled her against him. "I have a surprise waiting for you at the penthouse. And in the morning, I'll make that French toast you love."

Lorelei kept her hands at her sides. "No, I'm not coming over, Niles. I'm tired... and I've had a lot to drink... and I just want to go home."

"Please, Lor. We haven't made love in a couple of weeks and..."

"No."

Niles suddenly looked horrified. "Are you going home with *him*?"

"Have you not heard one word I've said?" Lorelei was beginning to lose her temper. "But even if I was going home with Frank it wouldn't be any of your business!"

"What if I want to make it my business?" Niles practically shouted.

"I don't know what that means!" Lorelei said through her teeth. "You need to back off. My life is *my* affair and I will conduct my personal relationships how I see fit. Who I choose to have friendships with is none of your concern."

"I think I want it to be," Niles said quickly.

"I'm sorry?"

"I said… I want it to be. Look, I've been doing a lot of thinking lately and…" He paused to take one of her hands. "What I'm saying is that maybe I should stop investing all my time in my career and start investing it in someone I care for deeply."

Lorelei pulled her hand away and crossed her arms.

Niles continued in a rush. "I can make you happy. You know I can. We get along so well… in every way."

"Niles, I'm not…"

"Think about it. I won't pressure you. I know our relationship has always been casual, but I fear I've taken you for granted." Niles searched her green eyes. "I want to be the only man in your life."

Before Lorelei could respond, Frank stepped between her and Niles and said, "I'm afraid I can't allow that to happen, Donovan."

Mary was sitting on one of the royal blue couches with Faith.

"I'm dying to know who sent us the champagne," Faith gushed excitedly. "It's very intriguing to have an admirer."

"Yes, but who in our group is being admired?" Mary wondered.

"Probably someone gawking at Lorelei from afar while they work up the nerve to come over here."

Mary giggled and pointed out Frank, Niles and Lorelei in a heated discussion about twenty feet away. "Whoever wants to impress her is going to have to get through those two guys first."

Faith sighed. "I like Niles and everything, but he needs to go away. Frank is Lor's soulmate."

Mary took another sip of the Boerl & Kroff from her champagne glass. It was delicious. Whoever had sent the bottles had impeccable taste.

"Uh oh," said Faith. She was watching Lorelei and Frank launch into a full-blown argument. Niles stood by looking smug.

"Should we go over there?" Mary asked, concerned.

Faith shook her head. "Nope. This is the dance."

"The dance?"

"Frank and Lor are denying their pent-up feelings of attraction and all that angst has to go somewhere so they're going to fight. Passion is passion."

Lorelei made a heated gesture and Mary saw her best friend's neck turn red with frustration. Niles was actually smiling now, clearly enjoying himself.

Frank reached for Lorelei to calm her down and she smacked his hand away. His expression went from irritated to pained and back to annoyed when Niles tried to butt into the conversation.

With a look of complete exasperation, Frank shoved Niles backward.

Faith and Mary jumped to their feet, rushing to Lorelei's side while Niles, totally caught off balance, toppled over sideways like a wobbly Armani penguin.

"What is *wrong* with you?" Lorelei yelled at Frank.

"YOU!" he yelled back at her. "YOU are what's wrong with me!"

"Are you okay?" Mary asked Niles, holding out her hand to help him up. He ignored her and stood quickly, his face stormy.

"How DARE you!" Niles shouted at Frank, advancing on him. "How dare you assault me in front of my girlfriend!"

"She's not your girlfriend!" Frank roared.

Lorelei had had enough. "I'm not anyone's girlfriend," she asserted, "because I'm moving. You both know that. You know I'm moving to Manhattan as soon as I can see my way clear to do it." This wasn't the way she'd wanted to announce her decision, but these two macho idiots had forced her into it.

Faith let loose with a heartbreaking wail. "No! No! We still have to talk about this, don't we?"

Mary felt all of the breath leave her lungs. She turned wet, amber eyes to Lorelei, her voice shaking. "When? Did Margaret retire?"

Everyone was staring at Lorelei, waiting for her to respond. She looked first at Mary. "I will be moving to New York, if Empire & Malkin allow it, in four weeks."

Faith uttered a horrendously pitiful sob and pushed her way through the crowds, stumbling toward the ladies' room.

"Why didn't you tell me?" Mary asked, deeply hurt.

"Because it's not firm yet." Lorelei's voice softened. "We knew we'd part one day, Mare, but that doesn't mean we'll stop being friends. I knew AirSec could send you and Owen to another state or another country before I ever got to Manhattan. San Diego has always been temporary- for both of us."

"But what if it's not?" Mary whispered.

Lorelei put her arm around her friend. "I don't understand."

Tears spilled down Mary's cheeks. "If I leave Owen, Lor, I'm going to need you more than ever."

Mitch, returning from the bar with a Shirley Temple for Faith, approached the little group just in time to overhear the exchange. And as Mary leaned her head on Lorelei's shoulder, Mitch finally understood how deeply his little girl was hurting- and how serious the problems between her and Owen were.

Much later, with everyone dispersed throughout the club, Frank took Lorelei's hand and pulled her into a dark corner. The dim lighting was murky, greyish, giving them the illusion that they were completely alone. They stared at one another, chemistry vibrating between them.

"I want to say I'm sorry," Frank apologized. "I was out of line earlier with Niles."

"I'm sorry too," Lorelei said. "I don't know why I'm so irritated and restless tonight."

"There's a lot going on."

"No… it's more than that. It's like… like I have all of these butterflies inside of me that are frantically trying to break free."

"I feel the same way," Frank said, his voice deep, powerfully magnetic.

Lorelei looked up at him, her heart in her eyes. She reached out and touched his cheek. His jaw clenched as she ran her fingers down his neck, trailed them over his chest, his biceps, taking her time, loving the feel of the hard muscle beneath her hand.

"Dance with me?" Lorelei asked, her voice teeming with emotions she no longer wanted to control.

Instead of answering, Frank took Lorelei in his muscular arms, holding her close. Goosebumps sprinkled over her body like a delicate dusting of sensual awareness. She rested her head on his shoulder and forgot about everything and everyone except the man who was breaking down all of her protective barriers.

Niles, standing off to the side, had seen the passion in Lorelei's eyes when she looked up at Frank, and as he watched the two of them dancing together he knew they were in their own space and time. Although their touches and movements were restrained, anyone could see there was so much more going on between them than mere friendship. Niles cursed himself for letting Lorelei Harper slip through his fingers. He'd had two years to win her over, but work had always been too important. Thinking back, Niles wondered even if he had wanted to make her his own would she have agreed?

Most likely not.

He regretfully acknowledged that Lorelei had never, in the entire time he'd known her, looked at him the way she was looking at Detective Frank Williams.

Niles wasn't used to losing, and he wasn't about to admit public defeat, but he recognized when a battle wasn't his to wage. There was no chance of victory. With a lump in his throat, and without saying goodbye to anyone, Niles quietly slipped out a side door and into the night air.

CHAPTER 50

T he next morning Lorelei's living room was littered with tired, hungover loved ones. Mitch was sleeping on one of the bright red sofas, Georgette was cozily snoring on the fainting couch and Mary and Lorelei were curled up together on the floor amidst a sea of fuzzy blankets and pillows.

Around nine a.m., a knock sounded at the front door and Faith rushed down the circular stairs from Lorelei's bedroom before the noise woke anyone.

"Shhhhhhh…." she said, opening the door. When she saw it was Frank she pulled him inside. "Everyone's still sleeping."

"You all came back to Lorelei's?" Frank was surprised.

"No one was able to drive except me. Lor said it was okay if we all just crashed here. I stayed because… because…"

"Because of Manhattan."

"Lor and I need to talk."

Frank nodded in understanding. He looked over at Lorelei peacefully sleeping, her blonde head cushioned on a lavender pillow, a downy blanket tucked around her voluptuous body. She looked so beautiful. What he wouldn't give to…

"Why did you come by?" Faith was asking in a low voice.

Sheepishly, Frank held up a paper bag filled with groceries. "I thought Lorelei might need a hearty, home cooked breakfast this morning after all that champagne last night."

"You're so sweet," Faith gushed.

Frank noticed someone was missing. "Where's Francesca?"

Faith's eyes took on a mischievous glint. "She's upstairs. We've been watching You Tube videos."

"What kind of videos?"

"Tutorials," Faith whispered excitedly. "Francesca said she was thinking about shaving her head and…"

Frank smothered a laugh. "She didn't!"

"No!" Faith said triumphantly. "*I* did!"

Mitch stirred and opened his eyes. His suit pants were wrinkled and his dress shirt was open down the front revealing his broad tanned chest and firm stomach. He sat up and massaged his temples.

"Are you okay?" Faith asked him, concerned. "Can I get you some water?"

Mitch attempted a smile. "Sounds good."

Faith gestured to Frank to follow her into the kitchen. "One of the perks of being pregnant," she said. "No hangovers."

Frank dumped the contents of his grocery bag on the counter. "If we stretch it, I'm pretty sure I can make enough breakfast for everyone."

Faith pawed through the contents eagerly. "Do it! I'm so hungry I could eat a hundred cows!"

Frank chuckled. "I'm afraid I've only got chicken and pig here. Does quiche sound okay?"

"Heavenly! And you brought a baguette and fruit and different kinds of cheeses…" Faith stopped, a jar of capers in her hand. "How are you so awake this morning?" she asked.

"I didn't drink that much last night." Frank cleared his throat. "I think it's a good idea if I keep control of all my faculties around Lorelei."

"Ah," said Faith. "Very respectable. You're just drawing lines and making rules all over the place, aren't you, Detective?"

Frank leaned against the counter and crossed his arms. "Boundaries are very, very important right now. I want Lorelei to trust me." He sought Faith's compassionate eyes. "I'm not going to hurt her. Please don't worry. I'm not Connor."

"Oh, I know," Faith reassured him. "You're Lor's soulmate."

Frank felt his heart constrict. "You don't know that."

"But I do! I swear it! I can tell." She moved toward the coffee pot, poured a cup of the dark liquid and handed it to Frank. Her voice dropped as her eyes became serious, pleading. "Please tell me you're going to convince Lorelei that you're her soulmate before she moves. Please tell me she'll stay in San Diego for you."

Frank took the coffee cup from Faith and set it down on the kitchen island. "Listen, Fay, Lorelei and I had a long talk in the back of the club last night and she told me how going to New York has been a goal of hers for a very long time. Now, that goal has nothing to do with you and nothing to do with me. She has to follow her dreams and we can't stand in the way."

Mitch stumbled into the kitchen, rubbing his eyes.

"Sir," Frank said to Mitch, moving away from Faith and pulling a chair out from under the lip of the island, "why don't you sit down? You look pretty out of it."

Mitch ran a hand over his face. "Reckon I don't feel too good."

"Just hungover, right?" Frank asked casually, but his eyes were watchful.

"Yeah," said Mitch, gingerly sipping the water Faith handed him, "I'm sure that's all it is."

A Herculean scream of anguish came from the living room and Frank and Faith rushed out of the kitchen.

Georgette, still prostrate on the fainting couch, was staring up at Francesca. "What have you *done*?" she demanded of her partner.

Francesca, a joyful grin on her wrinkly face, slowly turned in a circle to give Georgette a full view. "Faith shaved my head for me! Doesn't it look fantastic?"

Lorelei and Mary were sitting up in their makeshift bed of blankets on the floor, rapidly blinking sleep from their eyes, trying to make sense of what was happening.

"Well," said Faith proudly, "I only shaved half of her hair." She walked over and placed a hand on Francesca's grey head. "See," Faith indicated, "... the right side is completely bald, but then I faded in the spiky parts on the other side around the back with scissors. It's very chic."

Lorelei yawned and rubbed the back of her neck. "I would say I'm surprised this happened, but..."

Georgette was standing now, her hands on her hips. "Franny, I cannot *believe* you did this!"

"Well," said Francesca, cheerfully placing blame, "you guys all passed out and left Faith and me unsupervised."

Mary giggled. "It's kind of cute, Auntie."

Francesca preened. "You think so? I'm going to look so edgy for our couples' portrait next month."

"The photo shoot for our anniversary," Georgette mourned, sinking back down onto the chaise lounge. "You're going to have a shaved head in our pictures."

"*Half* shaved," Faith corrected.

Lorelei's green eyes focused on Frank in confusion. "I don't remember you coming home with us last night...?"

"I got here about ten minutes ago," Frank said, meeting her glance and then looking away. She was entirely too tempting with her tousled hair, sleepy, innocent expression and clingy, satin pajama shirt. He had a wild thought of pushing Mary out of the way and ordering her and everyone else to leave so he could lay Lorelei back on those soft blankets and cover her body with his own, explore her curves with his hands, feel the softness of her skin with his tongue, hear her moans of pleasure in his ear...

"What happened to Niles?" Mary asked the group, unwittingly dousing the flames of Frank's scorching hot daydream by mentioning Mr. Tall Dark and Fire Retardant. "He just kind of disappeared."

"I should call him," Lorelei said. She suspected he had left when he'd seen her dancing with Frank, his pride probably somewhat bruised.

Mitch came into the room holding a steaming mug of black coffee just as his cell phone rang. He dug it out of his pants pocket and when he saw who was calling a slow sexy smile crossed his lips. "I have to take this," he said distractedly to no one in particular and left the room.

"Did you see that?" Faith exclaimed. "Did you see the expression on his face? That man is totally in love."

"Bertie is one foxy lady," Francesca offered, giving a low wolf whistle. She tapped her chin thoughtfully. "You know if I weren't committed to someone else…"

"She's too young for you," George said, rolling her eyes. Then she said to Mary, "Bertie is very sweet, my dear. I think you two will get on wonderfully."

"I'm starving," Francesca announced suddenly. "We all need some hangover grub, stat."

"We could order out," Lorelei suggested. "I don't keep too much food around the house…"

Frank rubbed his hands together. "You ladies are all in luck. I brought groceries with me. Who wants chicken quiche Florentine with a side of bacon?"

Everyone looked excited and Lorelei gazed up at him, admiration shining from her green eyes. "You can cook?"

"Sure," Frank said easily. "When my son is with me I have to make sure he eats properly."

Lorelei's voice was low and husky. "Is there anything you can't do, Detective?"

"Nope. Wouldn't I be fool to admit otherwise?"

A few hours later, everyone except Faith had left Lorelei's condo. Blankets and pillows were stacked neatly on one of the red couches. The kitchen was spotless, thanks to Frank and Mary who had scrubbed the dishes, scoured bacon grease from the range top and swept up crumbs and fruit peelings from the counters and floors. Cloth napkins were piled up on top of Lorelei's washer waiting to become clean again and someone had opened all the windows to let in the sunny sea breezes.

Her head still aching slightly from the night's festivities, Lorelei reached into her medicine chest for two aspirin, then headed downstairs to find Faith sitting at the kitchen island, her chin resting in her hands, a glass of orange juice in front of her.

Lorelei poured herself a cup of coffee. "So, choking incident aside, did you have fun last night?" she asked, trying to keep things light, but dreading the conversation that was about to ensue.

Faith smiled. "It was great! Did you see that swimsuit model try to take Mitch away from me when we were dancing? I thought it was so funny when she looked all scared of me and ran off."

Lorelei laughed. "Because you shouted, 'Oh, HELL no, you whore! Scram or I'll cut a bitch!'"

"I heard some lady say that to another lady down at Guedo's a month or so ago. It kind of stuck with me."

"Isn't Guedo's that terrible bar with the awful jukebox?"

"Yes!" giggled Faith. "Jesse and I were role-playing during date night."

"What on earth were you role-playing at *Guedo's*? Certainly not royalty or international spies."

"We were hillbillies who met on the dance floor. My name was Wanette and I'd had a really hard day cooking meth and trying to sell it. Jesse - I mean, *Cletus* - walked in looking super-sexy in overalls and he offered to buy me a Schlitz, but I told him I couldn't drink because I was knocked up. And he said he'd like to be the one to impregnate me next time I needed a good boinking and then I heard the girl next to us call another girl a hooker and say she would cut her."

"I'm riveted. What happened next?"

"Well, Jesse- I mean, Cletus- thought we should leave because one of the women pulled a razorblade out of her ponytail and there was about to be a fight. We went outside to his truck - he borrowed an old beat-up Chevy from someone- and he drove me to an abandoned gas station on the outskirts of town. It was really dark and we could see all the stars in the sky. He spread a blanket in the bed of the pickup and he'd brought pillows and Funyuns and cheese-in-a-can and we talked and laughed and snacked and he told me silly jokes. And then he started kissing me and we had a really hard time getting his overalls off which was hysterical, and then we made love on the blanket and it was kind of funny because my red Lee Press-On nails started popping off when we were rolling around. We found a fake nail stuck to his butt when we got home."

"You know, I would normally make a smart-ass comment, but you two really take the cake in romance."

Faith grinned. "Are you softening, Lorelei Harper?"

"Absolutely not. But I love that you and Jesse are so happy."

"You could have the same…" Faith hinted.

Lorelei sat down on a chair next to Faith and took her hand. "Fay, I don't want to settle down. I have a very different dream for my life."

"You mean moving away?"

"Yes."

"But why? You could make a ton of money here in San Diego. It's not like Manhattan is the only place on earth you could be a CFO or a CEO."

"I know. But I guess I've always thought of getting to New York as truly 'making it.' Manhattan is incredible, always buzzing with energy, with life, with creativity. There are four million people on that little island and the competition is insane. I want to feel the adrenaline rush of not just working with the best of the best, but *becoming* the best of the best. Even if I don't get to New York through Empire & Malkin, I will find another way. Whether I move in four weeks or four years, it's my long-term goal. You've known this. I don't understand why it's suddenly become such a huge deal."

"Because I hoped it would never really happen, or that you would change your mind, or that you would meet someone and fall in love and not be able to leave them. I guess I've just been pretending for years that your moving wasn't really ever going to shake out. And now… now it's so REAL. And I thought… I mean…" Faith dipped her head and continued timidly, "… are you sure you're not just running away?"

Lorelei let go of Faith's hand. "What exactly would I be running away from?"

"Memories of Connor O'Cassidy."

There was a long silence and then Lorelei scraped back her chair. She walked to the kitchen window and gazed out over the vast blueness of the Pacific Ocean. She took her time in responding, trying to choose her words very carefully.

"It's because of Connor I don't want to pursue a committed relationship. That has nothing to do with my career."

"Can I suggest that throwing yourself into work is simply a distraction, rather than a goal?"

Lorelei turned around, her green eyes narrowed. "You can certainly suggest it but that doesn't mean it's true."

Faith stood up. "What if I told you that moving isn't going to make your life any better because you have to deal with your demons first?"

"I would say you're crossing a line you shouldn't."

"You have to get over Connor, Lor."

"I… am… over… him!" Lorelei ground out, her mouth tightening. "I'm warning you, Fay, don't do this…"

"I'm tired of pussy-footing around that jerk! I hate that he hurt you and I hate that he made you completely closed off to ever experiencing true love! And now… now he's not even around anymore and he's still affecting your decisions by chasing you out of San Diego… and out of my life!"

"I realize you're upset and I'm trying to be understanding, but, really, this is none of your business…"

"It is *so* my business! You're my family!" Faith cried passionately. "I told you - I told you that night you and Frank came over... that I can't lose you... I can't... you're going to abandon me and..."

Lorelei was becoming exasperated. "Why do you keep saying that? It's not like when I move we're never going to talk again! There are cars and airplanes and trains and phones and email... We will still be in each other's lives. I will still be there for you."

"No you won't!" Faith argued stubbornly. "You'll be working so hard trying to forget Connor and trying to get ahead that you won't even remember me, let alone have time to travel or make a call. I know you, Lor."

"If you know me so well," Lorelei said, her voice thick with hurt, "then you know I would never, *ever* turn my back on my family or my friends."

"That's what you say now." Faith pressed her hands against her heart and looked at Lorelei with haunted, wet eyes. "If you leave then I'll be orphaned a second time. Except... except this time it will be worse because I'll see it happening. When my family abandoned me I didn't know how awful it was since I was a baby. But now... I'll know. I know who you are and I know the love you've brought to my life." She began to sob, the floodgates opening.

"Fay..."

"Don't! Don't you dare tell me I'm wrong about how I feel! And don't tell me how I *should* feel! You with your perfect family and your perfect life! Don't tell me you know *anything* about what it's like being alone in this world because you don't!"

"You have Jesse and the children..."

"You were first! Don't you get that, Lor? You were the first person to love and accept me and make me feel like I had a family. You took me into your circle and showed me what it's like to belong, to have a sense of security, to know that there's someone who will always be there for me and always have my back. You moving away is just your selfish escape into a glitzy, glamour filled world where you can forget

Connor and become everything he'll be sorry he lost. That'll show him, won't it?" Faith's weeping came in heavier, deeper, her voice rising in desperate hysteria. "Connor deserted you and now you're deserting me!"

"No! No, that is not true -"

"I don't ever want to see you again!" Faith screamed, her emotions out of control.

Lorelei stood frozen with shock. "You don't mean that."

"You're *leaving* me, Lor! Whether it's next month or next year or whenever you go to New York, I'm losing you! And you don't even care!" Faith's voice broke and she tried to take big gulps of air. "I'm not watching you walk away from me. You're going to New York to forget. And it's only a matter of time before you forget me too."

Faith turned, stumbled through the kitchen into the living room, and let the front door slam behind her with a harsh thud of finality.

CHAPTER 51

"Daddy, are you sure you're all right?" Mary asked, kissing her father good-bye at the airport. She didn't like how tired he looked.

Mitch smiled. "It's been a long time since your old man had quite that much to drink." He hugged his little girl. "I'm fine. Don't you worry."

"Maybe you can rest this afternoon when you get home."

"Maybe I can," Mitch hedged.

"Oh," Mary said shyly, "you're probably seeing Bertie."

"Yes, tonight."

"I'd like to meet her."

"I'll try to come back out here for a long weekend in September. Do you want me to bring Bertie with me?"

"You'll still be dating her by then?" Mary teased.

"Without a doubt," Mitch said sincerely. "I've never felt this way about a woman before."

Mary's face grew serious and she lowered her eyes.

"Hey," Mitch said gently, his voice soft and reassuring, "I know what you're thinking." He tipped Mary's chin up with his finger so that two pairs of amber eyes met. "Your mother was a wonderful woman. She had so much to offer the world with her kindness and her artistic ability. She and I weren't... a good fit because our personalities were so different. But that doesn't mean I didn't think very, very highly of

Helene. And my relationship with her, such as it was, was the best thing that ever happened to me because she brought me you."

"Sometimes I think about her," Mary admitted. "Sometimes... sometimes I wish I had something that belonged to her, you know? Like one of her paintings... or, well, anything, I guess, to prove she was real. That I really did have a mother."

Mitch looked away uncomfortably as he thought about Helene's possessions sitting in a corner of his house right this very moment.

He quickly hugged Mary to his chest before she could see the shame of deceit washing over his handsome face.

Mary timidly entered the Crown Room at Hotel Del Coronado, her eyes sweeping over the exquisitely decorated restaurant. The grand space was exactly how Mary imagined the tearoom must look in Buckingham Palace, and the guests were beautifully dressed, their hair and makeup as immaculate as their table manners and social etiquette. Mary's anxiety stemmed not from her elegant surroundings, however, but rather the person she was there to meet.

Finally she spotted Ellen Crossfield at a far window, a porcelain plate full of scones before her, a steaming teapot at the ready next to her elbow. She stood in a cloud of expensive perfume as Mary approached, kissing her daughter-in-law on both cheeks with stiff, cold lips.

"Hello dear," Ellen said, her eyes moving critically over Mary's summer dress with its billowing pastel skirt and modest neckline. "Have you heard from my son?"

Mary shook her head as they both sat down. "No, but I don't expect to. He said communication would be very limited on this training mission."

"I see," said Ellen, crossing her legs gracefully.

A formally attired waiter sidled up to their table. "May I tell you about our brunch specials today?" he asked politely.

"No," said Ellen, waving him away, "we would both like the royal tea luncheon."

He bowed. "Yes, ma'am."

Mary felt very uneasy. She'd hated saying goodbye to her dad earlier at the airport and she still felt hungover from the club the night before. Ellen was never a pleasant conversationalist, even at the best of times. Now, across the table, Ellen's unblinking, almost reptilian eyes seemed to be broadcasting some sort of frigid dismissal.

"How are you feeling, dear?" Ellen inquired.

Mary shifted in her chair. "I'm still not pregnant."

Ellen's eyebrows raised. "My, we're not beating around the bush, are we?"

"I thought... that's why we're here. To discuss my... my..."

"Infertility?"

Mary blushed. She wanted to say Owen could be the infertile one, but that seemed like a disrespectful thing to say to his mother.

"You know," Ellen took a dainty sip of her tea, "I don't think you need to worry about it anymore."

Mary blinked in surprise.

"If I'm not mistaken, you're not really taking the idea of becoming pregnant too seriously. From what I've come to learn, my son's desire to carry on the family name isn't very important to you."

"I..."

"It's all right, dear," Ellen said loftily. "As we grow older our inclinations become more self-seeking. And I understand that- I truly do."

Their waiter appeared with tiny cucumber sandwiches. Deftly wielding a pair of engraved gold tongs, he placed two sandwiches on Mary's plate and two on Ellen's. When he discreetly turned away Mary tentatively confided, "It's just that... I'm not sure I want to be a mother right now -"

Ellen cut her off, her voice no-nonsense. "Well, then you shouldn't be! There's no reason for you to worry your pretty little head about something that is no longer your concern."

Mary was startled. "No longer my…?"

"How old are you now, dear?"

"Thirty-two, but I don't know what that has to do -"

"That's right. You're thirty-two. And did you know if a woman becomes pregnant after age thirty-five her chances of giving birth to a baby with Down Syndrome increases to one in three-hundred-fifty?" Ellen clucked her tongue and shook her head. "Such a shame. The statistics are frightening."

"What are you saying? That I shouldn't have a baby after thirty-five?"

"I'm saying your chances of having a healthy pregnancy decrease with every year that passes. Even if you decide you want to be a mother in a few years… well," Ellen paused, pursing her lips, "we wouldn't necessarily want to chance your having a baby with… defects… now would we? Just as Owen needs to pass on the Crossfield name, his children do as well."

Mary stared at her mother-in-law, her thoughts bouncing between hurt and anger.

"Or you could decide in a few years that you don't want children at all." She took another sip of tea. "And that just won't do."

"Have you… have you talked to Owen about this?"

"Not in so many words. Your husband," Ellen's lip curled slightly, "has taken desperate measures upon himself to try to ensure an heir. I'm not saying it's your fault he strayed, but you've certainly not made things easy for him."

Mary unsuccessfully stifled a gasp. "Owen wouldn't… are you implying… I'm… confused…"

"I know you are, dear, and I am deeply sorry for that, but you and I must come to an agreement before he leaves AirSec and moves back home."

"Leave the company? No! He loves flying! And we're not moving!" Mary's face had gone white.

"Well," said Ellen coolly, "*you're* not moving. I think, Mary, you need to be honest with me and with yourself. You and Owen have grown apart. You know this. And he has responsibilities to his family that he must fulfill. You," she paused for effect, "are standing in the way of that. I must say, dear… it's really time for you to withdraw from the entire situation."

"Did… does Owen know you were going to say these things to me?"

Ellen's eyes flickered ever so briefly. "Of course. And he is in complete agreement. We felt that it would be best if you begin the process while he is gone. If everything is set in motion now, then when he gets back he only has to sign a few documents. Of course, Charles and I are more than willing to give you a very large settlement."

Mary was speechless, her heart racing, her hands shaking. A cold sweat had broken out along her brow.

"Now," Ellen folded her hands and leaned forward as though negotiating a business deal, "once you file for divorce, a bank account will be set up in your name. We feel that two million dollars is more than fair."

Mary's head began to swim and dizziness washed over her. "I don't feel very good," she whispered, her stomach churning.

Ellen rolled her eyes. "Well, we know it's not morning sickness."

"I… ha-have to go," Mary stammered, clumsily getting to her feet.

"Fine. Call me next week when you've hired an attorney and we'll get the process started."

Mary stared at her mother-in-law, realization dawning. "You want me to divorce Owen so he is free to marry someone else. Someone… who can have a baby. Someone younger so there's more time without risk of… of the baby having a deformity…"

Ellen's glacial eyes didn't flinch. "That's right. And when all of this is over, Mary, you come out the winner. Imagine! So much money at your disposal and a whole new life to start. This is a very exciting time for you."

"What if I don't want a new life?" Mary asked, her lips quivering.

Ellen inclined her head, her face set. "And why wouldn't you? Tell me right here and right now that you are in love with my son."

Mary stood stock still, the blood draining from her face.

"That's what I thought. And I wonder, Mary, dear, if the decline of your marriage has anything to do with a certain famous author?"

A deathly silence fell between the two women and Mary stared at her mother-in-law in horror.

"You didn't honestly think I would meet you today without doing my due diligence, did you? 'Covering my bases,' I believe, is the more *common* term." Ellen stood, her eyes like molten steel. "You make one move against my family and I'll have Thomas McQuillan publicly humiliated in ways you never imagined. Understand, dearest Mary, the choice has already been made for you. File for the divorce." She leaned forward, her icy gaze threatening. "Are we clear?"

"Yes," Mary said quietly. "We are clear."

"Good." Ellen sat back down on her chair. "I'll see you in court."

CHAPTER 52

A knock sounded on Lorelei's office door and she looked up in annoyance. "Come in."

"Sorry to bother you, Miss Harper," said Langford Tufton, "but I'm heading back to New York shortly and there are a few items I'd like to discuss with you before I go."

Lorelei took off her reading glasses and stood. "Of course."

Langford closed the door behind him, then walked over to shake her hand before sitting down on one of the chairs in front of her desk. He was a distinguished gentleman in his fifties, very clean-cut and well-dressed. His claim to executive fame at Empire & Malkin was his longstanding role as Joe Thompson's right-hand man.

"I want you to know," Langford said as Lorelei sat back in her chair, her legs crossed, her posture poised and professional, "... that I talked to Joe today and he's very impressed with the way you've handled the Edmond Davies situation."

Lorelei raised an eyebrow. "Really?"

Langford smiled. "You intimidated Joe and that got his attention. He assigned the Davies case to me right after you called the first time. I'm sure you're aware that it's extremely unusual for a conflict of this nature to be taken so high up the chain, but as it turns out, this was no simple sexual harassment complaint. The expense reports and cash flow statements you sent to us reflected some pretty fishy numbers so we dug deep. Joe contracted a forensic accountant, and lo and behold, ol' Davies has been embezzling for years." He spread his hands. "Your instincts were right when you suspected he'd been playing dirty with the financials."

Lorelei kept her composure even though her heart had started to race. She'd never liked Edmond Davies, but... a criminal? "Can I ask how much he skimmed?"

"Somewhere in the neighborhood of a quarter of a million dollars." Lorelei's green eyes widened.

"Davies was cunning with his misappropriations; apparently he's one smart cookie when he's not drinking. When this whole thing's over he'll be convicted of a Class B Felony with up to twenty years in prison." Langford chuckled. "Now *he'll* be the one getting sexually harassed."

Lorelei smiled weakly.

Langford checked himself. "Sorry." He cleared his throat. "What I really came to tell you..."

Lorelei's whole body tensed. This was the moment she'd been waiting for. Would he inform her she was being dismissed from the company for putting her nose in where it didn't belong? Or would he say she could stay where she was, but could no longer be considered a candidate for Margaret's position? Or was he about to tell her she'd be moving to New York by the end of the month...?

"Your record here at Empire & Malkin is exemplary, Miss Harper, and your reputation among both your peers and your superiors has us confident..."

Lorelei took a deep breath.

"... that you're the perfect successor to assume Edmond Davies' position. The entire San Diego office has been interviewed during this investigation, and aside from finding a myriad of policy breaches by Davies, we also discovered, albeit indirectly, that you are a highly valued and respected individual. We've researched your skillset, your previous evaluations, your education level... and we spoke at length with the brokers both in this office and in your regional offices. After an exhaustive look into your history with Empire & Malkin, we have no doubt whatsoever in your ability to lead and," Langford rummaged around in his briefcase and pulled out a file, "we're pleased to present this offer letter to you." Langford pushed a typed, embossed paper across her desk and she looked at it with dull eyes, her heart sinking. "As you can see, the annual salary is five times your current income. You'll have full control over your own expenses and you'll receive quarterly bonuses. Oh! And we've bumped your paid vacation to six weeks per year." He rubbed his hands together. "This is a great opportunity, Miss Harper. I'm very happy for you."

Lorelei thought long and hard before she answered. Langford assumed she was simply speechless, overwhelmed by the generous offer.

"Mr. Tufton, I appreciate the proposal and I am grateful for the kind words, however, it has been my hope, my dream really, to live and work in New York."

Langford was taken aback. "*Why?*"

"Well, for one, it's where Empire & Malkin is headquartered. Our CEO and our president work from there. Our most powerful brokers. Our financial experts and marketing geniuses." She tilted her head slightly. "Surely you understand my ambition since you yourself reside there?"

"Well," he cleared his throat, "don't get me wrong, New York is an amazing city, but living there isn't quite like it's portrayed in the movies. I mean, just the weather alone is prohibitive, not to mention the cost of living. I'm not saying the city isn't magnificent, because it is, I'm just surprised you want to live in the concrete jungle. Think about it! Right now, you live in *paradise*! San Diego's weather is beautiful year-round. No snow, no sleet, no ice, no freezing winds. You have the Pacific just footsteps from this building… sandy beaches, gorgeous sunshine. Why would you ever want to leave Eden?"

Lorelei gazed at Langford Tufton shrewdly. "You had that speech ready, didn't you?"

He shifted uncomfortably.

"Who doesn't want me to take Margaret's position?" Lorelei demanded. "Is it Joe? Is this retaliation for overstepping my bounds by trying to help Tatum?"

"No!" Langford was starting to perspire. "No, you mustn't think that."

Lorelei stood up and placed her hands on her desk. "Then what am I supposed to think?"

"You're a valuable employee in this firm, Miss Harper, and -"

"I'm listening."

Langford's voice was placating. "You are more valuable to us here in San Diego. You see, this office is going to need someone strong and capable. There will probably be turnover with Davies gone. He wasn't a good leader, but oftentimes the devil you know is better than the devil you don't, and if we bring in an unknown manager from the outside that no one knows well enough to trust then we run the risk of employees and brokers jumping ship. That absolutely *cannot* happen. We won't position ourselves to allow the competition to poach our key players. We believe, since you're highly liked and respected here, if you stay on in a managerial capacity then the office won't experience any departing hits. Which means revenue will stay on track." He leaned forward. "It's a win-win if you take the position, Miss Harper. You'll be living and working in this gorgeous coastal paradise, making copious amounts of money. You will have the power and authority to not just keep this office in the black, but to make it truly sensational."

"No." Lorelei shook her head. "No. Absolutely not. You are not doing what's best for the company by squashing my growth potential."

"How can you say that? We're still promoting you. In fact," Langford shuffled through his briefcase and consulted an iPad, "Margaret's position pays significantly less than what we've offered you to stay on here."

Lorelei's eyes narrowed. "How do I even know that's true?" She held up her hands. "You know what? It doesn't matter." She walked to her office door and opened it, standing to the side so Langford could leave. "My answer is no."

Langford turned around in his seat to look at her. "But the commission analyst position in New York is off the table. They're going to force you into the managerial role here."

"We'll see about that," Lorelei said, indicating the hallway. "Good day, Mr. Tufton."

After Langford had slunk out of her office, Lorelei shut the door and sank down onto her chair. How ironic, she thought, that Davies had been the first to say he wouldn't let her leave San Diego and now she couldn't leave because she had to replace him. Usually one to work out her own problems, she found herself in the unfamiliar position of wanting to talk to someone, someone who would listen, give sound advice, and help her to organize her thoughts and her next course of action. The whole situation was complex and frustrating and... disappointing.

Lorelei picked up her phone to call her parents - they always offered a willing ear and solid guidance – then put it down again when she remembered they were on a Rhine Getaway cruise in the Netherlands. Mary? No, she was too fragile right now, what with Owen gone and her satanic mother-in-law pushing divorce. Faith? Lorelei's heart turned over at the thought. Faith wouldn't return any of her phone calls. Niles? No, he hadn't spoken to her since the night at the club.

Lorelei tapped her foot, impatient with herself. Why was she even running through a list of confidants? She'd known as soon as Langford Tufton walked through her doorway that Detective Frank Williams would be the first person she called, no matter what the outcome.

CHAPTER 53

Thomas was writing furiously in his den, the words flowing out of him like a cascade of hot lava rushing down a steep snow-covered mountain. He was in his element, happily pounding away at his laptop as storylines and characters and dialogue flashed through his mind in dreamlike rushes of creativity. It was like the old days, he thought, before *Souls in Collision* had made him a household name. Back when writing books had been fun and exciting. Back when there wasn't any pressure to top his previous work on a grand scale. Back when expectations weren't at an insanely high level. Now... now he was writing again just for the simple, pure joy of writing.

A part of Thomas wanted to credit Mary Crossfield and her family for the inspiration that overcame his writer's block. After all, it was watching her interact with her loved ones that had given him an idea about a family drama- a poignant plot chronicling the strength of love. He'd never written anything like it, and as the story poured forth, he wondered why he'd never considered such a narrative before. After all, he had strong bonds with his parents, his siblings and his nieces and nephews. And he'd been close with Grandpa Bob and Grandma Molly before their passing. Remembering his grandparents' relationship- the longest and most beautiful love affair he'd ever had the privilege of witnessing- he decided to weave their story into his new novel, losing himself in the mystical world of romantic soulmates.

Lennie would be coming by tomorrow with contracts for the book. Thomas had told him at the club the night before that he'd have the manuscript ready for editing in four weeks. That seemed a short amount of time, but with inspiration consuming him, Thomas knew he could easily crank out twenty-five hundred words a day, meaning he'd have an eighty-thousand-word novel constructed in a month. Piece of cake for a pro, if he could just silence the voices of self-doubt in his head; the voices that screamed he was already a failure both in career and in love.

A soft knock sounded at his door and Helga's voice called tentatively, "Thomas? I'm so sorry to bot'er you, but d'ere's someone here to see you. She said she apologize fer coming unannounced, but it's very important."

Irritated, Thomas called over his shoulder. "Who is it then?"

"Her name is Gemma Hamilton."

When Thomas wrote he couldn't care less about his appearance. He hadn't even showered yet. He was wearing old board shorts and a ratty t-shirt with holes along the bottom. Comfort was the order of the day when creativity struck. He truly believed that his muse couldn't flow naturally if he was constricted, constrained, worried about wrinkling something, or concerned with coffee spills. Frequently, he snacked while writing and instead of wasting time with a napkin, he'd hurriedly wipe his fingers on whatever shirt he was wearing, knowing stains didn't matter. In fact, looking like a hobo almost seemed to enhance the perceived starving artist persona and that put him in a better writing mood.

Gemma Hamilton.

Thomas sat perfectly still in his chair after he told Helga he'd be right out. He was numb with anticipation and blood was pounding in his ears. How long had it been since he and Gemma had been in the same room together? He'd seen her on the silver screen of course- he never missed one of her movies; the opportunity to gaze at her beautiful face with its adorable smattering of freckles and deep, charming dimples. But in person? Almost ten years.

When he stood up his legs were leaden and he had to force himself to the door. He was ashamed of the way he looked and briefly contemplated taking a quick shower. But, no, it wasn't fair to keep her waiting. Whatever reason Gemma had for showing up completely out of the blue had to be of utmost importance.

As he made his way down the hall and staircase to his living room, Thomas tried to calm his thoughts. He hoped Gemma was all right and not in some kind of trouble. Maybe she needed his help... no, what could she possibly need *his* help for? Maybe she had left Dick Rimmel and wanted to... no, NO. Thomas could not let his thoughts wander down that road. She had a family- children who needed a mother and father. And from all accounts, she and Dick were very happy together. Unusual for Hollywood. But Thomas expected nothing less from Gemma.

When Thomas walked into his living room, Gemma stood from where she'd been sitting on one of his oversized sofas. Neither knew what to do when their eyes met. They started forward as though to hug, but drew back at the same time. Thomas put out his hand in an awkward attempt at a handshake and Gemma took it ever so briefly and then let go as if their touch had given her a horrible jolt of pain. But then she smiled shyly and Thomas was transported back to those snowy nights in Wales when they'd been lovers and friends, when Gemma had warmed both his bed and his heart, when life had been simple and pleasurable and filled with the most delightful sounds. Like Gemma giggling at his stupid jokes, her laughter contagiously delightful. Like Gemma saying her lines on the set of *Souls in Collision- his* lines, the lines he had written- falling from her luscious mouth with such raw feeling. Like Gemma's breaths coming in low and quick as she moaned his name night after night when he made love to her as though he wanted to both consume her and fulfill her every desire.

And now she stood before him, a decade later, as lovely as ever in a blue silk scarf and a white shirt. White… the color of innocence. He remembered Mary Crossfield in her white dress from the night before. Two women so different, yet so much alike. It was intriguing. Perhaps he could use the comparison in his book somehow. As that thought entered his mind he became suddenly elated. He was thinking like an author again! Reality was beginning to infringe on imagination- the most genuine form of storytelling in action.

"I'm glad you're here," he said simply. "It's good to see you."

They both sat conspicuously far apart on the large sofa.

"You look the same, Thomas McQuillan," Gemma said, smiling. She gestured to his shabby clothing. "I see you're still dressing like a bum when you're on a writing jag."

Thomas grinned and spread his hands. "Haven't even showered."

At the same time they remembered a particularly erotic shared morning in Gemma's shower back in Wales. Their eyes locked for a moment and then they both looked quickly away.

After a stilted pause Gemma said, "I'm really very sorry to come over unannounced. I hope you don't mind that I made some private inquiries as to where you lived. I know how discreet you are and…"

Thomas rushed to reassure her. "It's okay, Gem, no worries."

"Thank you. It's just… I need to tell you something that happened today. And I didn't feel like it was a situation we should discuss over the phone."

"Is everything all right? Are you okay?"

"Yes, yes, I'm fine. Absolutely." Gemma turned toward Thomas, her eyes serious. "I had lunch with Katya Vetrov earlier."

Thomas' eyes narrowed. "Go on."

"Her assistant had called and asked if I would meet with her which I knew was fishy from the outset- especially so soon after your return to the spotlight thanks to that dumb celebrity gossip show."

"Yes," said Thomas, his fists clenching. "I have Katya to thank for that."

"I figured. She's extremely manipulative. I played the simpering fool during our lunch so I could draw her out and get the whole story. Tom, she's got dirt on you and on me and she was going to make it public. My bodyguard nabbed her outside of Cecelia's and found a mini Wi-Fi video camera in her purse. From the angle it looked like she must have hidden it somewhere on our table. She recorded our entire conversation which was highly private and sensitive. To give credit where credit is due, she's very intelligent and," Gemma broke eye contact, "she made some very accurate guesses about my past."

Thomas stood up and paced the room, his body rigid with anger. "Did she want money?"

"No. She never mentioned blackmail. I think she was out for some sort of revenge on you." Gemma fiddled with her purse strap. "She said you asked her to marry you."

"Oh, come *on*! That's such bullshit! You know I would never..." he stopped and ran his hands through his hair. "You know I'm not the marrying type."

"Yes, of course." Gemma cleared her throat delicately. "Like I said, the whole situation was very suspicious. So I just played along until I could find out what she was up to. After David took the camera away from her I told her my attorney will be in contact. If she ever tries to threaten you or me again, I will have her blackballed from Hollywood. And she knows I have the power to do so."

Thomas looked at Gemma approvingly. "Don't play a player, eh?"

"I've been in this business way too long to be naïve."

"I can't believe she didn't guess you were on to her."

"Oh really?" Gemma teased. "You do remember that I act for a living. I was merely playing a role." She rubbed her knuckles on her chest and stretched her hand out before her, examining her fingernails. "I'd say my performance was Oscar-worthy."

Thomas chuckled. "And hers?"

"Not even B movie level."

"Gem, I…" Thomas sat back down on the sofa, closer to her this time. "I'm really sorry this happened. I would never wish my baggage on you. I haven't handled my personal life very well since you and I... since… Anyway, I wish I'd never gotten involved with Katya and now she's dragged you into whatever game it is she's playing. I feel terrible."

"Tom, it's okay. No harm was done. And once my attorney scares the life out of her with invasion of privacy and intrusion of solitude lawsuits, neither of us should hear from her again. What she did was illegal and she knows it. My assumption is she was going to release the video anonymously and the public would have blamed it on the paparazzi. Katya would have never been implicated."

"But now?"

"The camera has her fingerprints on it."

"So what kind of dirt did she have on me? On you?"

Gemma reached over and took one of Thomas' hands in her own. The warmth of her touch brought back a profusion of memories and he longed to pull her against him, to feel her soft, graceful body against his own…

"Tommy," Gemma said tenderly, her eyes searching his, "it was nothing you need to worry about. But there is something I want to say, I need to say. I think you understand that you're the only man I'll ever be in love with. I love Dick, but I'm not *in love* with him." She took a deep breath. "But I know that you and I have different needs in life. Our paths were always meant to cross, but they're not going in the same direction. We're simply at a brief intersection right now and when I leave in a few minutes we may never see each other again. What we had was the purest form of love I've ever known and I came away from our relationship with more than you can imagine." Gemma leaned forward, her eyes serious, her lips inches from Thomas'. "What Katya knows is of no consequence to how our lives will continue. You have your direction to travel in and I have mine. But I will always, *always* love you."

Thomas couldn't breathe. The words she spoke were hurting his heart. The nearness of her beautiful face was sending his senses into complete overdrive. "I love you too, Gem," he said, his voice hoarse. "Katya was only a distraction. A total opposite of you- someone who would never remind me of what I gave up. I wish... I wish..."

Gemma laid her head on his shoulder. "I know. I wish too."

Thomas held her as they both became lost in the memories of the past, the circle of time rolling forward and backward, showering them in a peaceful serenity. Neither moved, not wanting to break the spell of nostalgia, and several moments passed before Gemma said huskily, "I should go..." She broke apart from Thomas and her eyes fell to his lips. Without thinking, she ran her hands over his strong forearms, loving the feel of his skin, the tautness of his muscles, the... she leaned in closer, her touch both sweet and suggestive. Thomas' jaw hardened as he tried to control what his body so desperately wanted, what his soul longed for, what his mind told him was only natural because he loved her, would always love her...

Suddenly Gemma stood, her face flushed. "I'm sorry. I'm so sorry."

Thomas dropped his head into his hands, his heart racing, his thoughts in frenetic turmoil.

Gemma placed a gentle hand on his shoulder. "I'll see myself out."

He couldn't look at her.

A quiet stillness followed. But before she turned away, Gemma whispered, "I love you, Tommy," and then she walked out of his life once again.

CHAPTER 54

⁓

Bonjour Mama,

It's been a week since Dad flew back to Arizona and so much has happened since then. I don't even know where to start really, but...

Have you ever felt like your life has become a total disaster? Like it's messy and chaotic and filled with disorganized thoughts, patterns and events? It's like there's an illusion of everything being out of control, yet somehow, in the back of my mind I think I must be able to calm all of the turbulence. Does life really just happen to us? Or is that a cop-out? I've been so sheltered, so taken care of and- well, coddled in a lot of ways- that I wonder if I'm even able to cope with adult problems. I think about Faith, who learned independence from a young age because she had to. There was no one for her to depend on when she was growing up, no one who she could run to if she needed a place to stay, no family unit who gathered around her when times got tough. And Lorelei... well, she's the ultimate woman, someone who knows what she wants and gets it. Lorelei is the person everyone turns to, not the person who relies on others. She has this amazing career laid out before her and she's going to run some financial company one day and be in Forbes magazine. And then there's me. I've never had to make it on my own. I've never been unloved. I've never had to worry about having a job, or being homeless or pushing myself to the limit just to survive. I'm grateful, of course, but in some ways I think it's stunted my growth. I know everyone looks at me like I need to be taken care of... they see me as fragile and innocent and, well, maybe a bit immature. Perhaps it's because I've never known what it means to have to truly grow up.

And even when I divorce Owen, I'll still be taken care of financially and I'll still have Daddy and Aunt George and Aunt Francesca, and Lorelei (who may soon be in New York, but I cannot even talk about that right now) and Faith as my emotional support system. I can't believe I just wrote the words "when I divorce Owen." It's so surreal and so... sad. A part of my life is ending and instead of a chapter closing, I feel like a whole book has been written, finished, and will now be placed on a bookshelf to gather cobwebs and dust. I have cried myself to sleep more than once this week, but I think my tears are for the final ending of something that used to be so beautiful. What Owen and I shared has been gone for a long time- but actually saying goodbye to the only man I ever thought I'd be with is tearing me up inside. I know it's the right thing to do... for both of us. But that doesn't mean it's easy. It doesn't mean I don't feel like I've failed in some way. It doesn't mean I'm not devastated that my life isn't turning out the way I thought it would.

I had brunch with Owen's mother last Sunday and she made it very clear she wants me out of the Crossfield's lives. They want nothing to do with me because I'm infertile. Or they perceive it that way. I'm no good to them if I can't have a child who will carry on their family name, go into their family business, bring continued honor and fortune to their legacy. I sort of get it, I guess. I mean, I've always known what Owen's background was. He just seemed so separate from it, you know? And I think he is- or used to be. He tried to break free in whatever limited way he could by joining the military and never taking money from them to support us. I wonder how much of the pressure from his family has driven him to become the person he is now? A person who is so different from the person I married.

I have contacted a divorce attorney. I had to. Ellen was threatening me. She must have hired a private detective because she knows

I'm working for Thomas McQuillan. I'm horrified that she's invaded my privacy (and his!), but I'm not completely surprised. She's looking out for her family the only way she knows how- by being aggressively hostile. I said above that I'll still be taken care of financially- what I meant by that is Ellen offered me two million dollars to leave her family. Pretty crazy, right? I've thought off and on over the past week about not taking it. After all, I was thinking of leaving Owen before this anyway. I should try to stand on my own two feet. This is my opportunity to learn how to take care of myself, to be truly independent, to see what I'm made of. But then... it would be nice to have a nest egg so I can try writing as a living. Once I finish my book who knows if a publisher will even pick it up? And even if it is picked up, will it sell?

Would you think me terribly weak if I told you that despite everything I still love Owen? I still care what happens to him and I hope he'll be happy. I don't feel a romantic love for him anymore- he's broken that in me- I feel... a wistful love. I think about the boy he was when we fell for each other all those years ago. He was so full of life! All he wanted was to fly planes and make love to me and be independent from his family. He was so in tune with his dreams and plans. And now that boy is gone. The present day Owen just isn't even the same person.

Loving someone and being in love with someone- it's funny how those are two distinct and separate emotions. I guess that's why it wasn't hard, when all was said and done and I knew what I had to do, to pick up the phone and call the divorce attorney. Because I love Owen I want him to be happy. And for him to be happy I think he needs to please his parents. I can't say whether that's right or wrong because I don't want to judge. He was just never able to completely break free from their chains of inherited responsibility. Perhaps when he fulfills his destiny he'll find the freedom he seeks. But somehow, some way, I think a part of his heart will remain imprisoned. And down the road he will think of those early days he and I shared and he'll remember true liberation, true autonomy... and true love. This past year I hoped so many times we could resurrect those days, but I knew... I knew all along what we had was slowly dying. I just never wanted to admit it to myself.

In the meantime, I've been trying to distract myself with work; in addition to walking Chuckles, Giggles and Patch (my regular clients), I have started babysitting Voltaire. It's gone surprisingly well. Voltaire is a good boy if I keep him very, very active. We take jogs around Thomas' property, do laps together in the Olympic-sized pool, play fetch over and over, and one day I drove him down to Del Mar Dog Beach and he ran around the sand like a possessed crab. It was hysterical!

As it turns out, the best part of the arrangement is that I have a room in Thomas' house all to myself - a lovely nook of a space – and I'm thinking about bringing my laptop and doing some writing at the little antique desk when Voltaire takes a nap (he usually falls asleep for a half an hour or so after our first workout). I think he'd love to be tucked into the double bed with its soft blankets and puffy throw pillows while I get some writing in.

Thomas has been giving me homework to do via email. Mostly he sends writing prompts or asks me to complete certain exercises to enhance my vocabulary. He's also trying to teach me "show not tell" which I've argued can look like bloated prose to the reader. He came out of his office and we got into a heated debate about it and despite his irritation with me I found the exchange highly engaging. It's like he makes me think- he stimulates me mentally. I'd love to spend more time with him, but he's been very distant this week. I haven't seen Katya at all and I wonder if they broke up? He's been walking around in raggedy clothes and he hasn't shaved (it doesn't look like) since the last time I saw him. His hazel eyes are sad and... troubled. He said he's been writing a lot so maybe he's just concentrating on his novel. I want to ask about the project he's working on because I'd like him to trust me and for us to be friends, but he's so closed off and not at all like he was Saturday by the pond. I sort of find the broody, aloof Thomas very mysterious and attractive (and somewhat reminiscent of our dinner at The Marine Room), but I'm trying very, very hard to not be one of those girls who fawns all over handsome celebrities. I'm sure he gets enough of that. Besides, I'm his employee, I'm still married, there's Katya (?) and... who am I even kidding? There's no way he would even be interested in someone like me. I'm just a simple girl and he's... well, he's Thomas McQuillan.

I've decided to write a novel about the love affair between my great-grandparents, George and Pauline Hulbert. Aunt Georgette brought me a letter when she was here that Great-Grandpa George wrote to Great-Grandma Pauline in 1908 before he proposed. It's SO romantic! My favorite part is when Great-Grandpa says, "I have got a good one on you." I know he means he adores and loves Great-Grandma more than any other woman and he's excited for their future. I will have to find out more about their life together from Aunt Georgette so I can draft an outline (one of my homework assignments from Thomas is on how to structure a plot using The Freytag Model). I'll make the story mostly fiction so that I have creative license to add drama and conflict where the historical facts need beefing up, but I can only imagine that my great-grandparents must have had a beautiful and enduring marriage. I'm so excited! I'll bring the letter with me to Thomas' house and keep it in my room to show him-- when and if he emerges in a semi-decent mood from his den.

CHAPTER 55

"That is the dumbest thing I've ever heard!" Mary yelled at Thomas.

"Oh really? And who between the two of us is the published author? Who has been writing professionally his whole adult life?" He got in her face. "Who is coaching *who*?!"

"I'm tired of you telling me I have to write a certain number of words per day! How am I supposed to write if my muse doesn't show up?!"

"How is your muse supposed to show up if you're not writing!?" Thomas bellowed back.

They stared at one another in the hallway outside of Thomas' den. Mary's face was flushed with indignation, and Thomas, who looked like he hadn't showered in a week, stood rigid and angry in exceptionally grungy clothes.

Mary picked up her purse, which she had dropped on the floor in order to better gesture wildly during their argument. "I should go," she said huffily.

"Hey," Thomas put out a hand to stop her, "I'm sorry. I don't know why we keep fighting like this."

"Because you're impossible! You're demanding and condescending and... and sometimes rude!" Mary shot back.

"Really?" Thomas looked surprised.

"Yes, really," Mary said, but the heat was gone from her words.

"Listen, why don't you come into my office for a minute. I want you to read something."

Mary's eyes widened. "You do?"

Thomas rubbed the back of his neck. "Yeah. I'd like your opinion on a chapter I wrote this morning. It's… it has to do with a family scene where the father and daughter find out the grandmother has a hidden secret in her past."

"That… doesn't sound like something you would write about."

"What is that supposed to mean?" Thomas snapped, his temper flaring again.

"It doesn't *mean* anything!" Mary said irritably. "It's just that all of your previous books have been suspenseful thrillers."

"So now you're pigeon-holing my authorship?"

"Stop baiting me, Thomas. I don't want to argue anymore today."

Thomas spun around and stalked into his office. "Close the door behind you," he instructed.

Annoyed, Mary gave him a mock salute. "Yes, sir!"

"Here." He plonked down six typed pages in front of her. "Read these and then give me your opinion of the diction. I just want to make sure I've thoroughly defined the tone."

Mary sat in a chair across from Thomas and began to read. The first page immediately grabbed her imagination and she forgot all about any expressions of style as she allowed herself to be transported to another place and time. She raced through the six pages at warp speed and put them down in breathless admiration. Her eyes shone when she looked at Thomas. "You are an incredible writer."

"How can I argue with that?" Thomas teased, a smile lighting up his broody hazel eyes.

Mary giggled. "So all you have to do to calm me down is let me read your work, and all I have to do to get you to be nice is compliment your writing."

Thomas leaned back in his chair and steepled his fingers. "Have I really been that bad?"

Mary averted her gaze. "I've had some things going on in my personal life that aren't pleasant and I know I've been on edge because of it. I'm sorry I've been fighting you on some of your coaching."

"Some?" Thomas cleared his throat pointedly.

"Okay. A lot."

"If you want to talk, I'm a good listener."

Mary shook her head. "I wouldn't want to burden you. I... have my best friends to confide in and..."

"And *we're* not friends?"

Mary blinked. "Are we?"

"I thought so."

"Oh! Yes, well... I'd like that..."

"I can trust you, right? I trust you with my house, my crazy dog and now my manuscript. I'm pretty sure, aside from Helga, you're the closest person in my sphere right now. I've got my buddies, of course, but they're for hanging out- surfing, drinking, concerts. And my siblings are all very busy with their kids."

"What about Katya?" The words flew out before she could catch them.

Thomas' eyes darkened. "Katya is no longer in my life."

"I'm sorry... I shouldn't have asked..." Flustered, Mary started to stand up.

"Hey, it's okay." He motioned for her to sit down. "Don't go."

Mary was very aware that she looked almost as disheveled as Thomas did. She'd taken Voltaire to the park earlier, chasing him around in the grass and sun until he was exhausted. The exercise was a welcome stress reliever, but it had wreaked havoc on her appearance. She tried to tuck a few stray hairs back into her ponytail. Her makeup had long since melted off in the heat of the day and her casual shorts and t-shirt seemed very tomboyish.

"You didn't tell me what you thought of my tone in the chapter you read," Thomas was saying. "How do you perceive the characters?"

Mary smiled encouragingly. "They're extremely relatable- almost familiar. I feel like I know them!"

Thomas cleared his throat. "Hmmm… well, that's good." He suddenly looked uncomfortable.

"Thank you for letting me read your draft. It means a lot to me. And I was serious when I said you are an incredible writer. You're amazingly talented." She stopped because she knew she was starting to gush. It was so hard not to when he was being pleasant and not an arrogant jerk.

"Thank you. And you have a lot of potential. You're going to make a great novelist one day."

Mary's mouth dropped open. "I can't believe you just said that."

Thomas chuckled. "Just stating facts."

Mary sighed dreamily. "Thank you. Coming from you… it's a huge boost to my confidence."

"Well, I'm glad we could call a truce- end your day here on a positive note."

"Yes…" The end of the day. Time to go home to her empty townhouse, her empty bed… another empty day slipping by.

Not even Roger would be home. Faith had picked him up earlier so he could have a slumber party tonight with Mrs. Fartington. The children insisted dogs enjoy sleepovers too. Mary knew Roger would have a grand time drinking weak tea with Maddy's dolls, playing baseball with Joel's buddies in the backyard and eating scraps from the dinner table thanks to Scotty's terrible fork-to-hand-to-mouth coordination.

"Are you sure you don't want to talk about something?" Thomas leaned forward. "You look a little pale, actually. Are you all right?"

"Yes, I'm fine, I'm… I'm…" she stuttered to a stop.

"What is it?"

"It's just that I'm feeling very alone right now… very…" The words came out in a blurted rush, "I'm getting a divorce. I'm getting a divorce because my mother-in-law is forcing me to. She's sort of blackmailing me, I guess, but I think I knew it was over with Owen anyway when..." She stared at Thomas, horrified. "I'm so sorry. I shouldn't have... you're my employer and..."

"And your friend. Didn't we establish that already? Lord knows I could use some goodness in my life."

"Goodness?"

"Sure. Genuine kindness. You're a very soothing person. When you're not yelling at me about bloated prose."

A giggle escaped. "I don't know why we fight so much."

Thomas smiled, and then, struck with an idea, said, "Hey, do you have to rush home? Helga's making reindeer stew with juniper berries tonight. Why don't you stay for dinner?"

"That sounds... interesting." Mary wrinkled her freckled nose.

"It's really good; she's cooked it before. Some old Swedish recipe with A LOT of butter in it."

Mary thought of her quiet townhouse. "Okay, I'll try it." Shyly, she glanced into Thomas' hazel eyes.

He held her gaze for a moment and then looked down at himself. "I should probably clean up a bit. Hate to have you sit across from me at the dinner table like this. Most unappetizing."

Mary gestured at her face and hair pointedly.

"That's different. You're naturally pretty. You don't need to dress up to look good."

An awkward silence fell between them.

"Say," said Thomas, "why don't we eat on the balcony off my game room? We can watch the sun set over the ocean. Have you ever seen the green flash?"

"No, but my friend Lorelei has."

"Well, maybe tonight is our night to witness it. Now, what kind of drink would you like with dinner? Do you have a favorite beer or wine or cocktail?"

"I'd love a gin rickey," Mary said. "That's what I usually order when I go out with the girls."

"You're kidding."

Mary blushed. "No. I know it's a silly old drink, but I tried one a long time ago because of…"

"F. Scott Fitzgerald," they said at the same time.

Surprised, they stared at one another.

"It's my drink of choice too," Thomas said, his eyes running over Mary curiously. "What an extraordinary coincidence."

Helga was very pleased that Mary was staying for dinner. The two women had bonded early, forging a pleasant rapport born of mutual fondness. They laughed and chatted together in the big kitchen whenever Mary and Voltaire passed through. Helga had made it her mission to fatten Mary up, but the girl was exercising with Voltaire so much that she hadn't gained an ounce even though she ate everything Helga put in front of her.

Thomas had retired to his bedroom to shower and change and Mary took Voltaire on a walk around the pond. The grey portly dog loved finding sticks and bringing them to Mary, snorting happily and nuzzling her fingers with his scrunched-up nose. She had quite a handful of twigs when Helga called out from the big house, "Dinner is ready!"

When Mary and Voltaire entered the fragrant kitchen, Helga gave Voltaire his supper and then she bustled Mary off to the stairway. "Now you go up to da game room. Helga set table on balcony already and Thomas is pouring da drinks." She patted Mary's hand maternally. "You two talk about da writing t'ings and haf fun."

Mary walked up the stairs to the second-floor balcony slowly, savoring the fact that she was about to dine with Thomas McQuillan. In his mansion. Overlooking the far-off ocean. At sunset. It was all so surreal. But it wasn't ideal. She was starting divorce proceedings against the only man she'd ever been with, the only man she'd loved, the only man she had poured her heart and soul into. A lump rose in her throat when she pictured Owen's bright blue eyes and she remembered all those nights long ago when he'd literally and figuratively swept her off her feet. She had thought he was her soulmate. Could he still be? Could soulmates fall out of love? Could they be... sometimes cruel to one another? Life wasn't perfect, so it only made sense relationships couldn't be either. Mary felt like damaged goods. Her identity was caught up in being Owen's wife, but that wasn't who she was anymore.

So, who was she?

Mary topped the stairs and followed the hallway to Thomas' game room. The door was open and she stepped inside, taking in the enormous room with all of its manly accoutrements. She trailed a hand along the pool table, the one she knew her dad would love, and wondered how often Thomas used it. She admired a group of paintings displayed on the east wall- there were seven compositions, each depicting one of The Seven Wonders of the World. She stopped in front of a mural of the Grand Canyon. Her home state.

With a start she realized she could move back to Arizona. Be close to her father and Aunt Georgette and Aunt Francesca. She didn't have to stay in San Diego. Or she could move to a different state altogether. In fact, she could go anywhere she wanted. The thought, instead of freeing, left her with a sense of displacement. Where *did* she belong?

"I need to start thinking of myself as independent," she whispered. "To... to... learn to... live without my husband." Footsteps sounded behind her, but she didn't hear them. Her eyes had filled with tears and she brushed them away impatiently, trying to remember a mantra Aunt Francesca had repeated over and over when she'd gone through an I-was-in-the-British-Armed-Forces-in-a-previous-life reincarnation phase a few years back. "Be tough!" Mary instructed herself sternly. Then, louder, "Hold fast! Stand firm! Soldier on!"

"Is this a private pep talk?" a voice behind her asked.

Mary clapped a hand to her mouth and slowly turned around, her face on fire.

Thomas handed her a gin rickey and tapped his glass to hers. "Cheers."

They both took sips of their drinks and Mary's amber eyes widened in delight. "This is delicious!"

"I'm glad you're pleased." Thomas smiled and gestured toward the balcony. "Hungry?"

"Yes." Mary nodded and for the first time noticed his appearance. "You look really...um..." she blushed prettily. "You changed out of your writing clothes."

Thomas rubbed his smooth jawline. "And shaved." He winked. "All for you."

Mary followed him numbly outside, her mind whirling in all different directions. Thomas smelled fresh and clean, his long sandy hair brushed back, his jeans and navy crew neck sweater casual, yet extremely sexy on his athletic body. He pulled her chair out for her and she sat up to the small, round table Helga had set. The food smelled delicious and when Thomas offered her a basket of fresh baked brown bread slices, her mouth began to water in earnest.

They were much too far from the ocean to hear the waves break, but the view before them was stunning as they shared an invigorating conversation, a few really bad jokes and a lot of laughs. Mary forgot all about being lonely. She forgot all about everything and everyone except Thomas McQuillan and how wonderful it was to talk to someone so interested in all the same things she was. He was intelligent and knowledgeable, and she excitedly asked his views and opinions on everything from poetry to crime dramas to song writing. Like a wilted and thirsty flower she soaked up his observations and his insights, as though his words were the most refreshing water she'd ever drunk.

Finding Mary an excellent conversationalist, as well as a superb sounding board, Thomas opened up in ways he hadn't for a very long time. They were enjoying each other's company so much, in fact, that neither realized the sun had put itself to bed long after they'd finished eating. Darkness now fell so heavily between them they could barely see each other through the shadows.

"It appears we missed the green flash," Thomas said dryly, standing and offering his hand to Mary.

Timidly she took it, and once he helped her up, he let go. They walked back inside the game room companionably and Thomas poured them both another gin rickey at the bar. He flipped on the classic rock station he normally listened to. "Is this okay?"

"Pink Floyd?" Mary nodded. "Absolutely."

"You're a Floyd fan?"

"My dad used to be before he got into country."

Thomas made a face. "Country?"

"The good stuff. Waylon Jennings, George Jones, Johnny Cash…"

"Ahhh… the outlaws," Thomas said approvingly. He turned off his stereo system and went to a control panel on the back wall.

Merle Haggard's voice drifted over the room and Mary smiled. "Daddy loves this song."

Thomas took a swallow of his gin rickey. "Tell me about your dad."

"He's a good man. That's what everyone says about him. 'Mitchell Morrison is a good man.' He's one of those people others are drawn to."

"Why is that?"

Thoughtfully, Mary replied, "Because he knows what he wants from life and he cares deeply for other people, but he never mixes the two."

"Meaning?" Thomas prompted.

"Well, sometimes we allow our choices to be dictated by how we think they will affect our loved ones."

"Your dad doesn't do that?"

"No, he makes decisions that will make him happy, even if they make others sad. But no one ever thinks he's being unkind or selfish because he's so loving."

"That's the secret to life, isn't it?"

"Maybe. Knowing who you are and owning it."

Thomas drained his glass and went to pour himself another. "And who are you, Mary Crossfield?"

"I was just asking myself that same question earlier."

"I think you can start by identifying yourself as a writer. You've got the raw talent. It just needs to be molded and honed."

"I feel like I'm in a dream." Mary finished the rest of her drink. It was strong and she could feel herself loosening up.

"Why?"

"Because I've admired you for so very long. And now I'm in your home, with your undivided attention, and you're coaching me in the one thing I've always loved and... you've said I have talent. I could die happy right now." She smiled at him, her eyes lighting up with gratefulness. "And it's all happened at the lowest point in my life. I feel... very blessed."

Thomas poured her another gin rickey and brought both glasses back to where Mary stood.

"These are pretty strong," Mary said, taking a tentative sip. "I'm not going to be able to drive if you keep giving these to me."

"Maybe I don't want you to drive. Maybe you should just stay the night."

As soon as the words were out of his mouth, Thomas regretted them. Mary looked almost frightened, shocked even.

After an uncomfortable pause, Thomas light-heartedly engaged Mary in a game of darts. They returned to the conviviality they'd shared over dinner, but Thomas knew his thoughtless words had shaken the poor girl. Mary Crossfield wasn't someone he should toy with- she wasn't the type who would be able to come away from an intimate evening without taking a blow to her delicate psyche. She wasn't even divorced yet, she was extremely emotionally vulnerable and Thomas was fairly confident she had a celebrity crush on him. He would not use her for his own physical pleasure. "But…" his bad boy nature pointed out to him, "you could show *her* pleasure too. And I seriously doubt she's ever experienced the heights of intensity you could lavish on her soft, sensual body. You could… comfort her. Yes! She *needs* comforting. It would be in her best interest for you to make her feel better, help her forget her problems for a few hours." Thomas watched Mary throw a dart and giggle when it fell short. She bent over to pick it up from the floor and his mind turned the corner of lust. "To hell with a few hours, probably all night."

No.

Absolutely not.

What had he overheard Mary saying to herself before dinner? Oh, yes! "Hold fast! Stand firm! Soldier on!"

Putting all thoughts of seduction from his mind, and repeating those phrases over and over in his head, Thomas poured two more gin rickeys and then engaged Mary in a rousing game of air hockey. She beat him soundly several times and he was impressed. He was also impressed with how natural and genuine she was, how easy it was to be around her. Mary's words, her demeanor, her very essence reflected compassion and a sweetness of spirit like…

Thomas was talking to himself again. "Ok, yes, she reminds me of Gemma, but… she doesn't. Mary has some fire in her, she likes to spar with me and Gemma and I never fought. Ever. Mary loves to talk about writing and books and art and music. Gemma discussed those things but not with passion like Mary does. Gemma was complimentary of my work, but she wasn't ever in awe, per say. When Mary looked at me after she read my manuscript… her eyes were like shining stars, like… Damnit! What is wrong with you, Tom McQuillan? Why are you making comparisons? Why are you even thinking about Gemma? She's out of your life. Again. She made her choice. You made yours."

But as Thomas said the words to himself, he knew he'd always be under Gemma's spell. Always. No woman would ever take her place in his heart. Gemma was special. She'd never hurt him, never lied to him... she was the epitome of authentic honesty. And she'd loved him when he was a virtual nobody.

Thomas studied Mary carefully. Did she really like him? Or did she only like who he represented in her mind? Stripped of fame and fortune, would she still want to hang out with him? Would she still look at him with those tempting, admiring glances?

Mary set her gin rickey down on the air hockey table. She laughed and then held the back of her hand to her pretty mouth. "I think I'm really tipsy." She laughed again as though what she had just said was the funniest thing in the world.

Thomas moved closer to her, his eyes searching hers. "Would you like me very much, Mary Crossfield, if I were a nobody?"

She giggled. "Of course! You like me and *I'm* a nobody." She twirled around in a circle and pulled the band from her ponytail. Her honey hair cascaded down her back and she smiled. "I feel so free tonight. Like all of my problems don't really exist. Like Owen never really hurt me that badly. Like I'm not worthless for not being able to have a baby. Like just because I'm only a boring ol' dog-walker doesn't mean I can't one day write a book that might be sort of good. Like... like..." She looked up at Thomas. "Like it doesn't matter that my mother didn't want me or that Lorelei wants to live far away or that my best friends aren't speaking to each other right now or that... I'm not as gorgeous as Katya Vetrov."

Startled, Thomas said, "You don't want to be anything like Katya, believe me."

Clearly, Mary had had way too much to drink. "But if I looked like her maybe you would be interested in me. You know, before Owen left on his training mission I used to have dreams about you, but now that he's gone I don't have them anymore for some reason."

Thomas couldn't help himself. "What kind of dreams?"

Even in her inebriated state Mary blushed. "Very sexy dreams. You... you did things to me that I've never experienced. You made me feel…" she looked unsteadily around the game room as though searching for inspiration, but simply slurred out, "…like I've never felt before."

Thomas ran his hands through his thick sandy hair. This was bad. This was so bad. How many freaking gin rickeys had he made her?

"You're a good person, Thomas," Mary said suddenly. "You know who you are. You know what you want out of life, but you care about other people. I've seen the way you treat Helga- how sweet you are to her. She loves you, you know? She told me she never had children of her own and she thinks of you like a son." Mary suddenly burst out laughing. "I think she hated Katya!"

"Katya isn't exactly on my list of favorite people either." Thomas eyed Mary. "I think we need to get you into bed. Your bed, not mine," he amended when her expression went from happily drunk to terrified.

"Okay. I'm so sorry. I was very irresponsible tonight."

"So was I." He guided her from the room, his strong hand on the small of her back. "Come on, you little boozer, let's try and get you up the stairs."

"Thomas?" she turned to face him and stumbled.

"Yes?"

"Thank you for letting me stay tonight. I… I've been having a hard time being alone in my house knowing… knowing my whole life is about to change."

"What you said earlier… about not being able to have a baby- is that why you're getting divorced? I know that's a personal question. You don't have to answer."

"Owen wants to have children and we can't. But, Thomas," she looked at him with pleading eyes, "I might not want to ever have a baby anyway. Do you think that's bad?"

"No!" Thomas said, shocked. "Why would that be bad?"

"Because what is a woman's purpose if she can't have children?"

Thomas sighed and led her across the room to a plush chair by the window. He kneeled before her. "I don't know if you're going to remember any of this tomorrow, but you need to know something straight up: a woman's purpose is not defined by whether she procreates or not. A female who gives birth is no better than one who does not."

"Some people wouldn't agree with you," Mary said sadly.

"Then those people are full of self-righteous shit."

"Did you ever want to have children, Thomas?"

"No, never."

"Because of your career?"

"Partly."

"What if you met the right woman? Would you want to start a family?"

Thomas looked up at the ceiling. "Apparently not."

"Oh," she murmured. Then she hiccupped loudly and giggled.

Thomas reached for her hand and helped her out of the chair. She swayed and then leaned into him, her head resting on his shoulder. He hesitated for only a split second before wrapping his arms around her in a warm hug. She relaxed against him and his body began to respond in ways he didn't want it to. Mary felt so good, so tender and soft and sweet. He hooked his chin over her shoulder and breathed in the scent of her hair... it smelled of sunshine and flowers. Without stopping to think, he ran his fingers through it like he'd seen her father do at the club. Just as he suspected, she stilled completely. He continued stroking her satiny tresses, and the trusting way she held on to him trounced his lascivious inclinations, chasing away all desire.

They stood holding one another for a very long time, two people with wrecked hearts, two people who felt lonely and exposed and vulnerable, two people who longed for escape from the pain of loss.

Eventually, Thomas picked Mary up and carried her to her room. He laid her on the double bed, pushing the extra pillows aside and covering her with a downy white blanket.

"Thank you," she mumbled, rubbing her eyes like a little girl. "I'm so sleepy, Thomas, I..." Her voice trailed off and ended in a deep, contented sigh.

He bent down and kissed her forehead and she stirred slightly, her breathing slowing as she drifted off to sleep. Thomas traced her freckles with his finger. She was so lovely. Both inside and out.

He straightened and walked to the door. He hesitated, his hand on the knob, and he looked back at Mary longingly. He wanted to hold her all night, to let her know she wasn't alone. To feel that *he* wasn't alone. But it would be too easy to make love to her when they woke up. The restraint he'd known this evening would all but disappear if he discovered Mary Crossfield in his arms after holding her body close to his own for several hours. He knew he could easily seduce her, could give her pleasure, could ravage and pillage her soft and beautiful body until she cried out rapturously over and over. He wondered what it would feel like to bridge her apparent innocence and storm the gates. He wanted to unlock her fantasies and do her bidding. What had Mary said tonight about the dreams she'd had of him? Something like "… you did things to me I've never experienced…"

And, oh, how he knew he could. He wanted to bring fulfillment to the desires she didn't even know she craved, to…

No.

He had to get out of this room.

Stepping over the threshold, Thomas closed her door behind him and stood outside. He would *not* take advantage of her. It would be wrong. He strode down the hallway and then stopped. Cursing, he punched the nearest wall. Turning around, he went back to Mary's room and rested his head against the closed door. He could hear her light breathing and his heart went out to the girl who thought she was unworthy as a woman because she hadn't had a child. A girl who hadn't said one bad thing about the husband she was divorcing. A girl who was hurting so badly that she'd stepped out of character and drank too much at the house of her employer. A girl who needed comfort and compassion. He put his hand on the doorknob and turned it. He would just slip into bed next to her, hold her close, keep her safe from sadness, even if only for the night. And then in the morning he would show her a whole new world of explosive ecstasy, working her body carefully, skillfully, toward erotic combustion at the highest level...

No. No!

Thomas sank down onto the carpeting and lay on his back. He'd sleep as close as he could to Mary without subjecting them both to a temptation that would surely only bring regret and pain. His heavy eyes closed and his last thought before drifting off was, "Hold fast! Stand firm! Soldier on!"

CHAPTER 56

9 November 1986

I'm as big as a house and my lower back hurts so much, but I don't care. I don't care! BECAUSE HE'S COMING TO VISIT!

He called me last night and said he wanted to be here for the birth of our baby.

He arrives in four weeks. Oh! I'm so excited I can hardly breathe.

10 December 1986

I only have a moment to write because I pick him up from the airport soon. I'm so nervous and flustered and so... certain that when he sees me he'll know we are meant to be together. He'll finally realize we share a love so pure that it will last forever. A love that will live on in our sweet baby girl.

13 December 1986

I can't stop crying as I write this. Not tears of sadness, but tears of joy. I was right.

He spotted me immediately when he got off the plane (how could he miss me, I'm so huge!) and he fell to his knees and kissed my big belly. It was the sweetest moment I've ever witnessed. Sweeter still, because it is me, Helene, who has the great honor of carrying his child. This truth makes me feel special, important, fulfilled. I know that he has women aplenty attracted to him, clamoring for his attention, but I am the only one who has a hold on him- I see that now. I can control his heart because I'm the one- the only one- giving him a baby.

He looks the same- handsome as ever, his amber eyes luminescent, his chest broad and confident. Despite my uncomfortable, swollen body I still wanted him, could feel the physical longing racing through my veins.

While he knelt before me, I lovingly put my palms on either side of his face. He placed his big hands on my stomach, smiling hugely when the baby kicked. He looked up at me, wonder and excitement illuminating his face, but then, as we stared at one another, his smile faded as he seemed to embrace the enormity of what was about to happen. We are going to be parents in the next few days. There is no turning back. The vista of responsibility opened up before us and it was frightening.

He stood up and put his arms around me and we held on to one another. Then he said he wanted to be there for our child; he wanted to be a good father, a present father. I asked if that meant he and I could be together now and he said yes. He said he would do anything for his baby. Anything at all.

⌒‿

20 December 1986

She is absolutely beautiful, our little Marion Grace. Perfect and healthy in every way. She was born four days ago and looks exactly like a Mabel Lucie Attwell painting. Her cheeks are chubby and pink, and she has big blue eyes and a rosebud mouth that's always hungry.

I was hoping she would inherit her father's dazzling amber eyes. I asked the doctor about it and he said to wait; often babies' eye color doesn't remain blue and we will know the permanent color in six to nine months.

Speaking of her father... he cannot stay away from his little girl. He is always holding Mary, cuddling her, reading her stories, trying to get her to smile. After I'm done nursing her, he takes Mary from me and burps her and she falls asleep on his big chest. I was crazy in love with him before, but now I love him all the more seeing how very tenderhearted he is; as though fatherhood were his greatest blessing.

As for me... now life wouldn't even be worth living without him in it.

When Thomas awoke the next morning, stiff and cold on the floor outside of Mary's bedroom, Voltaire was lightly scratching on the door to be let in.

Thomas grabbed him away quickly. "Shhhhhhh... let her sleep."

But Voltaire wasn't listening. He squirmed free of Thomas' arms and went back to the door. He sniffed under it and then whimpered pitifully.

Thomas stared at the stubborn, squat dog calmly asking to be let into Mary's room. Why wasn't Voltaire his usual hyper, berserk self? Thomas stood up and stretched, nudging Voltaire with his foot. "Come on, buddy, let's go see what Helga has for breakfast."

Voltaire looked up at him as if to say, "You go ahead," and he laid down, by the door, his head resting on his stubby legs.

"This giant house," Thomas muttered to himself as he ambled down the hallway, "and everyone wants to sleep on the floor outside of Mary Crossfield's room."

When Thomas entered the kitchen, smelling deliciously of bacon and sautéed onions, Helga handed him two cups of coffee.

He set one down and leaned against the counter. "How did you know?"

"Volpee run avay from me dis morning to da t'ird floor and Mary's Jeep is still parked outside."

Thomas took a sip of coffee and rubbed his face. "She's a light-weight. I shouldn't have given her so many drinks. I'll go back up and check on her in an hour."

Helga nodded. "She need her rest."

"Yes. Listen, Helga… you know that we didn't…"

"Helga knows dis. Helga knows nee'der of you vould cross boundaries you should not be." She went to the massive refrigerator and pulled out a wire basket full of speckled brown eggs and a crock of fresh butter.

Thomas remained silent and slowly finished his coffee while Helga bustled around the kitchen. At last he sighed and admitted in a very quiet voice, "But I wanted to."

Helga wiped her hands on a dish towel and stood before Thomas. "I know, mina älskling. But you are a good boy, vith a good heart." She patted his chest with her plump hand. "Helga proud of you."

⌒‿

26 February 1987

We made love for the first time since those days and nights we spent together in Christopher Creek. That seems so long ago now. So far away. My body was much different then- tight and firm, all sexy curves and voluptuous lines. My breasts before Baby were buoyant, soft and supple, but now they are gigantic, engorged with milk and sometimes hard. They are often painful and the only relief I find is in breastfeed-ing little Mary. My stomach is flabby now, no longer flat, and I have silver stretchmarks meandering across my belly like tiny roads that lead to nowhere.

But he treated my body as though it were no different, as though the changes were just part of the enjoyable scenery, an altered canvas in some ways, but the glorious paints of passion were still the same. Indeed, he brought me to the heavens so many times I could only lean against his shoulder and mumble words in French. They were grateful words, words of love, words of lust.

He told me afterward, while we lay together naked and entwined, that he is going back to America and Mary and I are to stay here in France with my family. He wants to set up a home for us in Arizona and when it's ready he will send for me. I did not tell him I already have my wedding gown because he hasn't spoken of marriage. I don't want to frighten him off. I'm afraid of saying anything that will ruin my chance at true happiness. The fact that he wants me in his life makes me believe that I was right all along—we do belong together.

He takes a different view, I think, although he is careful not to hurt my feelings with too much bluntness.

3 March 1987

I just said good-bye to him and it was very hard, but I have the hope and excitement now of knowing we are going to be a family soon.

He let a few tears fall as he held Mary and kissed her goodbye. I've never seen a more devoted father. He told me yesterday that his life now has more meaning than he ever dreamed. He said he would do anything for our little girl. I asked him if that included being with a woman he didn't love.

He changed the subject.

I know now.

I suppose I've known all along. But that doesn't make it hurt any less.

Bonjour Mama,

Have you ever liked a man who didn't like you in return? I think I humiliated myself last night, even though I don't remember everything I said. Which, actually, in and of itself, is humiliating.

Thomas and I are friends, nothing more. I would be lying if I said I didn't, as Happy would say, "fancy" him, but I'm sure I'm just one of many females who find him incredibly attractive. He dated a super-model, for heaven's sake! I'm not exactly competition in the world of the rich and famous.

Anyway, that's not the point. The point is that I'm lonely and con-fused and, well, really scared of what the future holds. There have been a few times where I've wished I had Owen to talk to and then I remember that he – and our impending divorce - is what I need to talk about most.

I keep replaying my conversation with Ellen over and over in my mind and some things just aren't adding up. Like how she said she and Owen had discussed the divorce. Is it possible she was lying to me?

No, that can't be right. I mean, he was so cold to me when he left on the mission. And that morning too… I never did find out where he was and why he was acting so strange. Ellen said something about him straying, but I blew that comment off as too horrible to even con-sider. Owen would never, ever think of infidelity. But if he knew we are about to embark on a divorce… would he? How long has his family been planning to ask me to leave? Maybe they have someone lined up for him already. Some fertile girl ecstatic to marry into a rich family.

I'm so sad about everything that's happening, Mama. It feels good to write all of my muddled thoughts out, but I need to call Daddy tonight and tell him everything. He needs to know. He's not just my father, he's one of my best friends. It's always been like that- ever since I can remember.

But I can't tell him about Thomas McQuillan. I signed a confidentiality agreement for starters but honestly, I wouldn't say anything anyway. Thomas is such a private person and I'm honored he thinks of me as a friend. He even let me read part of his new manuscript! It was... one of the most thrilling moments of my life. You must think that's so lame! But the fact that he trusts me is overwhelmingly complimentary and surreal.

We had the most amazing dinner last night. I could seriously talk to him for just hours. Our communication is on some weird plane... like we spur each other's thought processes and, when we're not fighting, he can really get me to delve deep into my convictions about life and writing. And everything he says is so interesting! He has this prodigiously fascinating insight and a hysterically funny sarcastic sense of humor and... I'm gushing, aren't I?

Anyway, I had way too much to drink and after playing darts I don't remember very much. I woke up in my room at Thomas' house with a pounding headache. Voltaire was scratching at my door and when I got up to let him in he jumped on the bed and stared at me. That's so unlike him! He's always such a colossal ball of insane energy. I sat back down on the blankets and he immediately cuddled into my lap, his little nose snorts soft and contented. I haven't known him to be so sweet before so I didn't want to move for fear of breaking the spell. I think he has bonded with me now and I felt this huge surge of affection for him. The next thing I knew an hour had passed. I woke up curled on my side with Voltaire sleeping and snoring in my arms, his wrinkly face pressed into my stomach. I hated to wake him- he looked so comfortably adorable- so I stayed where I was and glanced around my cozy little room. I wondered how I'd gotten into bed and hoped I hadn't made too big a fool of myself.

Thomas appeared in the doorway, leaning against the threshold, mugs of steaming coffee in each hand. He smiled at me and I knew then that everything was okay between us. He didn't seem angry with me for having too much to drink and crashing at his house- an employee, no less! How awful! And he wasn't avoiding my eyes or looking at me like I was some groupie so I felt better knowing I mustn't have betrayed my feelings for him.

He sat on the edge of the bed, careful not to wake Voltaire with any motion. Slowly, he passed me a cup of coffee and I tried to sit up slightly without disturbing my grey potato bedmate.

"Sleep well?" he asked.

I blushed. I couldn't help it. "Yes. But, Thomas, I'm sorry..."

He held up a hand. "No apologies. You've got a lot going on in your life right now."

"But you're my employer..."

He ignored me. "I'm sorry too. I shouldn't have mixed your drinks so strong. And I shouldn't have kept making them."

I took a sip of coffee. It was delicious! All dark and fragrant and rich. I smiled at Thomas and Voltaire shifted, burying his smooshed face into my hip. "You make the best gin rickeys I've ever had," I said. "Next time I'll make sure to tell the bartender I'm on a self-imposed two-drink maximum."

"The bartender concurs. And I hope there will be a next time." Thomas cleared his throat. "Helga would like you to stay for dinner again the night after next. But she asked if she could join us. Would you mind?"

"Of course not! That would be so nice." Suddenly a terrible thought struck and my mouth dropped open in horror. "Does Helga know I'm here? That I spent the night?" I started getting flustered. "She knows I wouldn't... that we didn't... that..."

Thomas put a hand on my leg and despite the blanket covering me, the warmth of his touch sent a chill through my body. Funny how contradictory that is, isn't it?

He said, "Please don't worry. She knows you spent the night in your room and I spent the night... elsewhere."

I felt all agitated and annoyed with myself for allowing the entire situation to have happened. My first reaction to this irritability was to pick a fight with Thomas just so I could release my pent-up energy on someone. No, that's not right. Not just on someone. On Thomas. Because there's this perverse part of me that gets really excited when we're arguing. Not excited sexually, but... I feel so alive! Like all of the neurons in my brain are pulsing with vitality. Pairing that with what I see when I look at him... all of my senses go totally radioactive. There's something about Thomas, I mean, aside from the fact that he's handsome and an amazing writer. It's like there's a magnet inside of him and a magnet inside of me and they're trying to get close to one another, but they keep repelling, fighting, pushing away from the other. It's scintillating.

And I haven't known scintillating my whole life. It's a new, very potent sensation.

When we went downstairs Helga had fixed a wonderful breakfast. I took two helpings because it was so absolutely scrumptious. I asked her how she made it and she said it's a simple savory strudel recipe with eggs, bacon, swiss chard and scallions. She said the secret to getting it just right is to combine powdered garlic and cornmeal in a pan with olive oil and to let the strudel sizzle in that for a few minutes after it's braided. I love learning her cooking tricks. Owen will be so upset if he finds out how much I've been eating lately.

Wait...

That's not his concern anymore.

Anyway, breakfast was so fun! Helga ate with Thomas and me and we chatted and laughed and teased each other and Voltaire tried to steal everyone's napkins from their laps. I felt so accepted and so part of the household. I was having such a nice time and then a landscaper knocked on the back door and handed Helga a big white envelope with Thomas' name written on it.

When Thomas saw the handwriting, he cursed loudly and grabbed the envelope from Helga, storming out of the kitchen. It was very tense after that. I helped Helga with the dishes even though she tried to shoo me away and then I left for home to shower and change. Thomas never did come back to the kitchen. I wonder if I will see him when I return for my shift later?

I hope he's okay.

CHAPTER 57

*T*homas took the envelope with Katya's handwriting into his den and slammed the door behind him. The skinny witch must have bribed one of the landscapers to bring it to the house.

Thomas' first instinct was to put the envelope through the shredder or set it on fire without even reading it, but curiosity got the better of him. What did she want? What could Katya Vetrov *possibly* want from him after she'd done everything in her power to hurt and betray him? Certainly she'd have taken Gemma's threats of legal action and Hollywood blacklisting seriously. Katya would know better than to contact Thomas at all.

Gingerly, as though the envelope were a demented scorpion hell bent on ferociously stinging his hands, he pulled out the contents and laid them on his desk. Weird. Katya had ripped out a full-page photo of Gemma with her oldest child, Colin, from a celebrity gossip magazine. Colin, dressed in a baseball uniform and carrying a bat, was looking directly at the camera as he and his mother strolled through a park. The headline at the top of the picture said: "Gemma Hamilton's Handsome Boy Hits a Home Run!"

Setting the picture down, Thomas picked up a hastily scrawled note in Katya's handwriting. The script was jerky and messy as though she'd been in a hurry or distraught when she'd written it. Thomas' face went from bright red to deathly pale as he read through the message and when he was done the piece of paper fell from his hand, fluttering through the air unnoticed. Excruciating silence closed in around him from every side. Cold with shock, he picked up the picture of Gemma and Colin from his desk and stared hard at Colin's chin- a chin so like his own. His gaze moved to the boy's broody hazel eyes. Why had he never noticed? Never guessed?

Thomas McQuillan buried his head in his hands and cried as if his heart were breaking.

"We have to stop meeting like this," Frank said as he caught Lorelei up in a big hug.

She smiled, comforted by the friendly embrace. "I can't tell you how much I've enjoyed exercising out of doors this past week," she told him when he set her down. "Aside from weekend hikes here and there I'd just been going to the gym every day." She looked out over the San Diego Bay and fluffed up her blonde curls. "Being in the fresh air is so much better."

Frank was pleased. "You're a great running partner. This is what... our fifth night in a row?"

Lorelei started stretching, propping one of her calves on a half wall and bending over it until she touched her toes. "Yup."

Frank looked away from the unintentionally sexy pose, turned around and pointed north. "I'll race you to The Midway."

"I run faster than you."

"I have more bulk to carry."

Lorelei ran her eyes appreciatively over Frank's muscular body. He was wearing running shorts and a sleeveless workout tank. "That's no excuse, Detective."

"Oh yeah?"

She sprinted down the sidewalk, grinning at him when he fell into place beside her. They jogged the next mile in comfortable silence, ocean breezes swirling around them, the cool night air invigorating their heated skin. The moon shone brightly above, highlighting the rippling waters of the Pacific.

Lorelei felt some of the stress leave her body as she concentrated on her breathing. She pushed herself to run faster, her strides becoming longer, quicker. Frank adjusted his speed to match hers as naturally as if they'd been pacing partners for years instead of mere days.

When they reached The Midway, a huge aircraft carrier docked at Navy Pier, Lorelei slowed to a walk. Frank jogged a few steps ahead of her and stopped, his hands on his hips. They stood apart, catching their breath, watching the twinkling lights of Coronado Island across the bay.

"What a gorgeous night," Lorelei said appreciatively. As her breathing returned to normal, she turned warm eyes to Frank. "Thank you for talking with me on the phone earlier- I felt better after we spoke. Actually, I should thank you for being such a great friend to me all week. I've been so stressed out about work and what's going on with Faith."

"I'm here for you as long as you want me around."

"Thank you… Listen, I didn't tell you everything on the phone." She had only shared with him the most painful part - that she wasn't going to be given Margaret's position. It had cost her a great deal to say the words out loud.

He raised an eyebrow at her. "Oh?"

Lorelei sighed. "Corporate wants me to run the San Diego office."

Frank stood very still. He wanted to tell her to take the offer so he didn't have to worry about her moving away. Instead he forced himself to be objective. "How do you feel about that?"

"I won't consider it," she replied, lightning-quick. "It wasn't in my game plan."

"So what's your next move?"

"What if I went to New York anyway? Not with Empire & Malkin, of course, but there are thousands of jobs in the city. Surely, if nothing else, I can get into an entry level accounting gig and start working my way up. At least I'd *be* there."

"That sounds like a career setback," Frank speculated tentatively. "Is Manhattan worth a possible demotion?"

Lorelei didn't answer. She began pacing up and down the board-walk and Frank watched her, wishing he could ease her agitation. She looked so confident and fit in her yoga pants and racerback sports cami. Her curls were in disarray from running in the sea breezes and her face was glowing with health and vitality. The thought of Lorelei leaving the state made Frank want to punch something, but he couldn't let his feelings get in the way of what was best for her. The only thing was... *was* moving the best thing for her?

After watching her silently for a few moments he grabbed her hand. "Hey, stop pacing. You're making me dizzy."

Lorelei smiled. "Sorry. It's my thing when I'm thinking."

"Try thinking out loud. That's what I'm here for."

She was acutely aware that Frank hadn't let go of her hand. She didn't want him to. He was so reassuring, so level-headed. She slid her fingers in between his and held on tightly. "I'm... confused," she admitted, her mind racing to try and place her anxious thoughts into their proper boxes.

Frank was very conscious of the way her hand felt in his, so small, so delicate.

"Okay, good," he said. "Let's start with that. What are you con-fused about?"

"Well, I'm very happy about the outcome of the investigation, and I regret nothing about my part in it. But... do you believe in fate, Frank? Why does it seem like everything is working against me as far as moving to New York? First with Faith and now with Margaret's position being denied me. And... Mary's got some pretty upsetting stuff going on right now and she's going to need me to be there for her... And..." She looked up at him, her green eyes softening, "... and I met you."

Frank squeezed her hand in silent encouragement, but Lorelei gently pulled back, unable to believe she'd just said those words- words that were a possible gateway into other words that should never be felt and never be expressed. Internally panicking, she mentally stored all of her thoughts - Faith, Mary, work, Manhattan - into their proper containers and closed the lids tightly. But the large box with Detective Frank Williams' name on it... that box remained open and unsealed. The more she tried to close off her feelings and shove them inside, the more they fought to be free. Her emotions for Frank were running rampant and she couldn't catch them, couldn't store them away, couldn't stop them from taking over. Why now? Why... The box with Frank's name suddenly disintegrated as she flashed back to all the kindnesses he'd shown her, the compassion, the patience, the strength. And she stood, transfixed, staring at him, conscious that the walls around her heart had begun to crumble. With absolute clarity she knew she didn't want to be locked up in the pain of the past anymore, she wanted to be free from the scars that bound her. Her soul cried out for what it had been denied for so long and in that instant she found the sweet release of clemency. Without fear, she let herself be consumed with affection for the man who stood before her.

Frank watched the changes in Lorelei's face and wondered what was going through that intelligent mind of hers. She seemed to be struggling with something and then, in the blink of an eye, a peace settled over her features. She gazed up at him with such adoration and such passion that he was taken aback.

"Frank?"

He couldn't speak. She'd infused so much feeling into the way she said his name.

"Frank, I think I can let go now. It's not surrender; it's acceptance. I want to -"

A shrill scream of laughter pierced the night air. Lorelei and Frank turned to see a yacht had docked at the pier and three people had disembarked. There was a man, thin, good-looking and dressed in expensive trendy clothes, with his arm around two young women, one on each side. The girls were scantily clad, their huge bosoms barely concealed. They hung on every word the man said, giggling and flirtatiously running their hands along his chest, his face and his back. The three were unmistakably nouveau riche, overly confident, hyped up on their own attractiveness and wealth. As they wandered down the boardwalk, closer to where Frank and Lorelei stood, the man's eyes suddenly grew wide. He put the two women from him and made a beeline for Lorelei.

Frank immediately stepped in front of Lorelei and crossed his arms.

"Hey!" the man said indignantly. "I just want to talk to her."

"Nope." Frank widened his stance. "Just keep moving."

"But I know her…" he peered around Frank's shoulder. "She looks so familiar…" He snapped his fingers. "Lorelei Harper!"

Frank turned around to look at Lorelei. Her face had gone paper white and she was staring at the man as if he were a ghost.

"Lor?" Frank was instantly concerned. "Lor? Honey, are you okay?"

"My band doesn't make it back to San Diego too often," the man said, extending a hand to Frank. "Connor O'Cassidy. Nice to meet you."

⌒

"Nice to meet you too," Frank snarled, glowering at the man who had hurt Lorelei. Deeply hurt her. He felt the burn of anger start in his toes and explode its way up his body until the muscles in his arms hardened with anger and malice. Connor's face was too perfect, too pretty. It needed to be roughed up a little. Fuck that. A LOT.

Without thinking, Frank's fists braced for action and his right elbow shot backward to gain peak momentum. Connor's eyes widened as he saw Frank's huge arm thrust through the air with strength and speed, but before Frank's knuckles made contact with Connor's jaw, Lorelei stepped between the men and yelled, "Stop!"

"Don't, Frank," Lorelei said, placing a hand on his arm.

To Connor she said, "Do you have a minute? I'd like to buy you a drink so we can talk."

—

Frank watched them walk away in disbelief. He sank down onto the seawall and rested his arms on his knees. Shoulders hunched, he studied his hands, clasping and unclasping them. His resentment toward Connor began to spill over into resentment for Lorelei. She had left him standing alone with no recourse for the fury he wanted to unleash. She had turned her back on him both literally and figuratively. Connor O'Cassidy had walked on stage a leading man while Frank faded into nothing more than part of the scenery.

He shook his head. No, that couldn't be right. Frank's back straightened and he sat up, his eyes searching for answers amongst the dark waves lapping over the rocks in front of the quay. He *knew* Lorelei Harper. She wouldn't turn her back on a friend. Ever.

Frank stood, ducked into the shadows, and stealthily followed the woman he was certain loved him, even though she couldn't say the words.

CHAPTER 58

onnor O'Cassidy held the door to Humphrey's Pub open for Lorelei. On the walk over he had told the two women from the yacht to go back to the boat and wait for him.

Lorelei stepped through the threshold and walked purposely through the old, dingy building to a discreet table at the far end of the bar. Connor followed her, appreciatively enjoying the view.

A pretty barmaid appeared and set down two beat-up menus.

"Special tonight is shepherd's pie," she said, snapping her gum. She gave Connor a special smile. "You look like a Guinness man."

Connor winked at her. "I can be any kind of man you like."

She flirtatiously flipped her hair off her shoulder and then turned to Lorelei. "And what will you have, darlin'?"

"Freedom."

The barmaid looked confused. "Is that some sort of mixed drink, or...?"

"I'd like a Templeton Rye Manhattan, up with a twist."

"Okay, sugar. That we can do."

As their server walked away from the table, Connor leaned forward and reached for Lorelei's hands. He stroked them, his fingers caressing hers the way he'd done when they were a couple all those years ago. Tingles ran up her arms at his touch, familiar little electromagnetic currents. Vivid flashbacks played through her mind- she and Connor snuggling on the beach or the couch or the theatre while he touched every part of her hands- her thumbs, her wrists, her finger-nails, her palms. She and Connor had been so in love. Every moment, every physical contact, every word had been magical and meaningful.

"You sure picked a classy place," Connor teased as he looked around the skeevy ambiance of Humphrey's.

"I'm wearing workout clothes," Lorelei said dryly.

Connor's gaze traveled over what he could see of her body from above the table. "And you look gorgeous in them."

"Stop it…"

He gripped her hands tighter. "Hey, I know our breakup was hard for you- it was for me too- but that doesn't mean we can't be complimentary to one another. Don't I look much better now than I did when we were dating?"

"Your teeth are whiter," Lorelei offered ungraciously.

Connor chuckled. "I guess I'll take what I can get in the flattery department from you."

She paused a moment, and when she spoke again her tone turned serious, almost beseeching. "I really need to talk, to clear some things up in my mind. I think running into you tonight was some sort of bizarre serendipity."

Connor's smile faded. "Hey, I'm really sorry about everything that happened between us, Lor, if that's what you want to chat about. I was… very young when we broke up. The world was just beginning to open up for me. It was natural that we no longer belonged together, don't you think?"

It was time to go all in. It was time to face her demons. It was time to let go. As much as it hurt, as much as it galled her to say the words that made her feel weak, she had to be open and honest. Honest with herself.

"No, Connor, it wasn't natural for me. I loved you. I loved you with everything that was in me. And none of that mattered to you. You took the best of me and just walked away with it."

Connor's eyes were full of sympathy. "I know I hurt you, Lor, but people grow and change and move on. The band was taking off and

I had a lot of crazy opportunity being flung my way. There was so much money, so many demands, so many girls…" He hung his head. "I was on the road all the time and it was hard for you and me to be together. Temptation was all around me constantly." He looked up and searched her eyes. "I was tired of saying no. I was tired of not giving in to everything life had to offer. It was all just being thrown in my lap and it was exciting and… as much as I loved you, having a girl waiting around for me back in my hometown wasn't… part of who I was anymore."

"If you had *really* loved me, Connor, do you think any of that would have mattered?"

"I don't know. Maybe some people aren't meant to be monogamous. But what you and I had was special, Lor." He smiled. "So very special. I loved you and we had a great time together, but it was fleeting; a part of our youth. We both had to grow up and move on."

Her eyebrow arched. "And you think you've grown up?"

Connor gave a sardonic smile. "I suppose that's debatable. Do musicians ever grow up? We have a blast on stage, give thousands of fans a good time and we get *paid* for it. Cash is pouring in like a never-ending waterfall to keep me doing the one thing I love most - performing with my band. Girls are constantly begging me for attention, hanging on me, trying to please me in every way possible. I have houses and cars and toys, and I've been to so many countries and exotic places… and… I'm deliriously happy. I have regrets of course, and you would be one of them, but… let me put it to you this way, Lor: if you were suddenly thrust into your dream life, wouldn't you willingly leave behind anything that didn't belong in your new world?"

"Not if it meant turning away from a friend." As soon as the words were out of her mouth she felt a twinge of conscience. *Faith.*

"I feel like you're not hearing me. I would have still wanted to have been your friend, Lor. We even discussed it when we broke up. But you told me no, remember? You said if we couldn't be together as a couple then you didn't want me in your life at all."

"Because it would hurt too much!"

Connor's voice rose. "And you don't think it hurt me to lose you? We were not just lovers, we were best friends. I only wanted to end half of our relationship but you ended it all."

Lorelei shook her head, the feelings from the past mingling with the pain she'd been harboring over the years. "I thought we were soul-mates, Connor. I thought we were going to be together forever- that nothing could separate us."

"*You* separated us. I still wanted a relationship with you, but you wanted it on your terms."

"That's not fair."

"But it's true nonetheless." Connor rubbed his thumbs over the backs of her hands in gentle circular motions. "What is it you really want to say to me? Why are we here?"

Lorelei took a deep breath and forced herself to embrace the powerlessness she felt in acknowledging the frailty of regret. "I want to know why... why I gave myself to you in every way possible and you found it so easy to walk away. It made me feel like... I was pathetic for being open and vulnerable and loving. That being one hundred and ten percent all-in with someone was weak and irrational."

"Come on, Lor. Think about what you're saying. Do you or do you not give one hundred and ten percent to your friends and family? Aren't they worth it?"

"Yes, but..."

"So how can giving of yourself ever be wrong?"

"When the other person takes advantage of your love."

"Is that what you think I did?" Connor drew back, appalled. "You think that I used you and then took off when I hit the jackpot, so to speak?"

"That's exactly what I think." Lorelei replied, her voice brittle. "I was just someone you wasted time with until your number was called in the music industry lottery."

"Good god! What kind of asshole do you think I am?"

Her face said it all.

"I see. Well, just for the record, I was in love with you. Our time together was some of the best I've ever known - and that's saying a lot coming from someone living the proverbial dream." Connor's hands were on hers once more, warmer, softer. "I remember everything about the fun we had together. I remember all the laughs, the silly fights, the nights we didn't sleep because I couldn't get enough of you. I remember it all and I'm glad. I'm *happy* that I shared my life for a brief time with someone as perfect - both inside and out - as you."

Lorelei squeezed Connor's hands and the thrill of touching him lessened as she admitted, "I haven't been able to love again since you left."

"Tell me why."

That simple request pierced something deep inside her. She began to expunge all of the repressed, restrained emotions she'd fostered toward Connor over the years. She laid it all out on the line and he sedately accepted every insult and condemnation. His eyes never left her face, his body language never shifted defensively. And when Lorelei's rush of words finally ebbed she stared at him in silence, the air around her heavy with the weight of bereavement.

Lorelei looked down, watching Connor's touch graze and caress her fingers, and she felt a surge of grief well up inside. The grief took on a life of its own, an internal tornado swallowing up and destroying everything beautiful around it. She let it happen- she felt its power. Her mind's eye saw the destruction of an innocent love as she watched the memories and the pain be swept away and obliterated. It was ugly. It was excruciating. Sadness filled her as she flashed back to the days and the nights she'd spent missing Connor, then the even harder days and nights where she'd achingly pieced her heart back together and closed it off forever. The recollections were shattering, awful to look at. She'd been letting the pain fester for so long that now her agony was monstrous, devastating, and she wanted to turn around and retreat back into the safety of her guarded walls. Instead, she threw back her shoulders and let the fierce winds of sorrow bluster in and around her and, as she faced the pain of her past, the tornado suddenly disbanded and dissolved, leaving a path of fresh, healthy ruination. Connor O'Cassidy's box had been permanently decimated, the images and suffering inside annihilated in the wake of her inner strength. She'd triumphed.

A smile of peaceful happiness spread across her face and she let go of Connor's hands. "Thank you for talking with me and thank you most of all for listening."

Connor returned the smile tentatively. "Does that mean we can be friends going forward?"

"I don't think I could trust you again. I would always wonder in the back of my mind if you were going to walk out of my life."

"But that shouldn't be a concern between true friends."

Lorelei's green eyes misted and she lowered her head as she thought once again of Faith. "You're right."

With that, she stood up. "I have to go, Connor. I'm sorry to leave so soon, but there's a very special redhead I need to talk to. And... I'm certain there's someone outside waiting for me. Someone who *has* earned my trust and my heart and my love."

Connor rose to his feet, then leaned in to brush the softest of kisses against her lips. "Goodbye, Lor."

She looked into his eyes and felt nothing. The sweet, glorious freedom of nothing at all.

Lorelei walked out of Humphrey's Pub and into the cool evening air. She inhaled deeply and looked around. The moon was full, fat and engorged with borrowed light. Stars twinkled above, peeking out from their dark, velvety blankets. The scent of the sea danced fragrantly on night breezes, lifting Lorelei's blonde curls and cooling her pink cheeks. It had been warm inside the bar, stuffy even. Coming outside had been freeing. Just as she was now. Free from the past and free from her self-imposed prison. She was free to love, free to...

Detective Frank Williams appeared before her and she smiled up at him, her heart in her eyes.

"I knew you'd be waiting," she said.

"No place I'd rather be."

"There's something I need to tell you, Frank..."

"And there's something you should know, Lor..."

"I love you," they said at the same time.

CHAPTER 59

"Why don't you just move in? You're here every night anyway," Mitch said, leaning sideways from his pillow and kissing Bertie's bare shoulder.

It was late in the evening and they were relaxing in bed together; Mitch with a Zane Grey book and Bertie on her Kindle reading *For Whom the Bell Tolls*, one of her favorite novels.

"But I like my condo." Bertie said, pulling her reading glasses down to the tip of her nose and sweeping her chocolate brown eyes over Mitch's face. "And I like my independence."

"Oh really?" Mitch ran his hand over the curve of her hip. "Don't you like this more?"

Pushing her glasses back up, Bertie returned to Hemingway. "Apples and oranges, Morrison."

Mitch groaned and tossed his book aside. "I can't concentrate when you're in my bed and naked."

"We literally just made love fifteen minutes ago!"

"That long?"

Bertie grinned and shook her head. "You are insatiable."

Mitch grabbed the Kindle out of her hands and nibbled her earlobe. "Only for you."

Bertie leaned into his touch. "We're not going to get any sleep tonight if you keep doing that."

"What else is new?" Mitch asked pushing her down into the sheets and nuzzling her stomach.

"Morrison, stop. I still have my glasses on… let me…"

"Shut up, Collins, I'm busy here." Mitch licked his way to her belly button with long, languid strokes. He peeked up at her, a voracious grin on his handsome face. "Leave those glasses on… then you can clearly see what I'm about to do to you…"

Mitch's cell phone rang, slicing through their loving banter.

"It's kind of late," Bertie said, looking at the clock on the bedside table in concern. "Maybe you should get that."

Mitch eyed her body longingly. "But…"

"I'll be right here when you get done talking to…" She wriggled away and grabbed his phone from the dresser on his side of the bed. She looked at the screen. "It's Mary."

Mitch was off the bed like a shot. "Go ahead and answer it," he said, pulling on a pair of shorts and rooting around his dresser for a t-shirt.

"Mary? It's Bertie. Your dad will be on in a moment. How are you?"

There was a long pause and Bertie's brown eyes held Mitch's amber gaze while she listened to what Mary was saying.

Eventually Bertie said, "I'm looking forward to meeting you too. And, yes, I'd love to talk about your book. Sounds like it's coming along nicely." A short silence and then, "Okay, you have a good evening too. Here's your dad."

Frank and Lorelei walked down the Embarcadero, lost in their own world. Their hands were clasped, fingers entwined, and they kept smiling at each other. Secret, enticing smiles that hinted they were about to become lovers.

Lorelei told Frank about her conversation with Connor. She left out no detail and hid no feelings. Frank accepted all she had to say with quiet understanding and when she was done pouring her heart out, he swept her up into a hug.

"I'm so proud of you, Lor. It's not easy to let go of the past."

She smiled as he set her down. "Turns out it was a lot easier than holding onto pain for years and years."

"Yeah, well hindsight is twenty-twenty."

"Frank?"

"Yes, Lor?"

"Will you walk me home?" Her green eyes shone bright, full of love.

"Are you sure that's what you want?"

"I want you."

"No regrets?"

She shook her head. "I love you so much it hurts."

Frank put his arms around her. "Then I'll spend the evening trying to ease your pain."

Bertie pulled on a silky robe and dropped a kiss on Mitch's head as she left the bedroom to give father and daughter privacy. She padded into the kitchen, poured herself a glass of wine and curled up on the couch with her Kindle, settling the sherpa blanket over her tan, shapely legs.

She tried to concentrate on the succinct, descriptive words Hemingway had written so long ago, but her mind kept wandering back to Mary Crossfield, the daughter of the man she was very much in love with. Bertie's heart had quickened in both excitement and hesitation when Mitch had asked her to move in with him. Had she really heard him say the words? Had he really meant them? It seemed like a dream. But it was too soon, wasn't it? Too soon to fall in love and commit and move in together. That's why she'd brushed him off, so that she could try to ignore the impulse to rush into anything smacking of hasty imprudence.

And what about Mary? The girl who'd never had a mother, not even a stepmother. How would Mary feel about her father allowing a woman so completely into his life? A woman living in the house Mary had grown up in? Would there be resentment? Jealousy? Mary didn't seem like a spoiled or selfish sort of girl, but then again, she'd never had to compete with another female for her dad's attention.

Bertie put down the Kindle and her glance fell on Helene's possessions still taking up temporary residence in a corner of the living room. Bertie stood and walked over to them, gently tugging at a white sheet draped over one of the paintings. The work of art was beautiful. Bertie admired the use of colors and the intricate details lavished on the canvas with complex brush strokes. Helene had been immensely talented.

A journal lay on top of one of the boxes to the side and Bertie picked it up, turning it over in her hands. Mary's mother's thoughts inhabited this book; thoughts about her life- a life that had ended willingly... and before its time.

Intrigued, Bertie brought the diary back to the couch and sat with it on her lap. She caressed the leather cover and wondered how Helene could have given up her child. How could she have stood it? And the even bigger question- *why* had she done it? Taking a sip of wine, Bertie carefully opened the journal, and its binding creaked lightly in protest.

"What were you like, Helene?" Bertie asked out loud. "You had Mitchell Morrison's child and then disappeared from their lives. What was going through your mind?"

Setting aside her natural inclination to correct grammar and analyze content, Bertie began to read, her eyes scanning the pages eagerly. So Mitch and Helene had met in Arizona. And Mitch had been a self-proclaimed bachelor with no intention of having a relationship with the French girl he'd bedded. Bertie smiled when she read what a devoted father Mitch had been in Paris and how he'd cried when he left Mary in France briefly. Bertie felt sorry for Helene, a woman so desperately in love that she'd been willing to sacrifice her self-respect by living with a man who didn't love her in return.

Bertie read on, intrigued by the events leading up to Helene and Mary's departure from France and then....

A small gasp escaped Bertie's throat and with one hand to her mouth, she devoured the next several pages in shock, her heart hammering, her mind whirling in all different directions. This was the secret. The heartbreaking secret Georgette wanted Mitch to tell his daughter.

⌒

Frank and Lorelei stared at one other in the elevator, mesmerized. Each floor they passed drew them closer to Lorelei's condo. Closer to love. Closer to pleasure. Closer to showing the depth of their emotions through the magic of touch. They were about to embark on a new and dazzling dimension, to step over the boundaries of resistance and into the enchanting world of mutual joy and elation.

The elevator stopped at the twenty-eighth floor and they stepped out into the hallway. Frank took Lorelei's hand and goosebumps rose all along her arm. Every nerve in her body was stretched to the breaking point, fire burned in her chest and her breath quickened. Overcome with the enormity of what they were about to do, she stopped walking and Frank turned, his eyes questioning. But when he saw the look on her face he said huskily, "I know. I feel it too."

Lorelei reached out and ran a hand along his arm, tracing his bicep with her fingertip. Loving the firmness of his strength, she put an inquisitive hand under Frank's shirt and explored the ridges of his stomach muscles. His eyes darkened with desire at her gentle perusal but he held still, allowing her to caress him as her hands moved upward, softly stroking his broad chest.

"Frank?" she was almost breathless. "That crazy electrical current... it happens every time we touch. It's like there's an inferno inside me and whenever you're close my whole body ignites."

Frank's jaw hardened, his muscles tensing. "You do the same to me." Slowly, seductively, he placed his large hands on either side of her ribcage, spanning them down over her hips and then around to her backside. Grasping her bottom roughly, possessively, he pulled her pelvis up to his own. She rasped his name in urgency when she felt his need and pressed into him, wrapping her arms around his neck. He lowered his head and she kissed him without inhibition, without restraint, and he pushed her against the wall, his hands roaming over her body, his lips moving to her eyes, her cheeks, her shoulders. She began to tremble, her clothed body aching to be released and devoured in every way by this man.

Frank swept her up into his arms and carried her the rest of the way to her condo. Unable to stop touching him, Lorelei massaged the muscles in his shoulders and upper back, kneading them sensually, captivated by the way they softened and then hardened under her touch. Her full lips brushed against his neck and she gently sucked the soft spot under his ear. He moaned in the back of his throat and she kissed her way to the exposed part of his chest above his tank top, tenderly nibbling at his delicious skin.

"I'm going to drop you if you keep doing that," Frank said huskily.

"I can't stop touching you... I want you so much," Lorelei whispered.

"I want you too, baby." Frank stopped in front of her door and set her down. Taking her face in his hands, he rubbed his thumbs against the delicate smoothness of her flushed cheeks. "Where is your key?"

Lorelei's eyes were hazed over, her body alert and responsive, but her mind completely shut down in the wake of the intense longing she felt. "Ummm..."

Frank chuckled. "Do you want me to just kick in the door?"

"You can do that?"

"Yes, but it will cause damage." He kissed the back of her hand. "It'll break the lock and you don't want anyone walking in and seeing the pleasure I'm about to lavish on that sexy body of yours."

Lorelei smiled coquettishly. "*I* can't wait to see that." She pulled his head down and said into his mouth, "And *feel* it."

Frank thrust his tongue between her beautiful lips and kissed her hard, his passion inflaming her beyond anything she'd ever experienced. Their kiss intensified, arousing both of them until they were shaking, panting with feverish yearning.

"Open the damn door," Frank managed hoarsely. "I can't take any more of this."

With trembling fingers, Lorelei reached into the small hidden pocket of her yoga pants, pulled out a key and unlocked her condo.

Frank drew Lorelei to his side with one muscular arm, lifting her over the threshold and slamming the door behind them. He set her down, turned the lock and said thickly, "Tell me where you want me, Lor."

"On my bed." Her face was both excited and shy.

"I was hoping you'd say that." Frank remembered all too well the plush round bed upstairs with its sheer canopy and incredibly luxurious scarlet duvet. He'd imagined ravishing Lorelei's body there more than once. He looked down at her now and saw that her eyes were bright, full of love. He embraced her in a warm hug and said into her hair, "I want this night to be perfect for you, Lorelei Harper."

She kissed his shoulder contentedly. "It already is."

⌒

Lorelei raked her green eyes over every part of Frank's naked body, from his strong calves up to his broad shoulders- and everything in between. Her gaze paused below his waistline and a delighted smile curved her luscious lips. "Impressive," she complimented with a hot look of desire.

By tacit agreement they headed to the shower, having both worked all day and jogged in the evening. Lorelei's bath was big and square, tiled in shiny blue iridescent pieces of glass. A rainfall shower head drenched the couple as they stood beneath it, locked in a deep and searching kiss. Gently, Frank pulled away and reached for Lorelei's body wash. He rubbed it between his hands and then ran them over her legs, her torso, her back. She sucked in her breath when he cupped her breasts, massaging each one with intense arousing pressure. His hands searched the poetic loveliness of her body, carefully reading every ardent response, moving over her rhythmically, lyrically, the composition of his touches harmonious with her needs. When she whispered his name his hands stilled for a moment before he allowed himself to trace the smoothness of her inner thighs, slowly, gently stroking, trailing upward until... Lorelei moaned as his fingers captured her, caressing every fold, every hidden crevasse, every chasm of her femininity. His touch was exploratory, reverent, so very capable, and then he kissed his way down the silken skin of her neck to the suppleness of her breasts. He kneeled before her and she placed her small hands on the top of his head. He brought his bold, masculine mouth to her most secret of places and ripples of pleasure raced through her body like lightning strikes.

"Frank..." she moaned, a million stars illuminating as she began the ascent into a new world, a sensually erotic world she'd never been to before. A world where only she and Frank existed, one in which she could be free and happy; one in which she knew she could enter without fear of abandonment or rejection. This world was only full of love, full of trust, full of both friendship and desire. And Frank was taking her there... slowly at first and then his sensitive ministrations grew assertive, dominant. Lorelei's groans turned to cries of delight and she dug her nails into his muscular shoulders. Her body began to vibrate with uncontrollable tremors as Frank brought her closer to the stars. Her eyes filled with tears as her mind and body slammed together in a paroxysm of recognition- she'd never felt like this before. *Never*.

Frank stopped for a moment- just a moment- the water above running over his rugged face. "I love you, Lorelei. Now. Tomorrow. Always." And then he sent her over the moon and into oblivion. Arching her back and crying out, she shuddered convulsively against him, light exploding all around her. She clutched his head closer, pressing herself against his lips and his tongue while he plunged his fingers into her over and over. Then, at the very height of her pinnacle, he left his fingers inside, crooking them slightly, beckoning her from within. She screamed his name and the new world detonated in a blinding sea of flames. Bursting over the crest of ecstasy, she cried out again and again, her sighs of pleasure gradually quieting, fading away into a new serenity.

Frank pulled her down and cradled her against his chest on the floor of the shower. Stroking her hair, he murmured words of love while she gently fell back to earth.

⁓

They finished showering, lovingly washing one another all over, their touches softer, sweeter than before. Their eyes glowing with a deeper affection, a stronger bond. Lorelei was all too aware that the pleasure she'd just felt was a small taste of the life Frank wanted to give her.

They took turns toweling each other off and then Lorelei led him by the hand to her sumptuous bed. She moved aside the wispy canopy and then pulled Detective Frank Williams into her arms. He covered her with his body and she cleaved into him. He moaned in raw desire when she reached down to caress him and she knew even though he was nearing the edge of his endurance, he would patiently take his time to ensure her pleasure. But why prolong what they both wanted so desperately?

"We have all night," she whispered seductively into his ear. "We can take our time later."

He searched her eyes and then kissed her until she was weak with need. "Lorelei…" he moaned and then he was inside her. She inhaled sharply, her senses pushed to their limit. He felt so good, so right, so absolutely perfect.

Frank didn't move. He allowed her to adjust, to take him in at her own pace, her own speed. She moved against him slightly and he braced his arms on either side of her, his biceps bulging with restrained anticipation. Lorelei pulled his face down to her own and bit his bottom lip seductively while she pushed her hips up and forward, fully taking Frank inside, loving the feel of being one with him, completely, wholly.

He eased his lips away from hers and looked into those brilliant green eyes. "Are you ready?"

"Oh yes."

"I feel like my entire life has led me to this moment."

"I love you, Frank Williams."

"And I love you, Lorelei Harper. So very much."

"I don't want this night to end." She was breathless.

"Oh, baby, it's only just beginning."

CHAPTER 60

*M*itch walked into the living room, his strong shoulders slightly hunched, the lines around his mouth showing signs of strain. "Mary is having a hard time…" he began and then stopped when he saw Helene's journal in Bertie's lap.

Quiet filled the room, reticent with secrecy.

Mitch's amber eyes flew to Bertie's face beseechingly, as though asking for absolution.

Bertie stretched out a hand to him. "If I'd been in your shoes all those years ago I wouldn't have told Mary the truth either."

Mitch sat heavily on the couch, pulling Bertie against his solid chest and kissing the top of her head. "Thank you." The words were simple but weighted with gratitude.

They held each other in the stillness for a few moments, then Mitch said, "Mary is divorcing Owen. Her mother-in-law is involved somehow, but she wouldn't give me details." His voice hardened. "You know, when Owen and Mary were first engaged I wasn't sure it was a good idea because of his parents. But I told myself that Mary was marrying a *person*, not a family. I wanted to believe that Owen was sincere when he told me he wasn't going to follow in his dad's footsteps- that loving Mary and providing for her was the one thing he cared about most in life; flying planes came second. I trusted him. He swore he'd never take money from Charles and Ellen or drag Mary into their elitist bullshit and I thought…" Mitch sighed. "I was such a fool. I should have known better than to believe him. What's more, I should have forbidden Mary from ever marrying that jackass."

"I don't think you can control adult children like that. And it doesn't sound like he was a jackass back then," Bertie said gently. "And Mary was in love, right? She might have run off with Owen whether you wanted her to or not."

"Maybe. Maybe not. Mary has always listened to me, never went against my rule as a child and never against my advice as an adult. She's a good girl and she trusts her old man."

"And what advice did you give her tonight?"

"Not much. I just listened. Told her I could be on a plane within a few hours if she needed me." Mitch scratched his chin thoughtfully. "There's something odd about the whole thing, though. Ellen claims she and Owen have already discussed the divorce, and Mary said Owen was acting very strange the morning he shipped out- like he was hiding something."

"He was hiding the fact that his mother was about to tell Mary she was out of the family?" Bertie suggested.

"Maybe." Mitch shifted and rubbed the side of his head with the heel of his hand. "Man, my mind feels a bit fuzzy for some reason."

Bertie's brow furrowed. "Probably because you need sleep. Let's get you into bed, Morrison, and not for any extracurricular activities."

"Okay," Mitch agreed, his tone sepulchral.

The strange inflection made Bertie sit up, her brown eyes intent. "Are you okay, sweetheart?" She placed a hand on his forehead and found it wet and clammy.

"Yeah, I think I'm just tired. And worried about Mary and..." Mitch sighed, "... and I feel guilty about not giving her Helene's things. But if she knew about them there would be questions and-"

"I understand. It's all right..."

"But she said the nicest things on the phone tonight and it made me feel guiltier than ever."

Bertie was becoming increasingly worried. Mitch's skin had taken on a greyish tinge and his speech was beginning to slur. Where was her cell phone...?

"Mary said," Mitch continued, "that I was the best daddy she could have ever asked for. She said she's so grateful that I've always been there for her." He paused, his words heavy with emotion. "She said she's proud to be my daughter."

Bertie kissed him on a pale cheek and stood. "You know what, my love? I'm very concerned about you right now so I'm just going to find my phone..."

"Why? I'm fine." Mitch stood drowsily and stumbled slightly.

"That's why," Bertie countered.

Mitch took an eerie breath of air and then said, confused, "I can't breathe."

"What do you mean?" Bertie was fully alarmed and warning bells clanged in her head sending shrieks of sirens down her spine.

Mitch fell backward into a sitting position on the couch, unable to hold himself upright any longer. "I can't..." he took a long, ragged gulp of air and then... "I can't breathe." His eyes closed and his head and mouth went slack.

Bertie shook him by the shoulders. "Mitch! Mitch! Wake up!" Her internal sirens had reached crescendo and she screamed above the horrific din in her head, "WAKE UP!!!"

With a cry of fear she ran to her cell phone and called 911 while Mitch sat unconscious on his couch looking for all the world like a patient father who had fallen asleep waiting for his beloved daughter to come home.

CHAPTER 61

⌒

The paramedics were wonderful. They rushed into Mitch's house and started CPR right away. One of them took Bertie aside and tried to distract her with questions regarding what Mitch had been doing that day, what had he eaten, what had he said before he'd become unconscious.

Then four policemen came through the door. There was a very nice officer called Keith. He stayed close to Bertie. He smelled like cigarette smoke and had kind eyes. He took Bertie in his police car to the hospital while Mitch rode lifelessly in the ambulance.

A chaplain was waiting in a small room by the ER for the family of the deceased. Bertie walked in and sat beside him. She couldn't speak. She couldn't think. Her body felt completely frozen. She looked at her fingers but they didn't seem like her own fingers. The chaplain asked if she would like to pray with him and she stared at him dumbly. "Why?"

"Your loved one is in heaven with the Lord, free from pain and free from the perils of this earth. We will ask God to be gracious to us in our time of sadness, and we will thank Him for the love He is bestowing on Mitchell Morrison tonight as he celebrates new life with our Father."

Bertie shook her head. It felt like it was full of wool. "But I want Mitch here. With me." Her lips trembled. "He loved me. He never loved a woman before. He called me by my last name and he liked country music and he has a daughter he adores and he enjoys working outside; he's been in construction his whole life and… he wanted me to move in…" Bertie's slender shoulders shook with sobs as the words tumbled out one after another, "…and I don't want Mitch to have new life, Father. I want him to come back and share life with *me*."

The chaplain placed his warm hands on Bertie's cold ones. "Seek comfort in remembering the great love Mitchell had for you and for others. Love never dies, my child. Love is for eternity."

It was like a dream. Like someone had ripped her heart out of her chest and left her to die. But it wasn't Mary who was dead. It was her father.

She sat on the floor, her cell phone in front of her. Aunt Georgette said Lorelei was coming over, would be there any second, not to hang up. Roger was in the house somewhere, completely oblivious to the fact that the entire world had changed. Hadn't just changed. It had imploded. Mary didn't understand. Understand any of it. How could someone be living and breathing one minute and gone forever the next? Death just didn't make sense. And it definitely didn't make any sense with regard to Mitchell Morrison.

Mary turned stormy eyes to a framed picture of her father on the other side of the room. Gone. He was gone. Gone forever. But how could that be? He was so healthy. So full of life. And now all that was left was death…

Tears coursed down Mary's cheeks. Dead. Her daddy was dead.

She wanted to be dead too so she could be with him.

That was crazy talk. But she didn't care.

Erupting into violent sobs, she curled in a ball on the floor, hugging her knees to her chest. All she could feel was pain, a horrible pain pressing her down. She gave into it, wishing the rug beneath her would open and swallow her up. The man she had always been able to count on. The man who had always been there for her. The man who loved her above all else. The man who was her anchor, her friend, her confidant, her strength. GONE. Mary's cries capsized into hysteria and she began to cough, choking on her tears.

"I NEED HIM!!!" she screamed through her sobs. "I NEED HIM!!! I NEED HIM!!! He can't leave me! Daddy!!! DADDY!!!"

⌒‿

"Franny, I can't do this again," Georgette wept into her pillow. "I can't..."

"Shhhhhh...." Francesca stroked Georgette's hair, tears pouring down her own cheeks. *"Sono qui. Ti amo. Calma la mia bella..."* The Italian words were soothing, lyrical.

"Mitch," George whimpered pitifully. "My darling brother..."

Francesca gathered Georgette into her arms. "He is at peace, *bellisima*, you must believe that."

Georgette pushed at her. *"I'm* not at peace!" Then she pulled Francesca back, her voice mournfully crestfallen. "Another brother! Oh, Franny, I've lost both my baby brothers! And my parents are already gone. I'm alone... the last of my family..."

⌒‿

Mary cried on the floor of her home until she thought she was empty, void of emotion, but the pain just kept oppressing her, the heel of its hand shoving her down further and further into the barren wasteland of sorrow. The tears wouldn't stop, the heartache wouldn't let up. Searing pain shot through her head, and her stomach ached from the constant sobbing. She didn't know how long she'd been on the ground, paralyzed with the wretchedness of total and complete loss, but she knew that at some point Roger had come into the room and, sensing her grief, had thrown his large floppy body next to hers.

Mary's phone lay where she'd left it. Aunt Francesca had been trying to reach Mary but she didn't think she was capable of speaking. She picked up the phone and stared at it as though she'd never seen it before. Her hands were numb and clumsy. It rang again. Aunt Francesca.

But where was Lorelei? Aunt George had said Lorelei would be there. Mary wanted her best friend more than anything. Lorelei would understand how Mary's universe had just collapsed upon itself with the death of her father. Death. Mary felt like she was going to throw up. Death. Her dad was dead.

Mary pushed at Roger and staggered to her feet. Lightheadedness rushed in and around her and she thought for a moment she might faint. Her face was hot and puffy, her lips dry and swollen. She stumbled into the kitchen and grabbed her keys from the counter. Opening the back door to the garage, she climbed into her Jeep. Roger, close on her heels, leapt into the backseat.

Mary pulled out of her driveway slowly, dazedly. She forgot to switch on the headlights. Her tears were still flowing. She didn't know if she'd ever stop crying; she felt anesthetized, as though all of her senses were trundling dully through a thick gel. Pulling onto the highway she headed straight for Thomas McQuillan's house. Mary wanted Helga- sweet, motherly Helga, who would hold Mary in her plump arms and say comforting things that had no meaning and make Mary feel like she wasn't completely alone in the world.

Misery had only just begun. Mary saw nothing ahead of her except the torture of painful loneliness.

Even Lorelei was absent when she was needed most.

⌒

Francesca shook Georgette's shoulders gently. "Georgie, I can't get a hold of Mary. Are you sure Lorelei is with her?"

George's face was buried in her pillow, her sobs soaking the satiny blue cover. "I called Lorelei... left messages... I'm sure she's with Mary."

"I'm very worried. Mary isn't answering." Francesca tentatively turned Georgette over. "You should have waited to call Mary until Lorelei was there."

"I know... I can't... I don't..." George's face crumpled as a fresh torrent of tears rolled down her wrinkled cheeks. "I can't do this, Franny, I can't handle the pain inside. It hurts... it hurts so much. Maybe this isn't real. Maybe Mitch isn't really gone." She clutched at Francesca's shoulders. "Tell me!" Her voice climbed to a high-pitched panic. "Tell me he's alive! TELL ME!!! Make this go away, Franny! I want to wake up! This is just a horrible dream!"

Francesca, weeping softly, pulled Georgette close. "It's real, *bellisima*, I'm so sorry. So very sorry." Francesca held her darling Georgie, rocking her back and forth like a child, uttering words of love and singing soft, soothing verses of Italian song, just as she had all those years ago when Claude had left them too.

Mary entered Thomas' gate code on the keypad and drove along the dark cobbled pathway to his home. Using her key, she let herself in the house and took Roger through the living room and down the hallway to the kitchen. A light was on, the smell of cinnamon wafting through the air. Mary burst through the swinging door and Helga swung around in alarm. She took one look at Mary's ravaged face and opened her consoling, motherly arms.

CHAPTER 62

*F*rank awoke the next morning to the sun brightly shining through the eastern window. The rays highlighted Lorelei's curls which were spread out like spun gold on his chest. She was sleeping as peacefully as a child, one hand under her beautiful face and one hand resting on Frank's hip. He looked down at her and his heart turned over with love.

The evening had been tantalizingly sensual and licentiously decadent as they had explored each and every inch of one another's bodies. Their touches had been both inquisitive and gentle, and both daring and demanding. Their lust was mutually insatiable, spurred on by the love that surged in and around them. The electrical currents never stopped, only intensified, and Frank and Lorelei brought one another to climax over and over, fascinated by the magnetic pull that enticingly led them on. Frank had never known such physical intimacy could exist- not simply pleasure, but an emotional connection that enhanced every moment of sexual seduction.

Lorelei stirred and he kissed the top of her head. She nuzzled into his chest and he held her close.

"How long have we been asleep?" she asked drowsily.

Frank looked at the bedside clock. "About an hour."

Lorelei looked up at him and smiled, her green eyes dreamy. "I loved falling asleep in your arms."

"It was the second-best thing that happened last night."

She giggled and raised up to kiss his lips softly. "I'm going to go downstairs and make coffee."

Frank rolled her over and pinned her beneath his powerful body. "I have a better idea."

Thomas was pacing in the kitchen, his hands running through his sandy hair in agitation. "I don't understand - why didn't you wake me up?"

"D'ere vas no reason to," Helga explained for the third time. "I gave her a sedative from when I haf dat surgery last year and den I tuck her into bed and stay vith her until she go to sleep."

"I could have…"

"You could haf v'hat?" Helga raised an eyebrow.

"I could have comforted her. Isn't that why she came here? For me?"

Helga shook her head. "It does not matter v'hy she came here as long as ve help her." She handed him a cup of fägring black tea. "You peek in on her and gif dis to her if she avake."

Thomas took the hot mug from Helga and stared at it thoughtfully. "You know, I saw him. That night I went to the club with Lennie. Mary and her father were there. At least I'm sure it was her dad- she looks just like him. And he has the same uncanny amber eyes." Thomas sighed in bewilderment. "He was healthy, Helga. Handsome guy, nice suit. He danced a lot with a redhead wearing a very short dress. I saw lots of women staring at him and a very famous supermodel hit on him at one point."

Helga's mouth opened and Thomas held up a hand. "Not Katya." His face darkened as he thought of her and what she'd suggested in that envelope. A suggestion he knew in his very heart was true.

"It is not our say when da Fadder calls us home, mina älskling, but I know dat does not make it any easier for da loved one's left behind."

Thomas thought sadly of his grandparents who he missed very much. "No, it's not easy."

"Mary's fadder was her whole vorld. You go upstairs and see if she okay. You tell Helga if Mary needs anyt'ing."

Thomas kissed Helga's plump cheek and she looked up at him in pleased surprise. "Thank you, Helga. I hope you know how special you are to me. I don't say it enough. Things like this happen and you realize how short life really is."

Lorelei poured Frank a steaming, fragrant cup of coffee and he took it from her, his hand grazing hers.

"I can still feel electricity," she marveled. "Even after all that happened last night."

Frank sipped his coffee, his eyes hot and tempting. "Why don't you come closer and I'll light up your world again. Ever seen a fireworks show at ten in the morning?"

Lorelei laughed. "Aren't you hungry? Because I'm famished." She opened the refrigerator door and looked inside sheepishly. "We could go out. I'll buy you breakfast at Nosh."

Frank put his mug down, placed his big hands on Lorelei's waist and bent to her ear. "Why don't we just order in?"

His deep voice sent chills down her back and she kissed him approvingly. "Mmmmm... I like the way you think, Detective." She glanced around her kitchen. "I wonder where I left my cell? I'll place a delivery request on the app."

"I don't think you had it last night when we were jogging," Frank remembered.

"Right. And I didn't even think about checking messages when we got back because..." she gave him a sly, intimate smile, "... because all I could think about was you." Walking into the living room, she called over her shoulder, "It's probably still in my attaché case."

Lorelei lifted her work portfolio from the plush red chair where she'd left it, unlatched the leather strappings and pulled her cell phone from the small pocket inside. She hadn't even turned the ringer back on since she'd left work. Entering her password, she waited for the home screen to pull up and to her surprise there were multiple calls from Georgette Morrison and another Arizona number she didn't recognize. A terrible feeling of trepidation washed over her and her stomach constricted in fear.

Tapping the voicemail button she listened to Georgette tearfully pleading for Lorelei to get to Mary as soon as possible.

Mitch had passed away.

No.

NO!

Lorelei waited for the next message, hoping this was some sort of cruel, inhumane joke. Georgette's voice was even shriller this time. "Where are you? Please go over to Mary's right now! Please, Lorelei, please! Hurry!"

Tears ran down Lorelei's face and she brushed at them with the back of her hand impatiently. This wasn't happening, this couldn't be…

Frank casually entered the room. "Did you find your…" He saw Lorelei, her green eyes wounded, her face wet with grief and rushed to her side. "Lor? What's wrong?"

"I have to get to Mary," she said absently as though Frank weren't even there. "I have to… Oh my god, what time did this message come in?" She scrolled through her phone, horrified. Mary had been alone all night. "I have to go," she said in shock. "I have to get to Mary…" With stiff, awkward steps she started toward her staircase.

"Lorelei!" Frank turned her around. "You're not going anywhere until you tell me what's happened."

"Mary needs me," she replied, her beautiful face sorrowful.

"I will take you to her. But tell me why she needs you." Frank's hands were warm and reassuring on her arms.

"Because Mitch died." The words choked in her throat as though the very breath of life couldn't admit to the death of such a dynamic, vigorous man.

Frank pulled Lorelei close. "Oh, honey, I'm so, so sorry." He lowered his head over Lorelei's in sympathetic reassurance and told her the one thing she wanted to hear most- that Mitch Morrison had cared for her. "When Mitch and I were alone at Sharky's he said something like, '… the nice lady in the red suit looks like she thinks you're pretty special… she's a good girl and you'd better not hurt her.'"

Lorelei pulled back and looked up at Frank. "He said that?"

"Sure did." Frank wiped a tear from her cheek. "He made it very clear he was looking out for your best interests and if I screwed up there'd be hell to pay. Very intimidating guy with the best of intentions."

"What did you say back?"

Frank chuckled. "I told him you and I were only friends. And he said, 'Reckon I don't kiss my friends like that.'"

Lorelei gave a watery smile. "Sounds like Mitch."

"Now, why don't you go upstairs and change and then I'll take you over to Mary's. Do you want to try calling her first?"

Lorelei nodded and picked up the phone again.

But Mary wasn't answering.

CHAPTER 63

⌒

Thomas gently opened Mary's bedroom door and a whoosh of air hit his face as a giant black furry monster jumped on him. Thomas grunted in startled surprise and the monster growled in warning.

Setting Mary's tea down on the table holding her laptop, Thomas edged toward the bed. It was a big black dog that had rushed him and the dog was now baring his teeth ever so slightly.

"Peace!" Thomas whispered, holding up his hands. "I'm friend, not foe."

Mary moaned and blinked confusedly. Roger's demeanor changed when he heard her and he whined, looking at Thomas with a befuddled expression on his big, dopey face. "Poor guy," Thomas said, patting him on the head. "You've had a rough night, haven't you?" He pointed toward the open bedroom door. "Why don't you go find Helga? She'll let you outside and get you some breakfast."

Thomas knew the dog couldn't be that smart, but Roger must have sensed some sort of kindness was being offered. He licked Thomas' arm and left the bedroom at a trot. Probably hoping for a tree in close proximity.

Thomas kneeled next to the bed and took Mary's hand. "Hey," he said softly.

She looked back at him with dull, lifeless eyes. "Hey."

"I brought you some tea."

"My dad died," she said in a wooden voice.

He stroked her tangled honey hair back from her face. "I know. I'm so sorry."

Tears welled up and spilled over. "I couldn't stop crying last night. I didn't know where to go."

"You were right to come here." Compassion squeezed Thomas' heart with a fierceness that took his breath away.

"I didn't want to be alone," she said hoarsely. "I don't know where Lorelei is and I thought I shouldn't go to Faith's house because I don't want to upset her children. I guess I could have gone to Corinne and Horse's, but Owen and Horse are best friends so that didn't seem like a good idea... I don't want to put Corinne in an uncomfortable position even though no one really knows yet that Owen and I are splitting up... and-"

"Shhhhh..." Thomas interrupted, trying to stop the flow of apologetic words. "It's okay that you're here, Mary."

"Thank you, Thomas." She looked up at him with trusting eyes and then a shadow crossed her face as though she remembered why she was there. Stricken, tears began coursing down her cheeks. "I'm sorry," she said, "I'm sorry to cry so much. I..." and her rosebud lips opened as though she were going to scream for help, but the only sound that came out was a keening so soft and so pitiful that it reminded Thomas of a newborn kitten calling for its mother.

Mary tightened her grip on his hand and she reached out for him with her other arm like a small child seeking comfort. In one swift movement, Thomas was beside her in the bed, taking her in his arms and pressing her head into his shoulder. "Cry as much as you want, Mary. It's okay. Let it all out. I'm not going anywhere."

And for the first time in years, Thomas forgot all about anything having to do with himself, his writing, his career or his struggles in missing Gemma. Not even his libido entered the picture, despite the fact that Mary's alluring body was draped forlornly over his own. The only thing that mattered to him was the grieving girl in his arms who needed to know she wasn't alone.

Thomas held Mary for close to an hour while she poured out her sorrow and anguish. Eventually her sobs quieted, but she was still clutching his shirt with both hands, her face buried in his chest. Thomas felt very protective of this gently broken woman who had turned to him for solace and strength.

After a few silent moments, Mary let out a breathy, mournful sigh. Hoping to soothe her, Thomas ran his hands through her hair over and over, the strokes tender and solicitous. She went completely still, relaxing into his touch and then she stiffened in recognition. "My dad used to brush my hair like that when I was a little girl."

"Do you want me to stop? Are the memories too painful?"

She didn't answer and Thomas tilted her chin up so that he could look in her eyes. "What can I do, Mary? What can I do for you? I want to help."

Her amber eyes spilled over with tears once again. "Take me home, Thomas," she begged. "Please take me home."

"Okay, just tell me where you live…"

"No." She shook her head, the waves of her hair rippling across his arms. "Take me home to Arizona."

Being affluent certainly had its perks, but in times of crisis, wealth and connections were invaluable. Thomas called in a favor and chartered a private plane. Mary didn't want to go to her townhouse to collect any clothing or toiletries. She said she never wanted to return to the place she'd lived with her controlling and indifferent husband. And it had been there, in the living room of that house, where she'd heard the shocking, horrific news that her father had passed away. Thomas asked if she would like to call any of her friends to let them know she was leaving the state and she looked at him painfully, hurt scattering across her lovely features.

"No. My best friend didn't come for me when I needed her the most. I don't want her now." Mary seemed to be on memory overload-not wanting to be reminded of anything that smacked of distress... her divorce, losing her father, the absent Lorelei.

Voltaire had been holed up in Helga's quarters all night and once Thomas and Mary were downstairs she let him out so he could meet Roger. At first Voltaire gaped in fright at the giant dog, and then, in true Boxer fashion, Roger swatted at Voltaire's head with a big paw. Voltaire's grey eyes widened in playful vengeance and he chomped down on one of Roger's front legs. The big black dog yipped, jumped straight in the air and Voltaire barked excitedly. The two raced out of the kitchen, slamming through the swinging door and crashing into a wall. There were a few yowling shrieks, a thunderous woof and then the tapping and skidding of claws tearing down the tiled hallway and fading out of earshot.

Thomas and Helga laughed, but Mary only turned sluggish eyes to Helga. "Thank you for taking care of Roger while I'm gone."

"You take care of v'hat you need to and don't vorry about huge dog. Helga make sure he eat good." She held Mary close and patted her back kindly. "I be right here v'hen you get back, okay?"

Mary nodded. "Okay."

Helga turned to Thomas. "You need anyt'ing at all you call me." In a low voice, she said in his ear, "V'hat about yer novel?"

"I already emailed Lennie and told him it won't be ready by dead-line," Thomas whispered back. "He's in freak-out mode over the contracts."

"Helga respect you. You learn dat being d'ere for o'ters is most important in life, yes? Even above vork?"

"Maybe the right person had to come along to show me."

"Maybe so, Thomas McQuillan, and we both know dat person was not da horrible vench Katya."

They exchanged a smile of amused agreement and then Thomas put his arm around Mary's limp waist. She looked up at him in confusion as though she'd forgotten where she was or what was happening around her.

"We're going to the airport now," Thomas said to her gently.

"Okay," Mary's voice was barely above a whisper.

Georgette had finally fallen into a restless slumber and she awoke the morning after Mitch's death groggy and disoriented.

Francesca came in the room with a tray of toast, jelly, orange juice and a shot of what looked like whiskey. She set it on the bed next to George and then pulled the curtains open, letting sunshine spill into their darkened bedroom.

"Don't, Franny. I just want to lie here and sleep. Go away."

Francesca sat on the bed and took the hands of her lover. "No, George. You need to get up and get yourself together."

"But -"

"I know. I really do. But with Claude it was different. You could take your time in grieving because there were no responsibilities. Our lives have changed since then, remember? Mary needs you. She's going to need you to be strong for her. You are the only mother she has."

Georgette closed her eyes. She knew Francesca was right but that didn't make it any easier. She wanted time to mourn and mend her own broken heart. She didn't even know if she had the energy or the capability to take on someone else's pain, even if it was her beloved niece.

"Franny, I don't think I can do this." Georgette squeezed Francesca's hands tightly, plaintively.

"Yes, you can. And I'll be right by your side every step of the way. Mary is our girl. Helene brought her to Mitch and then Mitch brought her to us. Remember that day at the villa? We promised him we'd always be there for Mary. In some ways we had the best of both worlds, didn't we? The freedom of being able to live our lives as we wanted, to travel when we wanted, have parties when we wanted... all because Mary belonged to her father. It was easy to arrange our schedules around her so that she felt like the center of attention when she was here, but we never had the total and complete responsibility of parenthood." Francesca's dark eyes softened, her words laden with intent. "Even though Mary is an adult, Georgie, she needs to know we're here for her, that she can always come to us, always rely on us. She's going to be lost and looking for comfort, for stability, for security. We must give that to her."

Georgette nodded but kept silent.

"Now," Francesca said, "let's get packed and I'll book us the first flight out of Phoenix to San Diego."

"Franny?"

"Yes, George?"

"Thank you. When you're not waving a gun around or shaving half your hair off you're really quite down to earth and levelheaded." A tiny sparkle of a smile graced her lips. "You're the best partner a girl could ever hope or wish for. And I love you."

"I love you too, *bellisima,*" Francesca replied with an affectionate pat to Georgette's cheek. "Now, is there anything we should pick up from Mitch's house on our way to the airport that Mary might want right away? Something special or sentimental that she'd like to hold on to today?"

Both women pondered for a few moments and then their eyes met, widening in consternation as they had the same thought.

"Helene's things," George whispered, the words like a talisman against secrecy.

"Oh god... that journal Mitch was talking about... I'll bet everything is in there- all of it."

"Franny, Mary absolutely *cannot* read that diary before we talk to her."

"She's in California, George. There's no way she's going to even know it exists until we tell her."

Thomas rented a car once he and Mary landed at Sky Harbor Airport and he drove them out to the address Mary provided. Aside from directions, she hadn't spoken either on the plane or in the vehicle. When Thomas pulled into the driveway of Mitch's house she let out a mournful cry and leapt from the car. Sprinting toward the porch, she lifted a small planter, pulled a key out from under it and unlocked the front door. Before Thomas could climb from the driver's seat he heard Mary's screams as she ran from room to room inside the house. "Daddy? Daddy?! DADDY!!! WHERE ARE YOU???"

"Faith won't answer my calls," Lorelei said to Frank in his truck. "Would you mind trying to reach her from your number? Mary is going to need both of us. I know Faith is still angry with me, but this is bigger than our little problem."

"It isn't little to Faith," Frank reminded her gently.

Lorelei dipped her head. "I know. And after my conversation with Connor I think I understand on a deeper level what she's going through. She and I will have a long talk, but Mary comes first right now."

Frank wanted to ask Lorelei if she was still entertaining the thought of moving to New York. Surely not. Not after all that had happened between them last night. The possibility of Lorelei being miles and miles away pained him. But this was not the time to get into the intricacies of their future and he kept silent.

When Frank pulled up to Mary's townhouse Lorelei jumped from his truck and ran across the driveway. Using her key, she unlocked the door and yelled for Mary. Getting no response, she began to panic, making a thorough search of both upstairs and downstairs. She found Mary's cell phone on the floor in the living room and, alarmed, she picked it up and took it back outside with her.

Frank was just ending his call with Faith when Lorelei climbed into the passenger seat. "Mary isn't here. She's not here." Lorelei's voice rose. "She needs me. I know she needs me! I've always been there for her. *Always*!" Staring at Mary's cell phone she forced her brain to remember the password. Frank was saying something but Lorelei tuned him out. The code was someone's birthday... whose birthday? Not hers, not Owen's... Oh! Roger's! Of course! She entered the date and Mary's phone unlocked. There were several missed calls from both Georgette and Francesca. Lorelei began scrolling through Mary's contacts until she found Corinne's number. No answer. She called Ricki and Happy but neither woman had heard from Mary, though they were both saddened to hear about Mitch – they knew how much he meant to her. Unsure what to do next, Lorelei searched through Mary's texts looking for clues. There were messages from herself, Mitch, Faith, Corinne, Georgette, Francesca, Willow Starflower regarding dog-walking... and there were several texts between Mary and a man named Thomas. Puzzled, Lorelei clicked into the contact info and a profile pulled up: Thomas McQuillan, phone number, address, dog's name, dog's breed, scheduling times... a link was also listed and Lorelei, perplexed, clicked into it and she was redirected to a scheduling app. Mary had blocked out times for writing, completing homework and reading books that had been assigned.

Dumbfounded, Lorelei turned to Frank. "Have you ever been shocked by a clue you've uncovered when you're investigating a case?"

"All the time."

Lorelei called Thomas' number and was sent straight to voicemail; he must have his phone turned off.

"We need to head east," Lorelei told Frank. "I think I know where Mary is." She put her seatbelt on and gave Frank an appraising glance. "But if she isn't there, are you up for interrogating a famous celebrity to see if *he* knows where she might be?"

"You never fail to intrigue me, Miss Harper. Where are we going?"

Lorelei gave him Thomas McQuillan's name and address. Frank raised his eyebrows, pulled out of Mary's driveway and sped toward the prosperous, exclusive community of Rancho Santa Fe.

CHAPTER 64

Thomas entered Mitchell Morrison's home, his heart heavy, his mind frantically trying to figure out how to calm the hysterical girl looking for her father. He shut the solid wood front door behind him and looked around the spacious home decorated in rich leathers and western décor. It was exactly the type of place a financially comfortable bachelor would live, masculine and expansive. Thomas could see the desert stretched out unendingly through the large windows and he wondered how many acres Mitch owned.

Walking over to a large wall covered in family photos surrounded by gorgeous pine frames, Thomas gazed at the many pictures of Mary growing up through the years. She'd been an adorably chubby baby, a pretty toddler, a lovely teenager and… there were photos of her as an adult with a tall, dark haired man, presumably her husband, Owen. Yes, there he was in his military uniform. Thomas leaned forward and scrutinized the Navy fighter pilot. Very good-looking, all-American, straight-laced. Not the type of man who broke rules. Mary and Owen looked happy together and Thomas felt a twinge of jealousy. He turned away and wandered over to the sofas. There was a leather-bound book on the coffee table that caught his eye. It appeared old and foreign, not like something he'd ever seen in the States.

Mary came into the room and she stared at Thomas, her face pale, her eyes red and swollen. "I'm sorry," she said softy. "I know he's gone, but there was a part of me that was hoping it wasn't real. I thought… I thought maybe he'd be here. Waiting for me. I wanted to tell him I love him one more time." Her voice caught. "I hope he knows. I hope he knows how much I loved him."

"From everything you've told me about your relationship with your father there's not a chance in hell he could have thought otherwise." Thomas reached for her hand and pulled her to a couch so that they were sitting together. "When was the last time you talked to your dad?"

"On the phone just yesterday."

"And what did you say?"

She thought back and her bottom lip trembled. "I said I was proud to be his daughter." Her shoulders straightened and her voice became clearer. "Because I am."

"Well, then, I'd say those are pretty great last words for a father to hear."

A trace of a smile touched her lips. "Yeah…"

Thomas put his arm around her and Mary leaned into him for comfort. Casting about for something benign to discuss he leaned forward slightly and picked up the leather-bound book from the coffee table. Handing it to her he said, "Has this been in your family for a long time? It's very unusual."

Mary took the old book from him, curiously turning it over in her hands. "I've never seen this before."

"Why don't you open it and read me what's inside?"

"Okay."

Anything to get their minds off the oppressive sadness of Mitch Morrison's death.

Mary turned to the first page and looked up at Thomas in surprise. "It's a journal."

"Your dad's?"

"I don't think so…" Mary began reading about a little girl who lived in Paris. Her father was teaching her English and she was having a rough go of it. "That's weird," Mary mused, "the only person I know who lived in France was…" Suddenly she gasped, her heart pounding.

Turning page after page, she read silently, devouring each entry like a famished youngster overindulging in sweets.

Eventually she said, "Thomas, this is my mother's diary! I wonder how it got here? Daddy told me he never knew where my mom was." Mary pointed to a page where Helene had been practicing her signature as a child. "This is her name- my mother's name is Helene." Mary read on without a sound, voraciously eating up every detail and every nuance.

After a while, her omnivorous perusal slowed and she said sadly, "My mother loved my father but he didn't love her in return. Daddy loved me so much he was going to live with her anyway." She raised her amber eyes to Thomas' hazel ones. "Dad was going to commit to a woman he didn't love for *me*. And he cried when he left us in France." She wiped a few wayward tears from her freckled cheeks.

Thomas kept silent, letting her talk when she needed. She unconsciously curled in closer and closer to his side, her body seeking the warmth and strength of his own as she discovered and shared with him the story of her mother. There were so many questions Thomas wanted to ask, but he kept his peace.

A few minutes passed and Mary started turning pages so fast Thomas couldn't be sure she was really comprehending what she was reading.

"Mary?"

She had gone completely motionless, her already pale skin now blanched white. The journal slipped from her lap and fell to the floor with a thudding echo.

Thomas put his hand on her cheek. It was cold as ice. "You're worrying me, Mary. Talk to me. Are you having physical pain?"

She shook her head no.

"Did you read something upsetting?"

She gave a small imperceptible nod.

"Can you tell me what it was?"

There was a long pause and then Mary took a deep, shuddering breath. "He wasn't my father."

"I don't understand…"

"Mitchell Morrison was not my biological father." The words left her pretty lips in a gut-wrenching whisper of anguish.

Thomas' brow furrowed. He looked over at the wall of pictures across from them to confirm what he remembered from the night at the club. "You and your father have the same eyes, Mary; a very unusual amber color. And your face has many of his same features. There's no way you two aren't related." Thomas hid his confusion with facts and reassurance.

A tear fell from Mary's eyelashes and splashed fragilely on Thomas' hand. "Daddy had a twin named Claude," she said, her tone vibrating with emotion. "Claude Morrison died when I was a baby and it was he who my mother loved; not Daddy."

For the first time in his intellectual, analytical and overly verbose life, Thomas McQuillan was at a loss for words. Mary seemed to have been shocked out of her grief and stunned into a new and frightening dimension full of uncertain enigmas. A dimension of secrets and lies. Not knowing what else to do, Thomas took her face in his hands and waited until she met his concerned gaze. She looked at him with such an expression of helplessness that he ran his fingers back into her hair and drew her head to his chest. He'd never felt the need to shelter and protect someone before, not like this; he wanted to shield Mary from all of the hurt surrounding her. He wanted to see her smile again, to laugh, to pepper him with questions about literature and music and art. He wanted her to fight with him, her skin flushed with indignation. The girl in his arms was merely a shadow of the girl who'd shown fire and spirit and innocence and compassion day after day in his home. He hugged her closer to his body.

"Do you have someone here in Arizona, Mary?" Thomas said tenderly. "Can I take you to your family?"

"Yes," her voice was muffled against his chest. "My aunties are in Tempe."

"Do you want me to drive you there?"

A very long silence followed and then, heartbroken, she said, "Do you think they know Daddy wasn't my father? Did they lie to me too?"

"Let's go see them and find out."

Mary struggled to sit upright. "Yes." Then she put her hands in his. "Thank you, Thomas."

"For what?"

"For being here for me. For being my friend. For getting me to Arizona. For not letting me do all of this alone. I'm sorry I've probably really messed up your writing schedule and I know you had gotten past your writer's block and..."

He stopped her. "Don't worry about that. You're more important."

"No, I'm not." She gave a weak little laugh. "I'm just an ordinary girl who happens to have a famous author as a guardian angel."

"I'd say that makes you extraordinary rather than ordinary."

Her eyes took on the slightest shine. "I appreciate everything you've done for me."

A blistering heat ran through Thomas' chest like a torrid river of magma. This woman had just experienced acute trauma and devastation over the last sixteen hours and here she was recognizing and expressing thankfulness. That kind of self-awareness wasn't intrinsic or learned- it came only of having a pure and beautiful soul.

Mary Crossfield, soon to be Mary Morrison, wasn't just a friend, or an indirect muse who'd led him back to his First Love of writing. No, he was unequivocally certain she was unintentionally knocking on the obscure door of his long-sequestered heart.

"One day you can return the favor," Thomas promised, helping her to her feet. "Let's go see your aunties."

CHAPTER 65

⌒

Frank and Lorelei sat idling in Frank's truck outside of Thomas McQuillan's large wrought iron gate.

Lorelei raised her eyebrows, impressed. "Posh."

There was a keypad in the brick wall next to the gate. Frank pushed the microphone button and waited.

A beeping noise sounded and then a female with a thick Scandinavian accent said, "Yes? How can I help you?"

"This is Detective Frank Williams with San Diego PD. I'm looking for a Mary Crossfield."

There was a long pause and then, "Mary Crossfield is not here."

"Was she here earlier?"

Another lengthy silence. Eventually the feminine Swedish voice said, "Do you see camera on da top left of da keypad? Can you please show Helga your identification?"

Frank pulled his credentials from the glove compartment. When he reached across the seat his hand brushed Lorelei's knees and the couple exchanged a smoldering look of instant desire at the innocent touch. The worry lines creasing Lorelei's brow eased for a moment as she felt the crackling spark of electricity sweep up her legs and spread warmth through her body.

Frank left one large hand on her thigh while he said into the microphone, "I'm with the major crimes division." He held up his badge and ID so they were visible to the eye of the camera. "If I could come inside and speak with you, I'd appreciate it."

Silence. Clearly the woman did not want to let him through.

"Is Thomas McQuillan home?" Frank persisted.

"No, he not home." There was a short pause and then, "Is Mary okay?" The voice was very concerned.

"That's what I'm trying to find out, ma'am. I have Mary's best friend with me, Lorelei Harper, and she's extremely worried."

"Oh!" said Helga. "Can she lean into da camera view? Mary tells Helga she loves Lorelei. Said she looks like Marilyn Monroe."

Frank chuckled. "She's more gorgeous than Marilyn," he said loyally.

Lorelei leaned across Frank's lap so Helga could see her. "Hi! Please let us in. I'm so sorry to intrude like this, but Mary's father passed away last night and we can't find her." Lorelei held Mary's cell phone up to the camera. "I found Thomas' name and address in Mary's contacts." She hesitated for a moment, not wanting to divulge any secrets she shouldn't. "I read a few texts between Thomas and Mary and it seems like they might be friends. I thought maybe she came here because I…" her voice lowered in remorse, "…wasn't there for her." With a start, Lorelei realized she hadn't been there for Mary much at all lately. Not with everything going on at work- the stresses of Davies' investigation, the uncertainty surrounding her possible promotion and move to New York. Not to mention she'd spent the last five evenings jogging with Frank. Lorelei felt her body stiffen in guilt. She hadn't been there for either of her friends. Faith wasn't speaking to her and Mary had fled, not to her best friend, but to someone else entirely. Lorelei's mind reeled with contrition. How had the three of them gone from close-knit sisters to solitary individuals with hidden agendas? Faith and Mary knew next to nothing of Lorelei's struggles at Empire & Malkin as of late. Lorelei and Faith had no clue Mary was not only working for a famous author, but writing her own book, a lifelong dream, with his guidance. What else were they all keeping from one another?

The gate opened. "Please come see Helga, Lorelei Harper. I wait outside for you."

⌒‿

Georgette and Mary sat at the large kitchen table in Tempe, mugs of hot tea in front of them despite the sizzling temps outside. It was always cool and fragrant in Francesca and George's house, scents of rosemary and lavender in the air, soft breezes from the overhead fans wrapping the occupants in comforting caresses. Italian music played faintly from the living room where Francesca had Thomas in her eager clutches. After Mary had introduced him to her aunts, Francesca immediately ran into the den, pulled her copy of *Souls in Collision* from a bookshelf and handed it to Thomas along with a pen. She dictated: "Write: Francesca Maria Benedetta Fogagnolo- thank you for the sexiest evening I've ever known. I'll never forget you and your gorgeous body. Love, Tom."

Mary raised wet amber eyes to Georgette over the freshly scrubbed wood table and pushed her mother's journal forward. "Did you know?"

Georgette looked from the leather-bound book to Mary's distraught face and asked anxiously, "Is this Helene's diary?" When Mary nodded, George placed a warm wrinkled hand over Mary's pale, tender one. "Yes, I knew. And, oh, honey, I'm so sorry. So sorry you found out like this. But you must remember you are Mitchell Morrison's daughter through and through. He was the one who loved you, raised you and has always been there for you. The genetics don't matter."

"Don't they? This changes everything…"

"No, it doesn't. It changes nothing," Georgette said firmly.

Mary's chin wavered, her mouth troubled and trembling. "He lied to me. You lied to me."

"Yes." Guilt etched George's features. "Your father didn't want you to know the truth because it was all too… too dramatic. Mitch and I were hurting so much when you came to us; we were raw and broken from losing our brother, and you brought us back to life, little girl. You were one last gift from Claude- a piece of him, a part of him. You gave us reason to heal, to find happiness again. And your dad feared the truth about your parents would only serve to hurt you. He's always wanted to protect you- right from the beginning."

"Yes, he was always looking out for me and now..." Mary's throat constricted, "...I'm going to miss him so much. I feel like the rug has been pulled out from under me. Like I don't have a foundation any-more. No anchor. No safe harbor."

"You have us," George said fiercely. "You have me and Aunt Fran-cesca. And this home is your home, just as it was when you were a child coming to visit. We will always be here for you."

Mary gave a small grateful smile and then allowed it to fade with her next words. "I finished reading Mama's journal in the car on the way over here. The last entry was rather cryptic, but not so much so that I can't hazard a guess as to what she meant. And how Dad wound up with her diary. Can we talk about my mother, please? Can you tell me the truth about what happened to her?"

Georgette took a careful sip of tea, her heart pounding in dread. She'd never thought she'd need to be accountable for sweet Mary's well-being all on her own. Mitch had been there always, Georgette was only a backup parent, so to speak. She understood a bit more now why Mitch had kept the secret of his daughter's beginnings veiled. Once told, a truth could wreak painful havoc that could never be taken back or assuaged. Georgette knew with her next statement she was taking Mary's mother away from her. George had been hounding Mitch to tell his daughter the truth for years, and now Georgette was the one having to do it herself. She had wanted Mary to know her past, but she hadn't wanted to be the one responsible for bearing the news; for taking on the repercussions. How naive she'd been! How insensi-tive to Mitch's reasons and motives.

Taking a deep breath, Georgette decided being direct was the best route. "Your mother committed suicide in France last month, my dear.

She was never well after Claude died. She was dependent upon her family. Her sister, Babette, mainly managed her care. I think 'obsessed' is a very accurate assessment for how Helene felt about Claude."

"But... but why didn't she... want me? How could a mother not want her own daughter?"

"I think Helene knew she wasn't going to be able to take care of you properly. In many ways, Helene was like a child herself."

"Is that who I am too? Is that how you see me? Like an adult child?"

"No," Georgette said staunchly. "No one thinks of you that way."

Mary wiped tears from her cheeks. "Maybe that's how I see myself. I feel so lost. My life started out complicated from the beginning- it turns out I was never really who I thought I was..."

"You will always be Mitchell Morrison's daughter."

"... and my in-laws don't want me because they think I can't have children..."

Georgette was incensed. "I will have Aunt Francesca shoot them..."

"... and I thought Owen was the love of my life but he isn't... and I think he cheated on me... something Ellen said..."

"I will have Aunt Francesca shoot Owen too."

Suddenly they looked at each other, Mary's eyes filled with tears and Georgette's filled with indignation. And, then, like a ray of sunshine bursting through the clouds they began to laugh, a sincere laugh that somehow, miraculously, cleansed some of their pain.

They grinned at one another affectionately and Mary felt lighthearted for the first time since the news of her father's death. She was free to ask the questions she'd never dared to.

"What was my mother like, Aunt George?"

"Well," Georgette said thoughtfully as she leaned back in her chair, "I only met her once, at a restaurant, and let me tell you, all of the men were watching her, looking at her as though they were enchanted. But she only had eyes for Claude- she was completely enamored with him. Then again, most girls were." George rolled her eyes in amusement. "My brothers were both ladies' men."

"Helene was beautiful?" Mary asked. It felt good to talk, to have an honest discussion about her mother.

"Very. And her movements were graceful, the way she carried herself was almost exotic. Her hair was a mess, like she'd just woken up from a night of passion and tied it up with a pretty French scarf and she wore no makeup, but somehow all of that made her very, very sexy. Her clothes were bohemian and faded and on anyone else they would have seemed shabby, but on her... they looked seductive. And she was incredibly sweet, she seemed an innocent soul in a lot of ways."

"Why didn't Uncle Claude love her?" Mary couldn't quite get herself to refer to him as her biological father.

"Probably because he was such a free spirit. He wanted to travel, to paint, to meet new people. Women flocked to him and he never tired of lavishing attention on them, but he wasn't one to be tied down."

"Until I came along?"

Georgette smiled. "Oh yes, Marion Grace. He loved you so very much and would have done anything for you."

Mary looked down at the table and made circles on it with her finger. "I feel sorry for my mom," she said contemplatively. "To love a man and not have him love you in return."

Georgette cleared her throat. "Speaking of men... you don't have to tell me, but that nice gentleman you brought home... I saw the way you looked at each other. Are you... is he..." she trailed off uncertainly, afraid of overstepping her bounds.

"It's okay, Aunt George, Thomas is just a friend. I... I needed someone after you and I got off the phone... when you told me that Daddy..." her voice broke.

"I am so sorry I called before Lorelei got there..." Georgette shook her head, her fine features etched with shame, "... I wasn't thinking... just out of my mind with grief..."

"I know, it's okay."

"Did Lorelei come over?"

"No," Mary whispered. "So I just went to the last place that felt like home."

"Thomas' house?"

"Yes."

Georgette took a thoughtful sip of her tea. "Tell me about Thomas, dear."

"I'm his pet nanny. He has a French Bulldog named Voltaire. And a really nice housekeeper called Helga."

"You two seem close," George observed carefully.

"He's been really good to me. We talk a lot about writing. He's helping me with my first novel."

Georgette remained silent, calculating that Mary would confide in her if she didn't appear too anxious. Italian song drifted in to them from the living room along with Francesca's sprightly chatter. There was the sound of wine being uncorked and the tinkling of crystal. Thomas chuckled and the deep sound was playful, comforting.

"I had sort of a celebrity crush on him," Mary began without looking up. "But now that I've gotten to know him better..." she faltered, a faint blush tinging her cheeks, "... it's just different now, I guess. He's... complicated, but I love sparring with him and listening to him talk about literature. He's so smart, Aunt George. He says stuff that just gets my brain reeling and it's... it's exciting, you know? Even when we fight it's exciting. And..." she dipped her head lower, "... he's so handsome."

"I noticed," Georgette said dryly, "even though he's not my type."

"And he's been nothing but a gentleman with me even though..." she met her aunt's eyes guiltily, "... even though sometimes I think I would cross a line I shouldn't if he pressed me."

"But he hasn't?" George asked anxiously.

"No. He hasn't. But... is it okay if we stay here tonight? I don't think I should be alone with him at Daddy's..."

"Of course, my dear! He can sleep in the spare room."

"And my room..."

"Is always waiting for you. I'm so glad you're here." Georgette stood and dropped a kiss on Mary's honey brown hair. "Now, let's see what Aunt Franny might rustle us up for dinner."

⌒

"And then I found this goat and I named him Steve and he lived in our house for a week," Francesca said dramatically, brandishing a fork full of pasta. She had cooked up a storm of Italian fare, spending much time in the kitchen singing, swearing and banging about in the pots and pans. She refused any help while preparing the mammoth meal, so Mary and Georgette poured over old family photos, smiling and weeping by turn when Mitch's strong, handsome face gazed back. Thomas was touched by Mary's bond with her aunt and he silently took part, only exclaiming over a picture if they shared one with him. He was content to lounge in a huge yellow chair with his wine, ensconced amongst cushiony throw pillows, his long legs propped up on a matching saffron colored foot stool.

When Francesca called them all into the dining room Thomas had been shocked by the amount of food on the large oak table. There were appetizers- artichoke flan with gorgonzola fondue and cappellacci with fresh tomato fillets, aubergines and light pesto. For the main course she had prepared lamb chops with black d'avola sauce and a delicious fresh vegetable salad. It was all presented beautifully and Thomas felt as though he'd been instantly transported to a Tuscan seaside village café.

As they ate, Francesca kept them entertained with her fun and silly anecdotes. She was particularly careful to catch Georgette's eye, as though sending strength through the airwaves, whenever Mary needed shoring up. Thomas was completely taken with Francesca, the small Italian woman whose dark eyes sparkled with mischief, her half-shaved head constantly turning or bobbing in concern or with naughty mirth. Earlier, she'd told Thomas the dirtiest joke in the living room about an Australian prison and he'd been laughing so hard he almost fell off his chair.

Mary treated both her aunties with daughterly deference, doting on them one minute and teasing them the next. Her amber eyes sought their approval when they discussed such matters as the details of handling her father's estate. Georgette and Francesca were clearly very take-charge women and Thomas had no doubt that everything from the planning of Mitch Morrison's funeral to the sale of his house would be handled with utmost efficiency and compassion.

When the foursome had eaten well past their capacity, Francesca presented a dessert and Mary, Georgette and Thomas groaned uncomfortably. Francesca called it *mele al forno* and said it was a simple recipe of baked apples soaked in red wine and sprinkled with cinnamon and sugar. After devouring this scrumptious concoction, they heaved themselves from the table and Georgette and Francesca, refusing any assistance, disappeared into the kitchen to wash the dishes. Thomas helped Mary from her chair and they walked outside to the back patio with their wine glasses. Francesca had lit candles all along the pool and fairy lights twinkled above them, swinging from the sloped overhang and gently swaying in the balmy evening air.

"Thank you for being here," Mary said, sitting down on the deck and dangling her feet in the pool. It was warm, like bath water, and she wiggled her toes in it contentedly.

"You have a very nice family," Thomas said, pulling off his shoes and setting them to the side.

They sat quietly for a moment, listening to the buzz of the cicadas in the trees.

"Will you go home tomorrow?" Mary asked shyly, sipping her wine.

"Is that what you would like me to do?"

Mary shivered even though she was far from cold. "No," she said honestly, "but maybe it would be best. You have your book to finish and…"

"And?"

"I… have a lot going on in my life right now and I feel very…" Her breath quickened at the sight of Thomas' hazel eyes, which in the moonlight appeared even darker and more intense.

"I'm not going to hurt you, Mary," he said, his voice deepening. "You know that, right?"

She nodded. "I know. But… I'm so confused about everything right now and…"

Thomas reached for her hand and as their fingers interlaced her heart picked up speed. He rubbed his thumb over her palm and she held on to him tenderly, her thoughts, her feelings, her emotions whirling around inside her like a heady tornado. She felt drawn to him, as though the mere joining of their hands was a powerful introduction to a new realm of exhilarating physical intrigue. She remembered thinking before how she and Thomas were like two magnets- constantly drawn together, yet repelling at the same time- and she wanted to both lean into him and run away from him for identical reasons.

They sat gazing out over the pool, lost in their own thoughts until eventually Thomas ventured curiously, "Was Aunt Georgette able to tell you about your mother and father's past?"

"Yes." Mary's voice was vulnerable. "My biological father loved me very much. And my mother… she loved me too, but she had a lot going on emotionally and wasn't able to care for me. That's why she gave me to my dad… to Mitch. He didn't *have* to take on the responsibility of raising me, you know? Daddy chose to love me even though I wasn't his."

"Choice is more beautiful than obligation. And it makes your relationship with Mitch even more special than it already was."

Mary smiled, her face blossoming with gratefulness. "It does, doesn't it?"

Thomas' brow furrowed in thought. "Your novel," he began ruminatively, "I think you should make it about your father."

"But I've already started…"

"I know. Set it aside for now. Use your writing to bleed, Mary. Talk about your pain through prose, your frustration through fiction. Writers have the gift of expression and we can use it for our own personal growth. You have so much going on right now and getting it all down on paper will be cathartic for you."

"And painful..."

"Pain is just weakness leaving the body, as the Marines say. You'll come away from all of this stronger. Your dad... I'm guessing he kept the secret that he wasn't your father because he thought he was doing what was best for you?"

Mary nodded. "That's what Aunt Georgette said."

Thomas' jaw clenched and unclenched. "He didn't want you to know your father was deceased and your mother was incapable of caring for you or for herself."

"Right." Mary looked up at him inquisitively. His eyes were far away, his mind on something other than her. His long, sandy hair rustled in the slight breeze, a few golden strands glinting in the moonlight and an unbidden thought crossed Mary's mind as she imagined him leaning in and settling his lips on her own. She looked down to clear her head, but saw Thomas' forearm, corded with muscle from surfing, very close to her lap as he held her hand. She wanted to bring his arm to her face, to press her cheek to it.

Thomas seemed to intuit her need for closeness; he let go of her hand and put his arm around her. She allowed her head to drop against his broad shoulder, her hair spilling in waves down his chest and resting on his leg.

"If I tell you something can you please promise to never tell a soul?" Thomas' voice said above her, deep, melodic, filled with pain.

Mary went very still. "Of course."

Silence fell between them, stretching on as they sat together, each hurting in different ways, each finding comfort in the nearness of the other.

"I have a son..." Thomas began and Mary listened quietly, intently, as he told her of his affair with Gemma, Gemma's pregnancy and marriage afterward, and Katya's recent revelation. "You know, the thing that hurts the most is that Gemma lied to me. Lied by omission. She should have told me she was pregnant- given me the chance to decide if I wanted to be a father or not. But she took my choice away and now if Colin ever found out the truth he'd be facing the same pain you are right now." Hurt slashed across Thomas' countenance, leaving anger in its wake. "She deceived me. It turns out she's just as deceptive as everyone else in Hollywood."

Mary pulled away to look into Thomas' face. "I don't know if that's fair. Daddy lied to me, but I don't think he's… a liar." Then, softly, "Why do you think she never told you?"

"Because I didn't want children. That's why we broke up. She wanted a family and I didn't."

"So Gemma was protecting you just as my dad was protecting me."

Thomas' eyes hardened.

Mary reached out a hand and touched his stubbled cheek gently. "And she was protecting her baby too."

"From what?"

"Rejection."

Thomas took her hand from his face and held it in both his own. "I always thought Gemma was perfect."

"No one can be perfect. That's what makes humans so interesting. We're all just walking around trying to do our best, to love and be loved, to make a difference, to become successful. To laugh… to…" She looked up at him, her eyes moist and sincere, "…to find a reason for living."

"And what's your reason for living, Mary Crossfield?" His tone was low and hushed.

She dipped her head, her honey hair falling over her pretty face. "I don't know," she whispered.

"Maybe we can find out together," Thomas said, taking hold of her chin and tilting her face up so he could look into her eyes. When he saw the fear mixed with passion in their amber depths he continued, "As friends, of course."

"Thomas," her sweet inflection made his heart constrict, "I have to stay in Arizona for a while, maybe a month, for the funeral and all of the legal things I'll need to take care of with Dad's estate. I know that my life is really complicated right now and I know that I'm just an average, simple girl, but..."

"But what?" he prompted, running his hands back into her silky hair. "And you're neither average, nor simple."

She smiled timidly. "I want you to know I admire your writing so much, and I love talking to you and hearing your ideas and your opinions, and your cynical sense of humor makes me laugh, and you've been so kind to me helping me with my book and then getting me home and being here to support me... and I admire and respect you and..."

He ran his fingers through her honey tresses, loving the feel of their velvety smoothness. "And?"

She blushed charmingly, relaxing into his touch. "You're not making this easy on me."

"Let me help you." His hands moved to the back of her neck and she gazed up at him with adoration. "Mary," he said, his lips inches from her own, "these last several years I've been running from feeling real emotion. I've been using indifference and hardness as a distraction, thinking that if certain needs were met then others would take a back seat. And then you came into my life and you reminded me of the good in this world, the innocence and..." He traced the contours of her face. "...the softness. You are softness and light and I want to spend all my time basking in it. I want to write about you, I want to feel you in my arms and I want to..." his eyes shadowed in lust, "give you pleasure."

"I want that too." She spoke in a sigh, as though she were dreaming.

"But we both know now is not the time. Maybe not for a while."

She nodded. "Yes." His breath on her face was intoxicating.

He brushed a kiss against her forehead then gathered her into his arms. They held one another protectively, as though warding off the intensity of their feelings as a unified front. Several moments passed and then Mary said, her voice muffled against his chest, "Will you tell Colin he's your son?"

"No," he said decisively. "He has a father who loves him. The truth would only bring pain."

"Do you have any regrets about not wanting to have children?"

Thomas ran his hands over her back in caressing strokes. "Not before. But now I do."

"What if I regret not wanting to have children when I'm older, but it's too late because I can't anymore?"

"It would be worse to have a child and then wish you hadn't."

Silence fell between them companionably and as their conversation ebbed, Mary felt the pressure of grief building inside and she knew she was about to cry again as thoughts of losing her father crowded out all other introspections. Tears began to run down her cheeks and splatter on Thomas' arms.

He held her tighter when he felt the wetness of her sorrow soaking into his shirt and he said softly, "How can I help you get through this, Mary?"

"You can't..."

"Surely there is something you need... or want... that will help ease the pain?"

She pulled away and looked up at him, imploring, trusting. "I want my best friends, Thomas. Do you think you could bring them here? I need them so much right now."

He kissed the top of her head. "Consider it done."

CHAPTER 66

"You were so strong tonight," Francesca said as she and Georgette stood before the double sink in their bathroom going through their nightly pre-bed ritual of moisturizing creams and mouthwash. "I'm proud of you."

Georgette smiled sadly. "Thank you, Franny. Can you believe Mary came home? I almost fainted from shock when I saw her on our doorstep."

"What I can't believe is that she has a new friend who is hot and famous," Francesca countered, giving a low whistle as she brushed the side of her head that had hair.

Georgette sighed in concern and applied face cream to her delicately wrinkled face. "Mary said there's nothing going on between them."

"I don't doubt that. Our Mary is a good girl. Did she say anything about Owen?"

"Divorce," Georgette said darkly, rubbing moisturizer into her cheeks with ferocious gestures. "Somehow Ellen is involved, on top of which Mary thinks Owen may have cheated."

Francesca's eyes narrowed threateningly. "I know a guy down at the range. He could take 'em both out. I've seen the dude fire and he's a real clean shot."

Georgette's frown cleared in amusement. "I was telling Mary you could do it yourself."

"Heh. Damn straight I could."

The women smiled, their eyes meeting in the mirror.

"We shouldn't joke about that," Georgette said, shaking her head in guilt and picking up her dental floss.

Francesca set down her hairbrush. "These next few weeks are going to be real hard, Georgie. We need to find humor wherever we can. Our girl is here and we gotta be strong for her. It's all up to us now."

"I just want to… crawl under the covers and not come out." Georgette let her tears fall. "I can't believe Mitch is gone. I loved him so much."

"You know what," Francesca said, coming toward George and holding both of her hands tenderly, "the best way to honor your brother's life is by taking care of Mary. That's what he would want. You do realize, my love, that the timeline has come full circle?"

"What do you mean?"

"Mitch showed up on our doorstep with Mary thirty-two years ago and she helped heal you from Claude's death. And now," Francesca reached up and brushed a grey curl from George's face, "Our little girl is back on our doorstep all these years later to help you heal from Mitch's death."

Georgette closed her eyes in nostalgic recognition. "Oh, Franny, you're right."

Mary lay alone in the darkness of her room. Nothing in it had changed since she'd left Arizona so long ago, newly married and excited to start Owen's adventures with the Navy. Georgette and Francesca kept Mary's bed, her pictures and posters, her writing desk and her stuffed animals just as they were. It was comforting, cozy, to be back in the room she'd spent countless nights in while growing up.

She rolled over and stared at the outline of her closed bedroom door. Thomas McQuillan was on the other side of the house in the spare room. Probably sleeping. She wondered how he slept? In a t-shirt and boxers? On his stomach? Bare-chested with shorts? His arms over his head? Naked? Her skin warmed at the thought. Maybe he wasn't even sleeping. Maybe he was writing. He'd brought his laptop. Perhaps he was working on his book.

They'd called Lorelei and Faith before turning in and Thomas had arranged flights for both women. Lorelei had been relieved beyond words to hear from her best friend. Mary was concerned about Lorelei's job, but Lorelei assured her the time off was warranted and not to worry. Faith had contacted Wicky whose parents agreed to let Wicky stay at the Dobbs' house as a live-in nanny for a week since school was still out of session for the summer.

Lorelei and Faith were scheduled to arrive the following evening.

Thomas had called Helga and she was full of news about meeting Detective Williams and Lorelei ("Such a nice couple, but da big black dog, he would not leef dat pretty Lorelei alone."). Helga reported that Voltaire and Roger had become inseparable, chasing one another, playing tug of war and swimming laps in the pool. Helga maintained Thomas should have thought to get another dog a long time ago for Voltaire was now constantly occupied and very happy to have a comrade. She said she would be grateful to keep Roger for the next month because he was a spectacular Frenchie babysitter and she was able to get all her housework done and even had time to plant new flowers along the pond border.

Throwing back her covers, Mary stood and opened her bedroom door. She couldn't sleep. There was way too much to think about. Sadness oppressed her and she felt like a heavily laden tumbrel burdened with the cargo of death, deceit and hopelessness. She wanted Thomas McQuillan's arms around her again so that her emotions could be comforted- and her desires inflamed; he was the perfect distraction from the harshness of reality. But...

Setting her shoulders and lifting her chin she tiptoed down the hallway and knocked on a door. Without waiting for an answer stepped through the threshold and flung herself on the bed.

"Help me. Please help me," she begged. "I don't know how to get past the pain... I miss my dad... help me..." She stretched out her arms like a wounded child and her aunties pulled her close, holding her and comforting her with loving words and embraces as tender as the gentle mothers they'd become.

⌒‿

"I'm so sorry, Fay. You were right about some of the things you said and I realize that now."

"I'm sorry too, Lor. I have no right to try and dictate your life. It's just that..."

"Can we call a truce?"

There was a long pause over the phone line and then, "So that we can provide a united front for Mary in Arizona tomorrow?"

"No, not for Mary. For us, Fay. For you and me. I love you. I'm not going to walk out of your life."

"It's just... it's just that you're my family..."

"That night you were choking at Sharky's... I was scared, so scared, and the only thing going through my mind was that I couldn't lose my sister. Not my 'friend'. My *sister*."

Faith began crying softly.

"I choose you, Fay. I will always choose you to be my family. Our relationship exists because we want it to, not because the ties of genetics bind us together."

Faith sniffled. "I choose you too."

"You're a part of me. Forever."

"Promise?"

"Now and always."

⌒‿

"Gemma?" Thomas said into his cell phone. "I'm sorry it's so late... no, I'm in Arizona... it's a long story... listen, we need to talk...

tomorrow, if possible, when I'm back in town... I understand, but... can't you make time...? No, I don't want to say what I have to say on the phone... I know, I'm not trying to be cryptic, it's just that... no, it's not about Katya, why?... Oh my god! Bhear fired her?... That's why she... no, never mind, I... Gem, just meet me tomorrow so we can talk... because... calm down..." His voice rose in anger, "Fine, Gemma! Fine, I'll tell you! Here it is: *Colin is my son*! You lied to me! ... Yes, you did!... I thought you could never hurt me, never deceive me, but it turns out you were the epitome of dishonesty all along... always so sanctimonious but in the end you... I don't care what you think is fair... how is it fair to me to not have a relationship with my son all these years... Oh really? Well, how would you know that since you didn't give me a chance?" Thomas' tone lowered, "Please stop crying, Gem, I'm sorry I raised my voice... yes, I'm very angry with you... no, no, I won't tell anyone the truth... I won't interfere... I know you're happy and Colin is happy... I understand... but this is the last time I ever want to talk to you because I can't... I won't... goodbye, Gemma."

"Did you and Frank do it?!" Faith shrieked, sending a giant bowl of popcorn flying in her exuberance. She, Lorelei and Mary were in their pajamas surrounded by blankets and pillows on the floor of George and Francesca's living room. They'd been watching old *Sex and the City* reruns, giggling and teasing one another while sipping Francesca's homemade bellinis (sans alcohol for Faith).

Lorelei shook her head primly. "A lady never tells."

"YOU DID!" Faith crowed. "How was it? I'll bet he's amazing in bed."

Mary removed a popcorn kernel that had landed in her hair. "Why do you think he's amazing in bed?"

"Because I was watching him during dessert at Sharky's. Did you see what he was doing to his fork?"

"Using it to eat his blackberry panna cotta like the rest of us," Lorelei said.

"Yes, but," Faith tossed her long red hair off both shoulders and launched into an animated explanation, "he would wrap his lips around the fork very thoughtfully and slowly whenever he took a bite. *Thoughtfully…*" Faith stressed, "and *slowwwwwly…*"

Mary giggled.

"And one time," Faith continued with a breathy sigh of romance, "he licked a bit of whipped cream off his finger and his tongue was very sensual and firm. *Sensual and firm, Lor.*"

Lorelei threw a lemon-colored pillow at her. "You're a nut, you know that?"

"So was he?" Faith wanted to know, ducking. "Was he thoughtful and slow and sensual and firm?"

"This conversation is closed."

Mary's back suddenly straightened. "Is that where you were?" she asked Lorelei. "Is that why my aunties couldn't get a hold of you when Dad passed away? You were… with Frank?"

A heavy silence hung in the air, then Lorelei reached over and squeezed Mary's arm. "I am so sorry I wasn't there for you when you needed me most, Mare," she said, her green eyes earnest. "But I'm with you now and I'm not going anywhere. I'm here for as long as you want me."

"I'm so glad you could come. But I know you have to get back to work…"

"Actually, I'm leaving Empire & Malkin."

"You quit?" Mary asked at the same time Faith wailed, "Are you moving to New York?"

"I took a leave of absence so I would be free to stay in Arizona as long as possible. But…" She paused for another sip of her bellini, "I've had some… issues arise over the past couple of weeks and I think it would be in my best interest for me and Empire to part ways."

"Wow," said Faith. "This is huge. Are you okay?"

Lorelei gave her a dazzling smile. "Never better."

Faith nodded. "Getting sexed-up by a thoughtful, slow, sensual, firm man will do that."

They erupted in laughter just as Francesca came into the room wearing a bright-red leotard and neon-green tights. "What do you chicks think about my elf outfit?" she asked, her hands on her hips. "They're holding tryouts next week down at the senior center for Santa Claus assistants."

"It's only August, Aunt Fran," Lorelei said.

"Yeah, but we elves are going to do a jazz dance routine while Abe Polinski - I mean, *Santa*- sings Tony Bennett-style Christmas carols so they want to leave lots of time for rehearsals."

"Is that what you're supposed to wear?" Mary ventured. "It's awfully tight on you, Auntie."

"I thought I'd have a better shot of making the cut if the judges could see my voluptuous curves when I shimmy for them."

Lorelei smothered a giggle and Faith said helpfully, "I think you need an elf's hat to complete your look."

Francesca snapped her fingers. "You're right!"

"Or," said Faith excitedly, "we could just dye your hair Christmas colors."

"YES!" Francesca agreed. "Great idea! Let's go to the drug store and get some holly green to try out tonight." She headed for the kitchen to get her keys. "I'll drive."

"Francesca Maria Benedetta Fogagnolo!" Georgette yelled from the hallway. "I can hear you and you are NOT dying your hair! Well, what's *left* of your hair. Now come back here and leave those sweet girls alone."

"Geesh," Francesca said, throwing Mary a look of exasperation, "your aunt can be such a buzzkill."

"FRANNY!"

"I'm coming!" She stomped out of the room.

"I'm going to need a lot more bellini after that," Lorelei said, pouring herself another glass from the large pitcher on the coffee table.

"Your aunties are a hoot," Faith said, smiling. "You have such a great family."

Mary nodded, her eyes softening. "I know. I just wish my dad were here."

"We do too," Lorelei agreed.

Faith pulled a fuzzy blanket over her legs. "I loved dancing with Mitch at Cobalt. Your dad was very handsome and suave, Mare. You know, if I hadn't been married and pregnant and he wasn't your father, I would have-"

"Faith!" Lorelei laughed, shaking her blonde head.

"What? It's a compliment." She wiggled her eyebrows lasciviously. "Mary had a hot dad."

"Gross!" Mary said, grimacing.

"Speaking of hot," Lorelei said, leaning back amongst the pile of pillows, "tell us about Famous Author Guy whisking you out here in a private jet, Mare."

Mary blushed. "I wanted to tell you both about him, but -"

"Confidentiality agreement. I know. He told us all about it. I thought he was going to make us sign one too."

Mary smiled. "I'll bet."

"We practically had to swear on a stack of bibles that we wouldn't call TMZ."

"But that doesn't mean we can't talk about him amongst ourselves," Faith suggested impishly.

"He's really nice," Mary said shyly. "And so talented. He's helping me write my first book. And I can talk to him about being an author and about art and music and... he's a really good listener and he's got this sarcastic sense of humor and he makes amazing gin rickeys and..."

Lorelei and Faith exchanged glances.

"I know what you're both thinking," Mary said defensively. "But I'm not stupid."

Faith jumped up and wrapped her arms around Mary. "We know. We're just really concerned about you. Especially with the divorce and your dad... we don't want anyone tall, tempting and surfer-like taking advantage of you."

"He wouldn't do that," Mary assured. Faith settled down next to her and began to braid Mary's honey hair into plaits.

"Okay," Lorelei nodded. "We won't nag. Just know if Thomas crosses any borders-"

"Like south of your panty line border," Faith interjected.

Lorelei rolled her eyes. "... we're here for you if you need to talk."

Mary smiled. "Thank you both. But nothing could happen between Thomas and me because he's... well, he's a celebrity and I'm..."

"About to receive a lot of Crossfield money and be rich!" Faith squealed happily.

"I was going to say 'married.'"

"Not for long," Lorelei maintained. "As soon as Owen gets back from his training mission and signs the divorce papers you'll be free as a bird."

"Will you move back to Arizona?" Faith asked tentatively, tying Mary's braids up with a blue ribbon.

"I don't know... I guess I'll need to start making plans after... after I'm done dealing with Dad's estate."

Lorelei sipped her bellini. "I'm assuming Mitch had a will?"

Mary nodded. "I'm not sure of the steps to take now, but I know Aunt Georgette will help me."

"In the meantime, we should go over to your father's house tomorrow and make a list of everything that's valuable. Does he have a safe?"

"Yes. There's documents inside, a few guns, some cash and my Great-Grandmother Pauline's diamond necklace."

"Anything of yours in there?"

"My birth certificate." Mary's mouth dropped open at the thought and she and Lorelei locked gazes. "I only needed it one time- for my driver's license. Then Daddy said he'd just keep it in the safe with his."

"Did you not look at it?" Faith wanted to know. "Surely Claude was listed as your father..."

Mary shook her head. "No, I just handed it over at the DMV. I didn't scrutinize it or anything."

"Wow," Lorelei mused. "Your dad must have been seriously nervous that day."

They all sat in thoughtful silence and then Faith said, "I think your mother being so in love with your father is terribly romantic, even if she was a bit obsessive. I mean, from what you said about the journal, Helene was head over heels for Claude and Claude positively adored you. There was a lot of love going on both before and after your birth. It's very sweet."

"If you think dysfunction is sweet," Lorelei said dryly.

"I only see love," Faith said dreamily.

Lorelei smiled at her friend affectionately. "Yes, that's all you would see, Fay."

"I'm so glad you guys are here," Mary said, her voice catching.

"No place we'd rather be," Lorelei asserted firmly.

And the three girls settled into their pillows and blankets, snuggled together as they giggled through a marathon night of Carrie, Samantha, Charlotte and Miranda. Wrapped up cozily both in blankets and in sisterly love, Mary felt her heart overflow. She wasn't alone. She had a rough road ahead, but with her two best friends and her beloved aunties supporting and encouraging her every step of the way, she wouldn't falter. Maybe she would even come out stronger.

It was time to make life happen *for* her, not *to* her.

CHAPTER 67

⌒

Bonjour Mama,

It seems silly to still be writing you now that I know you're gone. I mean, I never really knew the truth before about where you were or what you were doing, but now I know everything- or I should say, I know everything you wrote in your journal. Aunt Georgette filled in some of the blanks, but there are vast amounts of your life that I will maybe never know or understand. I've been thinking about contacting your sister, Babette, and making a trip to France to meet her, but I've got too much going on in my life right now to plan such an emotional journey.

It's been two months since Daddy passed away and I just got back to San Diego last week. I've been packing up the townhouse, separating my things from Owen's things. I had a terse email from Owen the other day- it's the first time I've heard from him since he's been gone. He was still very vague about the mission he's on. Corinne had told Horse about my dad passing away and apparently Horse told Owen, which is why he was emailing. His sympathy was very unemotional, almost detached, and that hurt me more than anything. He knew my father, knew what a great man he was- did Owen not feel any sadness at all? A personal loss? Maybe he's just too busy to even allow any kind of sentiment to penetrate his veneer of being in control? I don't know. And I'm tempted to say I don't care, but I do. He didn't even ask what happened... how it happened. It was a heart attack. Doesn't Owen want to know?

Aunt George and Aunt Franny were wonderful in helping me settle Daddy's estate, and Lorelei remained in Arizona for a month. Frank flew out one weekend to help us pack up my dad's house and Lorelei stayed with Frank at his hotel in the evenings instead of coming back to Aunt George's with me. If Faith had been there she would have been beside herself with curiosity and excitement, but I simply accepted their new relationship for what it obviously is- love. Frank is so sweet with Lei, Mama. One time I walked back into the living room where we were packing boxes and they didn't hear me come in. Frank was holding Lorelei, his hands in her curls, his deep voice reciting lines of poetry in her ear. Lei looked so content, so in love. I tiptoed out before they saw me. It kind of hurts my heart sometimes to be with them because their attraction and their affection are so genuine and beautiful. I wish I had that. Maybe I did in the beginning with Owen. I'm not sure anymore. But I'm so happy for Lorelei and at the same time a bit lonely for myself. I hope that doesn't make me sound too awfully selfish.

While I was in Arizona I referred Nancy and Willow to another dog-walker, and I think even though I'm back in San Diego I'm going to let go of my business. I really want to dedicate all my time to writing. I'm halfway through my novel about Dad- it's a fictional account of his life. It's been... really painful at times, but Thomas said this is healing so I have been trying to heed his advice and keep typing even though it hurts to do so.

And speaking of Thomas- he didn't return to Arizona. He stayed in San Diego and finished his book. But during our two months apart we emailed each other almost every day. I would reread each of Thomas' letters several times before responding just for the sheer pleasure of soaking in the creative way he crafts and molds words. He's such a genius when it comes to the English language.

However, not everyone thinks so.

Thomas wrote his book in record time, even beating his deadline, and his novel was published in September. I absolutely loved the manuscript, as did most literary critics, who applauded his courage in writing outside his genre. The public had the opposite reaction, however, most notably Souls in Collision *devotees, who pretty much vilified him on social media and sent his Amazon ranking plummeting with bad review after bad review.*

I was worried he would be upset, but he wrote in one of his letters:

I have faced my biggest fear – failure- and I'm still standing. I still want to write. I still want to create. I still have the desire and the drive to put words together for the sole purpose of touching another person and causing them to feel something. I still want to entertain with my prose- to take people away from their pain, their grief, their sorrow and give them an escape into a different world where they're accepted, where they belong. Isn't that what being a writer is all about? To give hope by providing a sense of community? I think I lost sight of that by trying to top Souls in Collision. *I was too scared of failing.*

Well, I've failed and now I'm free. Free to pursue my craft however I want. I'm whisked back to those days on Mission Beach when I was young and writing for the pure love of writing. I've overcome my demons because now I know they never really had any power. It was I who had the power all along.

I've only seen Thomas once since returning to San Diego, and that was when I went to his house to pick up Roger. Thomas and I stared at each other in his foyer and every nerve in my body was on fire. I didn't know whether to throw myself into his arms or run out the door. He didn't say anything, only looked into my eyes and there was so much passion in his gaze that my knees grew weak. We had discussed, as an unwritten rule, exclusively platonic topics in our emails, but there were a few times when one or both of us lightly touched on our emotional bond; a bond that's grown stronger through our missives. Thomas expresses himself so well and he's opened up to me in many ways. I imagine this must be what those great epistolary love affairs throughout history were like – a deepening of mutual regard and respect without the physical temptation.

I stood in front of him after almost eight weeks of absence, the building blocks of our deep friendship mountainous after the flurry of letters back and forth, and I felt that familiar magnetic pull between us pulsate and increase with each second that passed. I wanted him to touch me so badly that I was incapable of any speech.

Eventually he said, "Do you feel that?"

I said, "What?" very stupidly because my thoughts were all fuzzy and bursting with hormonal, inappropriate fantasies.

"The Law of Polarity."

This confused me. "Um…"

"Everything that exists has an equal and exact opposite."

I nodded but had no idea what he was talking about.

"There's a pull between us, Mary. Don't you feel it?" His hazel eyes were dusky and filled with a kind of wonder.

"Yes," I whispered.

"I've been doing a lot of thinking while you've been gone. About my life and what I want from it. The book tanking… well, that taught me something about myself that I needed to learn. My writing is important, but it's not the be all, end all in life."

"What is?" I asked, my mouth dry.

"Love."

A tear ran down my cheek and he stepped close to me, gently wiping it away.

"Mary, your relationships with your family and your friends made me realize how much I'd closed myself off. I've been denying love from anyone and everyone because I thought love had given up on me in Wales. I know now that wasn't the case."

Thomas began running his fingers through my hair and I went perfectly still.

"I've been calling my mom regularly again," he continued, "and we chat like old friends. My siblings and their kids are all coming to stay for a long weekend next month. I'm sending Helga to Sweden to see her family for three weeks over Christmas. I'm reaching out again, finding my way back to my roots." He pulled his hand from my hair and placed it on my cheek. "You've brought goodness back into my life both by example and with your sweet letters. I'm grateful to you."

"Thomas, I..."

And then his lips were on mine and I almost couldn't stand because I felt so weak with shock and desire. I thought I must have been dreaming because it wasn't possible Thomas McQuillan had said those things to me, Mary Crossfield, but he had and he was kissing me with so much passion that I lost all ability to think. His palms caught at my waist and then lowered to my bottom and I wound my arms around his neck until my breasts were pressed tightly against his chest. He moaned my name and bit my ear and my entire body went hot and cold at the same time. I've never felt such intensity before, such recklessness. As our kiss deepened our hands seemed to be of their own volition, roaming, exploring, seeking. Thomas pushed me up against a huge bookshelf and said, "You're my equal and exact opposite, Mary Morrison," and then he grabbed the front of my shirt and roughly pulled me in for an exquisitely erotic kiss. I was trapped between his strength and the hardness of the books behind me and I whimpered when he slipped his thigh between my legs. He watched the longing and desire swim across my face and then he suddenly released me, stepping back and running his hands through his sandy hair.

"I'm sorry, Mary. I'm so sorry."

He turned away and I was staring at his back, trying to collect my wits about me. My body was burned, branded by the fire of his touches and my emotions were inflamed and aching. I wasn't sure how to respond. I didn't think I could respond. Nothing seemed to be working- my voice, my legs, my thoughts. I just stood there, breathless and trembling.

Eventually Thomas looked at me and his hazel eyes were tortured, apologetic. "I would never hurt you," he said.

I managed to whisper that it was all right, but I wasn't exactly sure what was all right.

"This isn't going to work, Mary. You can't be here. I don't think we should see each other again until you have everything worked out that you need to. I won't take advantage of you."

"I know."

"Then come back to me when you're ready."

My heart was beating so fast I thought it would leap right from my chest. "How will I know?"

"You just will," he said, kissing me on the cheek. "And I'll be right here waiting."

He walked away from me, up the stairs and temporarily out of my life.

CHAPTER 68

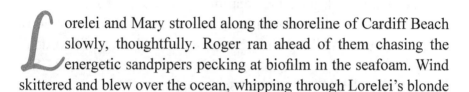

*L*orelei and Mary strolled along the shoreline of Cardiff Beach slowly, thoughtfully. Roger ran ahead of them chasing the energetic sandpipers pecking at biofilm in the seafoam. Wind skittered and blew over the ocean, whipping through Lorelei's blonde curls and rustling Mary's long, honey locks.

"What's on your mind, Mare? Something's up. You know I can read you like a book."

Mary glanced at her best friend guiltily. "I saw Thomas and... he kissed me."

"No surprise there. Aunt Fran told me when Thomas was in Arizona he kept looking at you like you were a delicious cannoli."

Mary giggled. "She said that?"

"Among other things," Lorelei said dryly. "But tell me about the kiss."

"It was... the most intense moment of my life... it was...magical. I know that sounds effusive, but I have all these feelings for Thomas that I don't know what to do with and since we'd been writing letters those feelings only grew stronger. So when we saw each other... it was," she sighed, "like forked lightning."

Lorelei took Mary's arm companionably. "And what happened after you kissed?"

"He apologized and said he wouldn't take advantage of me."

Lorelei raised a perfectly arched eyebrow. "Well, well, well, Thomas McQuillan really is a gentleman."

"And he said he didn't want to see me again until I was ready."

"Ah." She gazed out over the undulating waves of the ocean where a sailboat bobbed in the distant horizon. "He wants you to come to him uninhibited and free from any attachments or complications-when you're no longer vulnerable."

"Maybe when I finish my book..." Mary suggested uncertainly.

"How do you like writing full-time? No dogs to walk. No megalomaniac ex-husbands dictating your life...your dietary habits..."

Mary smiled. "It *is* nice eating whatever I want." She bent down and picked up a shell. "Writing the novel is hard. I feel like I don't really know what I'm doing and it's difficult to write about Dad." She looked at Lorelei. "Did I tell you Bertie called me?"

"When?"

"Four days ago. She asked if she could be my book editor. She said it would be her tribute to my father and she wants to be a part of the project." Mary tossed the shell into a wave. "She really loved my dad, Lor. Next time I go to Arizona we're going to have dinner."

"I think that's great." Lorelei smiled encouragingly.

Roger stopped chasing birds ahead of them and lifted his leg on a pile of washed up seaweed. When he was done he stared at Lorelei adoringly and then took off running toward a man walking a white poodle in the distance.

Mary called him back with a whistle and then said to Lorelei, "How did the meeting go yesterday at work?"

"My last day with Empire & Malkin is next Friday. They still won't budge on negotiating New York."

"Can I just say I'm ecstatic you're not moving?" Mary teased.

"Does that mean you're staying in San Diego too?"

"I think so. You and Faith are here and..."

"Owen is coming back soon from his training mission."

"Yes. There will be divorce court proceedings."

"What about Thomas McQuillan?"

"Oh Lei, by the time my life has settled down he probably won't be waiting for me anymore."

"I thought I made it clear two months ago that I didn't ever want to talk to you again, Gem," Thomas said. "Why the sudden urge to meet with me? I have nothing left to say to you."

They were sitting in a small set of bleachers at the equestrian center in Rancho Santa Fe. Gemma was wrapped up in a gigantic plaid jacket and sporting enormous, dark sunglasses so no one would recognize her; Thomas wore a baseball cap pulled low over his eyes for the same reason. Horsey people were all around them, more interested in the warmbloods and thoroughbreds than they were a random couple having a serious conversation in the stands.

"Dick left me," Gemma confided, her lips quivering. "I had Katya ousted after you told me you knew about Colin. No one would talk to her, hire her; she was even being shunned at A-list restaurants, clubs, bars. And do you know what she did in retaliation? Somehow snuck into Dick's production studio, cornered him and showed him a picture of Colin and a picture of you and told him he was a moron for not realizing the truth."

Thomas' fists clenched. "Where is Katya now?"

"Moved back to Russia."

"Poor Ruskies. Can't imagine they want that bitch on wheels back in their country."

Gemma toyed with the kleenex in her hands. "Dick was very angry with me."

Thomas was not sympathetic. "Of course he was. You lied to him just as you lied to me."

"I thought I was doing what was best for everyone." Her voice was very low and full of regret.

They sat quietly for several minutes, watching horses trot in the rings of the show arena until Thomas eventually said, "Listen, Gem, I'm really sorry for everything that's happened, but I'm not sure what you want from me. Why are we here?"

Gemma took a deep breath and then held one of Thomas' hands to her face. "I'm free now, Tommy. I'm free because you know the truth about your son. And Dick is…" She swallowed. "Dick said he's filing for separation."

"What are you saying?" Thomas felt a tug on his heart.

"I'm saying I want us to be together."

Imogen St. Perux had been spying on everyone in her association for years because, really, it was a benefit to all who lived within the Odiumscape HOA for the president to be aware of any impropriety or misconduct. That way Imogen could ward off and control the perils that befell so many lesser housing communities. She was the linchpin of the neighborhood and everything that went on in it was her business.

But as she hobbled down Sebastian Street and saw two men dressed in crisp black suits emerge from a black Hummer and knock on Owen and Mary Crossfield's front door, she wished, for the first time in her meddlesome career, that she wasn't so proactive. She wanted to unsee what she had just seen.

Because Imogen would never forget the grave faces and stoic movements of the men charged with the sorrowful assignment of telling young Mary Crossfield that her husband's plane had been shot down and he wasn't ever coming home.

Ellen Crossfield did not cry, even as a child. But now, as she and Charles sat across from one another, stunned into silence by the news of the death of their son, a tear gathered in her left eye ever so briefly and then quickly disappeared as though it had been sucked back into her body out of sheer will.

Charles looked at his wife. "Is the surrogate...?"

She shook her head no. "I talked to Dr. Rygert this morning."

"And Mary?"

"They were trying for a year and she never conceived. I highly doubt she is now."

The couple was sitting in their immense dining hall, sipping coffee at a long, expansive table. Ornate dishes, vases and mirrors decorated heavy, extravagant furniture all around them. Valuable artwork rose above oriental rugs and huge, vast windows allowed sunshine to spill in, highlighting the lavish interior and illuminating the unrealized dreams that hovered in the room.

A tall girl dressed in a grey uniform entered through a doorway and placed breakfast in front of Charles and Ellen Crossfield. She took a newspaper out from under her arm and set it to the left of Charles' plate. "Is there anything else you need?" she asked politely.

Neither the mister nor the missus responded so she left just as silently as she'd entered.

"It would seem," Charles said to his wife, putting on his reading glasses and picking up his fork, "that you and young Mary have quite a bit in common."

Ellen's face grew pallid, her features wary. "What do you mean?"

Charles turned his cold blue eyes on his wife, peering at her over his glasses. "How many children did you have, Ellie?"

Her back straightened. "I provided an heir... I..."

"One," Charles said with a sneer. "One goddamn son. And now look what's happened."

"I wanted more children, Charles! Lord knows we tried, but we kept having miscarriages and..." Ellen's lip curled in realization and she glared back at her husband. "Are you saying it's *my* fault we could only have one child?"

Charles took a bite of his vegetable frittata. "That's exactly what I'm saying." His fork clattered to his plate as he picked up the newspaper and shook it open.

Ellen's mouth thinned as she bit back the horrendous words she wanted to spew at her husband. She pushed her plate away and took a sip of coffee. The old pain was coming back, the pain she thought she'd buried when Owen had grown into a strong young man. She'd thought she'd been freed all those years ago, but now the recriminations of the past were taunting her, haunting her, once again.

"You know, Charles," she said eventually, "the meaning of life is not solely caught up in procreation."

To which he replied, "How else does the world know we were here unless we leave a legacy?"

"Maybe a legacy doesn't have to necessarily mean progeny."

Charles gazed at her with contempt. "You say that because you failed at being a woman."

Ellen felt like she'd been stabbed in the heart. Her mouth opened but nothing came out.

"Call Mary," Charles instructed his wife, "and see if there's any chance in hell she's pregnant."

And before Ellen could respond, Charles rattled his paper and disappeared behind it, signaling his exit from what he considered a pointless conversation.

CHAPTER 69

Thomas paced the floor of his game room in front of the pool table. He threw back his fifth shot of whiskey and slammed the empty glass down on a bar stool. He could hear Helga marching down the hallway, Voltaire snorting at her heels.

"Thomas," she said, striding into the room and standing before him, "enough of dis drinking. It not good for you. You tell Helga v'hat is wrong."

"No," Thomas said petulantly, bending down to pat Voltaire on the head affectionately. The squatty dog was so much calmer these days now that Thomas was exercising him regularly with daily hikes around the property.

Helga went to the French doors leading out to the balcony and flung them open. "It smell like alcohol in da room," she reprimanded.

"Yeah, well, a man's gotta do what a man's gotta do." Thomas walked over to a leather couch flanking a far wall and plunked down. Voltaire jumped up beside him, curling into a grey ball of fur.

Helga put her hands on her hips. "I not leefing dis room until you tell me v'hat's wrong."

Thomas clenched his jaw and looked away. "Women."

"Vomen?!" Helga exclaimed in surprise. "Dat's all?"

"That's *all*?" Thomas stared at her. "Do you realize how complicated the opposite sex is?"

"Ve not complicated," Helga said stoutly. She sat on the other side of the couch, her plump hands folded in her lap. "Now you tell Helga everyt'ing and Helga help you vith vomen problem."

Thomas shook his head. "If only it were that easy."

"Try to say v'hat is on your mind. Is it da sweet Mary Crossfield?"

"Morrison," Thomas corrected. "And I haven't heard from her since she left with Roger."

"You invite her here to dinner and I cook for you."

"It's not that simple."

"V'hy?"

"Because I don't want to pressure her. She needs to come here with a clear head."

"But *you* do not haf da clear head," Helga pointed out. "And v'hat about Gemma Hamilton? She call again?"

"Yes." Thomas ran his hands over his face. "She wants everything to go back to the way it was in Wales, but that's not possible."

"Because of Colin?"

"Because she lied to me."

"You must forgif in your heart, mina älskling."

"Forgiveness has nothing to do with it. I could never trust her again."

"If you really loved Gemma you vould want to be vith her."

Thomas looked at Helga, so calm, so cool, perched on the other side of the couch. How he wished things could be defined that easily. He'd been tempted to take Gemma into his arms and promise her forever right there in that equestrian center, but common sense had prevailed. There was too much water under the bridge between them and nothing to dam up the flowing river of deceit.

Helga continued knowingly. "Dis is not about Gemma d'ough. Dis is about Mary."

"You don't know that."

"I do know it because I know you, my Thomas. I see you happy, I see you write da words, I see you fall in love and now I see you miserable."

"I don't want to talk about this."

"V'hy?"

"Because it hurts."

"Love hurts."

Thomas stood up and ran his hands through his sandy hair. "And what if Mary never comes back?"

"Oh she vill. Helga knows."

"How do you know?"

"She left da letter from her great-grandpa in her room up da stairs."

"What letter?"

Mary had known as soon as she saw the officious-looking men on her porch, their black Hummer parked on the street behind them, why they were there and what they were about to tell her. Owen was gone. Killed in action. Died a hero. The particulars were classified.

The men, a notifications officer and the resident chaplain for Air-Sec, had stayed with Mary for over an hour - until Lorelei and Faith arrived - before taking their leave. A casualty assistance officer would be arriving the next day to go over funeral arrangements and to assist Mary with the submission of claims for Owen's pension and a rather substantial life insurance policy. The divorce paperwork was null and void since Owen had never signed it. She was a widow.

Lorelei and Faith had planted themselves on either side of Mary and the three girls sat silently on the boring brown couch Owen had delightedly chosen from a furniture store a few years back. Someone had turned on the television and *Top Gun* was playing. How apropos. And how sad. The lump in Mary's throat grew larger; it was getting harder to swallow.

Faith changed the channel to *I Love Lucy* reruns. They watched three episodes before anyone said anything. It was eerie in the town-house, as though the air was dense and charged with ambiguity.

"I don't know how to feel," Mary said into the stillness.

Lorelei pulled a tan and white checkered blanket from the back of the sofa and settled it over Mary, tucking it around her body. "You're in shock. What can I get you? Would you like something to drink?"

Before waiting for her to answer, Faith stood and went to the kitchen for a glass of cold water. She handed it to Mary, settled in close to her best friend and said, "Owen loved you in his own way, Mare. I think he loved you the best he could. Try to remember all of the good times you had together."

"I was going to divorce him," Mary said dully.

"That was not a decision you made lightly," Lorelei said gently. "And according to his mother, he wanted the divorce - he knew you would be filing while he was gone."

"Did he know he was going to die?" Mary asked. "Is that why he's been so insistent we have a baby?"

"I think it was just all the pressure from his parents," Faith surmised.

"I feel guilty," Mary said suddenly. "How am I supposed to reconcile my husband's death when I was going to leave him? Am I allowed to be sad? Allowed to grieve? Allowed to acknowledge our life together was over?"

Lorelei sighed. "I don't think there's an etiquette manual for this sort of experience. Any emotion you feel is allowable. We know you cared for Owen. We know you would never have wanted anything bad to happen to him."

"No," Mary whispered. "I would never want anything bad to happen to anyone."

"Do you want to be alone?" Lorelei asked, concerned. "Do you want us to go?"

Faith shook her head. "I'm not leaving. I don't care if you want me to stay or not, Mare."

Lorelei rolled her pretty green eyes.

"I want you both to stay," Mary assured her friends.

"Good!" Faith jumped up from the couch and skipped to Mary's cell phone on the hall table. "I'm going to order some pizza. Since my kiddos aren't here I don't have to share my slices or eat partially chewed crusts- that's pure Mom Heaven. Besides, the baby is craving pepperoni and breadsticks."

"Did the baby tell you this?" Lorelei said sarcastically.

"Oh sure!" Faith nodded, cell phone in hand. "He/she talks to me all the time. Mostly about food."

Mary's eyes went round. "What else does the baby say?"

Before Faith could answer, Mary's phone in her hand started ringing. When she saw who it was she made barfing noises. "It's Ellen."

"Oh!" Mary's face filled with compassion. "That poor woman."

Lorelei flattened her lips. "Don't talk to her if you don't want to, Mare. She might upset you. There's no reason…"

"No, I'd like to talk to her," Mary said, taking the phone from Faith. "AirSec would have called her and Charles as a courtesy. I want to tell her that I'm sorry for their loss and make sure there are no hard feelings between us. I hope she's all right…" Mary tapped the answer button and said, "Hello?"

"I assume you've heard the news," Ellen said frigidly. "Defense contractors make no distinction between happily married couples and soon-to-be-exes when sending their messengers of death."

Mary's fingers turned white as she gripped the phone. "Yes," she said softly, "I've heard."

"I am calling because I need to know if there's any possibility that you are pregnant?"

"No, I…" Mary's mouth went dry and no more words would come out.

"I didn't think so," Ellen said condescendingly. "It seems my son couldn't accomplish his familial obligations," she paused for effect, "even with another woman."

Mary sucked in her breath and it came out as a loud gasp.

"Yes, that's right," Ellen continued. "Owen hired a young girl to be a surrogate since you couldn't carry out your duty to this family. My *son*," she accentuated the word angrily, "took it upon himself to impregnate someone other than his wife."

When Mary didn't say anything Ellen went on, "I thought you should know what kind of man he was by telling you the *faithful* lie he wanted kept secret."

"I loved him," Mary whispered. "You have to know I loved Owen…"

"He was a stupid man for marrying you and a stupid man for joining the military, let alone working for that dreadful company. You couldn't fulfill his destiny and those mercenaries got him killed. And now where does that leave the Crossfields?"

"Is that all you care about?" Mary asked quietly. "Aren't you sad your son is gone? Aren't you proud that he died serving and protecting our country? I was going to tell you how sorry I am - I understand what loss is like, to lose a loved one, to grieve because you'll never see them again…"

"That's none of your concern. You were divorcing Owen anyway. Speaking of which, now that he's dead you can consider our cash deal off the table. Good day." And she hung up.

Charles walked into the luxurious living room where Ellen elegantly sat on an ornate ivory divan, her cell phone still in her hand.

"Is she with child?" he asked his wife, an eyebrow raised.

"No," Ellen said, setting her phone on a side table.

"Pity." He turned his back on her and started to leave the room.

Ellen's voice followed after him. "I hate what you've made me into."

He slowly swiveled back to her, immaculate in his three-piece suit, his grey hair perfectly arranged after an expensive cut. "You knew what you were getting into when you married me, Ellie."

Ellen nodded. "I did. I knew all about your family and their expectations."

"You wanted power and money."

"Yes," she agreed. "You're right. But, Charles, I also wanted you."

He snorted. "You don't know what love is."

"And you do?"

"I'm late for a meeting."

Ellen stood up and crossed the room to her husband, her fashionable heels sinking into the plush carpeting. When she was looking into his frosty blue eyes she said, "We were in love once. Before I lost the babies, before the pressures of life caved in on us and we both grew cold and distant. Don't you remember?"

"I remember you lied to me when you said on our wedding night that we would be happy and we'd have a houseful of children. There's more than one sort of betrayal, Ellie." He looked her up and down. "Don't ever speak to me of love again."

Ellen walked with dignified calmness to her bedroom and gently shut the door. She went in to her enormous bathroom and sat at the vanity, allowing her eyes to focus on her reflection. The woman looking back at her was dead inside. And as all of her hopes and dreams crashed around her it occurred to her that maybe, just maybe, those hopes and dreams had been misplaced. Perhaps the ambitions that had been of utmost importance weren't actually important at all. She thought of her handsome son, the son who had wanted to please both his parents and his adventurous nature. The son who had wanted to be free but remained imprisoned by expectation. The son who would now never reach his full potential.

For the first time in her entire life, Ellen Crossfield let tears flow. They fell, hot and remorseful, washing away her imperious expression and leaving in their wake a face shattered in defeat. And in her mind's eye all she could see was Owen kneeling before her pleading for a love she'd never been able to give.

CHAPTER 70

Bonjour Mama,

It's been three months since I've written in this journal. Three months since Owen passed away.

The funeral was lovely. I had to blink back my tears because the enormity of Owen's life having ended so soon and so tragically was overwhelming. Despite the fact that he and I were going our separate ways has no bearing on the unfairness of a life being cut short. He didn't deserve death.

Lorelei and Faith sat on either side of me during the service and afterward, at the reception, they never left my side. Aunt Georgette and Aunt Francesca had flown out for the ceremony and, of course, Frank and Jesse were there too. Corinne and Happy and Ricki gave me tearful hugs and said I would always be part of the AirSec family and I was to call on them for anything at all. Horse, Jambo and Tex are coming back to the States next week. I'm so glad they're safe. Corinne held on to me for a long time. I know she was thinking how awful it would have been to lose Horse; they love each other so very much.

You know who wasn't at the funeral? Charles and Ellen Crossfield. They didn't even come to their son's burial! I cried for Owen when I didn't see them. I was going to send Charles the medal AirSec gave me, as I felt it should stay in the family, but I decided to keep it; not because I loved Owen or because he was my husband, but because he bought that representation of patriotic symbolism with his innocent blood, and it deserves to be honored.

Ellen had told me the last time I spoke with her that Owen had had an affair in order to get another woman pregnant before he left on his mission. She alluded to it that time I met her for brunch at The Del as well. I don't know whether to believe her or not. On one hand, Owen wanted a baby desperately and if he was planning to divorce me anyway then I guess... but, no... deep down, in my heart of hearts, I don't think Owen would have touched another woman while we were still married. It wasn't in his nature to be disloyal- either to me or to his family. I think he wanted to please everyone and, in the process, ended up pleasing no one. Not even himself. I take some comfort knowing he lived the last moments of his life doing the one thing he adored- flying planes. At least in the end he was surrounded by the blue of the sky, where he'd always felt most at home.

I finished packing up my townhouse last month and I rented a small apartment by Moonlight Beach. It's a one bedroom with a skewed view of the ocean from my living room. Roger loves going out on the balcony and watching the waves and the seagulls.

Lorelei, Frank, Faith, Jesse, Horse and Corinne all spent a weekend helping me move. I donated Owen's clothes and most of our furniture to a local charity for resale. I found new bright, sunny couches, drapes and throw pillows for my tiny apartment in hues of blue and yellow and tangerine at a local beach store and I bought a double bed for my bedroom and covered it in a fluffy light green duvet with lots of matching pillows. Lorelei and I came across an old, antique writing desk at a vintage shop in Solana Beach and I sanded it down and refinished it, and it's been the perfect space for me to write my next novel. I hung your beautiful paintings in my living room and look at them every day. You were so talented, Mama.

The story about my dad didn't do very well, even after Bertie edited it and a small publishing house picked it up. Bertie said that's normal for a new author. Breakout hits are rare. She loved my manuscript, though, and encouraged me to keep writing. Between the money from Daddy's estate and Owen's life insurance policy, I'll be quite comfortable for another five years or so. If I'm not making a living from my books by then I'll look into taking some journalism classes and try to get a job writing articles for the local paper. Holokai offered me work at the coffee shop too which was very sweet. And Lorelei! Oh, Mama, she's opened up her own business! Can you believe it? I'm so happy for her. She's running an accounting agency specializing in business valuation and research analysis. She has so many new clients that she hired two more accountants last month. She's always dreamed of being a CEO or CFO of a major corporation. Turns out she just bypassed the middle man and went straight to the top on her own. I'm so proud of her. Anyway, she said she'd hire me on as a junior if I ever wanted to enroll in accounting courses down at SDSU. It would definitely be a great way to earn a living, and I could have that career I used to daydream about, but I'm really hoping writing will pan out. Writing is what I've always loved and it's how I want to pay my bills and spend my days.

It's been rather scary learning to be on my own, but it's freeing too. I make all my own decisions about everything from what I eat to what I spend my money on. I'm not accountable to anyone and I'm also not responsible for anyone other than Roger. I come and go as I please, stay up late if I want or wake up at noon if I want. Faith and Lorelei are constantly in and out of my apartment making sure I'm not lonely. They pick fresh flowers and set them in tiny vases around the living room or they bring over petit fours or coffee or a movie they want to watch. Sometimes we open all the windows, light a fire and huddle under the blankets together watching chick flicks and drinking hot cocoa and giggling until the wee hours of the night.

I placed Owen's medal in a place of honor above my little stone fireplace along with a picture of Daddy and me. I stare at that picture all the time and I wonder if Dad can see me from heaven. I wonder if you can see me too. I talk to both of you - you through this journal and Dad...well, Dad and I have one-sided conversations out loud. Another benefit of living alone.

I think about Thomas McQuillan all the time. I wonder how he is and what he's doing, but I'm frightened to reach out to him because I know I'm still healing from Dad's death and from the pain of what happened with Owen. I feel like I've grown so much in the months Thomas and I have been apart, but I don't know if it's enough. I also don't know if he even still wants me. I saw on the news that Gemma Hamilton and Dick Rimmel are divorcing. I feel sorry for them - celebrities have their personal lives splashed across social media and tawdry magazines, and the public eats it up and gossips about it. I especially feel sorry for Dick and Gemma's kids. And I wonder... I can't help but wonder if Thomas and Gemma are together now. There isn't anything stopping them. The thought makes my heart hurt.

I want to go to Thomas' house so I can get the letter Great-Grandpa George wrote to Great-Grandmother Pauline (I accidentally left it there when we rushed off to Arizona), but I'm too nervous to go back in case Thomas doesn't want to see me. In case he's with Gemma now. In case... in case I find out whatever it was between us wasn't real. I'd rather go on believing he really did feel something for me than face a harsh reality that he didn't wait for me. I'm remembering the words of Amy March again, but instead of applying it to art or to writing it's about Thomas: "I want to be great or nothing. I won't be a commonplace dauber, so I don't intend to try anymore."

I want to believe we could have been great together, that Thomas truly cared for me as much as I care for him. I dream of him often and I'd rather have those poignant fantasies rooted in hope than face the torment of knowing he's moved on.

"I don't think this is a good idea, Fay," Lorelei said, leaning back in her chair and sipping a dirty martini. She flashed an apologetic look at the chiseled and handsome Asian man across from her. "No offense, Wong."

He held up his hands. "None taken."

Faith, Jesse, Frank and Lorelei were at Bonita's Bistro waiting for Mary to arrive. Much to Lorelei's surprise, a well-spoken man in his late thirties wearing an expensively sleek pin striped suit joined them.

Faith crammed a breadstick into her mouth and spoke around it. "Wong and Jesse work together and Wong got divorced last year because his wife cheated on him with some dude in their spin class. But it's the wife's loss because Wong is sooooo nice and he has a lot of money since the firm just made him partner. He works out at the company gym every day and I've never seen him without his shirt, but Jesse said he has decent muscles. Oh! And he has a dog so I think he and Mary will get along great."

Wong cleared his throat and said, "You do know I'm sitting right here."

"Did I leave something out?" Faith asked, concerned.

Frank laughed and put his arm around Lorelei. "Well, Wong, this scenario is exactly how Lor and I met and I remember how uncomfortable it was and I extend my sincerest apologies." Frank raised his beer. "Just wait until Fay starts talking about sex. That's always a real treat."

Wong looked perplexed.

"Yes!" Faith screeched. "Sex! Speaking of which- it's getting harder to find angles that work for me and Jesse since my stomach is so huge now." She patted her broad belly. "But we've found that the 'sit and milk' position works best and then we can move into the 'spider' from there."

Wong stared. "What's the 'sit and milk'?"

"Well, it's when the man is sitting on the floor or the bed and the woman straddles him, and the balls of her feet are…"

"Oh look," Lorelei interrupted loudly. "Mary is here."

"Hi everyone," Mary said, kissing Frank on the cheek. "I'm so sorry I'm late." She hugged Lorelei and Jesse and then...

"Mary," Faith said excitedly, "this is Wong. Wong this is Mary."

Wong stood and shook Mary's hand and then pulled her chair out for her.

"Oh," Mary seemed flustered. "Hi. Nice to meet you."

"Fay has decided you need to start dating," Lorelei said, an edge to her tone. "*Surprise* dating. In fact, I would like to discuss this with Faith further. *In private*."

Faith looked around distractedly as though she hadn't heard and then fixated on a big, potted ficus across the room. She gazed at it raptly as though its leaves were profoundly fascinating. "Look at that plant," she said to Jesse, "it's so pretty and leafy and has lots of, um... fronds."

"NOW," Lorelei demanded.

"Okay, okay," Faith said, her hand on her lower back as she stood, belly protruding.

When they entered the ladies' restroom Lorelei turned on her friend. "What do you think you're doing? If Mary wanted to date then she would! Stop nosing in where you're not supposed to, Fay. The poor girl's been through enough."

"No, no, no, it's all right! I have a plan!" Faith said, grinning from ear to ear. "Tonight is just a test."

"I hate to even ask, but what kind of test?"

Faith grabbed Lorelei's hand and squeezed it exuberantly. "Mary is in love with Thomas McQuillan."

One of Lorelei's eyes twitched. "Wong is not Thomas McQuillan."

"I know, right? But Wong is super-handsome and successful and very nice. And Jesse said all the girls in the office have a crush on him."

"So why isn't he dating one of them?"

"Because he's gay!" Faith shouted triumphantly.

Lorelei rubbed her temples. "I'm getting a headache."

"Don't you see? Mary needs a night out with the perfect man so it pushes her to realize she'll never feel about anyone the way she feels about Thomas and then that will make her run back to Thomas and," she sighed whimsically, "straight into his arms."

"I'm so confused."

Faith was smug. "I called Thomas last week."

"You did what?" Lorelei practically yelled.

"Remember last time we were over at Mary's apartment and I ordered Thai food from her phone? Well, I just happened to sort of see Thomas' number in her contacts so when you guys weren't looking I wrote it on my hand."

"Oh dear lord…"

"When I got home I called Thomas and I told him how the three of us had talked about him one night and how Mary has all these feelings for him but she's scared he's back together with Gemma and I was like, '*Are* you back together with Gemma?' and he said no and I asked him if he wanted to see Mary and he said *very much* so I was like, 'Just leave everything to me!'"

Lorelei shook her head. "I can't believe you. I can't honestly believe you…"

"Mary seems really hesitant to put herself out there. I mean, she's only ever had sex with Owen and she's just so sweet and not very street smart about dating…"

"And you are?"

"…so I thought if she went out with someone non-threatening it would give her some confidence and make her see no one will ever measure up to Thomas because she and Thomas are soulmates."

"Fay, you really need to stop meddling and thinking people are soulmates when maybe they're not."

"Are you saying Frank isn't your soulmate?"

"That's different…"

Faith pointed a finger at her friend. "Ha! You don't deny it!"

Lorelei tried to hide a smile but couldn't. "You're incorrigible, you know that?"

"Wong agreed to go out tonight and pretend to be straight because he owes Jesse a favor and because I told him it was for a good cause: true love."

"And Wong's ex-wife...?"

"He really was married and got cheated on, but his wife wasn't a woman. Well, physically a woman, but Harvey-Ann did a lot of drag dressed as Rosemary Clooney."

"I really can't cope with this," Lorelei groaned. "I do not think there is enough alcohol..."

Suddenly Faith shrieked. "The baby is kicking!" She spread Lorelei's hand over her stomach. "Can you feel that?"

Lorelei stood perfectly still, her eyes riveted on Faith's in amazement. "Yes... I do... Oh, Fay," and her expression softened with tenderness, her irritation subsiding.

"It's a boy, Lor. We decided against being surprised and asked my OB yesterday." Her voice lowered, unsure. "Do you think it would be okay with Mary if we named the baby Mitchell? I feel like it would give Mary a bit of hope- to show her that her father isn't forgotten and that his memory will live on in new life."

"I think it's a beautiful gesture, Fay. Mary will love the idea."

"So you're not mad at me? About Wong?" Faith asked as they walked out of the restroom and through the dining area.

Lorelei sighed. "I think you are full of mischief, but you have the best of intentions and I can't be angry with that."

"Oh good," Faith gushed, "Because Thomas is going to show up at Mary's apartment tonight at eleven."

And Lorelei couldn't respond because they'd reached their table where Mary and Frank were chatting, Jesse was placing another drink order and Wong, applying chapstick to his lips as though it were lipstick, was checking out the backside of their waiter.

CHAPTER 71

⁓

Thomas sat in his office holding the letter Mary's great-grandfather had written to her great-grandmother. It was an endearing note from a long-ago era, penned by a man obviously in love.

Thomas re-read the letter again, especially intrigued by the phrase, "I have got a good one on you…"

Picacho, New Mexico
September 9, 1908

Miss Pauline Hulbert,

I sure wish you was here for I am having a time. I will be up Sunday and hope to find the same sweet Pauline as ever, and know I will. I don't believe anything that anybody tells me- if I did I would be the unhappiest boy in the world, but I believe you and not some at the news carrier. Don't know if you can read this or not. I am trying to cook dinner and write all at the same time and in a hurry also. I have got a good one on you and I think I shall hurrah you a little Sunday. I will not tell you now but will Sunday- it must be so for the most truthful man in the country told it.

All I wanted was just to let you know that I was all OK and just the same as your ever loving...

Geo

Thomas let the words soak into his soul as he thought of sweet, gentle Mary, the girl who gave love so freely to her family and friends without expecting anything in return. The girl who handled life with grace and innocence, accepting sadness just as she accepted happiness. He'd missed her terribly over the months – missed her gentle laughter, her passionate sparring, her deep insights into their mutual fascination with the written word. He missed her kind disposition and the way she looked up at him with those luminous amber eyes, eyes that were unable to hide what she was feeling inside. Thomas hadn't soon forgotten that intimate kiss they'd shared in his foyer, when he'd wanted to ravage her soft, sensuous body with his hands, his mouth, his... But, no, he knew he'd made the right decision by turning her away. She was so vulnerable, so heartbroken over the death of her father. It was the wrong time to start a romance - a *real* romance. Thomas didn't want Mary for just one night, or even for a few months. He wanted her by his side long-term. And he wanted her to come to him willingly, not because she had a crush or because she felt lost or lonely, but because she truly desired him for who he was. Too many years as a celebrity had made him cynical. And the messy, deceitful relationships he'd had with Katya and Gemma made him wary of jumping into anything too quickly.

Thomas had all but given up that Mary Morrison was coming back. He'd waited for her to call, to send an email, or to even show up on his doorstep. But she'd remained silent, distant, and he began to wonder if he'd simply imagined the chemistry between them.

The thought had occurred to him that Mary could be dating someone else; perhaps after divorcing Owen she'd met someone... but that was just too painful to even think about. Thomas decided to try going on a few dates himself, but he kept comparing the women to Mary and he lost all interest when he discovered they either only wanted to be seen with him or sleep with him or both. He'd had enough of casual sex. The thought of all the meaningless erotic encounters he'd had with Katya now made him feel ashamed. He'd used her to forget

Gemma, used her for his own purposes. And it turned out she'd ended up using him as well. In some ways he was grateful to Katya for telling him about Colin. It had been terrible at the time, but Thomas had begun to understand after a lot of soul searching why Gemma had lied. She hadn't done it to be malicious; she'd done it because she loved him and because she loved her son.

And then, just a few days ago, Mary's friend Faith had called and, with oddly endearing exuberance, told him Mary was in love with him and he needed to come see her. Faith said Mary was living alone in a small apartment by Moonlight Beach. She'd given Thomas the address and told him to be there in two days at eleven p.m. sharp.

"Does she know I'm coming over?" he'd asked warily.

"No," Faith replied, her tone confident, "but you two have been apart long enough. She's doing so much better now, Thomas. She's healing and she's finding her way. She has very strong feelings for you…"

That was all he'd needed to hear. "I'll be there," he said.

To which Faith replied, "I knew you would be. You're her soulmate."

His heart had almost leapt out of his chest.

And now, as he stared at the letter in his hands, knowing he was going to see Mary in just a few hours, he realized maybe it wasn't Mary who had needed to grow. It was him. He was the one who'd needed time to heal - time to lick his wounds from the disaster he'd made of his professional and his personal life.

He read the words again: "I have got a good one on you…"

That was exactly how he felt about Mary Morrison. And he couldn't wait to tell her so.

⌒

"I had a lovely evening, Wong," Mary said, shaking his hand and hoping he wasn't going to try and kiss her. It was ten-thirty and they were standing outside of her apartment door. She could hear Roger sniffing on the other side, probably wondering who she was with.

"I had a *fabulous* time," Wong said, straightening his tie. "Would you like me to come inside?"

"Oh," said Mary quickly, "no, that's okay. I should be going to bed…"

"Do you need me to hold you while you fall asleep?"

"Um…"

"I don't think I said that correctly." Wong pursed his lips. "I meant to say, I can be the man you need tonight. I'm at your disposal. Perhaps you'd like me to cuddle with you?"

Mary shook her head. "No, really, that's okay. Thank you, though. You've been such a gentleman and I appreciate how attentive and solicitous you've been. I haven't really gone on many dates and…"

"Would you like to go out again sometime?"

"Oh! Er, no, probably not. I mean, nothing against you or anything, I just… I'm really trying to focus on my career right now."

Did Wong look relieved?

"Soooo," Mary said, inching closer to her front door, "I should go…"

Wong smiled. "Until we meet again."

"Yes," she said faintly, "until then." She escaped into her apartment and shut the door hurriedly behind her. Roger licked Mary's hand and wagged his stub tail, glad she was home. She said to the big dog, "I'm not ready to date yet! I don't know what Faith was thinking!"

She threw her purse on a chair and pulled off her high heels. "I mean, I have so much going on, you know? I have my book to finish and I have my girlfriends to hang out with and I have… um, *you*." She patted Roger on the head and he looked at her lovingly. "I don't need a man. I've already established that. I'm doing fine on my own. The thought of kissing someone or…" she shivered in repulsion, "no, just no."

She slipped on a pair of old sneakers before opening the door and poking her head out. No sign of Wong.

Roger bounded outside, joyously running through the grass, stomping on wayward ice plants and watering every tree available. Mary picked up a stick and threw it and he chased after it in excitement. When he returned, Mary scratched his ear and confided, "That guy- Wong- was really nice tonight, and very handsome, but... being on a date, being next to a man... it just made me think about Thomas even more. No guy is ever going to measure up to Thomas McQuillan, you know? I'm just going to be single forever. Single is good."

Roger gazed up at her adoringly and panted in agreement.

"Single is easy. It's fun. It's freeing!"

Roger licked her hand and the pair made their way back into the apartment. Mary poured herself a glass of wine and took it into her bedroom. She stripped off all her clothes and donned an old, pink pajama top. It was huge on her small frame, cozily hiding all of her feminine curves with its soft and faded material.

Padding into her living room, she switched the TV on and selected a movie. Something to take her mind off of men. Well, one man. Definitely not romance. Maybe something scary, gory even.

Throwing a blanket over her legs, she settled on the sofa with her wine and Roger snuggled up next to her.

She chose a slasher film and the opening scene was suspenseful, frightening. Some crazy guy had escaped an insane asylum, donned a monkey suit and started hunting teenagers for sport. Just when the monkey made an "Eeep!" sound and raised his axe for a final blow, there was a knock on Mary's front door. She yelped, spilling a few drops of wine from her glass. Roger growled and ran to the door, but his protective angst eased when he sniffed at the doorjamb. He gave a happy little cry and his tail wagged ferociously.

So it's someone we know, Mary thought, relieved. Shakily, she turned the movie off. No more monkey murders tonight.

As she walked to the door she wondered who on earth could be coming over so late? It wasn't Lorelei or else Roger would have been throwing himself against the door deliriously. It couldn't be Faith because she and Jesse had gone out for hotel sex after dinner. Horse and Corinne were in Hawaii on a second honeymoon. Aunt Georgette and Aunt Francesca were in Arizona. Roger wouldn't be wiggling his butt around for Wong…

Curiously, Mary opened the door and Voltaire streaked inside like a fat grey rocket, right under Roger's legs. The two began racing around the coffee table, yipping in excitement, crashing into the sofas and chairs and then sprinting into the bedroom to jump on Mary's bed.

And Mary looked straight into the broody hazel eyes of Thomas McQuillan. He was holding a bouquet of Helga's tulips in one hand and a plate of butterkaka in the other. He wore a pair of faded jeans, a dark blue t-shirt and a charcoal blazer. His sandy hair was brushed back and tucked behind his ears. He looked incredibly handsome, as though he were somehow channeling a literary professor and a surfer at the same time. Mary was self-consciously aware that she was wearing only a nightshirt that fell to the middle of her thighs. Her hair was loose and tumbling messily around her shoulders. She stared at Thomas. She didn't know what to say. The words wouldn't come.

He handed her the flowers and the pastry and said, "May I come in?"

Mary moved aside and he stepped over the threshold. He seemed much too big for her small apartment. He must feel claustrophobic in such a confined space, especially being used to his gigantic house with all its amenities.

Thomas looked around appreciatively. "This place is so you - beachy artwork, books everywhere, soft pastel colors, flowers…"

Mary smiled. "I thought the same thing about your house when I saw it for the first time - that it looked exactly like how I would have pictured your home to be."

They stared at one another, a million unanswered questions thick between them. Mary wanted to touch him, to see if he was real. She wanted him to hold her, to talk to her, to debate with her, to tell her he missed her, to…

"These digs remind me of my old apartment in Mission Beach. I had good times there. Life was simpler. A lot of fun." He walked over to the fireplace and gazed at the picture of Mitch and Mary on the mantel. He turned after a few moments, his features gentle and filled with empathy. "How are you doing?"

She knew what he meant. "I'm okay. Learning to live without him day by day. Grief doesn't ever go away, does it?"

"No. We just learn how to manage it. Try to move forward even when our hearts are living in the past."

"And when we wish the memories were the present?"

"Yes." Thomas thoughtfully looked at the medal next to the photo of Mary with her father. "You never got divorced, did you?"

"No." Mary walked over to her small kitchen and put the butterkaka on the counter and the flowers in a vase. She hesitated for a moment and then, "Did you know, Thomas? That day we were sitting by the pond and you asked about the situation in the Middle East… you suspected Owen wasn't really going on a training mission."

Thomas met her eyes. "I wondered."

"Writer's intuition," Mary said softly. "Apparently I don't have it."

"Maybe that's a good thing." Thomas moved to a light blue chair and sat down, leaning his elbows on his legs. "Listen, I read your book. It was really good. I hope you're still writing."

She smiled as she came back into the living room. "I'm almost finished with the novel I started originally before you told me to write about Dad."

Thomas reached into an inside pocket of his jacket and pulled out a slender envelope. "You might need this to help you."

"Oh!" Mary exclaimed happily. "You brought the letter! Thank you! Thank you so much." She stood before him and reached for it, but he held it away from her.

"I read it. I hope that was all right."

She pulled her hand back, confused. "Yes, of course."

"You trusted me with this. You trusted me with Roger while you were in Arizona and I know he means the world to you. You trusted me to be there for you when Mitch passed away and when you found out Claude was your biological father. You trusted me with your heart and your feelings and your emotions through all of those letters you wrote me from Tempe. And *I* trusted *you*, Mary Morrison. I trust you still. But I don't know why you didn't come back to me. Tell me why you didn't return after I said I'd wait for you."

"I was scared…"

"Don't lie to me. I've had enough lies to last a lifetime."

Mary turned away and walked to the fireplace. She looked up at Owen's medal and then back at Thomas. "You know what my mother-in-law said to me? She said Owen had told me a 'faithful lie'. What do you think that means?"

"It could mean it was a lie that was given out of necessity and not with the intent to hurt."

"Like Gemma not telling you about Colin? Or my dad not telling me about Claude?"

"I suppose…"

She moved toward him, placing her small hands on his broad shoulders. "Thomas, I would never lie to you. A faithful lie or a malicious lie. The reason I didn't come back to you is because I didn't honestly think you meant what you said about us. I couldn't fathom the idea that someone like you could care for someone like me. And I thought… I was nervous that maybe you and Gemma would get back together. But either way, I was pretty sure you'd forgotten about me; that what we had wasn't real to you."

Thomas put the letter down on a side table and reached for Mary. He pulled her into his lap and settled her against his chest. "Gemma and I will never get back together. I was in love with the idea of her, but when faced with the truth I realized she wasn't who I wanted to spend the rest of my life with."

Mary breathed in Thomas' scent, resting her head against his shoulder, loving the feel of his warm body underneath her own. She placed a hand on his neck and he shivered.

"I waited for you, Mary. I've *been* waiting for you. I haven't stopped thinking about you or wanting you or wishing you would come back to me. There isn't anyone else in my life, Gemma or otherwise, because no other woman could touch my soul like you have."

Mary caressed Thomas' stubbled jaw and sighed. "I feel like I'm dreaming. Are you really here? Are you really saying these things to me?"

"Yes, my love." He put his large hands on either side of her face until he could see into her beautiful eyes. "I have got a good one on you."

And then he was kissing her, passionately, deeply, taking his time, seductively brushing his lips against Mary's, allowing his tongue to graze hers temptingly, teasingly. He ran his hands over her back and then down under her night shirt. He pulled away, his breathing ragged. "You're naked under there." His voice was gravelly, heavy with lust.

Mary giggled, her heart in her eyes. There was no longer fear in those amber depths like Thomas had seen in his game room when he'd suggested she spend the night, or when he'd implied they find out the meaning of life together in Arizona. She was looking at him with only joy and contentment... and voracious desire...

"Oh, hell," Thomas said gruffly, whipping the pink shirt up and over her head. She sat naked upon his lap, her face peaceful, her body relaxed.

"You're so soft," he said, running his hands along her arms, down her legs, over her stomach, across her collar bone. "I feel like there's so much we should discuss, but..." He brushed her hair off her shoulders, nuzzling her neck with his lips and then biting at a tender spot. She gasped and arched into the scorching heat of his mouth. He pulled her head down and kissed her again, forcefully this time, erotic thoughts pulsing out any sense of seduction or decorum. He wanted her, and from the way she was responding, she wanted him too.

Thomas gripped her thighs and pushed them apart so that she was straddling him. Grabbing her waist he pressed her hips down so that there would be no question in her mind as to how she was affecting him.

"Thomas..." she breathed.

"Tell me what you want me to do to you," he growled, his blood pumping hot. He wanted to consume her, he wanted her soft body enveloping him, surrounding him...

But before she could answer, there was a soft tapping noise at one of the living room windows. Then a scratch and a stifled squeak.

Thomas, startled out of his passionate thoughts, put Mary from him and stood, taking off his jacket and covering her with it. "Go into the bedroom with the dogs," he instructed.

Another scratch came from outside and then a muffled thud.

"Get away from that window," someone hissed.

A startled shriek sounded and then a loud whisper, "Lor! You scared me!"

"I *knew* you would be here! Leave Mary and Thomas alone!"

"I can't see anything," Faith complained. "She's got the drapes all closed. Do you think they're kissing?"

More scuffling noises ensued.

"Ma'am," Frank's deep voice said, "I'm going to have to ask you to vacate the premises. Your actions could be considered trespassing."

"Oh my god!" Faith squealed. "That was so freaking sexy! Say it again!"

"Shhhhh... Mary's going to hear you," Lorelei scolded.

"Maybe Frank should handcuff me," Faith suggested flirtatiously.

Then Jesse's hushed voice asked, "Hey, man, do you think I could borrow those just for tonight?"

"For hotel sex!" Faith agreed excitedly. "I'm not sure if the handcuffs will work during sit and milk though. I'll have to google it and see…" It sounded like she was pawing through her purse.

"We are all leaving *right now*," Lorelei commanded, her tightly controlled tone not brokering any argument.

There was a lot of subdued commotion, Faith giggled and was shushed, and then all was quiet.

Thomas and Mary looked at each other and then burst into laughter. While Mary wiped her eyes, Thomas took her in his arms and held her close. "May I stay the night?"

She nodded against him. "Yes."

He pulled back and cupped the back of her head with his hand. "I want an open invitation from here on out."

"Good."

"I don't want anyone but you, Mary."

Her amber eyes were sparkling, shining with all the longing she felt.

Thomas picked her up and carried her into her bedroom. He ordered Roger and Voltaire out and kicked the door shut behind them. He set Mary down tenderly, his big hands going into her hair. She looked up at him trustingly, her hands resting on his forearms.

"You make me feel things I've never felt before," Thomas began, "but most of all, you make me feel whole. You're soft where I'm rough. You're gentle where I'm hard. You're light where I'm dark. And I want you, I want you so much I can't see straight, but what's between us is so much more. You awakened a part of my heart that I never knew was dormant. I need you in my life, not just for now, but for always. Those letters we wrote back and forth- that's where our story began. And now… now I want to write our story together. Word by word. Chapter by chapter."

Tears welled in Mary's eyes and spilled down her cheeks.

"What are you feeling?" Thomas whispered huskily. "Please say something."

"I love you." Her sweet voice was bold, emotional, filled with promise.

Thomas felt the universe shift on its axis and he smiled, his soul catching fire. "And I love you, Mary Morrison."

ACKNOWLEDGMENTS

⌒

Faithful Lies would not be in existence it if weren't for the following phenomenal souls:

Shanda Trofe, my author coach and long-suffering cheerleader. Thank you for handling my neurosis and emotionalism like a champ. Without your encouragement, I would have given up on myself long before the second chapter was even written. Words will never express my deep appreciation to you for helping me push past my self-imposed limitations. You are truly an angel.

Dana Micheli, editor extraordinaire. Thank you for taking me on, for treating me kindly even when I made mistakes, and thank you for reading (and responding to) all of my silly, weird, volatile emails. Most of all, thank you for loving my book and my characters and for respecting my vision and voice. You're not just a spectacular editor, but a spectacular person, and I admire you tons.

Humongous gratitude and undying loyalty to Christina St. Arnold and Aggie Redkey, my sisters from different misters. Thanks for being at my side every step of the way- for letting me cry, for making me laugh, for being beta readers and proof readers, for talking about my characters as though they are real people, for showing me that the bond of love between girlfriends, *true girlfriends*, is unbreakable and unshakeable. You both have my heart now and always.

Special love to my mama, Jeannie Buckingham, who has told me from the beginning: *You can be whatever you want if you set your mind to it.* I hope this book makes you proud. And many thanks to you and Daddy for showing me, by example, that true love can, and does, exist. Looking back, I so clearly see where my love of romance started- right at home.

And to Mark Fousek, no longer the dream crusher, but the dream maker. There is no way I would have been able to complete this book without you. You supported me, encouraged me, displayed the patience of a saint, and never left the house each morning without saying: *Write good today, honey.* Thank you for the opportunity to create. I love you.

Many thanks to...

Verline Rader, my fabulous auntie, best friend and kindred spirit. Thank you for your constant love, your strength and your beauty within. I want to be just like you when I grow up.

My gorgeous stepmama, Cyndi Bosworth, who created (and maintains) my super awesome website. And oodles of thanks for your ninja-like photography skills. My author photos came out *bomb* even though I felt like an awkward emu during the shoot. Your talent is unparalleled.

Aaron Haslam, devoted friend, confidant and sounding board. Thank you for having my back during this venture, for accompanying me to a "possibly" haunted house, for laughing at my stupid jokes and, thanks too, for proofreading the final draft.

Michele McCammon who designed my book cover. You created something truly beautiful that I absolutely adore. Thank you for bringing Mary and Voltaire to life.

Jessica Arroyo Martinez who helped me write my back cover blurb. Jessica, you're a word wizard with a gift for pizazz. Thanks for working with me.

Jennifer Louden, busy author, self-care guru and all around badass supporter of women... thank you for plowing through my verbose emails and responding with grace and understanding. You are a messenger of hope to all writers who find the going tough.

And a GINORMOUS thank you to Chris "Snooze" Kurek for granting me permission to use his lyrics from *Jeremiah Weed*. I love your song so damn much. Additional thanks to Rob "Trip" Raymond for fielding my effusive emails and getting me in touch with Chris. You guys rock. Dos Gringos forever.

ABOUT THE AUTHOR

Chelly Bosworth is an American novelist and blogger. She uses her writing to give her readers a sense of community and an escape from the stresses and pressures of everyday life. A third-generation native, Chelly resides in Arizona with her husband and their three rescue dogs, Larry Marie, The Murf and Jovie Noel. She welcomes visitors and messages at her website www.ChellyBosworth.com and encourages her readers to join The Boz Babes, an online group of girlfriends who support one another through laughter and love: https://www.facebook.com/groups/bozbabes/.

9 781733 277327